PE

THE NEW PENGUIN BOOK OF
AMERICAN SHORT STORIES

KASIA BODDY teaches American literature at University College London. The author of *Boxing: A Cultural History* (2008) and *The American Short Story Since 1950* (2010), she has also co-edited three other anthologies of short fiction.

The New Penguin Book of American Short Stories

From Washington Irving to Lydia Davis

Edited and with an Introduction and Notes by KASIA BODDY

PENGUIN BOOKS

PENGUIN CLASSICS

Published by the Penguin Group
Penguin Books Ltd, 80 Strand, London WC2R ORL, England
Penguin Group (USA) Inc., 375 Hudson Street, New York, New York 10014, USA
Penguin Group (Canada), 90 Eglinton Avenue East, Suite 700, Toronto, Ontario, Canada M4P 2Y3
(a division of Pearson Penguin Canada Inc.)
Penguin Ireland, 25 St Stephen's Green, Dublin 2, Ireland (a division of Penguin Books Ltd)
Penguin Group (Australia), 250 Camberwell Road, Camberwell, Victoria 3124, Australia
(a division of Pearson Australia Group Pty Ltd)
Penguin Books India Pvt Ltd, 11 Community Centre,
Panchsheel Park, New Delhi – 110 017, India
Penguin Group (NZ), 67 Apollo Drive, Rosedale, Auckland 0632, New Zealand
(a division of Pearson New Zealand Ltd)
Penguin Books (South Africa) (Pty) Ltd, 24 Sturdee Avenue,
Rosebank, Johannesburg 2196, South Africa

Penguin Books Ltd, Registered Offices: 80 Strand, London WC2R ORL, England

www.penguin.com

This collection first published in Penguin Classics 2011
002

Introduction and editorial matter copyright © Kasia Boddy, 2011
The acknowledgements, pp. 280–2, constitute an extension of this copyright page
All rights reserved

The moral rights of the editor and authors of the stories have been asserted

Set in 10.25/12.25pt Postscript Adobe Sabon
Typeset by Jouve (UK), Milton Keynes
Printed in England by Clays Ltd, St Ives plc

ISBN: 978-0-141-19442-4

www.greenpenguin.co.uk

MIX
Paper from
responsible sources
FSC
www.fsc.org FSC® C018179

Penguin Books is committed to a sustainable
future for our business, our readers and our planet.
This book is made from Forest Stewardship
Council™ certified paper.

ALWAYS LEARNING   **PEARSON**

Contents

Chronology

1000 Leif Ericsson lands in Vinland, the modern Newfoundland.

1492 Christopher Columbus, financed by Spain, makes the first of four voyages to the New World.

1565 The first Spanish missions in what is now Florida begin soon after the Jesuit foundation of St Augustine.

1584 Sir Walter Raleigh sends a reconnaissance fleet to what is now North Carolina. In the following year, he authorizes a colonizing expedition to Roanoke Island, naming the new territory Virginia for the 'Virgin Queen', Elizabeth I. The colonists return to England eleven months later.

1607 Jamestown, the first permanent English settlement, is established in Virginia by the London Company.

1614 A Dutch trading post (New Amsterdam) is set up on the lower end of Manhattan Island.

1618–19 Smallpox wipes out 90 per cent of Native Americans in Massachusetts Bay. Imported disease would become a major cause of the devastation of the indigenous population.

1619 Twenty African indentured servants are brought to Jamestown.

1620 The Plymouth colony is established in Massachusetts by a group of separatists from the Church of England. The rules of the community are established by the 'Mayflower Compact' and signed by the forty-one men who travelled on the ship of that name.

1624 John Smith publishes *The General History of Virginia, New England, and the Summer Isles*.

1630 John Winthrop's sermon 'A Model of Christian Charity', published in 1638, describes the Puritan vision of the 'City upon a Hill'. The Massachusetts Bay Company is founded.

1682 Mary Rowlandson's narrative of her three-month captivity by Algonquin Indians during King Philip's War (1675–8) becomes one of America's first bestsellers.

1692 Witchcraft trials are held in Salem, Massachusetts.

1704 The Boston *News-Letter* is the first American newspaper.

1733 Benjamin Franklin begins publishing *Poor Richard's Almanac*.

1741 Jonathan Edwards' sermon 'Sinners in the Hands of an Angry God' is a key work in the period of intense religious fervour known as the First Great Awakening.

1770 The Boston Massacre, in which five men are shot by British soldiers. One is an escaped slave called Crispus Attucks.

1773 The Boston Tea Party. A group of colonists, disguised as Mohawk Indians, board three ships in Boston Harbor and throw more than 300 crates overboard as a protest against the British tea tax.

1775–83 The Revolutionary Wars are fought between the British and the thirteen colonies of the eastern seaboard of North America.

1776 Thomas Paine publishes *Common Sense*. The Continental Congress adopts the Declaration of Independence on 4 July and names the new country the United States two months later.

1782 J. Hector St John de Crèvecoeur publishes *Letters from an American Farmer*.

1783 American independence is formally recognized by the British in the Treaty of Paris. Slavery is abolished in Massachusetts, with several other Northern states following suit over the next few years.

1787 Publication of the first of the *Federalist Papers*: a series of essays by James Madison, Alexander Hamilton and John Jay promoting the ratification of the Constitution.

1789 The US Constitution is ratified and goes into effect. George Washington is elected the country's first President. A national day of Thanksgiving (26 November) is proclaimed. Publication in England of *The Interesting Narrative of the*

Life of Olaudah Equiano, or Gustavus Vassa, the African. Written by Himself.

1790 The Naturalization Act is passed, ruling that only 'free white persons' are allowed to become citizens. The first census records a population of four million, of which 700,000 are slaves.

1791 The first ten amendments to the Constitution, known as the Bill of Rights, are ratified.

1794 Eli Whitney patents the cotton gin, an invention which, over the next sixty years, contributes to the massive expansion of the cotton industry and plantation slavery in the South. Susanna Haswell Rowson's *Charlotte Temple* (published first in London and then in Philadelphia) becomes the first American novel to be a bestseller.

1800 The census records a US population of approximately 5.3 million.

1803 The geographical area of the US nearly doubles in size following the Louisiana Purchase from France.

1804–6 President Thomas Jefferson sponsors Meriwether Lewis and William Clark's expedition to explore the West and find a route to the Pacific Ocean.

1806 Noah Webster publishes his *Compendious Dictionary of the English Language*.

1808 The Atlantic slave trade is abolished.

1812–14 War with Britain over the effects of restrictions on US trade and westward expansion. After witnessing a bombardment by the British Navy, Francis Scott Key writes 'The Defence of Fort McHenry', which, under the title 'The Star Spangled Banner', is officially adopted as the US National Anthem in 1931.

1815 Thomas Jefferson sells his personal library to the government; it forms the basis of the Library of Congress.

1818 Publication of the first part of *The Autobiography of Benjamin Franklin*.

1825 Thomas Cole establishes the Hudson Valley school of landscape painting. Completion of the Erie Canal connecting the Great Lakes to New York City.

1826 Completion of the first (three-mile) railroad in Quincy, Massachusetts.

1827 John James Audubon publishes the first volume of *The Birds of America*.

1830 President Andrew Jackson's Indian Removal Act is passed, allowing the displacement of five tribes – the Cherokee, Seminole, Creeks, Chickasaw and Choctaw – from various desirable territories to 'Indian Territory' in Oklahoma. In 1838, about 15,000 Cherokees begin the 800-mile journey from the South-east, on what becomes known as the Trail of Tears. Four thousand die on the journey.

1831 Nat Turner's slave revolt results in the death of more than fifty whites. William Garrison founds the abolitionist newspaper *The Liberator*.

1837 Samuel F. B. Morse patents his idea for a telegraph, sending the message 'What hath God wrought?' from Washington to Baltimore in 1844.

1838 Transatlantic steamship service begins.

1840 The Transcendentalist Club, founded in 1836, begins to publish *The Dial*.

1841 Ralph Waldo Emerson publishes *Essays – Series One*, including 'Self Reliance'.

1845 Publication of the *Narrative of the Life of Frederick Douglass* and Margaret Fuller's *Woman in the Nineteenth Century*. John O'Sullivan, a New York newspaper editor, writes of 'our manifest destiny to overspread the continent allotted by Providence for the free development of our yearly multiplying millions'.

1846–8 The annexation of Texas in 1845 leads to the Mexican War, in which the US captures additional territory including New Mexico and California.

1848 The Seneca Falls convention on women's rights. Gold is found at Sutter's Mill in Coloma, California. By 1849 word has spread across the country, bringing around 90,000 'forty-niners' to California. Before the Gold Rush ends in 1855, some 300,000 people have tried their luck.

1850 The Fugitive Slave Law comes into effect. The census collects information about national origin for the first time. Nathaniel Hawthorne publishes *The Scarlet Letter*.

1851 Herman Melville publishes *Moby Dick*. The initial print run of 3,000 copies is not sold in his lifetime.

1852 Harriet Beecher Stowe publishes *Uncle Tom's Cabin*, which sells a million copies in the following year.

1853 William Wells Brown's *Clotel; or, The President's Daughter* is the first novel by an African American to be published – in England.

1854 Opponents of slavery – abolitionists – set up the Republican Party. Henry David Thoreau publishes *Walden*.

1855 Walt Whitman publishes *Leaves of Grass*.

1857 A slave called Dred Scott sues for his freedom. The case reaches the Supreme Court, which rules that slaves and their descendants are not citizens but chattels and hence cannot sue in court. The *Atlantic Monthly* is launched.

1860–61 The Republican candidate Abraham Lincoln is elected President. Eleven pro-slavery states secede from the Union to form the Confederate States of America. War breaks out with an attack on Fort Sumter.

1863 Lincoln issues the Emancipation Proclamation which declares that slaves in the Confederate States are free.

1865 The Civil War ends with the defeat of the Confederates and slavery is abolished under the Thirteenth Amendment. Abraham Lincoln is assassinated. Six Confederate veterans from Tennessee form the Ku Klux Klan.

1866 A telegraph cable is successfully laid across the Atlantic Ocean. The Civil Rights Act extends citizenship to African Americans.

1867 About 35,000 Texan longhorn cattle first follow the Chisholm Trail (mapped by Jesse Chisholm) to the railhead at Abilene, Kansas.

1868 Louisa May Alcott publishes *Little Women*.

1869 The Union Pacific–Central Pacific transcontinental railroad is completed when the two lines meet at Promontory Point, Utah.

1876 Sioux Indians defeat US troops at the Battle of the Little Bighorn. In Boston Alexander Graham Bell uses a telephone to transmit speech ('Mr Watson, come here! I want to see you!'). The first transcontinental telephone call, between New York and San Francisco, takes place in 1915.

1881 Booker T. Washington founds the Tuskegee Normal School for Colored Teachers – one of many such institutions established after the Civil War. Henry James publishes *The Portrait of a Lady*.

1883 Opening of the Brooklyn Bridge, then the world's longest suspension bridge.

1884 Mark Twain publishes *The Adventures of Huckleberry Finn*. Work begins on the first 'skyscraper' – the ten-storey Home Insurance Building in Chicago. George Eastman patents a flexible roll of film. The first Kodak box cameras are sold in 1888.

1886 The Statue of Liberty, a gift from France, is dedicated in New York Harbor. In 1903, a plaque is attached bearing Emma Lazarus's 1883 sonnet 'The New Colossus', including the much quoted lines: 'Give me your tired, your poor/Your huddled masses yearning to be free'.

1890 US Troops defeat the Sioux Indians at Wounded Knee. The census reports that the West has been settled, the frontier is closed, and that the Native American population is less than 225,000. Fifteen per cent of the population is foreign-born.

1891 The International Copyright Act is passed, meaning that, for the first time, it becomes more profitable for American publishers to print the work of local authors. Thomas Edison patents the kinetoscope, having patented the phonograph in 1877.

1893 Frederick Jackson Turner delivers his address, 'The Significance of the Frontier in American History'.

1896 In the case of *Plessey v. Ferguson*, the Supreme Court rules that a Louisiana law mandating 'separate but equal' accommodation for black and white passengers on interstate railroads is constitutional.

1898 The US gains Puerto Rico, Guam and the Philippines following the Spanish-American War. Spain renounces any claim to Cuba, which becomes formally independent in 1902 (although the US retains the right to intervene in its affairs). Hawaii is annexed.

1900 More than 6,000 people die after a hurricane hits the city of Galveston on the Gulf of Mexico. Theodore Dreiser publishes *Sister Carrie*.

1901 Oil discovered in Texas. The first transatlantic radio signal is received.

1906 More than 3,000 people die in the San Francisco earthquake and resulting fire. Upton Sinclair's novel *The Jungle* exposes corruption in the meat-packing industry.

1908 Henry Ford introduces the Model T car. His factories adopt assembly-line technology in 1913.

1909 W. E. B. DuBois founds the National Association for the Advancement of Colored People (NAACP). Bakelite, the first wholly synthetic plastic, is patented.

1910–30 About 2 million African Americans move from the rural South to the urban North to escape poverty and racial violence in what becomes known as the Great Migration.

1913 The Armory Show in Manhattan introduces modern European art to the US. Opening of the Lincoln Highway, which runs 3,389 miles from Times Square in New York to Lincoln Park in San Francisco.

1915 Re-emergence of the Ku Klux Klan, whose membership reaches a peak of over 4 million in the mid-1920s. Release of D. W. Griffiths' film about the 1870s Klan, *The Birth of a Nation*. The *Lusitania* is sunk by a German U-boat.

1917 The United States enters the First World War. Selective Service draft is introduced.

1918 At least 675,000 Americans die in the influenza pandemic.

1919 The Eighteenth Amendment to the Constitution is ratified, prohibiting the manufacture, sale and transport of alcohol. Prohibition is repealed in 1933.

1920 Women gain voting rights under the Nineteenth Amendment.

1922 T. S. Eliot publishes *The Waste Land*.

1924 The Indian Citizenship Act is passed. The Immigration Act limits the number of immigrants from any country to 2 per cent of the number of people from that country already living in the US in 1890. The aim is to restrict immigration by eastern and southern Europeans; immigration from East Asia is prohibited.

1925 The *New Yorker* is founded. F. Scott Fitzgerald publishes *The Great Gatsby*.

1927 *The Jazz Singer* is released as the first talking picture. Charles Lindbergh flies from New York to Paris.

1929 Between 24 October and 13 November, $30 million is lost in devalued stocks on Wall Street. In the 'Great Depression' that follows millions lose their jobs.

1933 President Franklin D. Roosevelt launches his 'New Deal' recovery programme, which includes major public works to tackle unemployment and stimulate the economy.

1936 Margaret Mitchell publishes *Gone with the Wind* and William Faulkner publishes *Absalom, Absalom!*

1937 Zora Neale Hurston publishes *Their Eyes Were Watching God*.

1940 Release of Orson Welles's film, *Citizen Kane*. Richard Wright's *Native Son* is the first book by an African American to be chosen for the Book-of-the-Month Club.

1941 The US declares war on Japan after Japanese warplanes attack the US fleet at Pearl Harbor in Hawaii. Germany then declares war on the US, which subsequently intervenes decisively in the Second World War.

1945 Germany surrenders in May; in August the US drops atomic bombs on Hiroshima and Nagasaki and Japan surrenders.

1946 President Harry S. Truman establishes the Central Intelligence Agency (CIA). The art critic Robert Coates coins the term 'abstract expressionism'.

1947 The announcement of the Truman Doctrine – a policy of providing aid for nations threatened by communism – signals the start of the Cold War with the Soviet Union. Jackie Robinson signs for the Brooklyn Dodgers, becoming the first African American to play for a major league baseball team. *A Streetcar Named Desire*, by Tennessee Williams, opens on Broadway.

1948 The Marshall Plan to revive ailing European economies is announced. Over the next four years, $13 billion is disbursed.

1949 Arthur Miller's play *Death of a Salesman* opens on Broadway.

1950–53 US forces play a leading role against North Korean and Chinese armies in the Korean War.

1950–54 Senator Joseph McCarthy carries out a crusade against alleged communists in government and public life.

1951 Launch of transcontinental television. J. D. Salinger publishes *The Catcher in the Rye*.

1952 Ralph Ellison publishes *Invisible Man*.

1953 Saul Bellow publishes *The Adventures of Augie March*. Ethel and Julius Rosenberg are executed for espionage. *Playboy* magazine is launched.

1954 *Plessey v. Ferguson* (1896) is overturned when, in *Brown v. Board of Education*, the Supreme Court rules that racial segregation in schools is unconstitutional. This decision marks the start of a concerted campaign to secure civil rights for African Americans.

1955 The first McDonald's restaurant opens in Illinois.

1956 Allen Ginsberg publishes *Howl and Other Poems*.

1957 The Civil Rights Act. The USSR launches *Sputnik 1*, initiating the Space Race: the US follows four months later with *Explorer 1*. The National Aeronautics and Space Administration (NASA) is established in 1958.

1961 Cuban exiles, organized and financed by the US government, make an unsuccessful attempt to invade Cuba's Bahía de Cochinos (Bay of Pigs).

1962 The US compels the Soviet Union to withdraw nuclear weapons from Cuba in what becomes known as the Cuban Missile Crisis.

1963 President John F. Kennedy is assassinated.

1964 The US intensifies its military intervention in Vietnam. The Civil Rights Act becomes law.

1965 The Immigration and Nationality Act abolishes quotas based on national origin. Preference is now given to those who have relatives in the US. The civil rights leader Malcolm X is assassinated.

1966 Truman Capote publishes *In Cold Blood*.

1967 The population of the US reaches 200 million.

1968 Civil rights leader Martin Luther King and Presidential candidate Robert Kennedy are assassinated in separate incidents. Anti-war protests intensify, marked by violent demonstrations, particularly at Columbia University in New York and the Democratic Convention in Chicago. Norman Mailer publishes *The Armies of the Night*.

1969 US astronaut Neil Armstrong is the first person to walk on the moon. Philip Roth publishes *Portnoy's Complaint* and Mario Puzo publishes *The Godfather*.

1970 The foreign-born population is 4.7 per cent, having fallen from 11.6 per cent in 1930 and 6.9 per cent in 1950.

1973 The Vietnam ceasefire agreement is signed.

1974 President Richard Nixon resigns in the wake of the Watergate scandal over a 1972 break-in at the Democratic Party headquarters. The first of three Cohen–Boyer recombinant DNA cloning patents is granted, leading to the beginnings of the biotechnology industry.

1976 Alex Haley publishes *Roots*.

1979 Radical students seize the US Embassy in Tehran, Iran. The hostages are released 444 days later.

1981 First reports of acquired immunodeficiency syndrome (AIDS), a disease caused by the human immunodeficiency virus (HIV). The disease is not named until 1982.

1986 The Iran–Contra scandal reveals that proceeds from secret US arms deals to Iran were used illegally to fund anti-government rebels in Nicaragua.

1987 Toni Morrison publishes *Beloved*.

1989 US troops invade Panama, oust its government and arrest its leader, one-time CIA informant General Manuel Noriega, on drug-trafficking charges.

1990 The first McDonald's restaurant opens in Moscow.

1991 US forces play a dominant role in the war triggered by Iraq's invasion of Kuwait and ending with the expulsion of Iraqi troops.

1992 US President George W. Bush and Russian President Boris Yeltsin declare a formal end to the Cold War.

1994 The North American Free Trade Agreement (NAFTA), between the United States, Canada and Mexico, creates the largest free trade zone in the world.

1999 The US plays a leading role in the NATO bombardment of Yugoslavia as a response to Serb violence against ethnic Albanians in the province of Kosovo.

2000 The census reports that the foreign-born population is 11 per cent, the highest proportion since 1930. The Human Genome Project publishes the first draft of the genome; President Bill Clinton announces that it cannot be patented. The sequence of Chromosome 1, the largest of the human chromosomes, is published in 2006.

2001 More than 3,000 people die when a terrorist attack on 11 September destroys the World Trade Center in Manhattan and damages the Pentagon in Arlington, Virginia.

2003 The bombing of Baghdad marks the start of a US-led campaign to overthrow the Iraqi leader Saddam Hussein.

2005 Hundreds of people die when Hurricane Katrina strikes New Orleans.

2006 The population of the US reaches 300 million. About 0.8 per cent are of Native American descent.

2008 Millions of dollars are wiped out in bad loans and several financial institutions collapse. The US faces its worst financial crisis since the Great Depression.

2009 Barack Obama is sworn in as the 44th President. He is the first African American to hold the post.

Introduction

NB: Readers who do not wish to learn details of the stories may prefer to treat the Introduction as an Epilogue.

Like many others, I've looked to Edgar Allan Poe for a starting point. One of the great champions of the American short story, Poe argued that what gave a collection of tales the edge over a novel or a book of poems was its capacity to represent a 'vast variety of modes or inflections of thought and expression'.[1] Variety has certainly been one of my main aims in making this selection. The following pages are populated with farm labourers, artists, aunts, soldiers, sons, witches, drunks, ghosts, property developers and vacuum cleaner salesmen. There's also a dog, a frog and a caterpillar. Their stories are, in Washington Irving's phrase, all 'short and quickly told'.[2]

An anthology not only contains stories, it also, inevitably, tells stories. One narrative is about time, about change and continuity in the forms and preoccupations of an important American genre, from its beginnings in the early nineteenth century. Another concerns space or, more specifically, the ways in which the short story became a favoured mode in which to explore the diversity of the United States. Underlining both of these rather abstract emphases is the material fact that the short story is 'normally too short to be published by itself'[3] and so needs to find a home among other pieces – in a collection by a single author, in an anthology, or, to start with, most often in a magazine. While there have been storytellers since the earliest times, the invention and development of the modern short story as we recognize it is a product of the invention and development of magazines.

Twenty different magazines are represented in this anthology (see Sources), and through them we can trace several important

shifts. Before anyone spoke much of 'tales' or 'sketches' –
never mind 'short stories' – periodicals published essays.[4] The
essay tradition that developed in eighteenth-century British
periodicals, and then crossed the Atlantic, used a wide variety of short prose forms – from the dream vision to the mock
advertisement – and often employed a rather whimsical elderly
bachelor as a continuing narrator. Washington Irving used the
bachelor-narrator to great effect and, in 1820, his *Sketch-Book
of Geoffrey Crayon, Gent.* became America's 'first literary
best-seller'.[5] This collection opens with one of Crayon's prede-
cessors, Launcelot Langstaff, telling the tale of 'The Little Man
in Black' (1807).[6]

By the middle of the nineteenth century, locally based journals (such as the *New-England Magazine*, which published
Nathaniel Hawthorne's 'Young Goodman Brown' in 1835)
gave way to magazines with a national circulation, including
the *Atlantic*, the *Ladies' Home Journal* and *Collier's*, where
Henry James's 'The Real Right Thing' first appeared in 1899.
What became known as the 'magazine story' – to be 'taken
down with a gulp' – reached a peak of popularity in the early
decades of the twentieth century, although its usual reliance on
a predictable range of characters and stock devices (such as a
sentimental or ironic conclusion) led some to dismiss it as a
typical modern 'mechanical product'.[7] In response, there emerged
a whole host of 'little magazines' that promoted an experimen-
tal modernism – 'form, not plot,' said Sherwood Anderson,
whose spare and elusive 'The Untold Lie' was published in the
Seven Arts in 1917.[8] (The magazine had a circulation of just
5,000 while *Collier's*, at its peak, reached nearly three million.)
Since that time, the American short story has maintained a
reputation as a genre that is peculiarly amenable to both commercial formula and avant-garde innovation. By the late
twentieth century, with fewer and fewer national platforms
available, the 'holy grail' for short story writers became the
New Yorker; four of our final ten stories appeared in that
magazine.[9] Little magazines, many of which are associated with
universities and creative writing programmes, nevertheless remain
the home of most American short fiction.[10] This selection closes

with Lydia Davis's 'The Caterpillar', which featured in a little magazine called *NOON* in 2006.

Places and Voices

The stories in this book cover a fair amount of ground, as do their characters. It's perhaps appropriate then that we begin with the story of an immigrant – Irving's little man in black – or rather, the story of his final days in an insular Hudson Valley community, which is deeply suspicious of his 'foreign aspect' and 'outlandish tongue'.[11] America is an end point too for the narrator of Jhumpa Lahiri's 'The Third and Final Continent' (1999), but this time we hear the immigrant's version of events. Set in 1969, just as the first Americans leave the planet to walk on the moon, the story explores the ways in which our experience of space and time expands and contracts. Lahiri's narrator first travels from Calcutta to London, but he devotes a mere page to the five years he spent there. Nor does he elaborate on the thirty years of family life that he subsequently spent in Massachusetts. His subject is rather the 'remote interlude' of his first six weeks in a Boston lodging house kept by Mrs Croft, a woman born in 1866. 'Compared to a century', the time he spends with her 'was no time at all' and yet he measures it precisely in 'minutes' and 'steps' and the 'eight one dollar bills' of his weekly rent. The house, like Irving's village, offers a metaphor of a nation coping with intrusion. Mrs Croft might be obsessed with locked doors – patrolling her boarders and borders – but nevertheless she welcomes travellers from India to America, and via the radio, travellers from America to the moon.

The stories in this collection range all over the United States: from Ohio to Texas, Montana to Georgia, California to Mississippi. Can we distinguish a Harlem story from a Cleveland story? Is there a difference between a story set on a New England local train (Edith Wharton's 'Atrophy') and a story whose action takes place on the Denver to Kansas City line, with Westerners and Easterners sitting side by side (O. Henry's tale-with-a-twist, 'Hearts and Hands')?

O. Henry was writing in 1903, at a time when many believed that the short story was the ideal form for educating one part of the population about another. Bret Harte, another popular story writer, even argued that what became known as 'local color' allowed the Union, 'for the first time', to recognize fully 'its component parts'.[12] It was a period of great change in the constitution of those parts. On the one hand, large waves of immigration meant that the United States had an increasingly diverse population; on the other hand, local folk traditions were thought to be under threat from modern networks of communication (railways, magazines and, later, the telephone). While some stories sought to preserve regional or ethnic 'types' in ethnographic case studies, others explored the new networks as metaphors for human connection and disconnection. In Wharton's 'Atrophy' (1927), Nora Frenway is thwarted in her attempt to visit her dying lover. His jealous sister only wants to discuss timetables, and, feigning anxiety that Nora will miss her train, sends her 'back to the Junction' and her life of propriety. In Dorothy Parker's version of a long-distance phone call, 'New York to Detroit' (1928), we know that Jack (in Detroit) is talking about more than the crackling line when he tells Jean (in New York) that they've got 'the damndest, lousiest connection I ever saw in my life'.

Voices have always been important to the American short story. Many borrow the form of the dramatic monologue – think of Poe's walled-up narrator in 'The Tell-Tale Heart' (1843), desperate to confess, or of Aunt Hetty lecturing her nieces about marriage in Fanny Fern's sketch 'Aunt Hetty on Matrimony' (1851). Others present a scene of dialogue. In 'Starving Again' (1990), Lorrie Moore stages an interrogation of romance, 1980s-style, in a macrobiotic restaurant. Her hungry-for-love protagonists might not get much sustenance from the miso, but conversation is another matter. Whether the back and forth takes place across a cornfield (Anderson's 'The Untold Lie') or a city street (Zora Neale Hurston's 'Now You Cookin' with Gas') or the living-room couch (John Updike's 'Sunday Teasing'), or even (in Parker's case) across a continent, in many cases the conversation *is* the story.

The clash between voices and points of view, fundamental to all exchanges, is further emphasized when the speakers use different dialects. Many humorous stories of the early to mid-nineteenth century rely on a gap between a sophisticated Eastern narrator and an uneducated 'regional' speaker.[13] By 1865, however, when Samuel L. Clemens launched his career (under the name Mark Twain), the balance of power between the recorder of the tale and its teller had become less straightforward. Twain fiddled endlessly with 'Jim Smiley and His Jumping Frog'. The version included here, his third go, takes the form of a letter addressed to 'A. Ward'.[14] Twain relates how he was sent by a friend to inquire after a minister called Smiley but instead found himself listening to 'garrulous' Simon Wheeler's 'infernal reminiscence' about a *gambler* called Smiley. Eventually, 'good-naturedly', he walked away.[15] Was the joke on him? Had the seemingly earnest Wheeler been playing him for a fool all along? Is Twain's own rather pompous deadpan for real? We can't tell. 'Jim Smiley and His Jumping Frog' is as much a story about the complicated games and performances involved in storytelling as a tall tale about a frog.

While Twain used the frame tale to play the wiliness of the Southwest against the expectations of his New York *Saturday Press* readers, Joel Chandler Harris attempted a post-Civil War rehabilitation of plantation life. Uncle Remus has 'nothing but pleasant memories of the discipline of slavery'.[16] Remus's intimacy with Miss Sally's seven-year-old boy – not entirely dissimilar to the alliance of Twain's Huck and Jim – appealed to readers looking for an escape from complicated modernity and to those determined to revive the 'natural' race relations of the antebellum era. And yet the tales told by Remus – originating in the African-derived tales Harris had heard in his own childhood[17] – invariably undercut that cosy picture. 'The Wonderful Tar-Baby Story' (1880), for example, isn't about harmony and co-operation but sticky and violent entanglement. Characteristically, Uncle Remus leaves the ending open – 'dat's all de fur de tale goes' – and Miss Sally's boy in suspense.[18] The teller, once more, is in control of the tale.

Charles W. Chesnutt was Harris's contemporary and the first African-American writer to 'find a substantial white readership' through his publication in the *Atlantic*.[19] His first book, *The Conjure Woman* (1899), involved another ex-slave 'uncle' (Julius MacAdoo) telling stories of plantation life; in this case to the white Yankee couple who buy the plantation. But Chesnutt soon rejected the stereotypical restrictions of the 'dialect tale' in favour of fictions that tackled the complexities of black urban bourgeois existence. 'The Wife of His Youth' (1898), the title story of his second collection, directly addresses the relationship between that middle-class professional world and the 'old plantation life'. Charles Ryder is a light-skinned 'refined type', fond of Tennyson's 'fair maidens', and a believer in the 'upward process of absorption' of his race. One day, his party preparations are interrupted by the arrival of a 'very black' and elderly-looking woman called Liza Jane. It is as if his past has been 'summoned up' by the 'wave of a magician's wand'. Ryder listens as she relates her life story and later repeats the tale to his guests, before revealing that, twenty-nine years earlier, she had been his wife. We are told that Ryder uses the 'same soft dialect' as Liza Jane did, but the narrative provides a report in Standard English. The past must be acknowledged, Chesnutt suggests, but so too must its pastness.

If the 'dialect tale' had had its day, the richness of vernacular speech continued to inspire American writers. Zora Neale Hurston, in particular, was adamant that folklore was 'not a thing of the past' but, in the 1930s, very much 'still in the making'.[20] She believed that language (or, at least, what she called 'Negro Expression') came alive in a kind of everyday 'acting out' in 'little plays by strolling players . . . in a dozen streets in a thousand cities'.[21] 'No one' on those dozen streets, she said, 'ever mistakes the meaning.' 'Now You Cookin' with Gas' (1942), about two men from the South who meet in Harlem to brag, argue and share their homesickness, opens as if the reader is there on the street corner too. 'Wait till I light my coal-pot,' the narrator says, 'and I'll tell you about this Zigaboo called Jelly.' But since the readers of the *American Mercury* might mistake the meaning, the narrative then moves between Harlem 'slanguage', Standard English and, as a kind of compromise, free indirect style. A glossary further helped the reader not to 'mistake

the meaning'.[22] Some have read 'Now You Cookin' with Gas'
as a demonstration of Hurston's mastery of the 'spy-glass of
Anthropology', arguing that it is 'less fiction than a linguistic
study', but this is too simple.[23] The story does not simply use
jive talk; it's about jive talk. Unable to make a successful deal
in either sex or money, Jelly and Sweet Back take pleasure in
exchanging words. 'Boogerbooing', 'bullskating', 'confidenc-
ing' and 'beating up' their gums is what they mostly do.

Secrets and Silences

One group of stories in this book explores the consolations and
vitality of language, another seems to suggest that it's better,
and truer, not to say too much. 'Whatever I told him would
have been a lie,' concludes Anderson's Ray Pearson in 'The
Untold Lie', keeping schtum. Anderson's protégé Ernest Hemingway went on to form a theory of not telling or, as he put it,
'omission'.[24] 'Out of Season' (1923), his first experiment in this
mode, is made up of fragments of conversations and actions,
leaving many 'mysterious' gaps in information and time. The
reader's inevitable disorientation reflects that of the story's
'young gentleman' and 'his wife' who always seem to be either
late or early, strangers in a strange land, but misunderstanding
each other as much as they do the German and Italian speakers
of the Dolomites. The point of the story is not to explain but
rather to create what Carlos Baker called a 'metaphorical conflu-
ence of emotional atmospheres'.[25] A similar effect is created by
John Updike's 'Sunday Teasing' (1956), although its articulate
discussions may seem a world away from Hemingway's cryptic,
stylized exchanges. Here, though, the very volume of talk –
about St Paul and Benny Goodman, Henry Green and Scarlatti,
the *New York Times* and Garbo in *Camille* – serves only to indicate what hasn't been, and can't be, said. While washing the
dishes at the end of the day, the protagonist has a 'perfect and
luminous thought: *You don't know anything.*'

Secrets have always been the great motivators of fiction. If
nineteenth-century works often presented confession as a great

relief – certainly in the case of Poe's 'very, very dreadfully nervous' murderer, and Mary Wilkins Freeman's devoted 'Two Friends' (1887), each of whom is 'keepin' something' from the other – the modernist story suggested that secrecy was almost a condition of life. The moral of Henry James's 'The Real Right Thing' might be 'Don't pry'. A great writer dies and his wife hires a biographer. But while initially believing that the writer's ghost has appeared to guide him in 'an intercourse closer than that of life', the biographer is finally forced to accept that the ghost's intention is not to reveal but rather to continue to conceal and thus '*save* His Life'.[26]

The best one could hope for, it seemed, was the momentary exposure of a 'real self' behind the 'automaton' of convention (as Wharton put it in 'Atrophy'). Fiction's capacity for inner exposure made it preferable to photography, maintained Eudora Welty, who worked in both forms. Only stories could 'part the veil between people' and show 'what comes from inside'.[27] The revelation of the private real self was more likely to come from actions than from words. Jason and Sara Morton, the protagonists of Welty's 'The Whistle' (1938), are 'no more communicative in their misery than a pair of window shutters beaten by a storm'. They once owned a farm in Mississippi but the ravages of the Depression forced them to sell it to a Mr Perkins, and now their lives are governed by his 'great whistle' – calling them out in the night to protect the tomato plants from frost with their own clothes. One evening Jason does a 'rare, strange thing' and sets fire to every piece of wood in their cabin. He gives his wife a 'wonderful' moment of 'extravagant warmth', but the intimate consolation of their silent communion is broken by the return of the whistle, 'as though it would extract something further from their lives'.

Short-Story Time

Those who prefer novels sometimes say that the short story ignores history. While it's certainly true that a detailed chronicle of the Civil War or the Great Depression or the immigrant experience can't be fitted into ten or twenty pages, short stories have a lot to say about these events and, more generally, about the ways in which time is experienced.

The modern short story often stages moments of crisis or transformation; moments which, at the very least, provide 'some point of vantage, from which past and future are equally visible'.[28] A classic example is Flannery O'Connor's 'A Late Encounter with the Enemy' (1953), in which George Poker Sash experiences a fatal stroke at his 63-year-old granddaughter's college graduation, while sitting on stage dressed as a Confederate general. Sash is 104 but he can't recall the Civil War 'at all', nor the Spanish-American War in which he lost a son. In fact his most vivid memory is of the premiere of *Gone with the Wind* when he also wore a fake general's outfit and was surrounded by pretty girls. If Sash seems to represent the South's willing commodification of history – his corpse is left by a Coca-Cola machine – his final moments suggest the possibility of another perspective. When the 'little hole in his head' opens, images of his family and the names of Civil War battle sites rush in – the 'entire' and genuine past – 'as if the past were the only future now and he had to endure it'.

Death might offer the ultimate (if late-arriving) vantage point, but night – in particular, what Poe calls the 'dead hour' of midnight – often serves an adequate educative purpose. The problem is that the adventure of just 'one night' is often more than a 'mere interlude in the main business of life'; it changes that life for ever.[29] Did Goodman Brown witness a 'witch-meeting' in the forest or was it just a 'wild dream'? Either way, he returns to village life, and his waiting wife, a stern, sad and no longer young man.

Since Hawthorne's day, the American woods have seen their fair share of initiations into awareness of sex and evil and limitation. In Alice Walker's 'The Flowers' (1973), ten-year-old Myop is skipping along a woodland path, where 'nothing existed for her but her song'. Until, that is, a few hundred words later, when she stumbles upon the corpse of a lynched man and summer is 'over'. A more complicated initiation takes place for the sixteen-year-old protagonist of Richard Ford's

'Communist' (1985). Twenty-five years later, he's still not sure what exactly he learnt from the day in November 1961 when he went hunting on the lake with his mother and her boyfriend, a paranoid veteran of 1950s CIA operations in Vietnam. The tension exists on both a personal and a national level between what 'I knew . . . even then' and 'what is clear to me now'.

Of course, the forest is not the only place in which fissures in lives are made and felt. Twentieth-century fiction was more likely to make use of the temporary hiatus of a hotel (Hemingway), a lodging house (Lahiri), or a railway station. In John Cheever's mordantly funny 'Reunion' (1962) a teenaged boy, 'between trains', meets his father for an hour and a half, and for the last time, at Grand Central Station. But that's all the time he needs to realize that he has seen his 'future' and his 'doom'. The narrator of Grace Paley's 'Wants' (1971), meanwhile, meets her ex-husband on the steps of the public library. Her books are overdue, but if the librarian is happy to wipe 'the record clean', the ex wants to pinpoint, to the hour, the end of the marriage. The story both suggests the absurdity of this 'want' and acknowledges that big changes can come of small decisions, albeit in a rather haphazard fashion.

Because sometimes the event that should change everything doesn't. Written seventy years before Paley's story, in 1899, Stephen Crane's 'An Episode of War' exemplifies, and to some extent paved the way towards, the modern short story's emphasis on the arbitrary and inexplicable. While engaged in the banal ritual of dividing the company's coffee ration during the Civil War, an unnamed Union lieutenant suffers a gunshot wound that will lead to another division – the amputation of his arm from his body. The soldiers, who are 'spectators' to both events, can't comprehend how one minute all was well and then, the next, a bullet appeared from a nearby forest: 'the men in silence stared at the wood, then at the departing lieutenant – then at the wood, then at the lieutenant'. This is a story of many gaps – in bodies, in knowledge and also in our understanding of the importance of bodies and knowledge.[30] How much does the loss of an arm matter? What happens after time has been broken?

The conceit of waking up to find the world 'strange and incomprehensible' has a long pedigree in the American short story, beginning with Washington Irving's 'Rip Van Winkle' (1819), whose eponymous hero sleeps through the Revolution.[31] F. Scott Fitzgerald updates the conceit in 'The Lost Decade' (1939), in which a man who spent the Depression 'every-which-way drunk' emerges onto the streets of Manhattan ten years on, and has to learn again 'how people walk and what their clothes and shoes and hats are made of'. Like 'An Episode of War', these stories suggest that, however difficult, rupture can be overcome.

But the short story is not only about turning points, or points that refuse to turn. Isolating an episode can merely confirm a sense of time's relentlessness. Like Chesnutt's tale, Bernard Malamud's 'The First Seven Years' (1950) is about a man whose 'dreams of a better life' are threatened by the embodiment of an 'ugly' past he had tried to forget. A Jewish shoemaker in New York, Feld wants his daughter to marry a go-getting Horatio Alger type, but she's in love with his assistant, Sobel – a bald and tearful Holocaust survivor with scholarly tendencies. This is a story less about the past than about the future – about 'wants', and the delays and disappointments that accompany them. In the tradition of the Talmudic Midrash (an explication of a piece of scripture), it is also an ironic retelling of the Genesis story of Jacob's labour to win Rachel as his wife. Jacob's first seven years of labour end when he is deceived by her father Laban; another seven will follow.[32]

Malamud's story ends as it began, with the sound of Sobel 'pounding leather for his love'. Such temporal reminders – and attempts to resist them – are not uncommon in this anthology. Poe writes about a murder undertaken to quieten an old man's thumping heart. But after the man is dead, the thump then emanates from the murderer's own chest, his 'tell-tale heart' an unceasing echo of the tick of his watch. Violent action also fails to make a full stop in William Faulkner's 'Barn Burning' (1939) – the unhyphenated title of which ambiguously suggests both a discrete event and a continuing process. It's a story about a man trapped in the economic paralysis of Southern sharecropping who moves from one place to another in a cycle of humiliation and barn burning, his 'one weapon for the preservation of integrity'. But fire's angry heat – here, as in Welty's 'The Whistle' – doesn't change anything. Faulkner's story ends at midnight, the 'dead hour', as the man's ten-year-old son leaves barn-burning behind, turning 'his face toward the dark woods' of an uncertain future.

Small Things

Not the least thing a short story can do is take heed of small things and impart an 'air of consequence' to the seemingly inconsequential.[33] The pleasure of reading does not always stem from 'high excitements' or 'ramified implications' or what Lorrie Moore calls the 'makeshift construction of holiness'.[34] Short stories can be about what happens when you finally get around to returning your library books, or watch the precious minutes of a rare encounter dwindle away in bar-room bickering.

The very form of the short story – the way it refuses to go on for very long – seems to debunk grandiosity, and deflation can also be its tone or theme. Fanny Fern's Aunt Hetty issues a warning to her nieces on the pitfalls of matrimony, although she knows before she begins that 'every one of you'll try it, the first chance you get!' 'What's the use of talking?' she concludes after less than a page. And it's not just stories featuring lecturing aunts or other kinds of storytellers that reflect on their own practice. In 'I Bought a Little City' (1974), Donald Barthelme presents a portrait of the artist as real estate developer.[35] The speaker recalls the time he took possession of the 'nice little city' of Galveston, Texas. 'It suited me fine so I started to change it,' he says, as if that made perfect sense. After killing 6,000 dogs, creating a housing complex that from the sky looks like a jigsaw of the *Mona Lisa*, and issuing all kinds of orders, 'just out of meanness', he realizes that no one is happy, not even himself. What's the use of 'big changes' when you're in love with a woman who only loves you a 'little bit'? When it comes to ruining lives, God clearly has a better imagination than he does, so he gives up and sells the city.

If it's a bad idea to be 'too imaginative' with the little cities of ordinary life, it's fatal not to make any space at all for art. Washington Irving wrote about a community that won't even accept a 'little man' within its 'narrow limits'. What most annoys the villagers about the stranger is that he doesn't work – 'nor even seemed ambitious of earning a farthing' – but prefers to sit and read his 'large' book.[36] The artist-as-loafer is a figure who would recur in many classic works of American fiction, including Irving's own 'Rip Van Winkle' and, more recently, Raymond Carver's 'Collectors' (1975). Carver's story is about an 'out of work' man who invites a vacuum cleaner salesman into his house and watches him going 'about his business' – 'sweeping, sweeping', collecting 'material' and 'stuff'. That's all that happens. And yet, partly through its title, the story also wants to suggest that observation is itself a kind of work and a kind of art. As if looking for a counterpoint to Barthelme's God-playing town planner, Carver presents the artist as accumulator, a methodical gatherer of human bits and pieces, such as the ring on the salesman's scalp, where his hat had been, or the fat that 'hung over his belt'. Vacuuming up details like this, and instructing us to do the same, short story writers are 'moralists at heart'. 'You!' shouts the short story. 'You're not paying attention to your life, parcelled out as it is in increments smaller and more significant than you seem aware of.'[37]

But even paying attention to your life has its limits – something every short story, and anthology, must acknowledge. The final piece, by Lydia Davis, features a woman who wakes to find a caterpillar in her bed. She tries to look after the creature but soon loses him. How 'far' will she go for this 'tiny thing', no bigger than a 'splinter of wood or a thick piece of thread'? It doesn't take very long for her to decide that 'he is simply too small, really, for me to go on thinking about him'. And so she stops.

Kasia Boddy, 2011

NOTES

1. Edgar Allan Poe, review of Nathaniel Hawthorne's *Twice-Told Tales* (1842), in *Essays and Reviews* (New York: Library of America, 1984), p. 573.

2. In order to showcase as many writers as possible within a compact book, I've left out longer works such as Herman Melville's 15,000-word 'Bartleby, the Scrivener' (1853).

3. Helmut Bonheim, *The Narrative Modes: Techniques of the Short Story* (Cambridge: Brewer, 1982), p. 166.

4. The term 'Short-story' first appeared in print in 1885, in an article by the American critic Brander Matthews. He used a capital and a hyphen to mark the form as distinct from stories which merely happened to be short. 'The Philosophy of the Short-Story', in *The New Short Story Theories*, ed. Charles E. May (Athens, OH: Ohio University Press, 1997), pp. 73–80.

5. Alfred Bendixen, 'The Emergence and Development of the American Short Story', in *A Companion to the American Short Story*, eds. Alfred Bendixen and James Nagel (Oxford: Blackwell, 2010), p. 4.

6. Irving's 'little man' takes his name and dress from Oliver Goldsmith's 'man in black', a disappointed bachelor whose story is related by a Chinese visitor to London in *The Citizen of the World* (1760), letters 26 and 27.

7. Ellen B. Ballou, *The Building of the House: Houghton Mifflin's Formative Years* (Boston: Houghton Mifflin, 1970), p. 444; Edward J. O'Brien, *The Dance of the Machines: The American Short Story and the Industrial Age* (New York: Macaulay, 1929), p. 124.

8. Sherwood Anderson, *A Story Teller's Story* (1924) (Ann Arbor: University of Michigan Press, 2005), p. 352.

9. Stephen King, Introduction to *The Best American Short Stories 2007* (Boston: Houghton Mifflin, 2007), p. xvi.

10. See Mark McGurl, *The Program Era: Postwar Fiction and the Rise of Creative Writing* (Cambridge, MA: Harvard University Press, 2009).

11. Frank O'Connor famously described the short story as the form best suited to outsiders and 'submerged population groups'. *The Lonely Voice: A Study of the Short Story* (1960) (Hoboken, NJ: Melville House, 2004), p. 39.

12. Bret Harte, 'The Rise of the "Short Story"', in *The Luck of Roaring Camp* (London: Penguin, 2001), p. 254.

13. See Kenneth S. Lynne (ed.), *The Comic Tradition in America: An Anthology of American Humor* (New York: Norton, 1958).

14. In later versions he dropped the conceit of the letter to Ward.

15. Twain later wrote of being told by Professor Van Dyck of Princeton that the story originated in classical Greece rather than nineteenth-century California. 'Private History of the "Jumping Frog" Story', in *The Best Short Stories of Mark Twain*, ed. Lawrence I. Berkove (New York: Modern Library, 2004), p. 331.

16. Joel Chandler Harris, Introduction to *Uncle Remus: His Songs and Sayings* (1880) (London: Penguin, 1986), p. 47.

17. At least twenty-five versions of the Tar-Baby tale have been recorded in the English and French West Indies alone. See Elsie Clews Parsons, *Folklore of the Antilles, French and English* (New York: American Folklore Society, 1943), pp. 48–52.

18. Two evenings later, Remus offers 'How Mr Rabbit was Too Sharp for Mr Fox', in which Brer Rabbit tricks the fox into helping him to escape. The Tar-Baby story provoked responses from several twentieth-century African-American writers. See, for example, Ralph Ellison's 1964 essay, 'Hidden Name and Complex Fate', and Toni Morrison's novel, *Tar Baby* (1981).

19. Ellery Sedgwick, *A History of the Atlantic Monthly, 1857–1909* (Boston: University of Massachusetts Press, 1994), p. 267.

20. Zora Neale Hurston, 'Characteristics of Negro Expression', in *Negro: An Anthology*, ed. Nancy Cunard (1934) (New York: Continuum, 2002), p. 24.

21. Ibid., p. 27. The story was adapted for the stage by George C. Wolfe in 1989.

22. Zora Neale Hurston, 'Glossary of Harlem Slang', in *The Collected Stories* (New York: Harper Perennial, 1996), pp. 134–8. See also the unedited version, 'Harlem Slanguage', pp. 227–32.

23. Zora Neale Hurston, *Mules and Men* (1935) (New York: Harper Perennial, 1990), p. 1; Robert E. Hemenway, *Zora Neale Hurston: A Literary Biography* (Urbana: University of Illinois Press, 1977), p. 291.

24. 'My new theory [was] that you could omit anything if you knew that you omitted and the omitted part would strengthen the story and make people feel more than they understood.' Ernest Hemingway, *A Moveable Feast* (1964) (London: Granada, 1977), p. 54.

25. Carlos Baker, *Ernest Hemingway: A Life Story* (New York: Scribner's, 1969), p. 109.

26. For a speculative account of the story's sources, see Hugh Stevens, 'The Resistance to Queory: John Addington Symonds and

"The Real Right Thing"', *The Henry James Review*, 20, no. 3 (1999), 255–64.

27. 'Eudora Welty Talking with Hermione Lee', in *Writing Lives: Conversations Between Women Writers*, ed. Mary Chamberlain (London: Virago, 1988), p. 257. Welty's photographs appeared in *Life* magazine and in two New York exhibitions. One – of a tomato-packer playing guitar – recalls the happiest scene in 'The Whistle'. Eudora Welty, 'Tomato-packers' recess (Copiah County)', in *One Time, One Place: Mississippi in the Depression: A Snapshot Album* (Jackson: University of Mississippi Press, 1996), p. 21.

28. Frank O'Connor, *The Lonely Voice*, p. 103.

29. Nathaniel Hawthorne, 'Wakefield' (1835), in *Tales and Sketches* (New York: Library of America, 1982), p. 297.

30. See David Trotter, 'Dis-enablement: subject and method in the modernist short story', *Critical Quarterly*, 52, no. 2 (July 2010), 4–13.

31. Washington Irving, 'Rip Van Winkle', in *The Sketch Book of Geoffrey Crayon, Gent.* (1819–20) (Oxford: Oxford University Press, 1996), p. 43.

32. See Genesis 29: 20.

33. Edgar Allan Poe, 'The Philosophy of Composition', in *Essays and Reviews*, p. 13.

34. Edgar Allan Poe, review of *Twice-Told Tales*, p. 571; Susan Lohafer, *Coming to Terms with the Short Story* (Baton Rouge: Louisiana State University Press, 1983), p. 97; Lorrie Moore, 'People Like That Are the Only People Here', in *Collected Stories* (London: Faber, 2008), p. 246.

35. 'I Bought a Little City' might be read in the context of late 60s and early 70s initiatives to revitalize Galveston. In particular, Barthelme may have been thinking of George P. Mitchell, the force behind the city's 'Strand Historic District' as well as The Woodlands, a planned community north of Houston.

36. Michael Gilmore describes the little man as 'the first fully differentiated artist in American literature' whose unfriendly reception was not unlike that felt by Irving in the get-ahead new republic. 'The Literature of the Early and Revolutionary Periods', in *The Cambridge History of American Literature, Volume 1: 1590–1820*, ed. Sacvan Bercovitch (Cambridge: Cambridge University Press, 1994), p. 663.

37. Richard Ford, Introduction to *The Granta Book of the American Short Story* (London: Granta, 1992), p. xvii.

Further Reading

Alfred Bendixen and James Nagel (eds.), *A Companion to the American Short Story* (Oxford: Blackwell, 2010)

Kasia Boddy, *The American Short Story Since 1950* (Edinburgh: Edinburgh University Press, 2010)

Robert Bone, *Down Home: Origins of the Afro-American Short Story* (1975) (New York: Columbia University Press, 1988)

Julie Brown (ed.), *Ethnicity and the American Short Story* (New York: Garland, 1997)

Julie Brown (ed.), *American Women Short Story Writers* (New York: Garland, 2000)

Kirk Curnutt, *Wise Economies: Brevity and Storytelling in American Short Stories* (Moscow, ID: University of Idaho Press, 1997)

Eugene Current-Garcia, *The American Short Story Before 1850: A Critical History* (Boston: Twayne, 1985)

Blanche Gelfant (ed.), *The Columbia Companion to the Twentieth-Century American Short Story* (New York: Columbia University Press, 2000)

Richard E. Lee and Patrick Meanor (eds.), *American Short-Story Writers Since World War II*, Fifth Series (Detroit: Thomson Gale, 2007)

Andrew Levy, *The Culture and Commerce of the American Short Story* (Cambridge: Cambridge University Press, 1993)

Charles E. May (ed.), *The New Short Story Theories* (Athens, OH: Ohio University Press, 1997)

Charles E. May, *The Short Story: The Reality of Artifice* (New York: Routledge, 2002)

Frank Luther Mott, *A History of American Magazines*, 3 vols.
(Cambridge, MA: Harvard University Press, 1957)

James Nagel, *The Contemporary American Short-Story Cycle:
The Ethnic Resurgence of a Genre* (Baton Rouge: Louisiana
State University Press, 2001)

Frank O'Connor, *The Lonely Voice: A Study of the Short Story*
(1960) (Hoboken, NJ: Melville House, 2004)

Fred Lewis Pattee, *The Development of the American Short
Story* (New York: Harper, 1923)

Martin Scofield, *The Cambridge Introduction to the American
Short Story* (Cambridge: Cambridge University Press, 2006)

Valerie Shaw, *The Short Story* (London: Longman, 1983)

Douglas Tallack, *The Nineteenth-Century American Short
Story* (London: Routledge, 1993)

Ben Yagoda, *About Town: The New Yorker and the World It
Made* (New York: Da Capo Press, 2001)

The Little Man in Black
by Launcelot Langstaff, Fsq.

WASHINGTON IRVING

The following story has been handed down by family tradition for more than a century. It is one on which my cousin Christopher dwells with more than usual prolixity; and, being in some measure connected with a personage often quoted in our work, I have thought it worthy of being laid before my readers.

Soon after my grandfather, Mr Lemuel Cockloft, had quietly settled himself at the hall, and just about the time that the gossips of the neighbourhood, tired of prying into his affairs, were anxious for some new tea-table topick, the busy community of our little village was thrown into a grand turmoil of curiosity and conjecture; (a situation very common to little gossiping villages) by the sudden and unaccountable appearance of a mysterious individual.

The object of this solicitude was a little black looking man of a foreign aspect, who took possession of an old building, which having long had the reputation of being haunted, was in a state of ruinous desolation, and an object of fear to all true believers in ghosts. He usually wore a high sugar-loaf hat,[1] with a narrow brim, and a little black cloak, which, short as he was, scarcely reached below his knees. He sought no intimacy or acquaintance with any one; appeared to take no interest in the pleasures or the little broils of the village, nor ever talked; except sometimes to himself in an outlandish tongue. He commonly carried a large book, covered with sheepskin, under his arm; appeared always to be lost in meditation, and was often met by the peasantry, sometimes watching the dawning of day, sometimes at noon seated under a tree poring over his volume, and sometimes at evening, gazing with a look of sober tranquility at the sun as it gradually sunk below the horizon.

The good people of the vicinity beheld something prodigiously singular in all this – a profound mystery seemed to hang about the stranger, which, with all their sagacity they could not penetrate, and in the excess of worldly charity they pronounced it a sure sign 'that he was no better than he should be' – a phrase innocent enough in itself, but which, as applied in common, signifies nearly every thing that is bad. The young people thought him a gloomy misanthrope, because he never joined in their sports – the old men thought still more hardly of him, because he followed no trade, nor even seemed ambitious of earning a farthing – and as to the old gossips, baffled by the inflexible taciturnity of the stranger, they unanimously decreed that a man who could not or would not talk, was no better than a dumb beast. The little man in black, careless of their opinions, seemed resolved to maintain the liberty of keeping his own secret; and the consequence was that, in a little while, the whole village was in an uproar – for in little communities of this description, the members have always the privilege of being thoroughly versed, and even of meddling in all the affairs of each other.

A confidential conference was held one Sunday morning after sermon, at the door of the village church, and the character of the unknown fully investigated. The schoolmaster gave as his opinion that he was the wandering Jew – the sexton was certain that he must be a free-mason from his silence – a third maintained, with great obstinacy, that he was a high german doctor, and that the book which he carried about with him, contained the secrets of the black art; but the most prevailing opinion seemed to be that he was a *witch* – a race of beings at that time abounding in those parts; and a sagacious old matron from Connecticut proposed to ascertain the fact by sousing him into a kettle of hot water.

Suspicion, when once afloat, goes with wind and tide, and soon becomes certainty. Many a stormy night was the little man in black seen by the flashes of lightning, frisking and curveting in the air upon a broomstick; and it was always observed that at those times the storm did more mischief than at any other. The old lady in particular, who suggested the humane ordeal of the boiling kettle, lost on one of these occasions a fine brindled cow; which accident was entirely ascribed to the vengeance of the little man in black. If ever a mischievous hireling rode his master's favourite horse to a distant frolick, and the animal was observed to be lame and jaded in the morning – the little man in black was sure to be at the bottom of the affair, nor could a high wind howl through the village at night, but the old women shrugged up their shoulders and observed 'the little man in black was in his *tantrums*.' In short he became the bugbear of every house, and was as effectual in frightening little children into obedience and hystericks, as the redoubtable Raw-head-and-bloody-bones himself;[2] nor could a house-wife of the village sleep in peace, except under the guardianship of a horse-shoe nailed to the door.

The object of these direful suspicions remained for some time totally ignorant of the wonderful quandary he had occasioned, but he was soon doomed to feel its effects. An individual who is once so unfortunate as to incur the odium of a village, is in a great measure outlawed and proscribed; and becomes a mark for injury and insult – particularly if he has not the power or the disposition to recriminate. The little venomous passions, which in the great world are dissipated and weakened by being widely diffused, act in the narrow limits of a country town with collected vigour, and become rancorous in proportion as they are confined in their sphere of action. The little man in black experienced the truth of this – every mischievous urchin returning from school, had full liberty to break his windows; and this was considered as a most daring exploit, for, in such awe did they stand of him, that the most adventurous schoolboy was never seen to approach his threshold, and at night would prefer going round by the cross-roads, where a traveller had been murdered by the indians, rather than pass by the door of his forlorn habitation.

The only living creature that seemed to have any care or affection for this deserted being, was an old turnspit[3] – the companion of his lonely mansion and his solitary wanderings – the sharer of his scanty meals, and, sorry am I to say it – the sharer of his persecutions. The turnspit, like his master, was peaceable and inoffensive; never known to bark at a horse, to growl at a traveller, or to quarrel with the dogs of the neighbourhood. He followed close at his master's heels when he went out, and when he returned stretched himself in the sunbeams at the door, demeaning himself in all things like a civil and well disposed turnspit. But notwithstanding his exemplary deportment he fell likewise under the ill report of the village, as being the familiar[4] of the little man in black, and the evil spirit that presided at his incantations. The old hovel was considered as the scene of their unhallowed rites, and its harmless tenants regarded with a detestation, which their inoffensive conduct never merited. Though pelted and jeered at by the brats of the village, and frequently abused by their parents, the little man in black never turned to rebuke them, and his faithful dog, when wantonly assaulted, looked up wistfully in his master's face, and there learned a lesson of patience and forbearance.

The movements of this inscrutable being had long been the subject of speculation at Cockloft-hall, for its inmates were full as much given to *wondering* as their descendants. The patience with which he bore his persecutions, particularly surprised them – for patience is a virtue but little known in the Cockloft family. My grandmother, who it appears was rather superstitious, saw in this humility nothing but the gloomy sullenness of a wizard, who restrained himself for the present, in hopes of midnight vengeance – the parson of the village, who was a man of some reading, pronounced it the stubborn insensibility of a stoick philosopher: – my grandfather, who, worthy soul, seldom wandered abroad in search of conclusions, took a data from his own excellent heart, and regarded it as the humble forgiveness of a christian. But however different were their opinions as to the character of the stranger, they agreed in one particular, namely, in never intruding upon his solitude; and my grandmother, who was at that time nursing my mother, never left the room, without wisely putting the large family bible in the cradle – a sure talisman, in her opinion, against witchcraft and necromancy.[5]

One stormy winter night, when a bleak north-east wind moaned about the cottages, and howled around the village steeple, my grandfather was returning from club, preceded by a servant with a lantern. Just as he arrived opposite the desolate abode of the little man in black, he was arrested by the piteous howling of a dog which, heard in the pauses of the storm, was exquisitely mournful; and he fancied now and then, that he caught the low and broken groans of some one in distress. He stopped for some minutes, hesitating between the benevolence of his heart and a sensation of genuine delicacy, which in spite of his eccentricity he fully possessed – and which forbade him to pry into the concerns of his neighbours. Perhaps too, this hesitation might have been strengthened by a little taint of superstition; for surely, if the unknown had been addicted to witchcraft, this was a most propitious night for his vagaries. At length the old gentleman's philanthropy predominated; he approached the hovel and pushing open the door – for poverty has no occasion for locks and keys – beheld, by the light of the lantern, a scene that smote his generous heart to the core.

On a miserable bed, with pallid and emaciated visage and hollow eyes – in a room destitute of every convenience – without fire to warm, or friend to console him, lay this helpless mortal who had been so long the terror and wonder of the village. His dog was crouching on the scanty coverlet, and shivering with cold. My grandfather stepped softly and hesitatingly to the bed side, and accosted the forlorn sufferer in his usual accents of kindness. The little man in black seemed recalled by the tones of compassion from the lethargy into which he had fallen; for, though his heart was almost frozen, there was yet one chord that answered to the call of the good old man who bent over him – the tones of sympathy, so novel to his ear, called back his wandering senses and acted like a restorative to his solitary feelings.

He raised his eyes, but they were vacant and haggard – he put forth his hand, but it was cold – he essayed to speak, but the sound died away in his throat – he pointed to his mouth with an expression of dreadful meaning, and, sad to relate! my grandfather understood that the harmless stranger, deserted by society, was perishing with hunger! – With the quick impulse of humanity he dispatched the servant to the hall for refreshment. A little warm nourishment renovated him for a short time – but not long; it was evident his pilgrimage was drawing to a close, and he was about entering that peaceful asylum, where 'the wicked cease from troubling.'[6]

His tale of misery was short and quickly told; infirmities had stolen upon him, heightened by the rigours of the season: he had taken to his bed without strength to rise and ask for assistance – 'and if I had,' said he, in a tone of bitter despondency, 'to whom should I have applied? I have no friend that I know of in the world! – the villagers avoid me as something loathsome and dangerous; and here, in the midst of christians, should I have perished without a fellow-being to soothe the last moments of existence, and close my dying eyes, had not the howlings of my faithful dog excited your attention.'

He seemed deeply sensible of the kindness of my grand-father, and at one time as he looked up into his old benefactor's face, a solitary tear was observed to steal adown the parched furrows of his cheek – poor outcast! – it was the last tear he shed – but I warrant it was not the first by millions! My grand-father watched by him all night. Towards morning he gradually declined, and as the rising sun gleamed through the window, he begged to be raised in his bed that he might look at it for the last time. He contemplated it for a moment with a kind of reli-gious enthusiasm, and his lips moved as if engaged in prayer. The strange conjectures concerning him rushed on my grand-father's mind: 'he is an idolator!' thought he, 'and is worshipping the sun!' – He listened a moment and blushed at his own uncharitable suspicion – he was only engaged in the pious devotions of a christian. His simple orison being finished, the little man in black withdrew his eyes from the east, and taking my grandfather's hand in one of his, and making a motion with the other, towards the sun – 'I love to contemplate it,' said he, ''tis an emblem of the universal benevolence of a true christian – and it is the most glorious work of him, who is philanthropy itself!' My grandfather blushed still deeper at his ungenerous surmises; he had pitied the stranger at first, but now he revered him – he turned once more to regard him, but his countenance had undergone a change – the holy enthusiasm that had lighted up each feature had given place to an expression of mysterious import – a gleam of grandeur seemed to steal across his gothick visage, and he appeared full of some mighty secret which he hesitated to impart. He raised the tattered nightcap that had sunk almost over his eyes, and waving his withered hand with a slow and feeble expression of dignity, – 'In me,' said he, with laconick solemnity – 'In me you behold the last descendant of the renowned Linkum Fidelius!'[7] My grandfather gazed at him with reverence, for though he had never heard of the illustrious personage thus pompously announced, yet there was a certain black-letter dignity in the name, that peculiarly struck his fancy and commanded his respect.

'You have been kind to me,' continued the little man in black, after a momentary pause, 'and richly will I requite your kindness, by making you heir to my treasures! In yonder large deal box are the volumes of my illustrious ancestor, of which I alone am the fortunate possessor. Inherit them – ponder over them – and be wise!' He grew faint with the exertion he had made, and sunk back almost breathless on his pillow. His hand, which, inspired with the importance of his subject, he had raised to my grandfather's arm, slipped from its hold and fell over the side of the bed, and his faithful dog licked it, as if anxious to soothe the last moments of his master, and testify his gratitude to the hand that had so often cherished him. The untaught caresses of the faithful animal were not lost upon his dying master – he raised his languid eyes – turned them on the dog, then on my grandfather, and having given this silent recommendation – closed them forever.

The remains of the little man in black, notwithstanding the objections of many pious people, were decently interred in the church-yard of the village, and his spirit, harmless as the body it once animated, has never been known to molest a living being. My grandfather complied as far as possible with his last request – he conveyed the volumes of Linkum Fidelius to his library – he pondered over them frequently – but whether he grew wiser the tradition does not mention. This much is certain, that his kindness to the poor descendant of Fidelius, was amply rewarded by the approbation of his own heart, and the devoted attachment of the old turnspit, who transferring his affection from his deceased master to his benefactor, became his constant attendant, and was father to a long line of runty curs that still flourish in the family. And thus was the Cockloft library first enriched by the invaluable folioes of the sage LINKUM FIDELIUS.

Young Goodman Brown

NATHANIEL HAWTHORNE

Young Goodman Brown came forth, at sunset, into the street of Salem village,[1] but put his head back, after crossing the threshold, to exchange a parting kiss with his young wife. And Faith, as the wife was aptly named, thrust her own pretty head into the street, letting the wind play with the pink ribbons of her cap, while she called to Goodman Brown.

'Dearest heart,' whispered she, softly and rather sadly, when her lips were close to his ear, 'pr'y thee, put off your journey until sunrise, and sleep in your own bed to-night. A lone woman is troubled with such dreams and such thoughts, that she's afeard of herself, sometimes. Pray, tarry with me this night, dear husband, of all nights in the year!'[2]

'My love and my Faith,' replied young Goodman Brown, 'of all nights in the year, this one night must I tarry away from thee. My journey, as thou callest it, forth and back again, must needs be done 'twixt now and sunrise. What, my sweet, pretty wife, dost thou doubt me already, and we but three months married!'

'Then, God bless you!' said Faith, with the pink ribbons, 'and may you find all well, when you come back.'

'Amen!' cried Goodman Brown. 'Say thy prayers, dear Faith, and go to bed at dusk, and no harm will come to thee.'

So they parted; and the young man pursued his way, until, being about to turn the corner by the meeting-house, he looked back, and saw the head of Faith still peeping after him, with a melancholy air, in spite of her pink ribbons.

'Poor little Faith!' thought he, for his heart smote him. 'What a wretch am I, to leave her on such an errand![3] She talks of dreams, too. Methought, as she spoke, there was trouble in her face, as if a dream had warned her what work is to be done to-night. But, no, no! 'twould kill her to think it. Well; she's a blessed angel on earth; and after this one night, I'll cling to her skirts and follow her to Heaven.'

With this excellent resolve for the future, Goodman Brown felt himself justified[4] in making more haste on his present evil purpose. He had taken a dreary road, darkened by all the gloomiest trees of the forest, which barely stood aside to let the narrow path creep through, and closed immediately behind. It was all as lonely as could be; and there is this peculiarity in such a solitude, that the traveller knows not who may be concealed by the innumerable trunks and the thick boughs overhead; so that, with lonely footsteps, he may yet be passing through an unseen multitude.

'There may be a devilish Indian behind every tree,' said Goodman Brown, to himself; and he glanced fearfully behind him, as he added, 'What if the devil himself should be at my very elbow!'

His head being turned back, he passed a crook of the road, and looking forward again, beheld the figure of a man, in grave and decent attire, seated at the foot of an old tree. He arose, at Goodman Brown's approach, and walked onward, side by side with him.

'You are late, Goodman Brown,' said he. 'The clock of the Old South[5] was striking as I came through Boston; and that is full fifteen minutes agone.'

'Faith kept me back awhile,' replied the young man, with a tremor in his voice, caused by the sudden appearance of his companion, though not wholly unexpected.

It was now deep dusk in the forest, and deepest in that part of it where these two were journeying. As nearly as could be discerned, the second traveller was about fifty years old, apparently in the same rank of life as Goodman Brown, and bearing a considerable resemblance to him, though perhaps more in expression than features. Still, they might have been taken for father and son. And yet, though the elder person was as simply clad as the younger, and as simple in manner too, he had an indescribable air of one who knew the world, and would not have felt abashed at the governor's dinner-table, or in King William's court,[6] were it possible that his affairs should call him thither. But the only thing about him, that could be fixed upon as remarkable, was his staff, which bore the likeness of a great black snake, so curiously wrought, that it might almost be seen to twist and wriggle itself, like a living serpent. This, of course, must have been an ocular deception, assisted by the uncertain light.

'Come, Goodman Brown!' cried his fellow-traveller, 'this is a dull pace for the beginning of a journey. Take my staff, if you are so soon weary.'

'Friend,' said the other, exchanging his slow pace for a full stop, 'having kept covenant[7] by meeting thee here, it is my purpose now to return whence I came. I have scruples, touching the matter thou wot'st of.'

'Sayest thou so?' replied he of the serpent, smiling apart. 'Let us walk on, nevertheless, reasoning as we go, and if I convince thee not, thou shalt turn back. We are but a little way in the forest, yet.'

'Too far, too far!' exclaimed the goodman, unconsciously resuming his walk. 'My father never went into the woods on such an errand, nor his father before him. We have been a race of honest men and good Christians, since the days of the martyrs. And shall I be the first of the name of Brown, that ever took this path, and kept—'

'Such company, thou wouldst say,' observed the elder person, interpreting his pause. 'Well said, Goodman Brown! I have been as well acquainted with your family as with ever a one among the Puritans; and that's no trifle to say. I helped your grandfather, the constable, when he lashed the Quaker woman[8] so smartly through the streets of Salem. And it was I that brought your father a pitch-pine knot, kindled at my own hearth, to set fire to an Indian village, in King Philip's war.[9] They were my good friends, both; and many a pleasant walk have we had along this path, and returned merrily after midnight. I would fain be friends with you, for their sake.'

'If it be as thou sayest,' replied Goodman Brown, 'I marvel

they never spoke of these matters. Or, verily, I marvel not, seeing that the least rumor of the sort would have driven them
from New-England. We are a people of prayer, and good
works, to boot, and abide no such wickedness.'

'Wickedness or not,' said the traveller with the twisted staff,
'I have a very general acquaintance here in New-England. The
deacons of many a church have drunk the communion wine
with me; the selectmen, of divers towns, make me their chair-
man; and a majority of the Great and General Court are firm
supporters of my interest. The governor and I, too – but these
are state-secrets.'

'Can this be so!' cried Goodman Brown, with a stare of
amazement at his undisturbed companion. 'Howbeit, I have
nothing to do with the governor and council; they have their
own ways, and are no rule for a simple husbandman, like me.
But, were I to go on with thee, how should I meet the eye of
that good old man, our minister, at Salem village? Oh, his voice
would make me tremble, both Sabbath-day and lecture-day!'

Thus far, the elder traveller had listened with due gravity,
but now burst into a fit of irrepressible mirth, shaking himself
so violently, that his snake-like staff actually seemed to wriggle
in sympathy.

'Ha! ha! ha!' shouted he, again and again; then composing
himself, 'Well, go on, Goodman Brown, go on; but pr'y thee,
don't kill me with laughing!'

'Well, then, to end the matter at once,' said Goodman
Brown, considerably nettled, 'there is my wife, Faith. It would
break her dear little heart; and I'd rather break my own!'

'Nay, if that be the case,' answered the other, 'e'en go thy
ways, Goodman Brown. I would not, for twenty old women
like the one hobbling before us, that Faith should come to any
harm.'

As he spoke, he pointed his staff at a female figure on the
path, in whom Goodman Brown recognized a very pious and
exemplary dame, who had taught him his catechism,[10] in youth,
and was still his moral and spiritual adviser, jointly with the
minister and Deacon Gookin.

'A marvel, truly, that Goody Cloyse[11] should be so far in the wilderness, at night-fall!' said he. 'But, with your leave, friend, I shall take a cut through the woods, until we have left this Christian woman behind. Being a stranger to you, she might ask whom I was consorting with, and whither I was going.'

'Be it so,' said his fellow-traveller. 'Betake you to the woods, and let me keep the path.'

Accordingly, the young man turned aside, but took care to watch his companion, who advanced softly along the road, until he had come within a staff's length of the old dame. She, meanwhile, was making the best of her way, with singular speed for so aged a woman, and mumbling some indistinct words, a prayer, doubtless, as she went. The traveller put forth his staff, and touched her withered neck with what seemed the serpent's tail.

'The devil!' screamed the pious old lady.

'Then Goody Cloyse knows her old friend?' observed the traveller, confronting her, and leaning on his writhing stick.

'Ah, forsooth, and is it your worship, indeed?' cried the good dame. 'Yea, truly is it, and in the very image of my old gossip,[12] Goodman Brown, the grandfather of the silly fellow that now is. But – would your worship believe it? – my broomstick hath strangely disappeared, stolen, as I suspect, by that unhanged witch, Goody Cory, and that, too, when I was all anointed with the juice of smallage and cinque-foil and wolf's-bane—'[13]

'Mingled with fine wheat and the fat of a new-born babe,' said the shape of old Goodman Brown.

'Ah, your worship knows the receipt,' cried the old lady, cackling aloud. 'So, as I was saying, being all ready for the meeting, and no horse to ride on, I made up my mind to foot it; for they tell me, there is a nice young man to be taken into communion to-night. But now your good worship will lend me your arm, and we shall be there in a twinkling.'

'That can hardly be,' answered her friend. 'I may not spare you my arm, Goody Cloyse, but here is my staff, if you will.'

So saying, he threw it down at her feet, where, perhaps, it assumed life, being one of the rods which its owner had formerly lent to the Egyptian Magi.[14] Of this fact, however,

Goodman Brown could not take cognizance. He had cast up his eyes in astonishment, and looking down again, beheld neither Goody Cloyse nor the serpentine staff, but his fellow-traveller alone, who waited for him as calmly as if nothing had happened.

'That old woman taught me my catechism!' said the young man; and there was a world of meaning in this simple comment.

They continued to walk onward, while the elder traveller exhorted his companion to make good speed and persevere in the path, discoursing so aptly, that his arguments seemed rather to spring up in the bosom of his auditor, than to be suggested by himself. As they went, he plucked a branch of maple, to serve for a walking-stick, and began to strip it of the twigs and little boughs, which were wet with evening dew. The moment his fingers touched them, they became strangely withered and dried up, as with a week's sunshine. Thus the pair proceeded, at a good free pace, until suddenly, in a gloomy hollow of the road, Goodman Brown sat himself down on the stump of a tree, and refused to go any farther.

'Friend,' said he, stubbornly, 'my mind is made up. Not another step will I budge on this errand. What if a wretched old woman do choose to go to the devil, when I thought she was going to Heaven! Is that any reason why I should quit my dear Faith, and go after her?'

'You will think better of this, by-and-by,' said his acquaintance, composedly. 'Sit here and rest yourself awhile; and when you feel like moving again, there is my staff to help you along.'

Without more words, he threw his companion the maple stick, and was as speedily out of sight, as if he had vanished into the deepening gloom. The young man sat a few moments, by the road-side, applauding himself greatly, and thinking with how clear a conscience he should meet the minister, in his morning-walk, nor shrink from the eye of good old Deacon Gookin. And what calm sleep would be his, that very night, which was to have been spent so wickedly, but purely and sweetly now, in the arms of Faith! Amidst these pleasant and praiseworthy meditations, Goodman Brown heard the tramp of horses along the road, and deemed it advisable to conceal himself within the verge of the forest, conscious of the guilty purpose that had brought him thither, though now so happily turned from it.

On came the hoof-tramps and the voices of the riders, two grave old voices, conversing soberly as they drew near. These mingled sounds appeared to pass along the road, within a few yards of the young man's hiding-place; but owing, doubtless, to the depth of the gloom, at that particular spot, neither the travellers nor their steeds were visible. Though their figures brushed the small boughs by the way-side, it could not be seen that they intercepted, even for a moment, the faint gleam from the strip of bright sky, athwart which they must have passed. Goodman Brown alternately crouched and stood on tip-toe, pulling aside the branches, and thrusting forth his head as far as he durst, without discerning so much as a shadow. It vexed him the more, because he could have sworn, were such a thing possible, that he recognized the voices of the minister and Deacon Gookin, jogging along quietly, as they were wont to do, when bound to some ordination or ecclesiastical council. While yet within hearing, one of the riders stopped to pluck a switch.

'Of the two, reverend Sir,' said the voice like the deacon's, 'I had rather miss an ordination-dinner than to-night's meeting. They tell me that some of our community are to be here from Falmouth and beyond, and others from Connecticut and Rhode-Island; besides several of the Indian powows, who, after their fashion, know almost as much deviltry as the best of us. Moreover, there is a goodly young woman to be taken into communion.'

'Mighty well, Deacon Gookin!' replied the solemn old tones of the minister. 'Spur up, or we shall be late. Nothing can be done, you know, until I get on the ground.'

The hoofs clattered again, and the voices, talking so strangely in the empty air, passed on through the forest, where no church had ever been gathered, nor solitary Christian prayed. Whither, then, could these holy men be journeying, so deep into the heathen wilderness? Young Goodman Brown caught hold of a tree, for support, being ready to sink down on the ground, faint and overburthened with the heavy sickness of his heart. He looked up to the sky, doubting whether there really was a Heaven above him. Yet, there was the blue arch, and the stars brightening in it.

'With Heaven above, and Faith below, I will yet stand firm against the devil!' cried Goodman Brown.

While he still gazed upward, into the deep arch of the firmament, and had lifted his hands to pray, a cloud, though no wind was stirring, hurried across the zenith, and hid the brightening stars. The blue sky was still visible, except directly overhead, where this black mass of cloud was sweeping swiftly northward. Aloft in the air, as if from the depths of the cloud, came a confused and doubtful sound of voices. Once, the listener fancied that he could distinguish the accents of town's-people of his own, men and women, both pious and ungodly, many of whom he had met at the communion-table, and had seen others rioting at the tavern. The next moment, so indistinct were the sounds, he doubted whether he had heard aught but the murmur of the old forest, whispering without a wind. Then came a stronger swell of those familiar tones, heard daily in the sunshine, at Salem village, but never, until now, from a cloud of night. There was one voice, of a young woman, uttering lamentations, yet with an uncertain sorrow, and entreating for some favor, which, perhaps, it would grieve her to obtain. And all the unseen multitude, both saints and sinners, seemed to encourage her onward.

'Faith!' shouted Goodman Brown, in a voice of agony and desperation; and the echoes of the forest mocked him, crying – 'Faith! Faith!' as if bewildered wretches were seeking her, all through the wilderness.

The cry of grief, rage, and terror, was yet piercing the night, when the unhappy husband held his breath for a response. There was a scream, drowned immediately in a louder murmur of voices, fading into far-off laughter, as the dark cloud swept away, leaving the clear and silent sky above Goodman Brown. But something fluttered lightly down through the air, and caught on the branch of a tree. The young man seized it, and beheld a pink ribbon.

'My Faith is gone!' cried he, after one stupefied moment. 'There is no good on earth; and sin is but a name. Come, devil! for to thee is this world given.'

And maddened with despair, so that he laughed loud and long, did Goodman Brown grasp his staff and set forth again, at such a rate, that he seemed to fly along the forest-path, rather than to walk or run. The road grew wilder and drearier, and more faintly traced, and vanished at length, leaving him in the heart of the dark wilderness, still rushing onward, with the instinct that guides mortal man to evil. The whole forest was peopled with frightful sounds; the creaking of the trees, the howling of wild beasts, and the yell of Indians; while, some-times, the wind tolled like a distant church-bell, and sometimes gave a broad roar around the traveller, as if all Nature were laughing him to scorn. But he was himself the chief horror of the scene, and shrank not from its other horrors.

'Ha! ha! ha!' roared Goodman Brown, when the wind laughed at him. 'Let us hear which will laugh loudest! Think not to frighten me with your deviltry! Come witch, come wizard, come Indian powow, come devil himself! and here comes Goodman Brown. You may as well fear him as he fears you!'

In truth, all through the haunted forest, there could be noth-ing more frightful than the figure of Goodman Brown. On he flew, among the black pines, brandishing his staff with frenzied gestures, now giving vent to an inspiration of horrid blas-phemy, and now shouting forth such laughter, as set all the echoes of the forest laughing like demons around him. The fiend in his own shape is less hideous, than when he rages in the breast of man. Thus sped the demoniac on his course, until, quivering among the trees, he saw a red light before him, as when the felled trunks and branches of a clearing have been set on fire, and throw up their lurid blaze against the sky, at the hour of midnight. He paused, in a lull of the tempest that had driven him onward, and heard the swell of what seemed a hymn, rolling solemnly from a distance, with the weight of many voices. He knew the tune; it was a familiar one in the choir of the village meeting-house. The verse died heavily away, and was lengthened by a chorus, not of human voices, but of all the sounds of the benighted wilderness, pealing in awful harmony together. Goodman Brown cried out; and his cry was lost to his own ear, by its unison with the cry of the desert.

In the interval of silence, he stole forward, until the light glared full upon his eyes. At one extremity of an open space, hemmed in by the dark wall of the forest, arose a rock, bearing some rude, natural resemblance either to an altar or a pulpit, and surrounded by four blazing pines, their tops aflame, their stems untouched, like candles at an evening meeting. The mass of foliage, that had overgrown the summit of the rock, was all on fire, blazing high into the night, and fitfully illuminating the whole field. Each pendent twig and leafy festoon was in a blaze. As the red light arose and fell, a numerous congregation alternately shone forth, then disappeared in shadow, and again grew, as it were, out of the darkness, peopling the heart of the solitary woods at once.

'A grave and dark-clad company!' quoth Goodman Brown.

In truth, they were such. Among them, quivering to-and-fro, between gloom and splendor, appeared faces that would be seen, next day, at the council-board of the province, and others which, Sabbath after Sabbath, looked devoutly heavenward, and benignantly over the crowded pews, from the holiest pulpits in the land. Some affirm, that the lady of the governor was there. At least, there were high dames well known to her, and wives of honored husbands, and widows, a great multitude, and ancient maidens, all of excellent repute, and fair young girls, who trembled, lest their mothers should espy them. Either the sudden gleams of light, flashing over the obscure field, bedazzled Goodman Brown, or he recognized a score of the church-members of Salem village, famous for their especial sanctity. Good old Deacon Gookin had arrived, and waited at the skirts of that venerable saint, his revered pastor. But, irreverently consorting with these grave, reputable, and pious people, these elders of the church, these chaste dames and dewy virgins, there were men of dissolute lives and women of spotted fame, wretches given over to all mean and filthy vice, and suspected even of horrid crimes. It was strange to see, that the good shrank not from the wicked, nor were the sinners abashed by the saints. Scattered, also, among their pale-faced enemies, were the Indian priests, or powows, who had often scared their native forest with more hideous incantations than any known to English witchcraft.

'But, where is Faith?' thought Goodman Brown; and, as hope came into his heart, he trembled.

Another verse of the hymn arose, a slow and mournful strain, such as the pious love, but joined to words which expressed all that our nature can conceive of sin, and darkly hinted at far more. Unfathomable to mere mortals is the lore of fiends. Verse after verse was sung, and still the chorus of the desert swelled between, like the deepest tone of a mighty organ. And, with the final peal of that dreadful anthem, there came a sound, as if the roaring wind, the rushing streams, the howling beasts, and every other voice of the unconverted wilderness, were mingling and according with the voice of guilty man, in homage to the prince of all. The four blazing pines threw up a loftier flame, and obscurely discovered shapes and visages of horror on the smoke-wreaths, above the impious assembly. At the same moment, the fire on the rock shot redly forth, and formed a glowing arch above its base, where now appeared a figure.[15] With reverence be it spoken, the figure bore no slight similitude, both in garb and manner, to some grave divine of the New-England churches.

'Bring forth the converts!' cried a voice, that echoed through the field and rolled into the forest.

At the word, Goodman Brown stept forth from the shadow of the trees, and approached the congregation, with whom he felt a loathful brotherhood, by the sympathy of all that was wicked in his heart. He could have well nigh sworn, that the shape of his own dead father beckoned him to advance, looking downward from a smoke-wreath, while a woman, with dim features of despair, threw out her hand to warn him back. Was it his mother? But he had no power to retreat one step, nor to resist, even in thought, when the minister and good old Deacon Gookin seized his arms, and led him to the blazing rock. Thither came also the slender form of a veiled female, led between Goody Cloyse, that pious teacher of the catechism, and Martha Carrier, who had received the devil's promise to be queen of hell.[16] A rampant hag was she! And there stood the proselytes, beneath the canopy of fire.

'Welcome, my children,' said the dark figure, 'to the communion of your race! Ye have found, thus young, your nature and your destiny. My children, look behind you!'

They turned; and flashing forth, as it were, in a sheet of flame, the fiend-worshippers were seen; the smile of welcome gleamed darkly on every visage.

'There,' resumed the sable form, 'are all whom ye have reverenced from youth. Ye deemed them holier than yourselves, and shrank from your own sin, contrasting it with their lives of righteousness, and prayerful aspirations heavenward. Yet, here are they all, in my worshipping assembly! This night it shall be granted you to know their secret deeds; how hoary-bearded elders of the church have whispered wanton words to the young maids of their households; how many a woman, eager for widow's weeds, has given her husband a drink at bed-time, and let him sleep his last sleep in her bosom; how beardless youths have made haste to inherit their fathers' wealth; and how fair damsels – blush not, sweet ones! – have dug little graves in the garden, and bidden me, the sole guest, to an infant's funeral. By the sympathy of your human hearts for sin, ye shall scent out all the places – whether in church, bed-chamber, street, field, or forest – where crime has been committed, and shall exult to behold the whole earth one stain of guilt, one mighty blood-spot. Far more than this! It shall be yours to penetrate, in every bosom, the deep mystery of sin, the fountain of all wicked arts, and which inexhaustibly supplies more evil impulses than human power – than my power, at its utmost! – can make manifest in deeds. And now, my children, look upon each other.'

They did so; and, by the blaze of the hell-kindled torches, the wretched man beheld his Faith, and the wife her husband, trembling before that unhallowed altar.

'Lo! there ye stand, my children,' said the figure, in a deep and solemn tone, almost sad, with its despairing awfulness, as if his once angelic nature could yet mourn for our miserable race. 'Depending upon one another's hearts, ye had still hoped, that virtue were not all a dream. Now are ye undeceived! Evil is the nature of mankind. Evil must be your only happiness. Welcome, again, my children, to the communion of your race!'

'Welcome!' repeated the fiend-worshippers, in one cry of despair and triumph.

And there they stood, the only pair, as it seemed, who were yet hesitating on the verge of wickedness, in this dark world. A basin was hollowed, naturally, in the rock. Did it contain water, reddened by the lurid light? or was it blood? or, perchance, a liquid flame? Herein did the Shape of Evil dip his hand, and prepare to lay the mark of baptism upon their foreheads, that they might be partakers of the mystery of sin, more conscious of the secret guilt of others, both in deed and thought, than they could now be of their own. The husband cast one look at his pale wife, and Faith at him. What polluted wretches would the next glance shew them to each other, shuddering alike at what they disclosed and what they saw!

'Faith! Faith!' cried the husband. 'Look up to Heaven, and resist the Wicked One!'

Whether Faith obeyed, he knew not. Hardly had he spoken, when he found himself amid calm night and solitude, listening to a roar of the wind, which died heavily away through the forest. He staggered against the rock and felt it chill and damp, while a hanging twig, that had been all on fire, besprinkled his cheek with the coldest dew.

The next morning, young Goodman Brown came slowly into the street of Salem village, staring around him like a bewildered man. The good old minister was taking a walk along the grave-yard, to get an appetite for breakfast and meditate his sermon, and bestowed a blessing, as he passed, on Goodman Brown. He shrank from the venerable saint, as if to avoid an anathema. Old Deacon Gookin was at domestic worship, and the holy words of his prayer were heard through the open window. 'What God doth the wizard pray to?' quoth Goodman Brown. Goody Cloyse, that excellent old Christian, stood in the early sunshine, at her own lattice, catechising a little girl, who had brought her a pint of morning's milk. Goodman Brown snatched away the child, as from the grasp of the fiend himself. Turning the corner by the meeting-house, he spied the head of Faith, with the pink ribbons, gazing anxiously forth, and bursting into such joy at sight of him, that she skipt along the street, and almost kissed her husband before the whole village. But, Goodman Brown looked sternly and sadly into her face, and passed on without a greeting.

Had Goodman Brown fallen asleep in the forest, and only dreamed a wild dream of a witch-meeting?

Be it so, if you will. But, alas! it was a dream of evil omen for young Goodman Brown. A stern, a sad, a darkly meditative, a distrustful, if not a desperate man, did he become, from the night of that fearful dream. On the Sabbath-day, when the congregation were singing a holy psalm, he could not listen, because an anthem of sin rushed loudly upon his ear, and drowned all the blessed strain. When the minister spoke from the pulpit, with power and fervid eloquence, and, with his hand on the open Bible, of the sacred truths of our religion, and of saint-like lives and triumphant deaths, and of future bliss or misery unutterable, then did Goodman Brown turn pale, dreading, lest the roof should thunder down upon the gray blasphemer and his hearers. Often, awakening suddenly at midnight, he shrank from the bosom of Faith, and at morning or eventide, when the family knelt down at prayer, he scowled, and muttered to himself, and gazed sternly at his wife, and turned away. And when he had lived long, and was borne to his grave, a hoary corpse, followed by Faith, an aged woman, and children and grand-children, a goodly procession, besides neighbors, not a few, they carved no hopeful verse upon his tomb-stone; for his dying hour was gloom.

The Tell-Tale Heart

EDGAR ALLAN POE

True! – nervous – very, very dreadfully nervous I had been and am; but why *will* you say that I am mad? The disease had sharpened my senses – not destroyed – not dulled them. Above all was the sense of hearing acute. I heard all things in the heaven and in the earth.[1] I heard many things in hell. How, then, am I mad? Hearken! and observe how healthily – how calmly I can tell you the whole story.

It is impossible to say how first the idea entered my brain; but once conceived, it haunted me day and night. Object there was none. Passion there was none. I loved the old man. He had never wronged me. He had never given me insult. For his gold I had no desire. I think it was his eye! yes, it was this! One of his eyes resembled that of a vulture – a pale blue eye, with a film over it.[2] Whenever it fell upon me, my blood ran cold; and so by degrees – very gradually – I made up my mind to take the life of the old man, and thus rid myself of the eye for ever.

Now this is the point. You fancy me mad. Madmen know nothing. But you should have seen *me*. You should have seen how wisely I proceeded – with what caution – with what foresight – with what dissimulation I went to work! I was never kinder to the old man than during the whole week before I killed him. And every night, about midnight, I turned the latch of his door and opened it – oh, so gently! And then, when I had made an opening sufficient for my head, I put in a dark lantern, all closed, closed, so that no light shone out, and then I thrust in my head. Oh, you would have laughed to see how cunningly I thrust it in! I moved it slowly – very, very slowly, so that I might not disturb the old man's sleep. It took me an hour to place my whole head within the opening so far that I could see him as he lay upon his bed. Ha! – would a madman have been so wise as this? And then, when my head was well in the room, I undid the lantern cautiously – oh, so cautiously – cautiously (for the hinges creaked) – I undid it just so much that a single thin ray fell upon the vulture eye. And this I did for seven long nights – every night just at midnight – but I found the eye always closed; and so it was impossible to do the work; for it was not the old man who vexed me, but his Evil Eye. And every morning, when the day broke, I went boldly into the chamber, and spoke courageously to him, calling him by name in a hearty tone, and inquiring how he had passed the night. So you see he would have been a very profound old man, indeed, to suspect that every night, just at twelve, I looked in upon him while he slept.

Upon the eighth night I was more than usually cautious in opening the door. A watch's minute hand moves more quickly than did mine. Never before that night had I *felt* the extent of my own powers – of my sagacity. I could scarcely contain my feelings of triumph. To think that there I was, opening the door, little by little, and he not even to dream of my secret deeds or thoughts. I fairly chuckled at the idea; and perhaps he heard me; for he moved on the bed suddenly, as if startled. Now you may think that I drew back – but no. His room was as black as pitch with the thick darkness (for the shutters were close fastened, through fear of robbers), and so I knew that he could not see the opening of the door, and I kept pushing it on steadily, steadily.

I had my head in, and was about to open the lantern, when my thumb slipped upon the tin fastening, and the old man sprang up in the bed, crying out – 'Who's there?'

I kept quite still and said nothing. For a whole hour I did not move a muscle, and in the meantime I did not hear him lie down. He was still sitting up in the bed listening; – just as I have done, night after night, hearkening to the death watches in the wall.[3]

Presently I heard a slight groan, and I knew it was the groan of mortal terror. It was not a groan of pain or of grief – oh, no! – it was the low stifled sound that arises from the bottom of the soul when overcharged with awe. I knew the sound well. Many a night, just at midnight, when all the world slept, it has welled up from my own bosom, deepening, with its dreadful echo, the terrors that distracted me. I say I knew it well. I knew what the old man felt, and pitied him, although I chuckled at heart. I knew that he had been lying awake ever since the first slight noise, when he had turned in the bed. His fears had been ever since growing upon him. He had been trying to fancy them causeless, but could not. He had been saying to himself – 'It is nothing but the wind in the chimney – it is only a mouse crossing the floor,' or 'it is merely a cricket which has made a single chirp.' Yes, he had been trying to comfort himself with these suppositions; but he had found all in vain. *All in vain*; because Death, in approaching him, had stalked with his black shadow before him, and enveloped the victim. And it was the mournful influence of the unperceived shadow that caused him to feel – although he neither saw nor heard – to *feel* the presence of my head within the room.

When I had waited a long time, very patiently, without hearing him lie down, I resolved to open a little – a very, very little crevice in the lantern. So I opened it – you cannot imagine how stealthily, stealthily – until, at length, a single dim ray, like the thread of the spider, shot from out the crevice and full upon the vulture eye.

It was open – wide, wide open – and I grew furious as I gazed upon it. I saw it with perfect distinctness – all a dull blue, with a hideous veil over it that chilled the very marrow in my bones; but I could see nothing else of the old man's face or person: for I had directed the ray as if by instinct, precisely upon the damned spot.

And now have I not told you that what you mistake for madness is but over-acuteness of the senses? – now, I say, there came to my ears a low, dull, quick sound, such as a watch makes when enveloped in cotton. I knew *that* sound well too. It was the beating of the old man's heart. It increased my fury, as the beating of a drum stimulates the soldier into courage.

But even yet I refrained and kept still. I scarcely breathed.

I held the lantern motionless. I tried how steadily I could maintain the ray upon the eye. Meantime the hellish tattoo[4] of the
heart increased. It grew quicker and quicker, and louder and
louder every instant. The old man's terror *must* have been
extreme! It grew louder, I say, louder every moment! – do you
mark me well? I have told you that I am nervous: so I am. And
now at the dead hour of the night, amid the dreadful silence of
that old house, so strange a noise as this excited me to uncon-
trollable terror. Yet, for some minutes longer I refrained and
stood still. But the beating grew louder, louder! I thought the
heart must burst. And now a new anxiety seized me – the sound
would be heard by a neighbor! The old man's hour had come!
With a loud yell, I threw open the lantern and leaped into the
room. He shrieked once – once only. In an instant I dragged
him to the floor, and pulled the heavy bed over him. I then
smiled gaily, to find the deed so far done. But, for many minutes, the heart beat on with a muffled sound. This, however,
did not vex me; it would not be heard through the wall. At
length it ceased. The old man was dead. I removed the bed and
examined the corpse. Yes, he was stone, stone dead. I placed
my hand upon the heart and held it there many minutes. There
was no pulsation. He was stone dead. His eye would trouble
me no more.

If still you think me mad, you will think so no longer when
I describe the wise precautions I took for the concealment of
the body. The night waned, and I worked hastily, but in silence.
First of all I dismembered the corpse. I cut off the head and the
arms and the legs.

I then took up three planks from the flooring of the chamber,
and deposited all between the scantlings.[5] I then replaced the
boards so cleverly, so cunningly, that no human eye – not even
his – could have detected any thing wrong. There was nothing
to wash out – no stain of any kind – no blood-spot whatever.
I had been too wary for that. A tub had caught all – ha! ha!

When I had made an end of these labors, it was four o'clock –
still dark as midnight. As the bell sounded the hour, there came
a knocking at the street door. I went down to open it with a
light heart, – for what had I *now* to fear? There entered three

men, who introduced themselves, with perfect suavity, as officers of the police. A shriek had been heard by a neighbor during
the night; suspicion of foul play had been aroused; information
had been lodged at the police office, and they (the officers) had
been deputed to search the premises.

I smiled, – for *what* had I to fear? I bade the gentlemen welcome. The shriek, I said, was my own in a dream. The old man,
I mentioned, was absent in the country. I took my visitors all
over the house. I bade them search – search *well*. I led them, at
length, to *his* chamber. I showed them his treasures, secure,
undisturbed. In the enthusiasm of my confidence, I brought
chairs into the room, and desired them *here* to rest from their
fatigues, while I myself, in the wild audacity of my perfect triumph, placed my own seat upon the very spot beneath which
reposed the corpse of the victim.

The officers were satisfied. My *manner* had convinced them.
I was singularly at ease. They sat, and while I answered cheer-
ily, they chatted familiar things. But, ere long, I felt myself
getting pale and wished them gone. My head ached, and I fancied a ringing in my ears: but still they sat and still chatted. The
ringing became more distinct: – it continued and became more
distinct: I talked more freely to get rid of the feeling: but it continued and gained definitiveness – until, at length, I found that
the noise was *not* within my ears.

No doubt I now grew *very* pale; – but I talked more fluently,
and with a heightened voice. Yet the sound increased – and
what could I do? It was *a low, dull, quick sound – much such a
sound as a watch makes when enveloped in cotton*. I gasped for
breath – and yet the officers heard it not. I talked more quickly –
more vehemently; but the noise steadily increased. I arose and
argued about trifles, in a high key and with violent gesticula-
tions, but the noise steadily increased. Why *would* they not be
gone? I paced the floor to and fro with heavy strides, as if
excited to fury by the observation of the men – but the noise
steadily increased. Oh God! what *could* I do? I foamed – I
raved – I swore! I swung the chair upon which I had been sitting, and grated it upon the boards, but the noise arose over all
and continually increased. It grew louder – louder – *louder!*

And still the men chatted pleasantly, and smiled. Was it possible they heard not? Almighty God! – no, no! They heard! – they
suspected! – they *knew!* – they were making a mockery of my
horror! – this I thought, and this I think. But any thing was
better than this agony! Any thing was more tolerable than this
derision! I could bear those hypocritical smiles no longer! I felt
that I must scream or die! – and now – again! – hark! louder!
louder! louder! *louder!*—

  'Villains!' I shrieked, 'dissemble no more! I admit the deed! –
tear up the planks! – here, here! – it is the beating of his hideous
heart!'

Aunt Hetty on Matrimony

FANNY FERN

'Now girls,' said Aunt Hetty, 'put down your embroidery and
worsted work; do something sensible, and stop building air-
castles, and talking of lovers and honey-moons. It makes me sick;
it is perfectly antimonial.[1] Love is a farce; matrimony is a hum-
bug; husbands are domestic Napoleons, Neroes, Alexanders, –
sighing for other hearts to conquer, after they are sure of yours.
The honey-moon is as short-lived as a lucifer-match;[2] after that
you may wear your wedding-dress at the wash tub, and your
night-cap to meeting, and your husband wouldn't know it. You
may pick up your own pocket-handkerchief, help yourself to a
chair, and split your gown across the back reaching over the
table to get a piece of butter, while he is laying in his breakfast
as if it was the last meal he should eat this side of Jordan. When
he gets through he will aid your digestion, – while you are sip-
ping your first cup of coffee, – by inquiring what you'll have
for dinner; whether the cold lamb was all ate yesterday; if the
charcoal is all out, and what you gave for the last green tea you
bought. Then he gets up from the table, lights his cigar with the
last evening's paper, that you have not had a chance to read;
gives two or three whiffs of smoke, – which are sure to give you
a headache for the forenoon, – and, just as his coat-tail is vanishing through the door, apologizes for not doing "that errand"
for you yesterday, – thinks it doubtful if he can to-day, – "so
pressed with business." Hear of him at eleven o'clock, taking
an ice-cream with some ladies at a confectioner's, while you are
at home new-lining his old coat-sleeves. Children by the ears all
day, can't get out to take the air, feel as crazy as a fly in a drum;
husband comes home at night, nods a "How d'ye do, Fan",

boxes Charley's ears, stands little Fanny in the corner, sits down in the easiest chair in the warmest corner, puts his feet up over the grate, shutting out all the fire, while the baby's little pug nose grows blue with the cold; reads the newspaper all to himself, solaces his inner man with a hot cup of tea, and, just as you are laboring under the hallucination that he will ask you to take a mouthful of fresh air with him, he puts on his dressing-gown and slippers, and begins to reckon up the family expenses! after which he lies down on the sofa, and you keep time with your needle, while he sleeps till nine o'clock. Next morning, ask him to leave you a "little money," – he looks at you as if to be sure that you are in your right mind, draws a sigh long enough and strong enough to inflate a pair of bellows, and asks you "what you want with it, and if a half a dollar won't do?" – Gracious king! as if those little shoes, and stockings, and petticoats could be had for half a dollar! Oh girls! set your affections on cats, poodles, parrots or lap dogs; but let matrimony alone. It's the hardest way on earth of getting a living – you never know when your work is done. Think of carrying eight or nine children through the measles, chicken pox, rash, mumps, and scarlet fever, some of 'em twice over; it makes my head ache to think of it. Oh, you may scrimp and save, and twist and turn, and dig and delve, and economise *and die*, and your husband will marry again, take what you have saved to dress his second wife with, and she'll take your portrait for a fireboard, and, – but, what's the use of talking? I'll warrant every one of you'll try it, the first chance you get! there's a sort of bewitchment about it, somehow. I wish one half the world warn't fools, and the other half idiots, I do. Oh, dear!'

Jim Smiley and His Jumping Frog

MARK TWAIN

Mr A. Ward,[1]

Dear Sir: – Well, I called on good-natured, garrulous old Simon Wheeler, and I inquired after your friend Leonidas W. Smiley, as you requested me to do, and I hereunto append the result. If you can get any information out of it you are cordially welcome to it. I have a lurking suspicion that your Leonidas W. Smiley is a myth – that you never knew such a personage, and that you only conjectured that if I asked old Wheeler about him it would remind him of his infamous *Jim* Smiley, and he would go to work and bore me nearly to death with some infernal reminiscence of him as long and tedious as it should be useless to me. If that was your design, Mr Ward, it will gratify you to know that it succeeded.

I found Simon Wheeler dozing comfortably by the bar-room stove of the little old dilapidated tavern in the ancient mining camp of Boomerang, and I noticed that he was fat and bald-headed, and had an expression of winning gentleness and simplicity upon his tranquil countenance. He roused up and gave me good-day. I told him a friend of mine had commissioned me to make some inquiries about a cherished companion of his boyhood named Leonidas W. Smiley – Rev. Leonidas W. Smiley – a young minister of the gospel, who he had heard was at one time a resident of this village of Boomerang. I added that if Mr Wheeler could tell me anything about this Rev. Leonidas W. Smiley, I would feel under many obligations to him.

Simon Wheeler backed me into a corner and blockaded me

there with his chair – and then sat down and reeled off the monotonous narrative which follows this paragraph. He never smiled, he never frowned, he never changed his voice from the quiet, gently-flowing key to which he tuned the initial sentence, he never betrayed the slightest suspicion of enthusiasm – but all through the interminable narrative there ran a vein of impressive earnestness and sincerity, which showed me plainly that so far from his imagining that there was anything ridiculous or funny about his story, he regarded it as a really important matter, and admired its two heroes as men of transcendent genius in finesse. To me, the spectacle of a man drifting serenely along through such a queer yarn without ever smiling was exquisitely absurd. As I said before, I asked him to tell me what he knew of Rev. Leonidas W. Smiley, and he replied as follows. I let him go on in his own way, and never interrupted him once:

There was a feller here once by the name of *Jim* Smiley, in the winter of '49[2] – or maybe it was the spring of '50 – I don't recollect exactly, some how, though what makes me think it was one or the other is because I remember the big flume[3] wasn't finished when he first come to the camp; but anyway, he was the curiosest man about always betting on anything that turned up you ever see, if he could get anybody to bet on the other side, and if he couldn't he'd change sides – any way that suited the other man would suit *him* – any way just so's he got a bet, *he* was satisfied. But still, he was lucky – uncommon lucky; he most always come out winner. He was always ready and laying for a chance; there couldn't be no solitry thing mentioned but what that feller'd offer to bet on it – and take any side you please, as I was just telling you: if there was a horse race, you'd find him flush or you find him busted at the end of it; if there was a dog-fight, he'd bet on it; if there was a cat-fight, he'd bet on it; if there was a chicken-fight, he'd bet on it; why if there was two birds setting on a fence, he would bet you which one would fly first – or if there was a camp-meeting he would be there reglar to bet on parson Walker, which he judged to be the best exhorter about here, and so he was, too, and a good man; if he even see a straddle-bug[4] start to go any wheres,

he would bet you how long it would take him to get wherever
he was going to, and if you took him up he would foller that
straddle-bug to Mexico but what he would find out where he
was bound for and how long he was on the road. Lots of the
boys here has seen that Smiley and can tell you about him.
Why, it never made no difference to *him* – he would bet on
anything – the dangdest feller. Parson Walker's wife laid very
sick, once, for a good while, and it seemed as if they warn't
going to save her; but one morning he come in and Smiley
asked him how she was, and he said she was considerable
better – thank the Lord for his inf'nit mercy – and coming on
so smart that with the blessing of Providence she'd get well
yet – and Smiley, before he thought, says, 'Well, I'll resk two-
and-a-half that she don't, anyway.'

Thish-yer Smiley had a mare – the boys called her the fifteen-
minute nag, but that was only in fun, you know, because, of
course, she was faster than that – and he used to win money on
that horse, for all she was so slow and always had the asthma,
or the distemper, or the consumption, or something of that
kind. They used to give her two or three hundred yards' start,
and then pass her under way; but always at the fag-end of the
race she'd get excited and desperate-like, and come cavorting
and spraddling up,[5] and scattering her legs around limber,
sometimes in the air, and sometimes out to one side amongst
the fences, and kicking up m-o-r-e dust, and raising m-o-r-e
racket with her coughing and sneezing and blowing her nose –
and always fetch up at the stand just about a neck ahead, as
near as you could cipher it down.

And he had a little small bull-pup, that to look at him you'd
think he warn't worth a cent, but to set around and look ornery,
and lay for a chance to steal something. But as soon as money
was up on him he was a different dog – his under-jaw'd begin to
stick out like the for'castle of a steamboat, and his teeth would
uncover, and shine savage like the furnaces. And a dog might
tackle him, and bully-rag him, and bite him, and throw him
over his shoulder two or three times, and Andrew Jackson[6] –
which was the name of the pup – Andrew Jackson would never
let on but what he was satisfied, and hadn't expected nothing

else – and the bets being doubled and doubled on the other side all the time, till the money was all up – and then all of a sudden he would grab that other dog just by the joint of his hind legs and freeze to it – not chaw, you understand, but only just grip and hang on till they throwed up the sponge, if it was a year. Smiley always came out winner on that pup till he harnessed a dog once that didn't have no hind legs, because they'd been sawed off in a circular saw, and when the thing had gone along far enough, and the money was all up, and he came to make a snatch for his pet holt, he saw in a minute how he'd been imposed on, and how the other dog had him in the door, so to speak, and he 'peared surprised, and then he looked sorter discouraged like, and didn't try no more to win the fight, and so he got shucked out bad. He gave Smiley a look as much as to say his heart was broke, and it was *his* fault, for putting up a dog that hadn't no hind legs for him to take holt of, which was his main dependence in a fight, and then he limped off a piece, and laid down and died. It was a good pup, was that Andrew Jackson, and would have made a name for hisself if he'd lived, for the stuff was in him, and he had genius – I know it, because he hadn't had no opportunities to speak of, and it don't stand to reason that a dog could make such a fight as he could under them circumstances, if he hadn't no talent. It always makes me feel sorry when I think of that last fight of his'on, and the way it turned out.

Well, thish-yer Smiley had rat-terriers and chicken cocks, and tom-cats, and all them kind of things, till you couldn't rest, and you couldn't fetch nothing for him to bet on but he'd match you. He ketched a frog one day and took him home and said he cal'lated to educate him; and so he never done nothing for three months but set in his back yard and learn that frog to jump. And you bet you he *did* learn him, too. He'd give him a little hunch behind, and the next minute you'd see that frog whirling in the air like a doughnut – see him turn one summerset, or maybe a couple, if he got a good start, and come down flat-footed and all right, like a cat. He got him up so in the matter of ketching flies, and kept him in practice so constant, that he'd nail a fly every time as far as he could see him. Smiley said all a frog wanted was education, and he could do most anything – and I believe him. Why, I've seen him set Dan'l Web-ster[7] down here on this floor – Dan'l Webster was the name of the frog – and sing out, 'Flies! Dan'l, flies,' and quicker'n you could wink, he'd spring straight up, and snake a fly off'n the counter there, and flop down on the floor again as solid as a gob of mud, and fall to scratching the side of his head with his hind foot as indifferent as if he hadn't no idea he'd done any more'n any frog might do. You never see a frog so modest and straightfor'ard as he was, for all he was so gifted. And when it come to fair-and-square jumping on a dead level, he could get over more ground at one straddle than any animal of his breed you ever see. Jumping on a dead level was his strong suit, you understand, and when it come to that, Smiley would ante up money on him as long as he had a red.[8] Smiley was monstrous proud of his frog, and well he might be, for fellers that had travelled and ben everywheres all said he laid over any frog that ever *they* see.

Well, Smiley kept the beast in a little lattice box, and he used to fetch him down town sometimes and lay for a bet. One day a feller – a stranger in the camp, he was – come across him with his box, and says:

'What might it be that you've got in the box?'

And Smiley says, sorter indifferent like, 'It might be a parrot, or it might be a canary, maybe, but it ain't – it's only just a frog.'

And the feller took it, and looked at it careful, and turned it round this way and that, and says, 'H'm – so 'tis. Well, what's *he* good for?'

'Well,' Smiley says, easy and careless, 'He's good enough for *one* thing I should judge – he can outjump ary frog in Calaveras county.'

The feller took the box again, and took another long, particular look, and give it back to Smiley and says, very deliberate, 'Well – I don't see no points about that frog that's any better'n any other frog.'

'Maybe you don't,' Smiley says. 'Maybe you understand frogs, and maybe you don't understand 'em; maybe you've had experience, and maybe you ain't only a amature, as it were.

Anyways, I've got *my* opinion, and I'll resk forty dollars that he can outjump ary frog in Calaveras county.'

And the feller studied a minute, and then says, kinder sad, like, 'Well – I'm only a stranger here, and I ain't got no frog – but if I had a frog I'd bet you.'

And then Smiley says, 'That's all right – that's all right – if you'll hold my box a minute I'll go and get you a frog;' and so the feller took the box, and put up his forty dollars along with Smiley's, and set down to wait.

So he set there a good while thinking and thinking to hisself, and then he got the frog out and prized his mouth open and took a teaspoon and filled him full of quail-shot – filled him pretty near up to his chin – and set him on the floor. Smiley he went out to the swamp and slopped around in the mud for a long time, and finally he ketched a frog and fetched him in and give him to this feller and says:

'Now if you're ready, set him alongside of Dan'l, with his fore-paws just even with Dan'l's, and I'll give the word.' Then he says, 'one – two – three – jump!' and him and the feller touched up the frogs from behind, and the new frog hopped off lively, but Dan'l give a heave, and hysted up his shoulders – so – like a Frenchman, but it wasn't no use – he couldn't budge; he was planted as solid as a anvil, and he couldn't no more stir than if he was anchored out. Smiley was a good deal surprised, and he was disgusted too, but he didn't have no idea what the matter was, of course.

The feller took the money and started away, and when he was going out at the door he sorter jerked his thumb over his shoulder – this way – at Dan'l, and says again, very deliberate, 'Well – *I* don't see no points about that frog that's any better'n any other frog.'

Smiley he stood scratching his head and looking down at Dan'l a long time, and at last he says, 'I do wonder what in the nation that frog throwed off for – I wonder if there ain't some-thing the matter with him – he 'pears to look mighty baggy, somehow' – and he ketched Dan'l by the nap of the neck, and lifted him up and says, 'Why blame my cats if he don't weigh five pound' – and turned him upside down, and he belched out about a double-handful of shot. And then he see how it was, and he was the maddest man – he set the frog down and took out after that feller, but he never ketched him. And—

[Here Simon Wheeler heard his name called from the front-yard, and got up to go and see what was wanted.] And turning to me as he moved away, he said: 'Just sit where you are, stranger, and rest easy – I ain't going to be gone a second.'

But by your leave, I did not think that a continuation of the history of the enterprising vagabond Jim Smiley would be likely to afford me much information concerning the Rev. Leonidas W. Smiley, and so I started away.

At the door I met the sociable Wheeler returning, and he buttonholed me and recommenced:

'Well, thish-yer Smiley had a yaller one-eyed cow that didn't have no tail only just a short stump like a bannanner, and—'

'O, curse Smiley and his afflicted cow!' I muttered, good-naturedly, and bidding the old gentleman good-day, I departed.

Yours, truly,
MARK TWAIN.

The Wonderful Tar-Baby Story

JOEL CHANDLER HARRIS

'Didn't the fox *never* catch the rabbit, Uncle Remus?' asked the little boy the next evening.

'He come mighty nigh it, honey, sho's you bawn – Brer Fox did. One day atter Brer Rabbit fool 'im wid dat calamus root,[1] Brer Fox went ter wuk en got 'im some tar, en mix it wid some turkentime, en fix up a contrapshun wat he call a Tar-Baby, en he tuck dish yer Tar-Baby en he sot 'er in de big road, en den he lay off in de bushes fer ter see wat de news wuz gwineter be. En he didn't hatter wait long, nudder, kaze bimeby here come Brer Rabbit pacin' down de road – lippity-clippity, clippity-lippity – dez ez sassy ez a jay-bird. Brer Fox, he lay low. Brer Rabbit come prancin' 'long twel he spy de Tar-Baby, en den he fotch up on his behime legs like he wuz 'stonished. De Tar-Baby, she sot dar, she did, en Brer Fox, he lay low.

'"Mawnin'!" sez Brer Rabbit, sezee – "nice wedder dis mawnin'," sezee.

'Tar-Baby ain't sayin' nuthin', en Brer Fox, he lay low.

'"How duz yo' sym'tums seem ter segashuate?" sez Brer Rabbit, sezee.

'Brer Fox, he wink his eye slow, en lay low, en de Tar-Baby, she ain't sayin' nuthin'.

'"How you come on, den? Is you deaf?" sez Brer Rabbit, sezee. "Kaze if you is, I kin holler louder," sezee.

'Tar-Baby stay still, en Brer Fox, he lay low.

'"Youer stuck up, dat's w'at you is," says Brer Rabbit, sezee, "en I'm gwineter kyore you, dat's w'at I'm a gwineter do," sezee.

'Brer Fox, he sorter chuckle in his stummuck, he did, but Tar-Baby ain't sayin' nuthin'.

' "I'm gwineter larn you howter talk ter 'specttubble fokes ef hit's de las' ack," sez Brer Rabbit, sezee. "Ef you don't take off dat hat en tell me howdy, I'm gwineter bus' you wide open," sezee.

'Tar-Baby stay still, en Brer Fox, he lay low.

'Brer Rabbit keep on axin' 'im, en de Tar-Baby, she keep on sayin' nuthin', twel present'y Brer Rabbit draw back wid his fis', he did, en blip he tuck 'er side er de head. Right dar's whar he broke his merlasses jug. His fis' stuck, en he can't pull loose. De tar hilt 'im. But Tar-Baby, she stay still, en Brer Fox, he lay low.

' "Ef you don't lemme loose, I'll knock you agin," sez Brer Rabbit, sezee, en wid dat he fotch 'er a wipe wid de udder han', en dat stuck. Tar-Baby, she ain't sayin' nuthin', en Brer Fox, he lay low.

' "Tu'n me loose, fo' I kick de natal stuffin' outen you," sez Brer Rabbit, sezee, but de Tar-Baby, she ain't sayin' nuthin'. She des hilt on, en den Brer Rabbit lose de use er his feet in de same way. Brer Fox, he lay low. Den Brer Rabbit squall out dat ef de Tar-Baby don't tu'n 'im loose he butt 'er cranksided. En den he butted, en his head got stuck. Den Brer Fox, he sa'ntered fort', lookin' des ez innercent ez wunner yo' mammy's mockin'-birds.

' "Howdy, Brer Rabbit," sez Brer Fox, sezee. "You look sorter stuck up dis mawnin'," sezee, en den he rolled on de groun', en laft en laft twel he couldn't laff no mo'. "I speck you'll take dinner wid me dis time, Brer Rabbit. I done laid in some cala-mus root, en I ain't gwineter take no skuse," sez Brer Fox, sezee.'

Here Uncle Remus paused, and drew a two-pound yam out of the ashes.

'Did the fox eat the rabbit?' asked the little boy to whom the story had been told.

'Dat's all de fur de tale goes,' replied the old man. 'He mout, en den agin he mountent. Some say Jedge B'ar come 'long en loosed 'im – some say he didn't. I hear Miss Sally callin'. You better run 'long.'

Two Friends

MARY WILKINS FREEMAN

'I wish you'd jest look down the road again, Mis' Dunbar, an' see if you see anything of Abby comin'.'

'I don't see a sign of her. It's a real trial for you to be so short-sighted, ain't it, Sarah?'

'I guess it is. Why, you wouldn't believe it, but I can't see anybody out in the road to tell who 'tis. I can see somethin' movin', an' that's all, unless there's somethin' peculiar about 'em that I can tell 'em by. I can always tell old Mr Whitcomb – he's got a kind of a hitch when he walks, you know; an' Mis' Addison White always carries a parasol, an' I can tell her. I can see somethin' bobbin' overhead, an' I know who 'tis.'

'Queer, ain't it, how she always carries that parasol? Why, I've seen her with it in the dead of winter, when the sun was shinin', an' 'twas freezin' cold; no more need of a parasol—'

'She has to carry it to keep off the sun an' wind, 'cause her eyes are weak, I s'pose.'

'Why, I never knew that.'

'Abby said she told her so. Abby giggled right in her face one day when she met her with it.'

'She didn't!'

'She did – laughed right out. She said she couldn't help it no-how: you know Abby laughs terrible easy. There was Mis' White sailin' along with her parasol h'isted, she said, as fine as a fiddle. You know Mis' White always walks kind of nippin' anyhow, an' she's pretty dressy. An' then it was an awful cold, cloudy day, Abby said. The sun didn't shine, an' it didn't storm, an' there wa'n't no earthly use for a parasol anyway, that she could see. So she kind of snickered. I s'pose it struck her funny all of a sudden. Mis' White took it jest as quick, Abby said, an' told her kind of short that her eyes were terrible weak, an' she had to keep 'em shaded all the time she was outdoors; the doctor had give her orders to. Abby felt pretty streaked about it. You don't see her comin' yet, do you?'

'No, I don't. I thought I see somebody then, but it ain't her. It's the Patch boy, I guess. Yes, 'tis him. What do you think of Abby, Sarah?'

'Think of Abby! What do you mean, Mis' Dunbar?'

'Why, I mean, how do you think she is? Do you think her cough is as bad as 'twas?'

Sarah Arnold, who was a little light woman of fifty, thin-necked and round-backed, with blue protruding eyes in her tiny pale face, pursed up her mouth and went on with her work. She was sewing some red roses on to a black lace bonnet.

'I never thought her cough was very bad anyhow, as far as I was concerned,' said she, finally.

'Why, you didn't? I thought it sounded pretty bad. I've been feelin' kind of worried about her.'

' 'Tain't nothin' in the world but a throat cough. Her mother before her used to cough jest the same way. It sounds kind of hard, but 'tain't the kind of cough that kills folks. Why, I cough myself half the time.'

Sarah hacked a little as she spoke.

'Old Mis' Vane died of consumption, didn't she?'

'Consumption! Jest about as much consumption as I've got. Mis' Vane died of liver complaint. I guess I know. I was livin' right in the house.'

'Well, of course you'd be likely to know. I was thinkin' that was what I'd heard, that was all.'

'Some folks did call it consumption, but it wa'n't. See anything of Abby?'

'No, I don't. You ain't worried about her, are you?'

'Worried? – no. I ain't got no reason to be worried that I know of. She's old enough to take care of herself. All is, the supper table's been settin' an hour, an' I don't see where she is. She jest went down to the store to git some coffee.'

'It's kind of damp to-night.'

' 'Tain't damp enough to hurt her, I guess, well as she is.'

'Mebbe not. That's a pretty bonnet you're makin'.'

'Well, I think it's goin' to look pretty well. I didn't know as 'twould. I didn't have much to do with.'

'I s'pose it's Abby's.'

'Course it's Abby's. I guess you wouldn't see me comin' out in no such bonnet as this.'

'Why, you ain't any older than Abby, Sarah.'

'I'm different-lookin',' said Sarah, with a look which might have meant pride.

The two women were sitting on a little piazza at the side of the story-and-a-half white house.

Before the house was a small green yard with two cherry-trees in it. Then came the road, then some flat green meadow-lands where the frogs were singing. The grass on these meadows was a wet green, and there were some clumps of blue lilies which showed a long way off in it. Beyond the meadows was the south-west sky, which looked low and red and clear, and had birds in it. It was seven o'clock of a summer evening.

Mrs Dunbar, tall and straight, with a dark, leathery face whose features were gracefully cut, sat primly in a wooden chair, which was higher than Sarah's little rocker.

'I know Abby looks well in 'most everything,' said she.

'I never saw her try on anything that she didn't look well in. There's good-lookin' women, but there ain't many like Abby. Most folks are a little dependent on their bonnets, but she wa'n't, never. Sky blue or grass green, 'twas jest made for her. See anything of her comin'?'

'I can see her,' said Sarah, joyfully, in a minute.

'Abby Vane, where have you been?' she called out.

The approaching woman looked up and laughed. 'Did you think you'd lost me?' she said, as she came up the piazza step. 'I went into Mis' Parson's, an' I stayed longer'n I meant to. Agnes was there – she'd jest got home – an'—' She began to cough violently.

'You hadn't ought to give way to that ticklin' in your throat, Abby,' said Sarah, sharply.

'She'd better go into the house out of this damp air,' said Mrs Dunbar.

'Land! the air won't hurt her none. But mebbe you had better come in, Abby. I want to try on this bonnet. I wish you'd come too, Mis' Dunbar. I want you to see if you think it's deep enough in the back.'

'There!' said Sarah, after the three women had entered, and she had tied the bonnet on to Abby's head, picking the bows out daintily.

'It's real handsome on her,' said Mrs Dunbar.

'Red roses on a woman of my age!' laughed Abby. 'Sarah's bound to rig me up like a young girl.'

Abby stood in the little sitting room before the glass. The blinds were wide open to let the evening light in. Abby was a large, well-formed woman. She held her bonneted head up, and drew her chin back with an air of arch pride. The red roses bloomed meetly enough[1] above her candid, womanly forehead.

'If you can't wear red roses, I don't know who can,' said Sarah, looking up at her with pride and resentment. 'You could wear a white dress to meetin' an' look as well as any of 'em.'

'Look here, where did you git the lace for this bonnet?' asked Abby, suddenly. She had taken it off and was examining it closely.

'Oh, 'twas some I had.'

'See here, you tell the truth now, Sarah Arnold. Didn't you take this off your black silk dress?'

'It don't make no odds where I took it from.'

'You did. What made you do it?'

''Tain't worth talkin' 'bout. I always despised it on the dress.'

'Why, Sarah Arnold! That's jest the way she does,' said Abby to Mrs Dunbar. 'If I didn't watch her, she wouldn't leave herself a thing to put on.'

After Mrs Dunbar had gone, Abby sat down in a large covered rocking chair and leaned her head back. Her lips were parted a little, and her teeth showed. She looked ghastly all at once.

'What ails you?' said Sarah.

'Nothin'. I'm a little tired, that's all.'

'What are you holdin' on to your side for?'

'Oh, nothin'. It ached a little, that's all.'

'Mine's been achin' all the afternoon. I should think you'd better come out an' have somethin' to eat; the table's been set-tin' an hour an' a half.'

Abby rose meekly and followed Sarah into the kitchen with a sort of weak stateliness. She had always had a queenly way of walking. If Abby Vane should fall a victim to consumption some day, no one could say that she had brought it upon herself by non-observance of hygienic rules. Long miles of country road had she traversed with her fine swinging step, her shoulders thrown well back, her head erect, in her day. She had had the whole care of their vegetable garden, she had weeded and hoed and dug, she had chopped wood and raked hay, and picked apples and cherries.

There had always been a settled and amicable division of labor between the two women. Abby did the rough work, the man's work of the establishment, and Sarah, with her little, slim, nervous frame, the woman's work. All the dress-making and millinery was Sarah's department, all the cooking, all the tidying and furbishing of the house. Abby rose first in the morn-ing and made the fire, and she pumped the water and brought the tubs for the washing. Abby carried the purse, too. The two had literally one between them – one worn black leather wallet. When they went to the village store, if Sarah made the purchase, Abby drew forth the money to pay the bill.

The house belonged to Abby; she had inherited it from her mother. Sarah had some shares in the village bank, which kept them in food and clothes.

Nearly all the new clothes bought would be for Abby, though Sarah had to employ many a subterfuge to bring it about. She alone could have unravelled the subtlety of that diplomacy by which the new cashmere was made for Abby instead of herself, by which the new mantle was fitted to Abby's full, shapely shoulders instead of her own lean, stooping ones.

If Abby had been a barbarous empress, who exacted her cook's head as a penalty for a failure, she could have found no more faithful and anxious artist than Sarah. All the homely

New England recipes which Abby loved shone out to Sarah as if written in letters of gold. That nicety of adjustment through which the appetite should neither be cloyed by frequency nor tantalized by desire was a constant study with her. 'I've found out just how many times a week Abby likes mince pie,' she told Mrs Dunbar, triumphantly, once. 'I've been studyin' it out. She likes mince pie jest about twice to really relish it. She eats it other times, but she don't really hanker after it. I've been keepin' count about six weeks now, an' I can tell pretty well.'

Sarah had not eaten her own supper tonight, so she sat down with Abby at the little square table against the kitchen wall. Abby could not eat much, though she tried. Sarah watched her, scarcely taking a mouthful herself. She had a trick of swallowing convulsively every time Abby did, whether she was eating herself or not.

'Ain't goin' to have any custard pie?' said Sarah. 'Why not? I went to work an' made it on purpose.'

Abby began to laugh. 'Well, I'll tell you what 'tis, Sarah,' said she, 'near's I can put it; I've got jest about as much feelin' about takin' vittles as a pillow-tick² has about bein' stuffed with feathers.'

'Ain't you been eatin' nothin' this afternoon?'

'Nothin' but them few cherries before I went out.'

'That was jest enough to take your appetite off. I never can taste a thing between meals without feelin' it.'

'Well, I dare say that was it. Any of them cherries in the house now?'

'Yes; there's some in the cupboard. Want some?'

'I'll git 'em.'

Sarah jumped up and got a plate of beautiful red cherries and set them on the table.

'Let me see, these came off the Sarah-tree,' said Abby, meditatively. 'There wa'n't any on the Abby one this year.'

'No,' said Sarah, shortly.

'Kind of queer, wa'n't it? It's always bore, ever since I can remember.'

'I don't see nothin' very queer about it. It was frost-bit that cold spell last spring; that's all that ails it.'

'Why, the other one wa'n't.'

'This one's more exposed.'

The two round, symmetrical cherry-trees in the front yard had been called Abby and Sarah ever since the two women could remember. The fancy had originated somehow far back in their childhood, and ever since it had been the 'Abby-tree' and the 'Sarah-tree.' Both had borne plentifully until this season, when the Abby-tree displayed only her fine green leaves in fruit-time, and the Sarah-tree alone was rosy with cherries. Sarah had picked some that evening standing primly on a chair under the branches, a little basket on her arm, poking her pale inquisitive face into the perennial beauties of her woody namesake. Abby had been used to picking cherries after a more vigorous fashion, with a ladder, but she had not offered to this season.

'I couldn't git many – couldn't reach nothin' but the lowest branches,' said Sarah to-night, watching Abby eat the cherries. 'I guess you'd better take the ladder out there tomorrow. They're dead ripe, an' the birds are gittin' 'em. I scared off a whole flock to-day.'

'Well, I will if I can,' said Abby.

'Will if you can! Why, there ain't no reason why you can't, is there?'

'No, not that I know of.'

The next morning Abby painfully dragged the long ladder around the house to the tree, and did her appointed task. Sarah came to the door to watch her once, and Abby was coughing distressingly up amongst the green boughs.

'Don't give up to that ticklin' in your throat, for pity's sake, Abby,' she called out.

Abby's laugh floated back in answer, like a brave song, from the tree.

Presently Mrs Dunbar came up the path; she lived alone herself, and was a constant visitor. She stood under the tree, tall and lank and vigorous in her straight-skirted brown cotton gown.

'For the land sake, Abby! you don't mean to say you're pickin' cherries?' she called out. 'Are you crazy?'

'Hush!' whispered Abby, between the leaves.

'I don't see why she's crazy,' spoke up Sarah; 'she always picks 'em.'

'You don't catch me givin' up pickin' cherries till I'm a hundred,' said Abby, loudly. 'I'm a regular cherry bird.'

Sarah went into the house soon, and directly Abby crawled down the ladder. She was dripping with perspiration, and trembling.

'Abby Vane, I'm all out of patience,' said Mrs Dunbar. 'There ain't no sense in your doin' so.'

'Well, I've picked enough for a while, I guess.'

'Give me that other basket,' said Mrs Dunbar, harshly, 'an' I'll go up an' pick.'

'You can pick some for yourself,' coughed Abby.

'I don't like 'em,' said Mrs Dunbar, jerking herself up the ladder. 'Git up off the ground, an' go in.'

Abby obeyed without further words. She sat down in the sitting-room rocker, and leaned her head back. Sarah was stepping about in the kitchen, and did not come in, and she was glad.

In the course of a few months this old-fashioned chair, with its green cushion, held Abby from morning till night. She did not go out any more. She had kept about as long as she could. Every summer Sunday she had sat smartly beside Sarah in church, with those brave red roses on her head. But when the cold weather came her enemy's arrows were too sharp even for her strong mail of love and resolution.

Sarah's behavior seemed inexplicable. Even now that Abby was undeniably helpless, she was constantly goading her to her old tasks. She refused to admit that she was ill. She rebelled when the doctor was called: 'No more need of a doctor than nothin' at all,' she said.

Affairs went on so till the middle of the winter. Abby grew weaker and weaker, but Sarah seemed to ignore it. One day she went over to Mrs Dunbar's. One of the other neighbors was sitting with Abby. Sarah walked in suddenly. The outer door opened directly in Mrs Dunbar's living-room, and a whiff of icy air came in with her.

'How's Abby?' asked Mrs Dunbar.

''Bout the same.' Sarah stood upright, staring. She had a blue
plaid shawl over her head, and she clutched it together with her
red bony fingers. 'I've got something on my mind,' said she, 'an'
I've got to tell somebody. I'm goin' crazy.'

'What do you mean?'

'Abby's goin' to die, an' I've got something on my mind.
I 'ain't treated her right.'

'Sarah Arnold, do, for pity's sake, sit down, an' keep calm!'

'I'm calm enough. Oh, what shall I do?'

Mrs Dunbar forced Sarah into a chair, and took her shawl.
'You mustn't feel so,' said she. 'You've been just devoted to
Abby all your life, an' everybody knows it. I know when folks
die we're very apt to feel as if we hadn't done right by 'em, but
there 'ain't no sense in your feelin' so.'

'I know what I'm talkin' about. I've got something awful on
my mind. I've got to tell somebody.'

'Sarah Arnold, what do you mean?'

'I've got to tell.'

There was a puzzled look on the other woman's thin, strong
face. 'Well, if you've got anything you want to tell, you can tell
it, but I can't think what you're drivin' at.'

Sarah fixed her eyes on the wall at the right of Mrs Dunbar.
'It begins 'way back when we was girls. You know I went to
live with Abby an' her mother after my folks died. Abby an' me
had always been together. You remember that John Marshall
that used to keep store where Simmons is, about thirty year
ago. When Abby was about twenty, he begun waitin' on her.
He was a good-lookin' fellar, an' I guess he was smart, though
I never took a fancy to him.

'He was crazy after Abby; but her mother didn't like him.
She talked again' him from the very first of it, and wouldn't
take no notice of him. She declared she shouldn't have him.
Abby didn't say much. She'd laugh an' tell her mother not to
fret, but she'd treat him pretty well when he came.

'I s'pose she liked him. I used to watch her, an' think she did.
An' he kep' comin' an' comin'. All the fellars were craz' 'bout
her anyhow. She was the handsomest girl that was ever seen,

about. She'd laugh an' talk with all of 'em, but I s'pose Marshall was the one.

'Well, finally Mis' Vane made such a fuss that he stopped comin'. 'Twas along about a year before she died. I never knew, but I s'pose Abby told him. He went right off to Mexico. Abby didn't say a word, but I knew she felt bad. She didn't seem to care much about goin' into company, an' didn't act jest like herself.

'Well, old Mis' Vane died sudden, you know. She'd had the consumption for years, coughed ever since I could remember, but she went real quick at last, an' Abby was away. She'd gone over to her Aunt Abby's in Colebrook to stay a couple of days. Her aunt wa'n't well neither, an' wanted to see her, an' her mother seemed comfortable so she thought she could go. We sent for her jest as soon as Mis' Vane was took worse, but she couldn't git home in time.

'So I was with Mis' Vane when she died. She had her senses, and she left word for Abby. She said to tell her she'd give her consent to her marryin' John Marshall.'

Sarah stopped. Mrs Dunbar waited, staring.

'I 'ain't told her from that day to this.'

'What!'

'I 'ain't never told what her mother said.'

'Why, Sarah Arnold, why not?'

'Oh, I couldn't have it nohow – I couldn't – I couldn't, Mis' Dunbar. Seemed as if it would kill me to think of it. I couldn't have her likin' anybody else, an' gittin' married. You don't know what I'd been through. All my own folks had died before I was sixteen years old, an' Mis' Vane was gone, an' she'd been jest like a mother to me. I didn't have nobody in the world but Abby. I couldn't have it so – I couldn't – I couldn't.'

'Sarah Arnold, you've been livin' with her all these years, an' been such friends, an' had this shut up in your mind. What are you made of?'

'Oh, I've done everything I could for Abby – everything.'

'You couldn't make it up to her in such a way as that.'

'I know it. Oh, Mis' Dunbar, have I got to tell her? Have I?'

Mrs Dunbar, with her intent, ascetic face, confronted Sarah like an embodied conscience.

'Tell her? Sarah Arnold, don't you let another sun go down over your head before you tell her.'

'Oh, it don't seem as if I could.'

'Don't you wait another minute. You go right home now an' tell her, if you ever want any more peace in this world.'

Sarah stood gazing at her a minute, trembling. Then she pulled her shawl up over her head and turned toward the door.

'Well, I'll see,' said she.

'Don't you wait a minute!' Mrs Dunbar called after her again. Then she stood watching the lean, pitiful figure slink down the street. She wondered a good many times afterward if Sarah had told; she suspected that she had not.

Sarah avoided her, and never alluded to the matter again. She fell back on her old philosophy. ' 'Tain't nothin' but Abby's goin' to git over,' she told people. ' 'Tain't on her lungs. She'll git up as soon as it comes warmer weather.'

She treated Abby now with the greatest tenderness. She toiled for her day and night. Every delicacy which the sick woman had ever fancied stood waiting on the pantry shelves. Sarah went without shoes and flannels to purchase them, though the chance that they would be tasted was small.

Every spare moment which she could get she sewed for Abby, and folded and hung away new garments which would never be worn. If Abby ventured to remonstrate, Sarah was indignant, and sewed the more; sitting up through long winter nights, she stitched and hemmed with fierce zeal. She ransacked her own wardrobe for material, and hardly left herself a whole article to wear.

Toward spring, when her little dividends came in, she bought stuff for a new dress for Abby – soft cashmere of a beautiful blue. She got patterns, and cut and fitted and pleated with the best of her poor country skill.

'There,' said she, when it was completed, 'you've got a decent dress to put on, Abby, when you get out again.'

'It's real handsome, Sarah,' said Abby, smiling.

Abby did not die till the last of May. She sat in her chair by the window, and watched feebly the young grass springing up and the green film spreading over the tree boughs. Way over across in a neighbor's garden was a little peach-tree. Abby could just see it.

'Jest see that peach-tree over there,' she whispered to Sarah one evening. It was all rosy with bloom. 'It's the first tree I've seen blowed out this year. S'pose the Abby-tree's goin' to blossom?'

'I guess so,' said Sarah; 'it's leavin' out.'

Abby seemed to dwell on the blossoming of the Abby-tree. She kept talking about it. One morning she saw some cherry-trees in the next yard had blossomed, and she called Sarah eagerly.

'Sarah, have you looked to see if the Abby-tree's blossomed?'

'Of course it has. What's to hender?'

Abby's face was radiant. 'Oh, Sarah, I want to see it.'

'Well, you wait till afternoon,' said Sarah, with a tremble in her voice. 'I'll draw you round to the front-room door after dinner, an' you can look through at it.'

People passing that morning stared to see Sarah Arnold doing some curious work in the front yard. Not one blossom was there on the Abby-tree, but the Sarah-tree was white. Its delicate garlanded boughs stirred softly, and gave out a sweet smell. Bees murmured through them. Sarah had a ladder plunged into the roadward side of all this bloom and sweet-ness, and she was sawing and hacking at the white boughs. Then she would stagger across to the other tree with her arms full of them. They trailed on the green turf, they lay over her shoulders like white bayonets. All the air around her was full of flying petals. She looked like some homely Spring Angel. Then she bound these fair branches and twigs into the houseward side of the Abby-tree. She worked hard and fast. That after-noon one looking at the tree from the house would have been misled. That side of the Abby-tree was brave with bloom.

Sarah drew Abby in her chair a little way into the front room. 'There!' said she.

'Oh! ain't it beautiful?' cried Abby.

The white branches waved before the window. Abby sat looking at it with a peaceful smile on her face.

When she was back in her old place in the sitting-room, she gave a bright look up at Sarah.

'It ain't any use to worry,' said she, 'the Abby-tree is bound to blossom.'

Sarah cried out suddenly, 'Oh, Abby! Abby! Abby! what shall I do! oh, what shall I do!' She flung herself down by Abby's chair, and put her face on her thin knees. 'Oh, Abby! Abby!'

'I ain't gon' to,' said Sarah, in a minute. She stood up, and wiped her eyes. 'I know you're better, Abby, an' you'll be out pretty soon. All is, you've been sick pretty long, an' it's kind of wore on me, an' it come over me all of a sudden.'

'Sarah,' said Abby, solemnly, 'what's got to come has got to. You've got to look at things reasonable. There's two of us, an' one would have to go before the other one; we've always known it. It ain't goin' to be so bad as you think. Mis' Dunbar is comin' here to live with you. I've got it all fixed with her. She's real strong, an' she can make up the fires, an' git the water an' the tubs. You're fifty years old, an' you're goin' to have some more years to live. But it's just goin' to be gittin' up one day after another an' goin' to bed at night, an' they'll be gone. It can be got through with. There's roads trod out through everything, an' there's folks ahead with lanterns, as it were. You—'

'Oh, Abby! Abby! stop!' Sarah broke in. 'If you knew all there was to it. You don't know — you don't know! I 'ain't treated you right, Abby, I 'ain't. I've been keepin' something from you.'

'What have you been keepin', Sarah?'

Then Abby listened. Sarah told. There had always been an arch curve to Abby's handsome mouth – a look of sweet amusement at life. It showed forth plainly toward the close of Sarah's tale. Then it deepened suddenly. The poor sick woman laughed out, with a charming, gleeful ring.

A look of joyful wonder flashed over Sarah's despairing face. She stood staring.

'Sarah,' said Abby, 'I wouldn't have had John Marshall if he'd come on his knees after me all the way from Mexico!'

The Wife of His Youth[1]

CHARLES W. CHESNUTT

I

Mr Ryder was going to give a ball. There were several reasons why this was an opportune time for such an event.

Mr Ryder might aptly be called the dean of the Blue Veins. The original Blue Veins were a little society of colored persons organized in a certain Northern city shortly after the war. Its purpose was to establish and maintain correct social standards among a people whose social condition presented almost unlimited room for improvement. By accident, combined perhaps with some natural affinity, the society consisted of individuals who were, generally speaking, more white than black. Some envious outsider made the suggestion that no one was eligible for membership who was not white enough to show blue veins. The suggestion was readily adopted by those who were not of the favored few, and since that time the society, though possessing a longer and more pretentious name, had been known far and wide as the 'Blue Vein Society,' and its members as the 'Blue Veins.'

The Blue Veins did not allow that any such requirement existed for admission to their circle, but, on the contrary, declared that character and culture were the only things considered; and that if most of their members were light-colored, it was because such persons, as a rule, had had better opportunities to qualify themselves for membership. Opinions differed, too, as to the usefulness of the society. There were those who had been known to assail it violently as a glaring example of the very prejudice from which the colored race had suffered most; and later, when such critics had succeeded in getting on the inside, they had been heard to maintain with zeal and earnestness that the society was a lifeboat, an anchor, a bulwark and a shield, – a pillar of cloud by day and of fire by night,[2] to guide their people through the social wilderness. Another alleged prerequisite for Blue Vein membership was that of free birth; and while there was really no such requirement, it is doubtless true that very few of the members would have been unable to meet it if there had been. If there were one or two of the older members who had come up from the South and from slavery, their history presented enough romantic circumstances to rob their servile origin of its grosser aspects.

While there were no such tests of eligibility, it is true that the Blue Veins had their notions on these subjects, and that not all of them were equally liberal in regard to the things they collectively disclaimed. Mr Ryder was one of the most conservative. Though he had not been among the founders of the society, but had come in some years later, his genius for social leadership was such that he had speedily become its recognized adviser and head, the custodian of its standards, and the preserver of its traditions. He shaped its social policy, was active in providing for its entertainment, and when the interest fell off, as it sometimes did, he fanned the embers until they burst again into a cheerful flame.

There were still other reasons for his popularity. While he was not as white as some of the Blue Veins, his appearance was such as to confer distinction upon them. His features were of a refined type, his hair was almost straight; he was always neatly dressed; his manners were irreproachable, and his morals above suspicion. He had come to Groveland[3] a young man, and obtaining employment in the office of a railroad company as messenger had in time worked himself up to the position of stationery clerk, having charge of the distribution of the office supplies for the whole company. Although the lack of early training had hindered the orderly development of a naturally fine mind, it had not prevented him from doing a great deal of reading or from forming decidedly literary tastes. Poetry was his passion. He could repeat whole pages of the great English

poets; and if his pronunciation was sometimes faulty, his eye,
his voice, his gestures, would respond to the changing senti-
ment with a precision that revealed a poetic soul and disarmed
criticism. He was economical, and had saved money; he owned
and occupied a very comfortable house on a respectable street.
His residence was handsomely furnished, containing among
other things a good library, especially rich in poetry, a piano,
and some choice engravings. He generally shared his house
with some young couple, who looked after his wants and were
company for him; for Mr Ryder was a single man. In the early
days of his connection with the Blue Veins he had been regarded
as quite a catch, and young ladies and their mothers had
manœuvred with much ingenuity to capture him. Not, however, until Mrs Molly Dixon visited Groveland had any woman
ever made him wish to change his condition to that of a married man.

Mrs Dixon had come to Groveland from Washington in the
spring, and before the summer was over she had won Mr
Ryder's heart. She possessed many attractive qualities. She was
much younger than he; in fact, he was old enough to have been
her father, though no one knew exactly how old he was. She
was whiter than he, and better educated. She had moved in the
best colored society of the country, at Washington, and had
taught in the schools of that city. Such a superior person had
been eagerly welcomed to the Blue Vein Society, and had taken
a leading part in its activities. Mr Ryder had at first been
attracted by her charms of person, for she was very good looking and not over twenty-five; then by her refined manners and
the vivacity of her wit. Her husband had been a government
clerk, and at his death had left a considerable life insurance. She
was visiting friends in Groveland, and, finding the town and
the people to her liking, had prolonged her stay indefinitely. She
had not seemed displeased at Mr Ryder's attentions, but on the
contrary had given him every proper encouragement; indeed, a
younger and less cautious man would long since have spoken.
But he had made up his mind, and had only to determine the
time when he would ask her to be his wife. He decided to give a
ball in her honor, and at some time during the evening of the

ball to offer her his heart and hand. He had no special fears
about the outcome, but, with a little touch of romance, he
wanted the surroundings to be in harmony with his own feelings when he should have received the answer he expected.

Mr Ryder resolved that this ball should mark an epoch in
the social history of Groveland. He knew, of course, – no one
could know better, – the entertainments that had taken place in
past years, and what must be done to surpass them. His ball
must be worthy of the lady in whose honor it was to be given,
and must, by the quality of its guests, set an example for the
future. He had observed of late a growing liberality, almost a
laxity, in social matters, even among members of his own set,
and had several times been forced to meet in a social way persons whose complexions and callings in life were hardly up to
the standard which he considered proper for the society to
maintain. He had a theory of his own.

'I have no race prejudice,' he would say, 'but we people of
mixed blood are ground between the upper and the nether mill-
stone. Our fate lies between absorption by the white race and
extinction in the black. The one does n't want us yet, but may
take us in time. The other would welcome us, but it would be
for us a backward step. "With malice towards none, with charity for all,"[4] we must do the best we can for ourselves and those
who are to follow us. Self-preservation is the first law of nature.'

His ball would serve by its exclusiveness to counteract lev-
eling tendencies, and his marriage with Mrs Dixon would help
to further the upward process of absorption he had been wishing and waiting for.

II

The ball was to take place on Friday night. The house had
been put in order, the carpets covered with canvas, the halls
and stairs decorated with palms and potted plants; and in the
afternoon Mr Ryder sat on his front porch, which the shade
of a vine running up over a wire netting made a cool and pleasant lounging place. He expected to respond to the toast 'The

Ladies' at the supper, and from a volume of Tennyson[5] – his favorite poet – was fortifying himself with apt quotations. The volume was open at 'A Dream of Fair Women.' His eyes fell on these lines, and he read them aloud to judge better of their effect: –

> 'At length I saw a lady within call,
>   Stiller than chisell'd marble, standing there;
> A daughter of the gods, divinely tall,
>   And most divinely fair.'

He marked the verse, and turning the page read the stanza beginning, –

> 'O sweet pale Margaret,
>   O rare pale Margaret.'

He weighed the passage a moment, and decided that it would not do. Mrs Dixon was the palest lady he expected at the ball, and she was of a rather ruddy complexion, and of lively disposition and buxom build. So he ran over the leaves until his eye rested on the description of Queen Guinevere: –

> 'She seem'd a part of joyous Spring;
> A gown of grass-green silk she wore,
> Buckled with golden clasps before;
> A light-green tuft of plumes she bore
> Closed in a golden ring.
>
> * * *
>
> 'She look'd so lovely, as she sway'd
> The rein with dainty finger-tips,
> A man had given all other bliss,
> And all his worldly worth for this,
> To waste his whole heart in one kiss
> Upon her perfect lips.'

As Mr Ryder murmured these words audibly, with an appreciative thrill, he heard the latch of his gate click, and a light footfall sounding on the steps. He turned his head, and saw a woman standing before his door.

She was a little woman, not five feet tall, and proportioned to her height. Although she stood erect, and looked around her with very bright and restless eyes, she seemed quite old; for her face was crossed and recrossed with a hundred wrinkles, and around the edges of her bonnet could be seen protruding here and there a tuft of short gray wool. She wore a blue calico gown of ancient cut, a little red shawl fastened around her shoulders with an old-fashioned brass brooch, and a large bonnet profusely ornamented with faded red and yellow artificial flowers. And she was very black, – so black that her toothless gums, revealed when she opened her mouth to speak, were not red, but blue. She looked like a bit of the old plantation life, summoned up from the past by the wave of a magician's wand, as the poet's fancy had called into being the gracious shapes of which Mr Ryder had just been reading.

He rose from his chair and came over to where she stood.

'Good-afternoon, madam,' he said.

'Good-evenin', suh,' she answered, ducking suddenly with a quaint curtsy. Her voice was shrill and piping, but softened somewhat by age. 'Is dis yere whar Mistuh Ryduh lib, suh?' she asked, looking around her doubtfully, and glancing into the open windows, through which some of the preparations for the evening were visible.

'Yes,' he replied, with an air of kindly patronage, unconsciously flattered by her manner, 'I am Mr Ryder. Did you want to see me?'

'Yas, suh, ef I ain't 'sturbin' of you too much.'

'Not at all. Have a seat over here behind the vine, where it is cool. What can I do for you?'

''Scuse me, suh,' she continued, when she had sat down on the edge of a chair, ''scuse me, suh, I's lookin' for my husban'. I heerd you wuz a big man an' had libbed heah a long time, an' I 'lowed you wouldn't min' ef I'd come roun' an' ax you ef you'd ever heerd of a merlatter man by de name er Sam Taylor 'quirin' roun' in de chu'ches ermongs' de people fer his wife 'Liza Jane?'

Mr Ryder seemed to think for a moment.

'There used to be many such cases right after the war,' he said, 'but it has been so long that I have forgotten them. There are very few now. But tell me your story, and it may refresh my memory.'

She sat back farther in her chair so as to be more comfortable, and folded her withered hands in her lap.

'My name's 'Liza,' she began, ''Liza Jane. W'en I wuz young I us'ter b'long ter Marse Bob Smif, down in ole Missoura. I wuz bawn down dere. W'en I wuz a gal I wuz married ter a man named Jim. But Jim died, an' after dat I married a merlatter man named Sam Taylor. Sam wuz free-bawn, but his mammy and daddy died, an' de w'ite folks 'prenticed him ter my marster fer ter work fer 'im 'tel he wuz growed up. Sam worked in de fiel', an' I wuz de cook. One day Ma'y Ann, ole miss's maid, came rushin' out ter de kitchen, an' says she, "'Liza Jane, ole marse gwine sell yo' Sam down de ribber."

' "Go way f'm yere," says I; "my husban''s free!"

' "Don' make no diff'ence. I heerd ole marse tell ole miss he wuz gwine take yo' Sam 'way wid 'im ter-morrow, fer he needed money, an' he knowed whar he could git a t'ousan' dollars fer Sam an' no questions axed."

'W'en Sam come home f'm de fiel' dat night, I tole him 'bout ole marse gwine steal 'im, an' Sam run erway. His time wuz mos' up, an' he swo' dat w'en he wuz twenty-one he would come back an' he'p me run erway, er else save up de money ter buy my freedom. An' I know he'd 'a' done it, fer he thought a heap er me, Sam did. But w'en he come back he didn' fin' me, fer I wuzn' dere. Ole marse had heerd dat I warned Sam, so he had me whip' an' sol' down de ribber.

'Den de wah broke out, an' w'en it wuz ober de cullud folks wuz scattered. I went back ter de ole home; but Sam wuzn' dere, an' I could n' l'arn nuffin' 'bout 'im. But I knowed he'd be'n dere to look fer me an' had n' foun' me, an' had gone erway ter hunt fer me.

'I's be'n lookin' fer 'im eber sence,' she added simply, as though twenty-five years were but a couple of weeks, 'an' I knows he's be'n lookin' fer me. Fer he sot a heap er sto' by me, Sam did, an' I know he's be'n huntin' fer me all dese years, – 'less'n he's be'n

sick er sump'n, so he could n' work, er out'n his head, so he
could n' 'member his promise. I went back down de ribber, fer I
'lowed he'd gone down dere lookin' fer me. I 's be'n ter Noo
Orleens, an' Atlanty, an' Charleston, an' Richmon'; an' w'en I 'd
be'n all ober de Souf I come ter de Norf. Fer I knows I 'll fin'
'im some er dese days,' she added softly, 'er he 'll fin' me, an'
den we 'll bofe be as happy in freedom as we wuz in de ole days
befo' de wah.' A smile stole over her withered countenance as
she paused a moment, and her bright eyes softened into a far-
away look.

This was the substance of the old woman's story. She had
wandered a little here and there. Mr Ryder was looking at her
curiously when she finished.

'How have you lived all these years?' he asked.

'Cookin', suh. I 's a good cook. Does you know anybody
w'at needs a good cook, suh? I 's stoppin' wid a cullud fam'ly
roun' de corner yonder 'tel I kin git a place.'

'Do you really expect to find your husband? He may be dead
long ago.'

She shook her head emphatically. 'Oh no, he ain' dead. De
signs an' de tokens tells me. I dremp three nights runnin' on'y
dis las' week dat I foun' him.'

'He may have married another woman. Your slave marriage
would not have prevented him, for you never lived with him
after the war, and without that your marriage does n't count.'

'Would n' make no diff'ence wid Sam. He would n' marry
no yuther 'ooman 'tel he foun' out 'bout me. I knows it,' she
added. 'Sump'n 's be'n tellin' me all dese years dat I 's gwine fin'
Sam 'fo' I dies.'

'Perhaps he's outgrown you, and climbed up in the world
where he wouldn't care to have you find him.'

'No, indeed, suh,' she replied, 'Sam ain' dat kin' er man. He
wuz good ter me, Sam wuz, but he wuz n' much good ter
nobody e'se, fer he wuz one er de triflin'es'[6] han's on de plantation. I 'spec's ter haf ter suppo't 'im w'en I fin' 'im, fer he nebber
would work 'less'n he had ter. But den he wuz free, an' he didn'
git no pay fer his work, an' I don' blame 'im much. Mebbe he's
done better sence he run erway, but I ain' 'spectin' much.'

'You may have passed him on the street a hundred times during the twenty-five years, and not have known him; time works great changes.'

She smiled incredulously. 'I'd know 'im 'mongs' a hund'ed men. Fer dey wuz n' no yuther merlatter man like my man Sam, an' I could n' be mistook. I's toted his picture roun' wid me twenty-five years.'

'May I see it?' asked Mr Ryder. 'It might help me to remember whether I have seen the original.'

As she drew a small parcel from her bosom he saw that it was fastened to a string that went around her neck. Removing several wrappers, she brought to light an old-fashioned daguerreotype in a black case. He looked long and intently at the portrait. It was faded with time, but the features were still distinct, and it was easy to see what manner of man it had represented.

He closed the case, and with a slow movement handed it back to her.

'I don't know of any man in town who goes by that name,' he said, 'nor have I heard of any one making such inquiries. But if you will leave me your address, I will give the matter some attention, and if I find out anything I will let you know.'

She gave him the number of a house in the neighborhood, and went away, after thanking him warmly.

He wrote the address on the fly-leaf of the volume of Tennyson, and, when she had gone, rose to his feet and stood looking after her curiously. As she walked down the street with mincing step, he saw several persons whom she passed turn and look back at her with a smile of kindly amusement. When she had turned the corner, he went upstairs to his bedroom, and stood for a long time before the mirror of his dressing-case, gazing thoughtfully at the reflection of his own face.

III

At eight o'clock the ballroom was a blaze of light and the guests had begun to assemble; for there was a literary programme and some routine business of the society to be gone through with before the dancing. A black servant in evening dress waited at the door and directed the guests to the dressing-rooms.

The occasion was long memorable among the colored people of the city; not alone for the dress and display, but for the high average of intelligence and culture that distinguished the gathering as a whole. There were a number of schoolteachers, several young doctors, three or four lawyers, some professional singers, an editor, a lieutenant in the United States army spending his furlough in the city, and others in various polite callings; these were colored, though most of them would not have attracted even a casual glance because of any marked difference from white people. Most of the ladies were in evening costume, and dress coats and dancing pumps were the rule among the men. A band of string music, stationed in an alcove behind a row of palms, played popular airs while the guests were gathering.

The dancing began at half past nine. At eleven o'clock supper was served. Mr Ryder had left the ballroom some little time before the intermission, but reappeared at the supper-table. The spread was worthy of the occasion, and the guests did full justice to it. When the coffee had been served, the toast-master, Mr Solomon Sadler, rapped for order. He made a brief introductory speech, complimenting host and guests, and then presented in their order the toasts of the evening. They were responded to with a very fair display of after-dinner wit.

'The last toast,' said the toast-master, when he reached the end of the list, 'is one which must appeal to us all. There is no one of us of the sterner sex who is not at some time dependent upon woman, – in infancy for protection, in manhood for companionship, in old age for care and comforting. Our good host has been trying to live alone, but the fair faces I see around me to-night prove that he too is largely dependent upon the gentler sex for most that makes life worth living, – the society and love of friends, – and rumor is at fault if he does not soon yield entire subjection to one of them. Mr Ryder will now respond to the toast, – The Ladies.'

There was a pensive look in Mr Ryder's eyes as he took the floor and adjusted his eyeglasses. He began by speaking of woman as the gift of Heaven to man, and after some general observations on the relations of the sexes he said: 'But perhaps the quality which most distinguishes woman is her fidelity and devotion to those she loves. History is full of examples, but has recorded none more striking than one which only to-day came under my notice.'

He then related, simply but effectively, the story told by his visitor of the afternoon. He gave it in the same soft dialect, which came readily to his lips, while the company listened attentively and sympathetically. For the story had awakened a responsive thrill in many hearts. There were some present who had seen, and others who had heard their fathers and grandfathers tell, the wrongs and sufferings of this past generation, and all of them still felt, in their darker moments, the shadow hanging over them. Mr Ryder went on: –

'Such devotion and confidence are rare even among women. There are many who would have searched a year, some who would have waited five years, a few who might have hoped ten years; but for twenty-five years this woman has retained her affection for and her faith in a man she has not seen or heard of in all that time.

'She came to me to-day in the hope that I might be able to help her find this long-lost husband. And when she was gone I gave my fancy rein, and imagined a case I will put to you.

'Suppose that this husband, soon after his escape, had learned that his wife had been sold away, and that such inquiries as he could make brought no information of her whereabouts. Suppose that he was young, and she much older than he; that he was light, and she was black; that their marriage was a slave marriage, and legally binding only if they chose to make it so after the war. Suppose, too, that he made his way to the North, as some of us have done, and there, where he had larger opportunities, had improved them, and had in the course of all these years grown to be as different from the ignorant boy who ran away from fear of slavery as the day is from the night. Suppose, even, that he had qualified himself, by industry, by thrift, and by study, to win the friendship and be considered worthy of the society of such people as these I see around me to-night, gracing my board and filling my heart with gladness; for I am old enough to remember the day when such a gathering would not have been possible in this land. Suppose, too, that, as the years went by, this man's memory of the past grew more and more indistinct, until at last it was rarely, except in his dreams, that any image of this bygone period rose before his mind. And then suppose that accident should bring to his knowledge the fact that the wife of his youth, the wife he had left behind him, – not one who had walked by his side and kept pace with him in his upward struggle, but one upon whom advancing years and a laborious life had set their mark, – was alive and seeking him, but that he was absolutely safe from recognition or discovery, unless he chose to reveal himself. My friends, what would the man do? I will presume that he was one who loved honor, and tried to deal justly with all men. I will even carry the case further, and suppose that perhaps he had set his heart upon another, whom he had hoped to call his own. What would he do, or rather what ought he to do, in such a crisis of a lifetime?

'It seemed to me that he might hesitate, and I imagined that I was an old friend, a near friend, and that he had come to me for advice; and I argued the case with him. I tried to discuss it impartially. After we had looked upon the matter from every point of view, I said to him, in words that we all know: –[7]

> "This above all: to thine own self be true,
> And it must follow, as the night the day,
> Thou canst not then be false to any man."

'Then, finally, I put the question to him, "Shall you acknowledge her?"

'And now, ladies and gentlemen, friends and companions, I ask you, what should he have done?'

There was something in Mr Ryder's voice that stirred the hearts of those who sat around him. It suggested more than mere sympathy with an imaginary situation; it seemed rather in the nature of a personal appeal. It was observed, too, that his look rested more especially upon Mrs Dixon, with a mingled expression of renunciation and inquiry.

She had listened, with parted lips and streaming eyes. She was the first to speak: 'He should have acknowledged her.'

'Yes,' they all echoed, 'he should have acknowledged her.'

'My friends and companions,' responded Mr Ryder, 'I thank you, one and all. It is the answer I expected, for I knew your hearts.'

He turned and walked toward the closed door of an adjoining room, while every eye followed him in wondering curiosity. He came back in a moment, leading by the hand his visitor of the afternoon, who stood startled and trembling at the sudden plunge into this scene of brilliant gayety. She was neatly dressed in gray, and wore the white cap of an elderly woman.

'Ladies and gentlemen,' he said, 'this is the woman, and I am the man, whose story I have told you. Permit me to introduce to you the wife of my youth.'

The Real Right Thing

HENRY JAMES

I

When, after the death of Ashton Doyne – but three months after – George Withermore was approached, as the phrase is, on the subject of a 'volume,' the communication came straight from his publishers, who had been, and indeed much more, Doyne's own; but he was not surprised to learn, on the occurrence of the interview they next suggested, that a certain pressure as to the early issue of a Life had been brought to bear upon them by their late client's widow. Doyne's relations with his wife had been, to Withermore's knowledge, a very special chapter – which would present itself, by the way, as a delicate one for the biographer; but a sense of what she had lost, and even of what she had lacked, had betrayed itself, on the poor woman's part, from the first days of her bereavement, sufficiently to prepare an observer at all initiated for some attitude of reparation, some espousal even exaggerated of the interests of a distinguished name. George Withermore was, as he felt, initiated; yet what he had not expected was to hear that she had mentioned him as the person in whose hands she would most promptly place the materials for a book.

These materials – diaries, letters, memoranda, notes, documents of many sorts – were her property, and wholly in her control, no conditions at all attaching to any portion of her heritage; so that she was free at present to do as she liked – free, in particular, to do nothing. What Doyne would have arranged had he had time to arrange could be but supposition and guess. Death had taken him too soon and too suddenly, and there was all the pity that the only wishes he was known to have expressed were wishes that put it positively out of account. He had broken short off – that was the way of it; and the end was ragged and needed trimming. Withermore was conscious, abundantly, how close he had stood to him, but he was not less aware of his comparative obscurity. He was young, a journalist, a critic, a hand-to-mouth character, with little, as yet, as was vulgarly said, to show. His writings were few and small, his relations scant and vague. Doyne, on the other hand, had lived long enough – above all had had talent enough – to become great, and among his many friends gilded also with greatness were several to whom his wife would have struck those who knew her as much more likely to appeal.

The preference she had, at all events, uttered – and uttered in a roundabout, considerate way that left him a measure of freedom – made our young man feel that he must at least see her and that there would be in any case a good deal to talk about. He immediately wrote to her, she as promptly named an hour, and they had it out. But he came away with his particular idea immensely strengthened. She was a strange woman, and he had never thought her an agreeable one; only there was something that touched him now in her bustling, blundering impatience. She wanted the book to make up, and the individual whom, of her husband's set, she probably believed she might most manipulate was in every way to help it to make up. She had not taken Doyne seriously enough in life, but the biography should be a solid reply to every imputation on herself. She had scantly known how such books were constructed, but she had been looking and had learned something. It alarmed Withermore a little from the first to see that she would wish to go in for quantity. She talked of 'volumes' – but he had his notion of that.

'My thought went straight to *you*, as his own would have done,' she had said almost as soon as she rose before him there in her large array of mourning – with her big black eyes, her big black wig, her big black fan and gloves, her general gaunt, ugly, tragic, but striking and, as might have been thought from a certain point of view, 'elegant' presence. 'You're the one he liked

most; oh, *much*!' – and it had been quite enough to turn Withermore's head. It little mattered that he could afterward wonder
if she had known Doyne enough, when it came to that, to be
sure. He would have said for himself indeed that her testimony
on such a point would scarcely have counted. Still, there was
no smoke without fire; she knew at least what she meant, and
he was not a person she could have an interest in flattering.
They went up together, without delay, to the great man's vacant
study, which was at the back of the house and looked over the
large green garden – a beautiful and inspiring scene, to poor
Withermore's view – common to the expensive row.

'You can perfectly work here, you know,' said Mrs Doyne:
'you shall have the place quite to yourself – I'll give it all up
to you; so that in the evenings, in particular, don't you see?
for quiet and privacy, it will be perfection.'

Perfection indeed, the young man felt as he looked about –
having explained that, as his actual occupation was an evening
paper and his earlier hours, for a long time yet, regularly taken
up, he would have to come always at night. The place was full
of their lost friend; everything in it had belonged to him; everything they touched had been part of his life. It was for the
moment too much for Withermore – too great an honour and
even too great a care; memories still recent came back to him,
and, while his heart beat faster and his eyes filled with tears, the
pressure of his loyalty seemed almost more than he could carry.
At the sight of his tears Mrs Doyne's own rose to her lids, and
the two, for a minute, only looked at each other. He half
expected her to break out: 'Oh, help me to feel as I know you
know I want to feel!' And after a little one of them said, with
the other's deep assent – it didn't matter which: 'It's here that
we're *with* him.' But it was definitely the young man who put
it, before they left the room, that it was there he was with *them*.

The young man began to come as soon as he could arrange
it, and then it was, on the spot, in the charmed stillness, between
the lamp and the fire and with the curtains drawn, that a certain intenser consciousness crept over him. He turned in out of
the black London November; he passed through the large,
hushed house and up the red-carpeted staircase where he only

found in his path the whisk of a soundless, trained maid, or the reach, out of a doorway, of Mrs Doyne's queenly weeds and approving tragic face; and then, by a mere touch of the well-made door that gave so sharp and pleasant a click, shut himself in for three or four warm hours with the spirit – as he had always distinctly declared it – of his master. He was not a little frightened when, even the first night, it came over him that he had really been most affected, in the whole matter, by the prospect, the privilege and the luxury, of this sensation. He had not, he could now reflect, definitely considered the question of the book – as to which there was here, even already, much to consider: he had simply let his affection and admiration – to say nothing of his gratified pride – meet, to the full, the temptation Mrs Doyne had offered them.

How did he know, without more thought, he might begin to ask himself, that the book was, on the whole, to be desired? What warrant had he ever received from Ashton Doyne himself for so direct and, as it were, so familiar an approach? Great was the art of biography, but there were lives and lives, there were subjects and subjects. He confusedly recalled, so far as that went, old words dropped by Doyne over contemporary compilations, suggestions of how he himself discriminated as to other heroes and other panoramas. He even remembered how his friend, at moments, would have seemed to show himself as holding that the 'literary' career might – save in the case of a Johnson and a Scott, with a Boswell and a Lockhart to help[1] – best content itself to be represented. The artist was what he *did* – he was nothing else. Yet how, on the other hand, was not *he*, George Withermore, poor devil, to have jumped at the chance of spending his winter in an intimacy so rich? It had been simply dazzling – that was the fact. It hadn't been the 'terms,' from the publishers – though these were, as they said at the office, all right; it had been Doyne himself, his company and contact and presence – it had been just what it was turning out, the possibility of an intercourse closer than that of life. Strange that death, of the two things, should have the fewer mysteries and secrets! The first night our young man was alone in the room it seemed to him that his master and he were really for the first time together.

II

Mrs Doyne had for the most part let him expressively alone, but she had on two or three occasions looked in to see if his needs had been met, and he had had the opportunity of thanking her on the spot for the judgment and zeal with which she had smoothed his way. She had to some extent herself been looking things over and had been able already to muster several groups of letters; all the keys of drawers and cabinets she had, moreover, from the first placed in his hands, with helpful information as to the apparent whereabouts of different matters. She had put him, in a word, in the fullest possible possession, and whether or no her husband had trusted her, she at least, it was clear, trusted her husband's friend. There grew upon Withermore, nevertheless, the impression that, in spite of all these offices, she was not yet at peace, and that a certain unappeasable anxiety continued even to keep step with her confidence. Though she was full of consideration, she was at the same time perceptibly *there*: he felt her, through a supersubtle sixth sense that the whole connection had already brought into play, hover, in the still hours, at the top of landings and on the other side of doors, gathered from the soundless brush of her skirts the hint of her watchings and waitings. One evening when, at his friend's table, he had lost himself in the depths of correspondence, he was made to start and turn by the suggestion that some one was behind him. Mrs Doyne had come in without his hearing the door, and she gave a strained smile as he sprang to his feet. 'I hope,' she said, 'I haven't frightened you.'

'Just a little – I was so absorbed. It was as if, for the instant,' the young man explained, 'it had been himself.'

The oddity of her face increased in her wonder. 'Ashton?'

'He does seem so near,' said Withermore.

'To you too?'

This naturally struck him. 'He does then to you?'

She hesitated, not moving from the spot where she had first stood, but looking round the room as if to penetrate its duskier angles. She had a way of raising to the level of her nose the big black fan which she apparently never laid aside and with which she thus covered the lower half of her face, her rather hard eyes, above it, becoming the more ambiguous. 'Sometimes.'

'Here,' Withermore went on, 'it's as if he might at any moment come in. That's why I jumped just now. The time is so short since he really used to – it only *was* yesterday. I sit in his chair, I turn his books, I use his pens, I stir his fire, exactly as if, learning he would presently be back from a walk, I had come up here contentedly to wait. It's delightful – but it's strange.'

Mrs Doyne, still with her fan up, listened with interest. 'Does it worry you?'

'No – I like it.'

She hesitated again. 'Do you ever feel as if he were – a – quite – a – personally in the room?'

'Well, as I said just now,' her companion laughed, 'on hearing you behind me I seemed to take it so. What do we want, after all,' he asked, 'but that he shall be with us?'

'Yes, as you said he would be – that first time.' She stared in full assent. 'He *is* with us.'

She was rather portentous, but Withermore took it smiling. 'Then we must keep him. We must do only what he would like.'

'Oh, only that, of course – only. But if he *is* here—?' And her sombre eyes seemed to throw it out, in vague distress, over her fan.

'It shows that he's pleased and wants only to help? Yes, surely; it must show that.'

She gave a light gasp and looked again round the room. 'Well,' she said as she took leave of him, 'remember that I too want only to help.' On which, when she had gone, he felt sufficiently – that she had come in simply to see he was all right.

He was all right more and more, it struck him after this, for as he began to get into his work he moved, as it appeared to him, but the closer to the idea of Doyne's personal presence. When once this fancy had begun to hang about him he welcomed it, persuaded it, encouraged it, quite cherished it, looking forward all day to feeling it renew itself in the evening, and waiting for the evening very much as one of a pair of lovers might wait for the hour of their appointment. The smallest accidents humoured and confirmed it, and by the end of three or four weeks he had come quite to regard it as the consecration of his enterprise. Wasn't it what settled the question of what Doyne would have thought of what they were doing? What they were doing was what he wanted done, and they could go on, from step to step, without scruple or doubt. Withermore rejoiced indeed at moments to feel this certitude: there were times of dipping deep into some of Doyne's secrets when it was particularly pleasant to be able to hold that Doyne desired him, as it were, to know them. He was learning many things that he had not suspected, drawing many curtains, forcing many doors, reading many riddles, going, in general, as they said, behind almost everything. It was at an occasional sharp turn of some of the duskier of these wanderings 'behind' that he really, of a sudden, most felt himself, in the intimate, sensible way, face to face with his friend; so that he could scarcely have told, for the instant, if their meeting occurred in the narrow passage and tight squeeze of the past, or at the hour and in the place that actually held him. Was it '67, or was it but the other side of the table?

Happily, at any rate, even in the vulgarest light publicity could ever shed, there would be the great fact of the way Doyne was 'coming out.' He was coming out too beautifully – better yet than such a partisan as Withermore could have supposed. Yet, all the while, as well, how would this partisan have represented to any one else the special state of his own consciousness? It wasn't a thing to talk about – it was only a thing to feel. There were moments, for instance, when, as he bent over his papers, the light breath of his dead host was as distinctly in his hair as his own elbows were on the table before him. There were moments when, had he been able to look up, the other side of the table would have shown him this companion as vividly as the shaded lamplight showed him his page. That he couldn't at such a juncture look up was his own affair, for the situation was ruled – that was but natural – by deep delicacies and fine timidities, the dread of too sudden or too rude an advance. What was intensely in the air was that if Doyne *was* there it was not nearly so much for himself as for the young priest of his altar. He hovered and lingered, he came and went, he might almost have been, among the books and the papers, a hushed, discreet librarian, doing the particular things, rendering the quiet aid, liked by men of letters.

Withermore himself, meanwhile, came and went, changed his place, wandered on quests either definite or vague; and more than once, when, taking a book down from a shelf and finding in it marks of Doyne's pencil, he got drawn on and lost, he had heard documents on the table behind him gently shifted and stirred, had literally, on his return, found some letter he had mislaid pushed again into view, some wilderness cleared by the opening of an old journal at the very date he wanted. How should he have gone so, on occasion, to the special box or drawer, out of fifty receptacles, that would help him, had not his mystic assistant happened, in fine prevision, to tilt its lid, or to pull it half open, in just the manner that would catch his eye? – in spite, after all, of the fact of lapses and intervals in which, *could* one have really looked, one would have seen somebody standing before the fire a trifle detached and over-erect – somebody fixing one the least bit harder than in life.

III

That this auspicious relation had in fact existed, had continued, for two or three weeks, was sufficiently proved by the dawn of the distress with which our young man found himself aware that he had, for some reason, from a certain evening, begun to miss it. The sign of that was an abrupt, surprised sense – on the occasion of his mislaying a marvellous unpublished page which, hunt where he would, remained stupidly, irrecoverably lost – that his protected state was, after all, exposed to some confusion and even to some depression. If, for the joy of the business, Doyne and he had, from the start, been together, the situation had, within a few days of his first new suspicion of it, suffered the odd change of their ceasing to be so. That was what was the matter, he said to himself, from the moment an impression of mere mass and quantity struck him as taking, in his happy

outlook at his material, the place of his pleasant assumption of
a clear course and a lively pace. For five nights he struggled;
then, never at his table, wandering about the room, taking up
his references only to lay them down, looking out of the window, poking the fire, thinking strange thoughts and listening
for signs and sounds not as he suspected or imagined, but as he
vainly desired and invoked them, he made up his mind that he
was, for the time at least, forsaken.

The extraordinary thing thus became that it made him not
only sad not to feel Doyne's presence, but in a high degree
uneasy. It was stranger, somehow, that he shouldn't be there
than it had ever been that he *was* – so strange indeed at last that
Withermore's nerves found themselves quite inconsequently
affected. They had taken kindly enough to what was of an
order impossible to explain, perversely reserving their sharpest
state for the return to the normal, the supersession of the false.
They were remarkably beyond control when, finally, one night,
after resisting an hour or two, he simply edged out of the room.
It had only now, for the first time, become impossible to him to
remain there. Without design, but panting a little and positively
as a man scared, he passed along his usual corridor and reached
the top of the staircase. From this point he saw Mrs Doyne
looking up at him from the bottom quite as if she had known
he would come; and the most singular thing of all was that,
though he had been conscious of no notion to resort to her, had
only been prompted to relieve himself by escape, the sight of
her position made him recognize it as just, quickly feel it as a
part of some monstrous oppression that was closing over both
of them. It was wonderful how, in the mere modern London
hall, between the Tottenham Court Road rugs and the electric
light, it came up to him from the tall black lady, and went again
from him down to her, that he knew what she meant by looking
as if he would know. He descended straight, she turned into her
own little lower room, and there, the next thing, with the door
shut, they were, still in silence and with queer faces, confronted
over confessions that had taken sudden life from these two or
three movements. Withermore gasped as it came to him why he
had lost his friend. 'He has been with *you*?'

With this it was all out – out so far that neither had to explain and that, when 'What do you suppose is the matter?' quickly passed between them, one appeared to have said it as much as the other. Withermore looked about at the small, bright room in which, night after night, she had been living her life as he had been living his own upstairs. It was pretty, cosy, rosy; but she had by turns felt in it what he had felt and heard in it what he had heard. Her effect there – fantastic black, plumed and extravagant, upon deep pink – was that of some 'decadent'[2] coloured print, some poster of the newest school. 'You understood he had left me?' he asked.

She markedly wished to make it clear. 'This evening – yes. I've made things out.'

'You knew – before – that he was with me?'

She hesitated again. 'I felt he wasn't with *me*. But on the stairs—'

'Yes?'

'Well – he passed, more than once. He was in the house. And at your door—'

'Well?' he went on as she once more faltered.

'If I stopped I could sometimes tell. And from your face,' she added, 'to-night, at any rate, I knew your state.'

'And that was why you came out?'

'I thought you'd come to me.'

He put out to her, on this, his hand, and they thus, for a minute, in silence, held each other clasped. There was no peculiar presence for either, now – nothing more peculiar than that of each for the other. But the place had suddenly become as if consecrated, and Withermore turned over it again his anxiety. 'What *is* then the matter?'

'I only want to do the real right thing,' she replied after a moment.

'And are we not doing it?'

'I wonder. Are *you* not?'

He wondered too. 'To the best of my belief. But we must think.'

'We must think,' she echoed. And they did think – thought, with intensity, the rest of that evening together, and thought,

independently – Withermore at least could answer for himself –
during many days that followed. He intermitted for a little his
visits and his work, trying, in meditation, to catch himself in the
act of some mistake that might have accounted for their disturbance. Had he taken, on some important point – or looked as if
he might take – some wrong line or wrong view? had he somewhere benightedly falsified or inadequately insisted? He went
back at last with the idea of having guessed two or three questions he might have been on the way to muddle; after which he
had, above stairs, another period of agitation, presently followed by another interview, below, with Mrs Doyne, who was
still troubled and flushed.

'He's there?'

'He's there.'

'I knew it!' she returned in an odd gloom of triumph. Then
as to make it clear: 'He has not been again with *me*.'

'Nor with me again to help,' said Withermore.

She considered. 'Not to help?'

'I can't make it out – I'm at sea. Do what I will, I feel I'm
wrong.'

She covered him a moment with her pompous pain. 'How
do you feel it?'

'Why, by things that happen. The strangest things. I can't
describe them – and you wouldn't believe them.'

'Oh yes, I would!' Mrs Doyne murmured.

'Well, he intervenes.' Withermore tried to explain. 'However
I turn, I find him.'

She earnestly followed. '"Find" him?'

'I meet him. He seems to rise there before me.'

Mrs Doyne, staring, waited a little. 'Do you mean you see him?'

'I feel as if at any moment I may. I'm baffled. I'm checked.'
Then he added: 'I'm afraid.'

'Of *him*?' asked Mrs Doyne.

He thought. 'Well – of what I'm doing.'

'Then what, that's so awful, *are* you doing?'

'What you proposed to me. Going into his life.'

She showed, in her gravity, now, a new alarm. 'And don't
you *like* that?'

'Doesn't *he*? That's the question. We lay him bare. We serve him up. What is it called? We give him to the world.'

Poor Mrs Doyne, as if on a menace to her hard atonement, glared at this for an instant in deeper gloom. 'And why shouldn't we?'

'Because we don't know. There are natures, there are lives, that shrink. He mayn't wish it,' said Withermore. 'We never asked him.'

'How *could* we?'

He was silent a little. 'Well, we ask him now. That's, after all, what our start has, so far, represented. We've put it to him.'

'Then – if he has been with us – we've had his answer.'

Withermore spoke now as if he knew what to believe. 'He hasn't been "with" us – he has been against us.'

'Then why did you think—'

'What I *did* think, at first – that what he wishes to make us feel is his sympathy? Because, in my original simplicity, I was mistaken. I was – I don't know what to call it – so excited and charmed that I didn't understand. But I understand at last. He only wanted to communicate. He strains forward out of his darkness; he reaches toward us out of his mystery; he makes us dim signs out of his horror.'

' "Horror"?' Mrs Doyne gasped with her fan up to her mouth.

'At what we're doing.' He could by this time piece it all together. 'I see now that at first—'

'Well, what?'

'One had simply to feel he was there, and therefore not indifferent. And the beauty of that misled me. But he's there as a protest.'

'Against *my* Life?' Mrs Doyne wailed.

'Against *any* Life. He's there to *save* his Life. He's there to be let alone.'

'So you give up?' she almost shrieked.

He could only meet her. 'He's there as a warning.'

For a moment, on this, they looked at each other deep. 'You *are* afraid!' she at last brought out.

It affected him, but he insisted. 'He's there as a curse!'

With that they parted, but only for two or three days; her

last word to him continuing to sound so in his ears that, between his need really to satisfy her and another need presently to be noted, he felt that he might not yet take up his stake. He finally went back at his usual hour and found her in her usual place. 'Yes, I *am* afraid,' he announced as if he had turned that well over and knew now all it meant. 'But I gather that you're not.'

She faltered, reserving her word. 'What is it you fear?'

'Well, that if I go on I *shall* see him.'

'And then—?'

'Oh, then,' said George Withermore, 'I *should* give up!'

She weighed it with her lofty but earnest air. 'I think, you know, we must have a clear sign.'

'You wish me to try again?'

She hesitated. 'You see what it means – for me – to give up.'

'Ah, but *you* needn't,' Withermore said.

She seemed to wonder, but in a moment she went on. 'It would mean that he won't take from me—' But she dropped for despair.

'Well, what?'

'Anything,' said poor Mrs Doyne.

He faced her a moment more. 'I've thought myself of the clear sign. I'll try again.'

As he was leaving her, however, she remembered. 'I'm only afraid that to-night there's nothing ready – no lamp and no fire.'

'Never mind,' he said from the foot of the stairs; 'I'll find things.'

To which she answered that the door of the room would probably, at any rate, be open; and retired again as if to wait for him. She had not long to wait; though, with her own door wide and her attention fixed, she may not have taken the time quite as it appeared to her visitor. She heard him, after an interval, on the stair, and he presently stood at her entrance, where, if he had not been precipitate, but rather, as to step and sound, backward and vague, he showed at least as livid and blank.

'I give up.'

'Then you've seen him?'

'On the threshold – guarding it.'

'Guarding it?' She glowed over her fan. 'Distinct?'

'Immense. But dim. Dark. Dreadful,' said poor George Withermore.

She continued to wonder. 'You didn't go in?'

The young man turned away. 'He forbids!'

'You say *I* needn't,' she went on after a moment. 'Well then, need I?'

'See him?' George Withermore asked.

She waited an instant. 'Give up.'

'You must decide.' For himself he could at last but drop upon the sofa with his bent face in his hands. He was not quite to know afterwards how long he had sat so; it was enough that what he did next know was that he was alone among her favourite objects. Just as he gained his feet, however, with this sense and that of the door standing open to the hall, he found himself afresh confronted, in the light, the warmth, the rosy space, with her big black perfumed presence. He saw at a glance, as she offered him a huger, bleaker stare over the mask of her fan, that she had been above; and so it was that, for the last time, they faced together their strange question. 'You've seen him?' Withermore asked.

He was to infer later on from the extraordinary way she closed her eyes and, as if to steady herself, held them tight and long, in silence, that beside the unutterable vision of Ashton Doyne's wife his own might rank as an escape. He knew before she spoke that all was over. 'I give up.'

An Episode of War

STEPHEN CRANE

The lieutenant's rubber blanket lay on the ground, and upon it he had poured the company's supply of coffee. Corporals and other representatives of the grimy and hot-throated men who lined the breastwork had come for each squad's portion.

The lieutenant was frowning and serious at this task of division. His lips pursed as he drew with his sword various crevices in the heap, until brown squares of coffee, astoundingly equal in size, appeared on the blanket. He was on the verge of a great triumph in mathematics, and the corporals were thronging forward, each to reap a little square, when suddenly the lieutenant cried out and looked quickly at a man near him as if he suspected it was a case of personal assault. The others cried out also when they saw blood upon the lieutenant's sleeve.

He had winced like a man stung, swayed dangerously, and then straightened. The sound of his hoarse breathing was plainly audible. He looked sadly, mystically, over the breastwork at the green face of a wood, where now were many little puffs of white smoke. During this moment the men about him gazed statue-like and silent, astonished and awed by this catastrophe which happened when catastrophes were not expected – when they had leisure to observe it.

As the lieutenant stared at the wood, they too swung their heads, so that for another moment all hands, still silent, contemplated the distant forest as if their minds were fixed upon the mystery of a bullet's journey.

The officer had, of course, been compelled to take his sword into his left hand. He did not hold it by the hilt. He gripped it at the middle of the blade, awkwardly. Turning his eyes from the hostile wood, he looked at the sword as he held it there, and seemed puzzled as to what to do with it, where to put it. In short, this weapon had of a sudden become a strange thing to him. He looked at it in a kind of stupefaction, as if he had been endowed with a trident, a scepter, or a spade.

Finally he tried to sheathe it. To sheathe a sword held by the left hand, at the middle of the blade, in a scabbard hung at the left hip, is a feat worthy of a sawdust ring. This wounded officer engaged in a desperate struggle with the sword and the wobbling scabbard, and during the time of it, he breathed like a wrestler.

But at this instant the men, the spectators, awoke from their stone-like poses and crowded forward sympathetically. The orderly-sergeant took the sword and tenderly placed it in the scabbard. At the time, he leaned nervously backward, and did not allow even his finger to brush the body of the lieutenant. A wound gives strange dignity to him who bears it. Well men shy from this new and terrible majesty. It is as if the wounded man's hand is upon the curtain which hangs before the revelations of all existence, the meaning of ants, potentates, wars, cities, sunshine, snow, a feather dropped from a bird's wing, and the power of it sheds radiance upon a bloody form, and makes the other men understand sometimes that they are little. His comrades look at him with large eyes thoughtfully. Moreover, they fear vaguely that the weight of a finger upon him might send him headlong, precipitate the tragedy, hurl him at once into the dim, gray unknown. And so the orderly-sergeant, while sheathing the sword, leaned nervously backward.

There were others who proffered assistance. One timidly presented his shoulder and asked the lieutenant if he cared to lean upon it, but the latter waved him away mournfully. He wore the look of one who knows he is the victim of a terrible disease and understands his helplessness. He again stared over the breastwork at the forest, and then, turning, went slowly rearward. He held his right wrist tenderly in his left hand as if the wounded arm was made of very brittle glass.

And the men in silence stared at the wood, then at the departing lieutenant – then at the wood, then at the lieutenant.

As the wounded officer passed from the line of battle, he was enabled to see many things which as a participant in the fight were unknown to him. He saw a general on a black horse gazing over the lines of blue infantry[1] at the green woods which veiled his problems. An aide galloped furiously, dragged his horse suddenly to a halt, saluted, and presented a paper. It was, for a wonder, precisely like a historical painting.

To the rear of the general and his staff a group, composed of a bugler, two or three orderlies, and the bearer of the corps standard, all upon maniacal horses, were working like slaves to hold their ground, preserve their respectful interval, while the shells boomed in the air about them, and caused their chargers to make furious quivering leaps.

A battery, a tumultuous and shining mass, was swirling toward the right. The wild thud of hoofs, the cries of the riders shouting blame and praise, menace and encouragement, and, last, the roar of the wheels, the slant of the glistening guns, brought the lieutenant to an intent pause. The battery swept in curves that stirred the heart; it made halts as dramatic as the crash of a wave on the rocks, and when it fled onward this aggregation of wheels, levers, motors, had a beautiful unity, as if it were a missile. The sound of it was a war chorus that reached into the depths of man's emotion.

The lieutenant, still holding his arm as if it were of glass, stood watching this battery until all detail of it was lost, save the figures of the riders, which rose and fell and waved lashes over the black mass.

Later, he turned his eyes toward the battle, where the shooting sometimes crackled like bush-fires, sometimes sputtered with exasperating irregularity, and sometimes reverberated like the thunder. He saw the smoke rolling upward and saw crowds of men who ran and cheered, or stood and blazed away at the inscrutable distance.

He came upon some stragglers, and they told him how to find the field hospital. They described its exact location. In fact, these men, no longer having part in the battle, knew more of it than others. They told the performance of every corps, every division, the opinion of every general. The lieutenant, carrying his wounded arm rearward, looked upon them with wonder.

At the roadside a brigade was making coffee and buzzing with talk like a girls' boarding school. Several officers came out to him and inquired concerning things of which he knew nothing. One, seeing his arm, began to scold. 'Why, man, that's no way to do. You want to fix that thing.' He appropriated the lieutenant and the lieutenant's wound. He cut the sleeve and laid bare the arm, every nerve of which softly fluttered under his touch. He bound his handkerchief over the wound, scolding away in the meantime. His tone allowed one to think that he was in the habit of being wounded every day. The lieutenant hung his head, feeling, in this presence, that he did not know how to be correctly wounded.

The low white tents of the hospital were grouped around an old school-house. There was here a singular commotion. In the foreground two ambulances interlocked wheels in the deep mud. The drivers were tossing the blame of it back and forth, gesticulating and berating, while from the ambulances, both crammed with wounded, there came an occasional groan. An interminable crowd of bandaged men were coming and going. Great numbers sat under the trees nursing heads or arms or legs. There was a dispute of some kind raging on the steps of the school-house. Sitting with his back against a tree a man with a face as gray as a new army blanket was serenely smoking a corn-cob pipe. The lieutenant wished to rush forward and inform him that he was dying.

A busy surgeon was passing near the lieutenant. 'Good morning,' he said, with a friendly smile. Then he caught sight of the lieutenant's arm, and his face at once changed. 'Well, let's have a look at it.' He seemed possessed suddenly of a great contempt for the lieutenant. This wound evidently placed the latter on a very low social plane. The doctor cried out impatiently. What mutton-head had tied it up that way anyhow. The lieutenant answered: 'Oh, a man.'

When the wound was disclosed the doctor fingered it disdainfully. 'Humph,' he said. 'You come along with me and I'll 'tend to you.' His voice contained the same scorn as if he were saying: 'You will have to go to jail.'

The lieutenant had been very meek but now his face flushed,

and he looked into the doctor's eyes. 'I guess I won't have it amputated,' he said.

'Nonsense, man! nonsense! nonsense!' cried the doctor. 'Come along, now. I won't amputate it. Come along. Don't be a baby.'

'Let go of me,' said the lieutenant, holding back wrathfully, his glance fixed upon the door of the old school-house, as sinister to him as the portals of death.

And this is the story of how the lieutenant lost his arm. When he reached home, his sisters, his mother, his wife, sobbed for a long time at the sight of the flat sleeve. 'Oh, well,' he said, standing shamefaced amid these tears, 'I don't suppose it matters so much as all that.'

Hearts and Hands

O. HENRY

At Denver there was an influx of passengers into the coaches on the eastbound B. & M. express.[1] In one coach there sat a very pretty young woman dressed in elegant taste and surrounded by all the luxurious comforts of an experienced traveler. Among the newcomers were two young men, one of handsome presence with a bold, frank countenance and manner; the other a ruffled, glum-faced person, heavily built and roughly dressed. The two were handcuffed together.

As they passed down the aisle of the coach the only vacant seat offered was a reversed one facing the attractive young woman. Here the linked couple seated themselves. The young woman's glance fell upon them with a distant, swift disinterest; then with a lovely smile brightening her countenance and a tender pink tingeing her rounded cheeks, she held out a little gray-gloved hand. When she spoke her voice, full, sweet, and deliberate, proclaimed that its owner was accustomed to speak and be heard.

'Well, Mr Easton, if you *will* make me speak first, I suppose I must. Don't you ever recognize old friends when you meet them in the West?'

The younger man roused himself sharply at the sound of her voice, seemed to struggle with a slight embarrassment which he threw off instantly, and then clasped her fingers with his left hand.

'It's Miss Fairchild,' he said, with a smile. 'I'll ask you to excuse the other hand; it's otherwise engaged just at present.'

He slightly raised his right hand, bound at the wrist by the shining 'bracelet' to the left one of his companion. The glad look in the girl's eyes slowly changed to a bewildered horror.

The glow faded from her cheeks. Her lips parted in a vague, relaxing distress. Easton, with a little laugh, as if amused, was about to speak again when the other forestalled him. The glum-faced man had been watching the girl's countenance with veiled glances from his keen, shrewd eyes.

'You'll excuse me for speaking, miss, but, I see you're acquainted with the marshal here. If you'll ask him to speak a word for me when we get to the pen he'll do it, and it'll make things easier for me there. He's taking me to Leavenworth prison. It's seven years for counterfeiting.'

'Oh!' said the girl, with a deep breath and returning color. 'So that is what you are doing out here? A marshal!'

'My dear Miss Fairchild,' said Easton, calmly, 'I had to do something. Money has a way of taking wings unto itself, and you know it takes money to keep step with our crowd in Washington. I saw this opening in the West, and – well, a marshalship isn't quite as high a position as that of ambassador, but—'

'The ambassador,' said the girl, warmly, 'doesn't call any more. He needn't ever have done so. You ought to know that. And so now you are one of these dashing Western heroes, and you ride and shoot and go into all kinds of dangers. That's different from the Washington life. You have been missed from the old crowd.'

The girl's eyes, fascinated, went back, widening a little, to rest upon the glittering handcuffs.

'Don't you worry about them, miss,' said the other man. 'All marshals handcuff themselves to their prisoners to keep them from getting away. Mr Easton knows his business.'

'Will we see you again soon in Washington?' asked the girl.

'Not soon, I think,' said Easton. 'My butterfly days are over, I fear.'

'I love the West,' said the girl, irrelevantly. Her eyes were shining softly. She looked away out the car window. She began to speak truly and simply, without the gloss of style and manner: 'Mamma and I spent the summer in Denver. She went home a week ago because father was slightly ill. I could live and be happy in the West. I think the air here agrees with me. Money isn't everything. But people always misunderstand things and remain stupid—'

'Say, Mr Marshal,' growled the glum-faced man. 'This isn't quite fair. I'm needin' a drink, and haven't had a smoke all day. Haven't you talked long enough? Take me in the smoker now, won't you? I'm half dead for a pipe.'

The bound travelers rose to their feet, Easton with the same slow smile on his face.

'I can't deny a petition for tobacco,' he said, lightly. 'It's the one friend of the unfortunate. Good-bye, Miss Fairchild. Duty calls, you know.' He held out his hand for a farewell.

'It's too bad you are not going East,' she said, reclothing herself with manner and style. 'But you must go on to Leavenworth, I suppose?'

'Yes,' said Easton, 'I must go on to Leavenworth.'

The two men sidled down the aisle into the smoker.

The two passengers in a seat near by had heard most of the conversation. Said one of them: 'That marshal's a good sort of chap. Some of these Western fellows are all right.'

'Pretty young to hold an office like that, isn't he?' asked the other.

'Young!' exclaimed the first speaker, 'why – Oh! didn't you catch on? Say – did you ever know an officer to handcuff a prisoner to his *right* hand?'

The Untold Lie

SHERWOOD ANDERSON

Ray Pearson and Hal Winters were farm hands employed on a farm three miles north of Winesburg. On Saturday afternoons they came into town and wandered about through the streets with other fellows from the country.

Ray was a quiet, rather nervous man of perhaps fifty with a brown beard and shoulders rounded by too much and too hard labor. In his nature he was as unlike Hal Winters as two men can be unlike.

Ray was an altogether serious man and had a little sharp-featured wife who had also a sharp voice. The two, with half a dozen thin-legged children, lived in a tumble-down frame house beside a creek at the back end of the Wills farm where Ray was employed.

Hal Winters, his fellow employee, was a young fellow. He was not of the Ned Winters family, who were very respectable people in Winesburg, but was one of the three sons of the old man called Windpeter Winters who had a sawmill near Union-ville, six miles away, and who was looked upon by everyone in Winesburg as a confirmed old reprobate.

People from the part of Northern Ohio in which Winesburg lies will remember old Windpeter by his unusual and tragic death. He got drunk one evening in town and started to drive home to Unionville along the railroad tracks. Henry Bratten-burg, the butcher, who lived out that way, stopped him at the edge of the town and told him he was sure to meet the down train[1] but Windpeter slashed at him with his whip and drove on. When the train struck and killed him and his two horses a farmer and his wife who were driving home along a nearby road saw the accident. They said that old Windpeter stood up on the seat of his wagon, raving and swearing at the onrushing locomotive, and that he fairly screamed with delight when the team, maddened by his incessant slashing at them, rushed straight ahead to certain death. Boys like young George Willard and Seth Richmond will remember the incident quite vividly because, although everyone in our town said that the old man would go straight to hell and that the community was better off without him, they had a secret conviction that he knew what he was doing and admired his foolish courage. Most boys have seasons of wishing they could die gloriously instead of just being grocery clerks and going on with their humdrum lives.

But this is not the story of Windpeter Winters nor yet of his son Hal who worked on the Wills farm with Ray Pearson. It is Ray's story. It will, however, be necessary to talk a little of young Hal so that you will get into the spirit of it.

Hal was a bad one. Everyone said that. There were three of the Winters boys in that family, John, Hal, and Edward, all broad-shouldered big fellows like old Windpeter himself and all fighters and woman-chasers and generally all-around bad ones.

Hal was the worst of the lot and always up to some devilment. He once stole a load of boards from his father's mill and sold them in Winesburg. With the money he bought himself a suit of cheap, flashy clothes. Then he got drunk and when his father came raving into town to find him, they met and fought with their fists on Main Street and were arrested and put into jail together.

Hal went to work on the Wills farm because there was a country school teacher out that way who had taken his fancy. He was only twenty-two then but had already been in two or three of what were spoken of in Winesburg as 'women scrapes.' Everyone who heard of his infatuation for the school teacher was sure it would turn out badly. 'He'll only get her into trouble, you'll see,' was the word that went around.

And so these two men, Ray and Hal, were at work in a field on a day in the late October. They were husking corn and occasionally something was said and they laughed. Then came silence.

Ray, who was the more sensitive and always minded things more, had chapped hands and they hurt. He put them into his coat pockets and looked away across the fields. He was in a sad, distracted mood and was affected by the beauty of the country. If you knew the Winesburg country in the fall and how the low hills are all splashed with yellows and reds you would understand his feeling. He began to think of the time, long ago when he was a young fellow living with his father, then a baker in Winesburg, and how on such days he had wandered away into the woods to gather nuts, hunt rabbits, or just to loaf about and smoke his pipe. His marriage had come about through one of his days of wandering. He had induced a girl who waited on trade in his father's shop to go with him and something had happened. He was thinking of that afternoon and how it had affected his whole life when a spirit of protest awoke in him. He had forgotten about Hal and muttered words. 'Tricked by Gad, that's what I was, tricked by life and made a fool of,' he said in a low voice.

As though understanding his thoughts, Hal Winters spoke up. 'Well, has it been worth while? What about it, eh? What about marriage and all that?' he asked and then laughed. Hal tried to keep on laughing but he too was in an earnest mood. He began to talk earnestly. 'Has a fellow got to do it?' he asked. 'Has he got to be harnessed up and driven through life like a horse?'

Hal didn't wait for an answer but sprang to his feet and began to walk back and forth between the corn shocks. He was getting more and more excited. Bending down suddenly he picked up an ear of the yellow corn and threw it at the fence. 'I've got Nell Gunther in trouble,' he said. 'I'm telling you, but you keep your mouth shut.'

Ray Pearson arose and stood staring. He was almost a foot shorter than Hal, and when the younger man came and put his two hands on the older man's shoulders they made a picture. There they stood in the big empty field with the quiet corn shocks standing in rows behind them and the red and yellow hills in the distance, and from being just two indifferent workmen they had become all alive to each other. Hal sensed it and because that was his way he laughed. 'Well, old daddy,' he said awkwardly, 'come on, advise me. I've got Nell in trouble. Perhaps you've been in the same fix yourself. I know what everyone would say is the right thing to do, but what do you say? Shall I marry and settle down? Shall I put myself into the harness to be worn out like an old horse? You know me, Ray. There can't anyone break me but I can break myself. Shall I do it or shall I tell Nell to go to the devil? Come on, you tell me. Whatever you say, Ray, I'll do.'

Ray couldn't answer. He shook Hal's hands loose and turning walked straight away toward the barn. He was a sensitive man and there were tears in his eyes. He knew there was only one thing to say to Hal Winters, son of old Windpeter Winters, only one thing that all his own training and all the beliefs of the people he knew would approve, but for his life he couldn't say what he knew he should say.

At half-past four that afternoon Ray was puttering about the barnyard when his wife came up the lane along the creek and called him. After the talk with Hal he hadn't returned to the corn field but worked about the barn. He had already done the evening chores and had seen Hal, dressed and ready for a roistering night in town, come out of the farmhouse and go into the road. Along the path to his own house he trudged behind his wife, looking at the ground and thinking. He couldn't make out what was wrong. Every time he raised his eyes and saw the beauty of the country in the failing light he wanted to do something he had never done before, shout or scream or hit his wife with his fists or something equally unexpected and terrifying. Along the path he went scratching his head and trying to make it out. He looked hard at his wife's back but she seemed all right.

She only wanted him to go into town for groceries and as soon as she had told him what she wanted began to scold. 'You're always puttering,' she said. 'Now I want you to hustle. There isn't anything in the house for supper and you've got to get to town and back in a hurry.'

Ray went into his own house and took an overcoat from a hook back of the door. It was torn about the pockets and the

collar was shiny. His wife went into the bedroom and presently
came out with a soiled cloth in one hand and three silver dollars in the other. Somewhere in the house a child wept bitterly
and a dog that had been sleeping by the stove arose and yawned.
Again the wife scolded. 'The children will cry and cry. Why are
you always puttering?' she asked.

Ray went out of the house and climbed the fence into a field.
It was just growing dark and the scene that lay before him was
lovely. All the low hills were washed with color and even the
little clusters of bushes in the corners of the fences were alive
with beauty. The whole world seemed to Ray Pearson to have
become alive with something just as he and Hal had suddenly
become alive when they stood in the corn field staring into each
other's eyes.

The beauty of the country about Winesburg was too much
for Ray on that fall evening. That is all there was to it. He
could not stand it. Of a sudden he forgot all about being a quiet
old farm hand and throwing off the torn overcoat began to run
across the field. As he ran he shouted a protest against his life,
against all life, against everything that makes life ugly. 'There
was no promise made,' he cried into the empty spaces that lay
about him. 'I didn't promise my Minnie anything and Hal
hasn't made any promise to Nell. I know he hasn't. She went
into the woods with him because she wanted to go. What he
wanted she wanted. Why should I pay? Why should Hal pay?
Why should anyone pay? I don't want Hal to become old and
worn out. I'll tell him. I won't let it go on. I'll catch Hal before
he gets to town and I'll tell him.'

Ray ran clumsily and once he stumbled and fell down. 'I
must catch Hal and tell him,' he kept thinking, and although
his breath came in gasps he kept running harder and harder. As
he ran he thought of things that hadn't come into his mind for
years – how at the time he married he had planned to go west
to his uncle in Portland, Oregon – how he hadn't wanted to be
a farm hand, but had thought when he got out West he would
go to sea and be a sailor or get a job on a ranch and ride a horse
into Western towns, shouting and laughing and waking the
people in the houses with his wild cries. Then as he ran he

remembered his children and in fancy felt their hands clutching at him. All of his thoughts of himself were involved with the thoughts of Hal and he thought the children were clutching at the younger man also. 'They are the accidents of life, Hal,' he cried. 'They are not mine or yours. I had nothing to do with them.'

Darkness began to spread over the fields as Ray Pearson ran on and on. His breath came in little sobs. When he came to the fence at the edge of the road and confronted Hal Winters, all dressed up and smoking a pipe as he walked jauntily along, he could not have told what he thought or what he wanted.

Ray Pearson lost his nerve and this is really the end of the story of what happened to him. It was almost dark when he got to the fence and he put his hands on the top bar and stood staring. Hal Winters jumped a ditch and coming up close to Ray put his hands into his pockets and laughed. He seemed to have lost his own sense of what had happened in the corn field and when he put up a strong hand and took hold of the lapel of Ray's coat he shook the old man as he might have shaken a dog that had misbehaved.

'You came to tell me, eh?' he said. 'Well, never mind telling me anything. I'm not a coward and I've already made up my mind.' He laughed again and jumped back across the ditch. 'Nell ain't no fool,' he said. 'She didn't ask me to marry her. I want to marry her. I want to settle down and have kids.'

Ray Pearson also laughed. He felt like laughing at himself and all the world.

As the form of Hal Winters disappeared in the dusk that lay over the road that led to Winesburg, he turned and walked slowly back across the fields to where he had left his torn over-coat. As he went some memory of pleasant evenings spent with the thin-legged children in the tumble-down house by the creek must have come into his mind, for he muttered words. 'It's just as well. Whatever I told him would have been a lie,' he said softly, and then his form also disappeared into the darkness of the fields.

Out of Season

ERNEST HEMINGWAY

On the four lire Peduzzi had earned by spading the hotel garden he got quite drunk. He saw the young gentleman coming
down the path and spoke to him mysteriously. The young
gentleman said he had not eaten but would be ready to go as
soon as lunch was finished. Forty minutes or an hour.

At the cantina near the bridge they trusted him for three
more grappas because he was so confident and mysterious
about his job for the afternoon. It was a windy day with the
sun coming out from behind clouds and then going under in
sprinkles of rain. A wonderful day for trout fishing.

The young gentleman came out of the hotel and asked him
about the rods. Should his wife come behind with the rods?
'Yes,' said Peduzzi, 'let her follow us.' The young gentleman
went back into the hotel and spoke to his wife. He and Peduzzi
started down the road. The young gentleman had a musette[1]
over his shoulder. Peduzzi saw the wife, who looked as young
as the young gentleman, and was wearing mountain boots and
a blue beret, start out to follow them down the road, carrying
the fishing rods, unjointed, one in each hand. Peduzzi didn't
like her to be way back there. 'Signorina,' he called, winking at
the young gentleman, 'come up here and walk with us. Signora,
come up here. Let us all walk together.' Peduzzi wanted them
all three to walk down the street of Cortina[2] together.

The wife stayed behind, following rather sullenly. 'Signorina,'
Peduzzi called tenderly, 'come up here with us.' The young gentleman looked back and shouted something. The wife stopped
lagging behind and walked up.

Everyone they met walking through the main street of the

town Peduzzi greeted elaborately. Buon' di, Arturo! Tipping his hat. The bank clerk stared at him from the door of the Fascist café. Groups of three and four people standing in front of the shops stared at the three. The workmen in their stone-powdered jackets working on the foundations of the new hotel looked up as they passed. Nobody spoke or gave any sign to them except the town beggar, lean and old, with a spittle-thickened beard, who lifted his hat as they passed.

Peduzzi stopped in front of a store with the window full of bottles and brought his empty grappa bottle from an inside pocket of his old military coat. 'A little to drink, some marsala for the Signora, something, something to drink.' He gestured with the bottle. It was a wonderful day. 'Marsala, you like marsala, Signorina? A little marsala?'

The wife stood sullenly. 'You'll have to play up to this,' she said. 'I can't understand a word he says. He's drunk, isn't he?'

The young gentleman appeared not to hear Peduzzi. He was thinking, what in hell makes him say marsala? That's what Max Beerbohm[3] drinks.

'Geld,' Peduzzi said finally, taking hold of the young gentleman's sleeve. 'Lire.'[4] He smiled, reluctant to press the subject but needing to bring the young gentleman into action.

The young gentleman took out his pocketbook and gave him a ten-lira note. Peduzzi went up the steps to the door of the Specialty of Domestic and Foreign Wines shop. It was locked.

'It is closed until two,' someone passing in the street said scornfully. Peduzzi came down the steps. He felt hurt. Never mind, he said, we can get it at the Concordia.

They walked down the road to the Concordia three abreast. On the porch of the Concordia, where the rusty bobsleds were stacked, the young gentleman said, 'Was wollen sie?'[5] Peduzzi handed him the ten-lira note folded over and over. 'Nothing,' he said, 'anything.' He was embarrassed. 'Marsala, maybe. I don't know. Marsala?'

The door of the Concordia shut on the young gentleman and the wife. 'Three marsalas,' said the young gentleman to the girl behind the pastry counter. 'Two, you mean?' she asked. 'No,' he said, 'one for a vecchio.' 'Oh,' she said, 'a vecchio,'[6] and laughed,

getting down the bottle. She poured out the three muddy looking drinks into three glasses. The wife was sitting at a table
under the line of newspapers on sticks. The young gentleman
put one of the marsalas in front of her. 'You might as well drink
it,' he said, 'maybe it'll make you feel better.' She sat and looked
at the glass. The young gentleman went outside the door with a
glass for Peduzzi but could not see him.

'I don't know where he is,' he said, coming back into the
pastry room carrying the glass.

'He wanted a quart of it,' said the wife.

'How much is a quarter litre?' the young gentleman asked
the girl.

'Of the bianco? One lira.'

'No, of the marsala. Put these two in, too,' he said, giving
her his own glass and the one poured for Peduzzi. She filled the
quarter litre wine measure with a funnel. 'A bottle to carry it,'
said the young gentleman.

She went to hunt for a bottle. It all amused her.

'I'm sorry you feel so rotten, Tiny,' he said. 'I'm sorry I
talked the way I did at lunch. We were both getting at the same
thing from different angles.'

'It doesn't make any difference,' she said. 'None of it makes
any difference.'

'Are you too cold?' he asked. 'I wish you'd worn another
sweater.'

'I've got on three sweaters.'

The girl came in with a very slim brown bottle and poured
the marsala into it. The young gentleman paid five lire more.
They went out the door. The girl was amused. Peduzzi was
walking up and down at the other end out of the wind and
holding the rods.

'Come on,' he said, 'I will carry the rods. What difference
does it make if anybody sees them? No one will trouble us. No
one will make any trouble for me in Cortina. I know them at
the municipio. I have been a soldier. Everybody in this town
likes me. I sell frogs. What if it is forbidden to fish? Not a thing.
Nothing. No trouble. Big trout, I tell you. Lots of them.'

They were walking down the hill toward the river. The town

was in back of them. The sun had gone under and it was sprink-
ling rain. 'There,' said Peduzzi, pointing to a girl in the doorway
of a house they passed. 'My daughter.'

'His doctor,' the wife said, 'has he got to show us his doctor?'

'He said his daughter,' said the young gentleman.

The girl went into the house as Peduzzi pointed.

They walked down the hill across the fields and then turned
to follow the river bank. Peduzzi talked rapidly with much
winking and knowingness. As they walked three abreast the
wife caught his breath across the wind. Once he nudged her in
the ribs. Part of the time he talked in d'Ampezzo dialect and
sometimes in Tyroler German dialect. He could not make out
which the young gentleman and his wife understood the best so
he was being bilingual. But as the young gentleman said, Ja, Ja,
Peduzzi decided to talk altogether in Tyroler. The young gentleman and the wife understood nothing.

'Everybody in the town saw us going through with these
rods. We're probably being followed by the game police now. I
wish we weren't in on this damn thing. This damned old fool is
so drunk, too.'

'Of course you haven't got the guts to just go back,' said the
wife. 'Of course you have to go on.'

'Why don't you go back? Go on back, Tiny.'

'I'm going to stay with you. If you go to jail we might as well
both go.'

They turned sharp down the bank and Peduzzi stood, his
coat blowing in the wind, gesturing at the river. It was brown
and muddy. Off on the right there was a dump heap.

'Say it to me in Italian,' said the young gentleman.

'Un' mezz' ora. Piu d' un' mezz' ora.'

'He says it's at least a half hour more. Go on back, Tiny.
You're cold in this wind anyway. It's a rotten day and we aren't
going to have any fun, anyway.'

'All right,' she said, and climbed up the grassy bank.

Peduzzi was down at the river and did not notice her till she
was almost out of sight over the crest. 'Frau!' he shouted.
'Frau! Fräulein! You're not going.'

She went on over the crest of the hill.

'She's gone!' said Peduzzi. It shocked him.

He took off the rubber bands that held the rod segments together and commenced to joint up one of the rods.

'But you said it was half an hour further.'

'Oh, yes. It is good half an hour down. It is good here, too.'

'Really?'

'Of course. It is good here and good there, too.'

The young gentleman sat down on the bank and jointed up a rod, put on the reel and threaded the line through the guides. He felt uncomfortable and afraid that any minute a game-keeper or a posse of citizens would come over the bank from the town. He could see the houses of the town and the campa-nile over the edge of the hill. He opened his leader box. Peduzzi leaned over and dug his flat, hard thumb and forefinger in and tangled the moistened leaders.

'Have you some lead?'

'No.'

'You must have some lead.' Peduzzi was excited. 'You must have piombo. Piombo. A little piombo. Just here. Just above the hook or your bait will float on the water. You must have it. Just a little piombo.'

'Have you got some?'

'No.' He looked through his pockets desperately. Sifting through the cloth dirt in the linings of his inside military pock-ets. 'I haven't any. We must have piombo.'

'We can't fish then,' said the young gentleman, and un-jointed the rod, reeling the line back through the guides. 'We'll get some piombo and fish tomorrow.'

'But listen, caro, you must have piombo. The line will lie flat on the water.' Peduzzi's day was going to pieces before his eyes. 'You must have piombo. A little is enough. Your stuff is all clean and new but you have no lead. I would have brought some. You said you had everything.'

The young gentleman looked at the stream discolored by the melting snow. 'I know,' he said, 'we'll get some piombo and fish tomorrow.'

'At what hour in the morning? Tell me that.'

'At seven.'

The sun came out. It was warm and pleasant. The young gentleman felt relieved. He was no longer breaking the law. Sitting on the bank he took the bottle of marsala out of his pocket and passed it to Peduzzi. Peduzzi passed it back. The young gentleman took a drink of it and passed it to Peduzzi again. Peduzzi passed it back again. 'Drink,' he said, 'drink. It's your marsala.' After another short drink the young gentleman handed the bottle over. Peduzzi had been watching it closely. He took the bottle very hurriedly and tipped it up. The gray hairs in the folds of his neck oscillated as he drank, his eyes fixed on the end of the narrow brown bottle. He drank it all. The sun shone while he drank. It was wonderful. This was a great day, after all. A wonderful day.

'Senta, caro![7] In the morning at seven.' He had called the young gentleman caro several times and nothing had happened. It was good marsala. His eyes glistened. Days like this stretched out ahead. It would begin at seven in the morning.

They started to walk up the hill toward the town. The young gentleman went on ahead. He was quite a way up the hill. Peduzzi called to him.

'Listen, caro, can you let me take five lire for a favor?'

'For today?' asked the young gentleman frowning.

'No, not today. Give it to me today for tomorrow. I will provide everything for tomorrow. Pane, salami, formaggio,[8] good stuff for all of us. You and I and the Signora. Bait for fishing, minnows, not worms only. Perhaps I can get some marsala. All for five lire. Five lire for a favor.'

The young gentleman looked through his pocketbook and took out a two-lira note and two ones.

'Thank you, caro. Thank you,' said Peduzzi, in the tone of one member of the Carleton Club[9] accepting the *Morning Post* from another. This was living. He was through with the hotel garden, breaking up frozen manure with a dung fork. Life was opening out.

'Until seven o'clock then, caro,' he said, slapping the young gentleman on the back. 'Promptly at seven.'

'I may not be going,' said the young gentleman putting his purse back in his pocket.

'What,' said Peduzzi, 'I will have minnows, Signor. Salami, everything. You and I and the Signora. The three of us.'

'I may not be going,' said the young gentleman, 'very probably not. I will leave word with the padrone at the hotel office.'

Atrophy

EDITH WHARTON

I

Nora Frenway settled down furtively in her corner of the Pullman and, as the express plunged out of the Grand Central
Station, wondered at herself for being where she was. The
porter came along. 'Ticket?' 'Westover.' She had instinctively
lowered her voice and glanced about her. But neither the porter
nor her nearest neighbours – fortunately none of them known
to her – seemed in the least surprised or interested by the statement that she was travelling to Westover.

Yet what an earth-shaking announcement it was! Not that
she cared, now; not that anything mattered except the one
overwhelming fact which had convulsed her life, hurled her out
of her easy velvet-lined rut, and flung her thus naked to the
public scrutiny . . . Cautiously, again, she glanced about her to
make doubly sure that there was no one, absolutely no one, in
the Pullman whom she knew by sight.

Her life had been so carefully guarded, so inwardly conven-
tional in a world where all the outer conventions were tottering,
that no one had ever known she had a lover. No one – of that
she was absolutely sure. All the circumstances of the case had
made it necessary that she should conceal her real life – her
only real life – from everyone about her; from her half-invalid
irascible husband, his prying envious sisters, and the terrible
monumental old chieftainess, her mother-in-law, before whom
all the family quailed and humbugged and fibbed and fawned.

What nonsense to pretend that nowadays, even in big cities,
in the world's greatest social centres, the severe old-fashioned

standards had given place to tolerance, laxity and ease! You took up the morning paper, and you read of girl bandits, movie-star divorces, 'hold-ups' at balls, murder and suicide and elopement, and a general welter of disjointed disconnected impulses and appetites; then you turned your eyes onto your own daily life, and found yourself as cribbed and cabined, as beset by vigilant family eyes, observant friends, all sorts of embodied standards, as any white-muslin novel heroine of the 'sixties![1]

In a different way, of course. To the casual eye Mrs Frenway herself might have seemed as free as any of the young married women of her group. Poker playing, smoking, cocktail drinking, dancing, painting, short skirts, bobbed hair and the rest – when had these been denied to her? If by any outward sign she had differed too markedly from her kind – lengthened her skirts, refused to play for money, let her hair grow, or ceased to make up – her husband would have been the first to notice it, and to say: 'Are you ill? What's the matter? How queer you look! What's the sense of making yourself conspicuous?' For he and his kind had adopted all the old inhibitions and sanctions, blindly transferring them to a new ritual, as the receptive Romans did when strange gods were brought into their temples . . .

The train had escaped from the ugly fringes of the city, and the soft spring landscape was gliding past her: glimpses of green lawns, budding hedges, pretty irregular roofs, and miles and miles of alluring tarred roads slipping away into mystery. How often she had dreamed of dashing off down an unknown road with Christopher!

Not that she was a woman to be awed by the conventions. She knew she wasn't. She had always taken their measure, smiled at them – and conformed. On account of poor George Frenway, to begin with. Her husband, in a sense, was a man to be pitied; his weak health, his bad temper, his unsatisfied vanity, all made him a rather forlornly comic figure. But it was chiefly on account of the two children that she had always resisted the temptation to do anything reckless. The least self-betrayal would have been the end of everything. Too many eyes were watching her, and her husband's family was so strong, so united – when there was anybody for them to hate – and at all times so influential, that she would have been defeated at every point, and her husband would have kept the children.

At the mere thought she felt herself on the brink of an abyss. 'The children are my religion,' she had once said to herself; and she had no other.

Yet here she was on her way to Westover ... Oh, what did it matter now? That was the worst of it – it was too late for anything between her and Christopher to matter! She was sure he was dying. The way in which his cousin, Gladys Brincker, had blurted it out the day before at Kate Salmer's dance: 'You didn't know – poor Kit? Thought you and he were such pals! Yes; awfully bad, I'm afraid. Return of the old trouble! I know there've been two consultations – they had Knowlton down. They say there's not much hope; and nobody but that forlorn frightened Jane mounting guard ...'

Poor Christopher! His sister Jane Aldis, Nora suspected, forlorn and frightened as she was, had played in his life a part nearly as dominant as Frenway and the children in Nora's. Loyally, Christopher always pretended that she didn't; talked of her indulgently as 'poor Jenny'. But didn't she, Nora, always think of her husband as 'poor George'? Jane Aldis, of course, was much less self-assertive, less demanding, than George Frenway; but perhaps for that very reason she would appeal all the more to a man's compassion. And somehow, under her unobtrusive air, Nora had – on the rare occasions when they met – imagined that Miss Aldis was watching and drawing her inferences. But then Nora always felt, where Christopher was concerned, as if her breast were a pane of glass through which her trembling palpitating heart could be seen as plainly as holy viscera in a reliquary. Her sober afterthought was that Jane Aldis was just a dowdy self-effacing old maid whose life was filled to the brim by looking after the Westover place for her brother, and seeing that the fires were lit and the rooms full of flowers when he brought down his friends for a week-end.

Ah, how often he had said to Nora: 'If I could have you to myself for a week-end at Westover' – quite as if it were the easiest thing imaginable, as far as his arrangements were concerned! And they had even pretended to discuss how it could be done. But somehow she fancied he said it because he knew that the plan, for her, was about as feasible as a week-end in the moon. And in reality her only visits to Westover had been made in the company of her husband, and that of other friends, two or three times, at the beginning . . . For after that she wouldn't. It was three years now since she had been there.

Gladys Brincker, in speaking of Christopher's illness, had looked at Nora queerly, as though suspecting something. But no – what nonsense! No one had ever suspected Nora Frenway. Didn't she know what her friends said of her? 'Nora? No more temperament than a lamp-post. Always buried in her books . . . Never very attractive to men, in spite of her looks.' Hadn't she said that of other women, who perhaps, in secret, like herself . . .?

The train was slowing down as it approached a station. She sat up with a jerk and looked at her wrist-watch. It was half-past two, the station was Ockham; the next would be Westover. In less than an hour she would be under his roof, Jane Aldis would be receiving her in that low panelled room full of books, and she would be saying – what would she be saying?

She had gone over their conversation so often that she knew not only her own part in it but Miss Aldis's by heart. The first moments would of course be painful, difficult; but then a great wave of emotion, breaking down the barriers between the two anxious women, would fling them together. She wouldn't have to say much, to explain; Miss Aldis would just take her by the hand and lead her upstairs to the room.

That room! She shut her eyes, and remembered other rooms where she and he had been together in their joy and their strength . . . No, not that; she must not think of that now. For the man she had met in those other rooms was dying; the man she was going to was some one so different from that other man that it was like a profanation to associate their images . . . And yet the man she was going to was her own Christopher, the one who had lived in her soul; and how his soul must be needing hers, now that it hung alone on the dark brink! As if anything else mattered at such a moment! She neither thought nor cared what Jane Aldis might say or suspect; she wouldn't

have cared if the Pullman had been full of prying acquaint-
ances, or if George and all George's family had got in at that
last station.

She wouldn't have cared a fig for any of them. Yet at the
same moment she remembered having felt glad that her old
governess, whom she used to go and see twice a year, lived at
Ockham – so that if George did begin to ask questions, she
could always say: 'Yes, I went to see poor old Fräulein; she's
absolutely crippled now. I shall have to give her a Bath chair.[2]
Could you get me a catalogue of prices?' There wasn't a pre-
caution she hadn't thought of – and now she was ready to
scatter them all to the winds . . .

Westover – *Junction!*

She started up and pushed her way out of the train. All the
people seemed to be obstructing her, putting bags and suitcases
in her way. And the express stopped for only two minutes. Suppose she should be carried on to Albany?

Westover Junction was a growing place, and she was fairly
sure there would be a taxi at the station. There was one – she just
managed to get to it ahead of a travelling man with a sample
case and a new straw hat. As she opened the door a smell of
damp hay and bad tobacco greeted her. She sprang in and gasped:
'To Oakfield. You know? Mr Aldis's place near Westover.'

II

It began exactly as she had expected. A surprised parlour
maid – why surprised? – showed her into the low panelled
room that was so full of his presence, his books, his pipes, his
terrier dozing on the shabby rug. The parlour maid said she
would go and see if Miss Aldis could come down. Nora wanted
to ask if she were with her brother – and how he was. But she
found herself unable to speak the words. She was afraid her
voice might tremble. And why should she question the parlour
maid, when in a moment, she hoped, she was to see Miss Aldis?

The woman moved away with a hushed step – the step
which denotes illness in the house. She did not immediately

return, and the interval of waiting in that room, so strange yet so intimately known, was a new torture to Nora. It was unlike anything she had imagined. The writing table with his scattered pens and letters was more than she could bear. His dog looked at her amicably from the hearth, but made no advances; and though she longed to stroke him, to let her hand rest where Christopher's had rested, she dared not for fear he should bark and disturb the peculiar hush of that dumb watchful house. She stood in the window and looked out at the budding shrubs and the bulbs pushing up through the swollen earth.

'This way, please.'

Her heart gave a plunge. Was the woman actually taking her upstairs to his room? Her eyes filled, she felt herself swept forward on a great wave of passion and anguish . . . But she was only being led across the hall into a stiff lifeless drawing-room – the kind that bachelors get an upholsterer to do for them, and then turn their backs on forever. The chairs and sofas looked at her with an undisguised hostility, and then resumed the moping expression common to furniture in unfrequented rooms. Even the spring sun slanting in through the windows on the pale marquetry of a useless table seemed to bring no heat or light with it.

The rush of emotion subsided, leaving in Nora a sense of emptiness and apprehension. Supposing Jane Aldis should look at her with the cold eyes of this resentful room? She began to wish she had been friendlier and more cordial to Jane Aldis in the past. In her intense desire to conceal from everyone the tie between herself and Christopher she had avoided all show of interest in his family; and perhaps, as she now saw, excited curiosity by her very affectation of indifference.

No doubt it would have been more politic to establish an intimacy with Jane Aldis; and today, how much easier and more natural her position would have been! Instead of groping about – as she was again doing – for an explanation of her visit, she could have said: 'My dear, I came to see if there was anything in the world I could do to help you.'

She heard a hesitating step in the hall – a hushed step like the parlour maid's – and saw Miss Aldis pause near the half-open door. How old she had grown since their last meeting! Her hair, untidily pinned up, was gray and lanky. Her eyelids, always reddish, were swollen and heavy, her face sallow with anxiety and fatigue. It was odd to have feared so defenseless an adversary. Nora, for an instant, had the impression that Miss Aldis had wavered in the hall to catch a glimpse of her, take the measure of the situation. But perhaps she had only stopped to push back a strand of hair as she passed in front of a mirror.

'Mrs Frenway – how good of you!' She spoke in a cool detached voice, as if her real self were elsewhere and she were simply an automaton wound up to repeat the familiar forms of hospitality. 'Do sit down,' she said.

She pushed forward one of the sulky arm-chairs, and Nora seated herself stiffly, her hand-bag clutched on her knee, in the self-conscious attitude of a country caller.

'I came—'

'So good of you,' Miss Aldis repeated. 'I had no idea you were in this part of the world. Not the slightest.'

Was it a lead she was giving? Or did she know everything, and wish to extend to her visitor the decent shelter of a pretext? Or was she really so stupid—

'You're staying with the Brinckers, I suppose. Or the Northrups? I remember the last time you came to lunch here you motored over with Mr Frenway from the Northrups'. That must have been two years ago, wasn't it?' She put the question with an almost sprightly show of interest.

'No – three years,' said Nora, mechanically.

'Was it? As long ago as that? Yes – you're right. That was the year we moved the big fern-leaved beech. I remember Mr Frenway was interested in tree moving, and I took him out to show him where the tree had come from. He *is* interested in tree moving, isn't he?'

'Oh yes; very much.'

'We had those wonderful experts down to do it. "Tree doctors," they call themselves. They have special appliances, you know. The tree is growing better than it did before they moved it. But I suppose you've done a great deal of transplanting on Long Island.'

'Yes. My husband does a good deal of transplanting.'

'So you've come over from the Northrups'? I didn't even know they were down at Maybrook yet. I see so few people.'

'No; not from the Northrups'.'

'Oh – the Brinckers'? Hal Brincker was here yesterday, but he didn't tell me you were staying there.'

Nora hesitated. 'No. The fact is, I have an old governess who lives at Ockham. I go to see her sometimes. And so I came on to Westover—' She paused, and Miss Aldis interrogated brightly: 'Yes?' as if prompting her in a lesson she was repeating.

'Because I saw Gladys Brincker the other day, and she told me that your brother was ill.'

'Oh.' Miss Aldis gave the syllable its full weight, and set a full stop after it. Her eyebrows went up, as if in a faint surprise. The silent room seemed to close in on the two speakers, listening. A resuscitated fly buzzed[3] against the sunny window pane. 'Yes; he's ill,' she conceded at length.

'I'm so sorry; I . . . he has been . . . such a friend of ours . . . so long . . .'

'Yes; I've often heard him speak of you and Mr Frenway.' Another full stop sealed this announcement. ('No, she knows nothing,' Nora thought.) 'I remember his telling me that he thought a great deal of Mr Frenway's advice about moving trees. But then you see our soil is so different from yours. I suppose Mr Frenway has had your soil analyzed?'

'Yes; I think he has.'

'Christopher's always been a great gardener.'

'I hope he's not – not very ill? Gladys seemed to be afraid—'

'Illness is always something to be afraid of, isn't it?'

'But you're not – I mean, not anxious . . . not seriously?'

'It's so kind of you to ask. The doctors seem to think there's no particular change since yesterday.'

'And yesterday?'

'Well, yesterday they seemed to think there might be.'

'A change, you mean?'

'Well, yes.'

'A change – I hope for the better?'

'They said they weren't sure; they couldn't say.'

The fly's buzzing had become so insistent in the still room that it seemed to be going on inside of Nora's head, and in the confusion of sound she found it more and more difficult to regain a lead in the conversation. And the minutes were slipping by, and upstairs the man she loved was lying. It was absurd and lamentable to make a pretense of keeping up this twaddle. She would cut through it, no matter how.

'I suppose you've had – a consultation?'

'Oh, yes; Dr Knowlton's been down twice.'

'And what does he—'

'Well; he seems to agree with the others.'

There was another pause, and then Miss Aldis glanced out of the window. 'Why, who's that driving up?' she enquired.

'Oh, it's your taxi, I suppose, coming up the drive.'

'Yes. I got out at the gate.' She dared not add: 'For fear the noise might disturb him.'

'I hope you had no difficulty in finding a taxi at the Junction?'

'Oh, no; I had no difficulty.'

'I think it was so kind of you to come – not even knowing whether you'd find a carriage to bring you out all this way. And I know how busy you are. There's always so much going on in town, isn't there, even at this time of year?'

'Yes; I suppose so. But your brother—'

'Oh, of course my brother won't be up to any sort of gaiety; not for a long time.'

'A long time; no. But you do hope—'

'I think everybody about a sick bed ought to hope, don't you?'

'Yes; but I mean—'

Nora stood up suddenly, her brain whirling. Was it possible that she and that woman had sat thus facing each other for half an hour, piling up this conversational rubbish, while upstairs, out of sight, the truth, the meaning of their two lives hung on the frail thread of one man's intermittent pulse? She could not imagine why she felt so powerless and baffled. What had a woman who was young and handsome and beloved to fear from a dowdy and insignificant old maid? Why, the antagonism that these very graces and superiorities would create in the other's breast, especially if she knew they were all spent in charming the being on whom her life depended. Weak in herself, but powerful from her circumstances, she stood at bay on the ruins of all that Nora had ever loved. 'How she must hate me – and I never thought of it,' mused Nora, who had imagined that she had thought of everything where her relation to her lover was concerned. Well, it was too late now to remedy her omission; but at least she must assert herself, must say something to save the precious minutes that remained and break through the stifling web of platitudes which her enemy's tremulous hand was weaving around her.

'Miss Aldis – I must tell you – I came to see—'

'How he was? So very friendly of you. He would appreciate it, I know. Christopher is so devoted to his friends.'

'But you'll – you'll tell him that I—'

'Of course. That you came on purpose to ask about him. As soon as he's a little bit stronger.'

'But I mean – now?'

'Tell him now that you called to enquire? How good of you to think of that too! Perhaps tomorrow morning, if he's feeling a little bit brighter . . .'

Nora felt her lips drying as if a hot wind had parched them. They would hardly move. 'But now – now – today.' Her voice sank to a whisper as she added: 'Isn't he conscious?'

'Oh, yes; he's conscious; he's perfectly conscious.' Miss Aldis emphasized this with another of her long pauses. 'He shall certainly be told that you called.' Suddenly she too got up from her seat and moved toward the window. 'I must seem dreadfully inhospitable, not even offering you a cup of tea. But the fact is, perhaps I ought to tell you – if you're thinking of getting back to Ockham this afternoon there's only one train that stops at the Junction after three o'clock.' She pulled out an old-fashioned enamelled watch with a wreath of roses about the dial, and turned almost apologetically to Mrs Frenway. 'You ought to be at the station by four o'clock at the latest; and with one of those old Junction taxis . . . I'm so sorry; I know I must appear to be driving you away.' A wan smile drew up her pale lips.

Nora knew just how long the drive from Westover Junction

had taken, and understood that she was being delicately dismissed. Dismissed from life – from hope – even from the dear
anguish of filling her eyes for the last time with the face which
was the one face in the world to her! ('But then she does know
everything,' she thought.)

'I mustn't make you miss your train, you know.'

'Miss Aldis, is he – has he seen any one?' Nora hazarded in
a painful whisper.

'Seen any one? Well, there've been all the doctors – five of
them! And then the nurses. Oh, but you mean friends, of
course. Naturally.' She seemed to reflect. 'Hal Brincker, yes; he
saw our cousin Hal yesterday – but not for very long.'

Hal Brincker! Nora knew what Christopher thought of his
Brincker cousins – blighting bores, one and all of them, he
always said. And in the extremity of his illness the one person
privileged to see him had been – Hal Brincker! Nora's eyes
filled; she had to turn them away for a moment from Miss
Aldis's timid inexorable face.

'But today?' she finally brought out.

'No. Today he hasn't seen any one; not yet.' The two women
stood and looked at each other; then Miss Aldis glanced uncer-
tainly about the room. 'But couldn't I – Yes, I ought at least to
have asked you if you won't have a cup of tea. So stupid of me!
There might still be time. I never take tea myself.' Once more
she referred anxiously to her watch. 'The water is sure to be
boiling, because the nurses' tea is just being taken up. If you'll
excuse me a moment I'll go and see.'

'Oh, no; no!' Nora drew in a quick sob. 'How can you? . . .
I mean, I don't want any . . .'

Miss Aldis looked relieved. 'Then I shall be quite sure that
you won't reach the station too late.' She waited again, and
then held out a long stony hand. 'So kind – I shall never forget
your kindness. Coming all this way, when you might so easily
have telephoned from town. Do please tell Mr Frenway how I
appreciated it. You will remember to tell him, won't you? He
sent me such an interesting collection of pamphlets about tree
moving. I should like him to know how much I feel his kindness in letting you come.' She paused again, and pulled in her

lips so that they became a narrow thread, a mere line drawn across her face by a ruler. 'But, no; I won't trouble you; I'll write to thank him myself.' Her hand ran out to an electric bell on the nearest table. It shrilled through the silence, and the parlour maid appeared with a stage-like promptness.

'The taxi, please? Mrs Frenway's taxi.'

The room became silent again. Nora thought: 'Yes; she knows everything.' Miss Aldis peeped for the third time at her watch, and then uttered a slight unmeaning laugh. The blue-bottle banged against the window, and once more it seemed to Nora that its sonorities were reverberating inside her head. They were deafeningly mingled there with the explosion of the taxi's reluctant starting-up and its convulsed halt at the front door. The driver sounded his horn as if to summon her.

'He's afraid too that you'll be late!' Miss Aldis smiled.

The smooth slippery floor of the hall seemed to Nora to extend away in front of her for miles. At its far end she saw a little tunnel of light, a miniature maid, a toy taxi. Somehow she managed to travel the distance that separated her from them, though her bones ached with weariness, and at every step she seemed to be lifting a leaden weight. The taxi was close to her now, its door was open, she was getting in. The same smell of damp hay and bad tobacco greeted her. She saw her hostess standing on the threshold. 'To the Junction, driver – back to the Junction,' she heard Miss Aldis say. The taxi began to roll toward the gate. As it moved away Nora heard Miss Aldis calling: 'I'll be sure to write and thank Mr Frenway.'

New York to Detroit

DOROTHY PARKER

'All ready with Detroit,' said the telephone operator.

'Hello,' said the girl in New York.

'Hello?' said the young man in Detroit.

'Oh, Jack!' she said. 'Oh, darling, it's so wonderful to hear you. You don't know how much I—'

'Hello?' he said.

'Ah, can't you hear me?' she said. 'Why, I can hear you just as if you were right beside me. Is this any better, dear? Can you hear me now?'

'Who did you want to speak to?' he said.

'You, Jack!' she said. 'You, you. This is Jean, darling. Oh, please try to hear me. This is Jean.'

'Who?' he said.

'Jean,' she said. 'Ah, don't you know my voice? It's Jean, dear. Jean.'

'Oh, hello there,' he said. 'Well. Well, for heaven's sake. How are you?'

'I'm all right,' she said. 'Oh, I'm not, either, darling. I – oh, it's just terrible. I can't stand it any more. Aren't you coming back? Please, when are you coming back? You don't know how awful it is, without you. It's been such a long time, dear – you said it would be just four or five days, and it's nearly three weeks. It's like years and years. Oh, it's been so awful, sweetheart – it's just—'

'Hey, I'm terribly sorry,' he said, 'but I can't hear one damn thing you're saying. Can't you talk louder, or something?'

'I'll try, I'll try,' she said. 'Is this better? Now can you hear?'

'Yeah, now I can, a little,' he said. 'Don't talk so fast, will you? What did you say, before?'

'I said it's just awful without you,' she said. 'It's such a long time, dear. And I haven't had a word from you. I – oh, I've just been nearly crazy, Jack. Never even a post-card, dearest, or a—'

'Honestly, I haven't had a second,' he said. 'I've been working like a fool. God, I've been rushed.'

'Ah, have you?' she said. 'I'm sorry, dear. I've been silly. But it was just – oh, it was just hell, never hearing a word. I thought maybe you'd telephone to say good-night, sometimes, – you know, the way you used to, when you were away.'

'Why, I was going to, a lot of times,' he said, 'but I thought you'd probably be out, or something.'

'I haven't been out,' she said. 'I've been staying here, all by myself. It's – it's sort of better, that way. I don't want to see people. Everybody says, "When's Jack coming back?" and "What do you hear from Jack?" and I'm afraid I'll cry in front of them. Darling, it hurts so terribly when they ask me about you, and I have to say I don't—'

'This is the damndest, lousiest connection I ever saw in my life,' he said. 'What hurts? What's the matter?'

'I said, it hurts so terribly when people ask me about you,' she said, 'and I have to say – Oh, never mind. Never mind. How are you, dear? Tell me how you are.'

'Oh, pretty good,' he said. 'Tired as the devil. You all right?'

'Jack, I – that's what I wanted to tell you,' she said. 'I'm terribly worried. I'm nearly out of my mind. Oh, what will I do, dear, what are we going to do? Oh, Jack, Jack, darling!'

'Hey, how can I hear you when you mumble like that?' he said. 'Can't you talk louder? Talk right into the what-you-call-it.'

'I can't scream it over the telephone!' she said. 'Haven't you any sense? Don't you know what I'm telling you? Don't you know? Don't you know?'

'I give up,' he said. 'First you mumble, and then you yell. Look, this doesn't make sense. I can't hear anything, with this rotten connection. Why don't you write me a letter, in the morning? Do that, why don't you? And I'll write you one. See?'

'Jack, listen, listen!' she said. 'You listen to me! I've got to talk to you. I tell you I'm nearly crazy. Please, dearest, hear what I'm saying. Jack, I—'

'Just a minute,' he said. 'Someone's knocking at the door. *Come in. Well, for cryin' out loud! Come on in, bums. Hang your coats up on the floor, and sit down. The Scotch is in the closet, and there's ice in that pitcher. Make yourselves at home – act like you were in a regular bar. Be with you right away.* Hey, listen, there's a lot of crazy Indians just come in here, and I can't hear myself think. You go ahead and write me a letter tomorrow. Will you?'

'Write you a letter!' she said. 'Oh, God, don't you think I'd have written you before, if I'd known where to reach you? I didn't even know that, till they told me at your office today. I got so—'

'Oh, yeah, did they?' he said. 'I thought I – *Ah, pipe down, will you? Give a guy a chance. This is an expensive talk going on here.* Say, look, this must be costing you a million dollars. You oughtn't to do this.'

'What do you think I care about that?' she said. 'I'll die if I don't talk to you. I tell you I'll die, Jack. Sweetheart, what is it? Don't you want to talk to me? Tell me what makes you this way. Is it – don't you really like me any more? Is that it? Don't you, Jack?'

'Hell, I can't hear,' he said. 'Don't what?'

'Please,' she said. 'Please, please. Please, Jack, listen. When are you coming back, darling? I need you so. I need you so terribly. When are you coming back?'

'Why, that's the thing,' he said. 'That's what I was going to write you about tomorrow. *Come on, now, how about shutting up just for a minute? A joke's a joke.* Hello. Hear me all right? Why, you see, the way things came out today, it looks a little bit like I'd have to go on to Chicago for a while. Looks like a pretty big thing, and it won't mean a very long time, I don't believe. Looks as if I'd be going out there next week, I guess.'

'Jack, no!' she said. 'Oh, don't do that! You can't do that. You can't leave me alone like this. I've got to see you, dearest. I've got to. You've got to come back, or I've got to come there to you. I can't go through this. Jack, I can't, I—'

'Look, we better say good-night now,' he said. 'No use trying to make out what you say, when you talk all over yourself like that. And there's so much racket here – *Hey, can the harmony, will you? God, it's terrible. Want me to be thrown out of here?* You go get a good night's sleep, and I'll write you all about it tomorrow.'

'Listen!' she said. 'Jack, don't go 'way! Help me, darling. Say something to help me through tonight. Say you love me, for God's sake say you still love me. Say it. Say it.'

'Ah, I can't talk,' he said. 'This is fierce. I'll write you first thing in the morning. 'By. Thanks for calling up.'

'Jack!' she said. 'Jack, don't go. Jack, wait a minute. I've got to talk to you. I'll talk quietly. I won't cry. I'll talk so you can hear me. Please, dear, please—'

'All through with Detroit?' said the operator.

'No!' she said. 'No, no, no! Get him, get him back again right away! Get him back. No, never mind. Never mind it now. Never—'

The Whistle

EUDORA WELTY

Night fell. The darkness was thin, like some sleazy dress that has been worn and worn for many winters and always lets the cold through to the bones. Then the moon rose. A farm lay quite visible, like a white stone in water, among the stretches of deep woods in their colorless dead leaf. By a closer and more searching eye than the moon's, everything belonging to the Mortons might have been seen – even to the tiny tomato plants in their neat rows closest to the house, gray and featherlike, appalling in their exposed fragility. The moonlight covered everything, and lay upon the darkest shape of all, the farm-house where the lamp had just been blown out.

Inside, Jason and Sara Morton were lying between the quilts of a pallet which had been made up close to the fireplace. A fire still fluttered in the grate, making a drowsy sound now and then, and its exhausted light beat up and down the wall, across the rafters, and over the dark pallet where the old people lay, like a bird trying to find its way out of the room.

The long-spaced, tired breathing of Jason was the only noise besides the flutter of the fire. He lay under the quilt in a long shape like a bean, turned on his side to face the door. His lips opened in the dark, and in and out he breathed, in and out, slowly and with a rise and fall, over and over, like a conversation or a tale – a question and a sigh.

Sara lay on her back with her mouth agape, silent, but not asleep. She was staring at the dark and indistinguishable places among the rafters. Her eyes seemed opened too wide, the lids strained and limp, like openings which have been stretched shapeless and made of no more use. Once a hissing yellow flame stood erect in the old log, and her small face and pale hair, and one hand holding to the edge of the cover, were illuminated for a moment, with shadows bright blue. Then she pulled the quilt clear over her head.

Every night they lay trembling with cold, but no more communicative in their misery than a pair of window shutters beaten by a storm. Sometimes many days, weeks went by without words. They were not really old – they were only fifty; still, their lives were filled with tiredness, with a great lack of necessity to speak, with poverty which may have bound them like a disaster too great for any discussion but left them still separate and undesirous of sympathy. Perhaps, years ago, the long habit of silence may have been started in anger or passion. Who could tell now?

As the fire grew lower and lower, Jason's breathing grew heavy and solemn, and he was even beyond dreams. Completely hidden, Sara's body was as weightless as a strip of cane, there was hardly a shape to the quilt under which she was lying. Sometimes it seemed to Sara herself that it was her lack of weight which kept her from ever getting warm.

She was so tired of the cold! That was all it could do any more – make her tired. Year after year, she felt sure that she would die before the cold was over. Now, according to the Almanac,[1] it was spring . . . But year after year it was always the same. The plants would be set out in their frames, transplanted always too soon, and there was a freeze . . . When was the last time they had grown tall and full, that the cold had held off and there was a crop?

Like a vain dream, Sara began to have thoughts of the spring and summer. At first she thought only simply, of the colors of green and red, the smell of the sun on the ground, the touch of leaves and of warm ripening tomatoes. Then, all hidden as she was under the quilt, she began to imagine and remember the town of Dexter in the shipping season. There in her mind, dusty little Dexter became a theater for almost legendary festivity, a place of pleasure. On every road leading in, smiling farmers were bringing in wagonloads of the most beautiful tomatoes. The packing sheds at Dexter Station were all decorated – no, it was simply that the May sun was shining. Mr Perkins, the tall, gesturing figure, stood in the very center of everything, buying, directing, waving yellow papers that must be telegrams, shouting with grand impatience. And it was he, after all, that owned their farm now. Train after train of empty freight cars stretched away, waiting and then being filled. Was it possible to have saved out of the threat of the cold so many tomatoes in the world? Of course, for here marched in a perfect parade of Florida packers, all the way from Florida, tanned, stockingless, some of them tattooed. The music box was playing in the café across the way, and the crippled man that walked like a duck was back taking poses for a dime of the young people with their heads together. With shouts of triumph the men were getting drunk, and now and then a pistol went off somewhere. In the shade the children celebrated in tomato fights. A strong, heady, sweet smell hung over everything. Such excitement! Let the packers rest, if only for a moment, thought Sara. Stretch them out, stained with sweat, under the shade tree, and one can play the guitar. The girl wrappers listen while they work. What small brown hands, red with juice! Their faces are forever sleepy and flushed; when the men speak to them they laugh ... And Jason and Sara themselves are standing there, standing under the burning sun near the first shed, giving over their own load, watching their own tomatoes shoved into the process, swallowed away – sorted, wrapped, loaded, dispatched in a freight car – all so fast ... Mr Perkins holds out his hard, quick hand. Shake it fast! How quickly it is all over!

Sara, weightless under the quilt, could think of the celebrations of Dexter and see the vision of ripe tomatoes only in brief snatches, like the flare-up of the little fire. The rest of the time she thought only of cold, of cold going on before and after. She could not help but feel the chill of the here and now, which was not to think at all, but was for her only a trembling in the dark.

She coughed patiently and turned her head to one side. She peered over the quilt just a little and saw that the fire had at last gone out. There was left only a hulk of red log, a still, red, bent shape, like one of Jason's socks thrown down to be darned somehow. With only this to comfort her, Sara closed her eyes and fell asleep.

The husband and wife now lay perfectly still in the dark room, with Jason's hoarse, slow breathing, like the commotion of some clumsy nodding old bear trying to climb a tree, heard by nobody at all.

Every hour it was getting colder and colder. The moon, intense and white as the snow that does not fall here, drew higher in the sky, in the long night, and more distant from the earth. The farm looked as tiny and still as a seashell, with the little knob of a house surrounded by its curved furrows of tomato plants. Cold like a white pressing hand reached down and lay over the shell.

In Dexter there is a great whistle which is blown when a freeze threatens. It is known everywhere as Mr Perkins' whistle. Now it sounded out in the clear night, blast after blast. Over the countryside lights appeared in the windows of the farms. Men and women ran out into the fields and covered up their plants with whatever they had, while Mr Perkins' whistle blew and blew.

Jason Morton was not waked up by the great whistle. On he slept, his cavernous breathing like roars coming from a hollow tree. His right hand had been thrown out, from some deepness he must have dreamed, and lay stretched on the cold floor in the very center of a patch of moonlight which had moved across the room.

Sara felt herself waking. She knew that Mr Perkins' whistle was blowing, what it meant – and that it now remained for her to get Jason and go out to the field. A soft laxity, an illusion of warmth, flowed stubbornly down her body, and for a few moments she continued to lie still.

Then she was sitting up and seizing her husband by the shoulders, without saying a word, rocking him back and forth. It took all her strength to wake him. He coughed, his roaring was over, and he sat up. He said nothing either, and they both sat with bent heads and listened for the whistle. After a silence it blew again, a long, rising blast.

Promptly Sara and Jason got out of bed. They were both fully dressed, because of the cold, and only needed to put on their shoes. Jason lighted the lantern, and Sara gathered the bedclothes over her arm and followed him out.

Everything was white, and everything looked vast and extensive to them as they walked over the frozen field. White in a shadowed pit, abandoned from summer to summer, the old sorghum mill stood like the machine of a dream, with its long prostrate pole, its blunted axis.

Stooping over the little plants, Jason and Sara touched them and touched the earth. For their own knowledge, by their hands, they found everything to be true – the cold, the rightness of the warning, the need to act. Over the sticks set in among the plants they laid the quilts one by one, spreading them with a slow ingenuity. Jason took off his coat and laid it over the small tender plants by the side of the house. Then he glanced at Sara, and she reached down and pulled her dress off over her head. Her hair fell down out of its pins, and she began at once to tremble violently. The skirt was luckily long and full, and all the rest of the plants were covered by it.

Then Sara and Jason stood for a moment and stared almost idly at the field and up at the sky.

There was no wind. There was only the intense whiteness of moonlight. Why did this calm cold sink into them like the teeth of a trap? They bent their shoulders and walked silently back into the house.

The room was not much warmer. They had forgotten to shut the door behind them when the whistle was blowing so hard. They sat down to wait for morning.

Then Jason did a rare, strange thing. There long before morning he poured kerosene over some kindling and struck a light to it. Squatting, they got near it, quite gradually they drew together, and sat motionless until it all burned down. Still Sara did not move. Then Jason, in his underwear and long blue trousers, went out and brought in another load, and the big cherry log which of course was meant to be saved for the very last of winter.

The extravagant warmth of the room had sent some kind of

agitation over Sara, like her memories of Dexter in the shipping season. She sat huddled in a long brown cotton petticoat,
holding onto the string which went around the waist. Her
mouse-colored hair, paler at the temples, was hanging loose
down to her shoulders, like a child's unbound for a party. She
held her knees against her numb, pendulant breasts and stared
into the fire, her eyes widening.

On his side of the hearth Jason watched the fire burn too.
His breath came gently, quickly, noiselessly, as though for a
little time he would conceal or defend his tiredness. He lifted
his arms and held out his misshapen hands to the fire.

At last every bit of the wood was gone. Now the cherry log
was burned to ashes.

And all of a sudden Jason was on his feet again. Of all things,
he was bringing the split-bottomed chair over to the hearth. He
knocked it to pieces . . . It burned well and brightly. Sara never
said a word. She did not move . . .

Then the kitchen table. To think that a solid, steady four-
legged table like that, that had stood thirty years in one place,
should be consumed in such a little while! Sara stared almost
greedily at the waving flames.

Then when that was over, Jason and Sara sat in darkness
where their bed had been, and it was colder than ever. The fire
the kitchen table had made seemed wonderful to them – as if
what they had never said, and what could not be, had its life,
too, after all.

But Sara trembled, again pressing her hard knees against her
breast. In the return of winter, of the night's cold, something
strange, like fright, or dependency, a sensation of complete
helplessness, took possession of her. All at once, without turning her head, she spoke.

'Jason . . .'

A silence. But only for a moment.

'Listen,' said her husband's uncertain voice.

They held very still, as before, with bent heads.

Outside, as though it would exact something further from
their lives, the whistle continued to blow.

Barn Burning

WILLIAM FAULKNER

The store in which the Justice of the Peace's court was sitting smelled of cheese. The boy, crouched on his nail keg at the back of the crowded room, knew he smelled cheese, and more: from where he sat he could see the ranked shelves close-packed with the solid, squat, dynamic shapes of tin cans whose labels his stomach read, not from the lettering which meant nothing to his mind but from the scarlet devils and the silver curve of fish[1] – this, the cheese which he knew he smelled and the hermetic meat which his intestines believed he smelled coming in intermittent gusts momentary and brief between the other constant one, the smell and sense just a little of fear because mostly of despair and grief, the old fierce pull of blood. He could not see the table where the Justice sat and before which his father and his father's enemy (*our enemy* he thought in that despair; *ourn! mine and hisn both! He's my father!*) stood, but he could hear them, the two of them that is, because his father had said no word yet:

'But what proof have you, Mr Harris?'

'I told you. The hog got into my corn. I caught it up and sent it back to him. He had no fence that would hold it. I told him so, warned him. The next time I put the hog in my pen. When he came to get it I gave him enough wire to patch up his pen. The next time I put the hog up and kept it. I rode down to his house and saw the wire I gave him still rolled on to the spool in his yard. I told him he could have the hog when he paid me a dollar pound fee. That evening a nigger came with the dollar and got the hog. He was a strange nigger. He said, "He say to tell you wood and hay kin burn." I said, "What?" "That whut he say to tell you," the nigger said. "Wood and hay kin burn." That night my barn burned. I got the stock out but I lost the barn.'

'Where is the nigger? Have you got him?'

'He was a strange nigger, I tell you. I don't know what became of him.'

'But that's not proof. Don't you see that's not proof?'

'Get that boy up here. He knows.' For a moment the boy thought too that the man meant his older brother until Harris said, 'Not him. The little one. The boy,' and, crouching, small for his age, small and wiry like his father, in patched and faded jeans even too small for him, with straight, uncombed, brown hair and eyes gray and wild as storm scud, he saw the men between himself and the table part and become a lane of grim faces, at the end of which he saw the Justice, a shabby, collarless, graying man in spectacles, beckoning him. He felt no floor under his bare feet; he seemed to walk beneath the palpable weight of the grim turning faces. His father, stiff in his black Sunday coat donned not for the trial but for the moving, did not even look at him. *He aims for me to lie*, he thought, again with that frantic grief and despair. *And I will have to do hit.*

'What's your name, boy?' the Justice said.

'Colonel Sartoris Snopes,'[2] the boy whispered.

'Hey?' the Justice said. 'Talk louder. Colonel Sartoris? I reckon anybody named for Colonel Sartoris in this country can't help but tell the truth, can they?' The boy said nothing. *Enemy! Enemy!* he thought; for a moment he could not even see, could not see that the Justice's face was kindly nor discern that his voice was troubled when he spoke to the man named Harris: 'Do you want me to question this boy?' But he could hear, and during those subsequent long seconds while there was absolutely no sound in the crowded little room save that of quiet and intent breathing it was as if he had swung outward at the end of a grape vine, over a ravine, and at the top of the swing had been caught in a prolonged instant of mesmerized gravity, weightless in time.

'No!' Harris said violently, explosively. 'Damnation! Send him out of here!' Now time, the fluid world, rushed beneath him again, the voices coming to him again through the smell of cheese and sealed meat, the fear and despair and the old grief of blood:

'This case is closed. I can't find against you, Snopes, but I can give you advice. Leave this country and don't come back to it.'

His father spoke for the first time, his voice cold and harsh, level, without emphasis: 'I aim to. I don't figure to stay in a country among people who . . .' he said something unprintable and vile, addressed to no one.

'That'll do,' the Justice said. 'Take your wagon and get out of this country before dark. Case dismissed.'

His father turned, and he followed the stiff black coat, the wiry figure walking a little stiffly from where a Confederate provost's man's[3] musket ball had taken him in the heel on a stolen horse thirty years ago, followed the two backs now, since his older brother had appeared from somewhere in the crowd, no taller than the father but thicker, chewing tobacco steadily, between the two lines of grim-faced men and out of the store and across the worn gallery and down the sagging steps and among the dogs and half-grown boys in the mild May dust, where as he passed a voice hissed:

'Barn burner!'

Again he could not see, whirling; there was a face in a red haze, moonlike, bigger than the full moon, the owner of it half again his size, he leaping in the red haze toward the face, feeling no blow, feeling no shock when his head struck the earth, scrabbling up and leaping again, feeling no blow this time either and tasting no blood, scrabbling up to see the other boy in full flight and himself already leaping into pursuit as his father's hand jerked him back, the harsh, cold voice speaking above him: 'Go get in the wagon.'

It stood in a grove of locusts[4] and mulberries across the road. His two hulking sisters in their Sunday dresses and his mother and her sister in calico and sunbonnets were already in it, sitting on and among the sorry residue of the dozen and more movings which even the boy could remember – the battered stove, the broken beds and chairs, the clock inlaid with mother-of-pearl, which would not run, stopped at some fourteen minutes past two o'clock of a dead and forgotten day and time, which had been his mother's dowry. She was crying, though when she saw him she drew her sleeve across her face and began to descend from the wagon. 'Get back,' the father said.

'He's hurt. I got to get some water and wash his . . .'

'Get back in the wagon,' his father said. He got in too, over the tail-gate. His father mounted to the seat where the older brother already sat and struck the gaunt mules two savage blows with the peeled willow, but without heat. It was not even sadistic; it was exactly that same quality which in later years would cause his descendants to over-run the engine before putting a motor car into motion, striking and reining back in the same movement. The wagon went on, the store with its quiet crowd of grimly watching men dropped behind; a curve in the road hid it. *Forever* he thought. *Maybe he's done satisfied now, now that he has* . . . stopping himself, not to say it aloud even to himself. His mother's hand touched his shoulder.

'Does hit hurt?' she said.

'Naw,' he said. 'Hit don't hurt. Lemme be.'

'Can't you wipe some of the blood off before hit dries?'

'I'll wash to-night,' he said. 'Lemme be, I tell you.'

The wagon went on. He did not know where they were going. None of them ever did or ever asked, because it was always somewhere, always a house of sorts waiting for them a day or two days or even three days away. Likely his father had already arranged to make a crop on another farm before he . . . Again he had to stop himself. He (the father) always did. There was something about his wolflike independence and even courage when the advantage was at least neutral which impressed strangers, as if they got from his latent ravening ferocity not so much a sense of dependability as a feeling that his ferocious conviction in the rightness of his own actions would be of advantage to all whose interest lay with his.

That night they camped, in a grove of oaks and beeches where a spring ran. The nights were still cool and they had a fire against it, of a rail lifted from a nearby fence and cut into lengths – a small fire, neat, niggard almost, a shrewd fire; such fires were his father's habit and custom always, even in freezing

weather. Older, the boy might have remarked this and wondered why not a big one; why should not a man who had not
only seen the waste and extravagance of war, but who had in
his blood an inherent voracious prodigality with material not
his own, have burned everything in sight? Then he might have
gone a step farther and thought that that was the reason: that
niggard blaze was the living fruit of nights passed during those
four years in the woods hiding from all men, blue or gray,[5] with
his strings of horses (captured horses, he called them). And older
still, he might have divined the true reason: that the element of
fire spoke to some deep mainspring of his father's being, as the
element of steel or of powder spoke to other men, as the one
weapon for the preservation of integrity, else breath were not
worth the breathing, and hence to be regarded with respect and
used with discretion.

But he did not think this now and he had seen those same
niggard blazes all his life. He merely ate his supper beside it and
was already half asleep over his iron plate when his father
called him, and once more he followed the stiff back, the stiff
and ruthless limp, up the slope and on to the starlit road where,
turning, he could see his father against the stars but without
face or depth – a shape black, flat, and bloodless as though cut
from tin in the iron folds of the frockcoat which had not been
made for him, the voice harsh like tin and without heat like tin:

'You were fixing to tell them. You would have told him.' He
didn't answer. His father struck him with the flat of his hand on
the side of the head, hard but without heat, exactly as he had
struck the two mules at the store, exactly as he would strike
either of them with any stick in order to kill a horse fly, his
voice still without heat or anger: 'You're getting to be a man.
You got to learn. You got to learn to stick to your own blood
or you ain't going to have any blood to stick to you. Do you
think either of them, any man there this morning, would? Don't
you know all they wanted was a chance to get at me because
they knew I had them beat? Eh?' Later, twenty years later, he
was to tell himself, 'If I had said they wanted only truth, justice,
he would have hit me again.' But now he said nothing. He was
not crying. He just stood there. 'Answer me,' his father said.

'Yes,' he whispered. His father turned.

'Get on to bed. We'll be there to-morrow.'

To-morrow they were there. In the early afternoon the wagon stopped before a paintless two-room house identical almost with the dozen others it had stopped before even in the boy's ten years, and again, as on the other dozen occasions, his mother and aunt got down and began to unload the wagon, although his two sisters and his father and brother had not moved.

'Likely hit ain't fitten for hawgs,' one of the sisters said.

'Nevertheless, fit it will and you'll hog it and like it,' his father said. 'Get out of them chairs and help your Ma unload.'

The two sisters got down, big, bovine, in a flutter of cheap ribbons; one of them drew from the jumbled wagon bed a battered lantern, the other a worn broom. His father handed the reins to the older son and began to climb stiffly over the wheel. 'When they get unloaded, take the team to the barn and feed them.' Then he said, and at first the boy thought he was still speaking to his brother: 'Come with me.'

'Me?' he said.

'Yes,' his father said. 'You.'

'Abner,' his mother said. His father paused and looked back – the harsh level stare beneath the shaggy, graying, irascible brows.

'I reckon I'll have a word with the man that aims to begin to-morrow owning me body and soul for the next eight months.'[6]

They went back up the road. A week ago – or before last night, that is – he would have asked where they were going, but not now. His father had struck him before last night but never before had he paused afterward to explain why; it was as if the blow and the following calm, outrageous voice still rang, repercussed, divulging nothing to him save the terrible handicap of being young, the light weight of his few years, just heavy enough to prevent his soaring free of the world as it seemed to be ordered but not heavy enough to keep him footed solid in it, to resist it and try to change the course of its events.

Presently he could see the grove of oaks and cedars and the other flowering trees and shrubs where the house would be, though not the house yet. They walked beside a fence massed with honeysuckle and Cherokee roses[7] and came to a gate swinging open between two brick pillars, and now, beyond a sweep of drive, he saw the house for the first time and at that instant he forgot his father and the terror and despair both, and even when he remembered his father again (who had not stopped) the terror and despair did not return. Because, for all the twelve movings, they had sojourned until now in a poor country, a land of small farms and fields and houses, and he had never seen a house like this before. *Hit's big as a courthouse* he thought quietly, with a surge of peace and joy whose reason he could not have thought into words, being too young for that: *They are safe from him. People whose lives are a part of this peace and dignity are beyond his touch, he no more to them than a buzzing wasp: capable of stinging for a little moment but that's all; the spell of this peace and dignity rendering even the barns and stable and cribs which belong to it impervious to the puny flames he might contrive . . .* this, the peace and joy, ebbing for an instant as he looked again at the stiff black back, the stiff and implacable limp of the figure which was not dwarfed by the house, for the reason that it had never looked big anywhere and which now, against the serene columned backdrop, had more than ever that impervious quality of something cut ruthlessly from tin, depthless, as though, sidewise to the sun, it would cast no shadow. Watching him, the boy remarked the absolutely undeviating course which his father held and saw the stiff foot come squarely down in a pile of fresh droppings where a horse had stood in the drive and which his father could have avoided by a simple change of stride. But it ebbed only for a moment, though he could not have thought this into words either, walking on in the spell of the house, which he could even want but without envy, without sorrow, certainly never with that ravening and jealous rage which unknown to him walked in the ironlike black coat before him: *Maybe he will feel it too. Maybe it will even change him now from what maybe he couldn't help but be.*

They crossed the portico. Now he could hear his father's stiff foot as it came down on the boards with clocklike finality, a sound out of all proportion to the displacement of the body it bore and which was not dwarfed either by the white door before it, as though it had attained to a sort of vicious and ravening minimum not to be dwarfed by anything – the flat, wide, black hat, the formal coat of broadcloth which had once been black but which had now that friction-glazed greenish cast of the bodies of old house flies, the lifted sleeve which was too large, the lifted hand like a curled claw. The door opened so promptly that the boy knew the Negro must have been watching them all the time, an old man with neat grizzled hair, in a linen jacket, who stood barring the door with his body, saying, 'Wipe yo foots, white man, fo you come in here. Major ain't home nohow.'

'Get out of my way, nigger,' his father said, without heat too, flinging the door back and the Negro also and entering, his hat still on his head. And now the boy saw the prints of the stiff foot on the doorjamb and saw them appear on the pale rug behind the machinelike deliberation of the foot which seemed to bear (or transmit) twice the weight which the body compassed. The Negro was shouting 'Miss Lula! Miss Lula!' somewhere behind them, then the boy, deluged as though by a warm wave by a suave turn of carpeted stair and a pendant glitter of chandeliers and a mute gleam of gold frames, heard the swift feet and saw her too, a lady – perhaps he had never seen her like before either – in a gray, smooth gown with lace at the throat and an apron tied at the waist and the sleeves turned back, wiping cake or biscuit dough from her hands with a towel as she came up the hall, looking not at his father at all but at the tracks on the blond rug with an expression of incredulous amazement.

'I tried,' the Negro cried. 'I tole him to . . .'

'Will you please go away?' she said in a shaking voice. 'Major de Spain is not at home. Will you please go away?'

His father had not spoken again. He did not speak again. He did not even look at her. He just stood stiff in the center of the rug, in his hat, the shaggy iron-gray brows twitching slightly above the pebble-colored eyes as he appeared to examine the house with brief deliberation. Then with the same deliberation he turned; the boy watched him pivot on the good leg and saw the stiff foot drag round the arc of the turning, leaving a final long and fading smear. His father never looked at it, he never once looked down at the rug. The Negro held the door. It closed behind them, upon the hysteric and indistinguishable woman-wail. His father stopped at the top of the steps and scraped his boot clean on the edge of it. At the gate he stopped again. He stood for a moment, planted stiffly on the stiff foot, looking back at the house. 'Pretty and white, ain't it?' he said. 'That's sweat. Nigger sweat. Maybe it ain't white enough yet to suit him. Maybe he wants to mix some white sweat with it.'

Two hours later the boy was chopping wood behind the house within which his mother and aunt and the two sisters (the mother and aunt, not the two girls, he knew that; even at this distance and muffled by walls the flat loud voices of the two girls emanated an incorrigible idle inertia) were setting up the stove to prepare a meal, when he heard the hooves and saw the linen-clad man on a fine sorrel mare, whom he recognized even before he saw the rolled rug in front of the Negro youth following on a fat bay carriage horse – a suffused, angry face vanishing, still at full gallop, beyond the corner of the house where his father and brother were sitting in the two tilted chairs; and a moment later, almost before he could have put the axe down, he heard the hooves again and watched the sorrel mare go back out of the yard, already galloping again. Then his father began to shout one of the sisters' names, who presently emerged backward from the kitchen door dragging the rolled rug along the ground by one end while the other sister walked behind it.

'If you ain't going to tote, go on and set up the wash pot,' the first said.

'You, Sarty!' the second shouted. 'Set up the wash pot!' His father appeared at the door, framed against that shabbiness, as he had been against that other bland perfection, impervious to either, the mother's anxious face at his shoulder.

'Go on,' the father said. 'Pick it up.' The two sisters stooped, broad, lethargic; stooping, they presented an incredible expanse of pale cloth and a flutter of tawdry ribbons.

'If I thought enough of a rug to have to git hit all the way from France I wouldn't keep hit where folks coming in would have to tromp on hit,' the first said. They raised the rug.

'Abner,' the mother said. 'Let me do it.'

'You go back and git dinner,' his father said. 'I'll tend to this.'

From the woodpile through the rest of the afternoon the boy watched them, the rug spread flat in the dust beside the bubbling wash-pot, the two sisters stooping over it with that profound and lethargic reluctance, while the father stood over them in turn, implacable and grim, driving them though never raising his voice again. He could smell the harsh homemade lye they were using; he saw his mother come to the door once and look toward them with an expression not anxious now but very like despair; he saw his father turn, and he fell to with the axe and saw from the corner of his eye his father raise from the ground a flattish fragment of field stone and examine it and return to the pot, and this time his mother actually spoke: 'Abner. Abner. Please don't. Please, Abner.'

Then he was done too. It was dusk; the whippoorwills[8] had already begun. He could smell coffee from the room where they would presently eat the cold food remaining from the mid-afternoon meal, though when he entered the house he realized they were having coffee again probably because there was a fire on the hearth, before which the rug now lay spread over the backs of the two chairs. The tracks of his father's foot were gone. Where they had been were now long, water-cloudy scoriations resembling the sporadic course of a lilliputian mowing machine.

It still hung there while they ate the cold food and then went to bed, scattered without order or claim up and down the two rooms, his mother in one bed, where his father would later lie, the older brother in the other, himself, the aunt, and the two sisters on pallets on the floor. But his father was not in bed yet. The last thing the boy remembered was the depthless, harsh silhouette of the hat and coat bending over the rug and it seemed to him that he had not even closed his eyes when the silhouette was standing over him, the fire almost dead behind it, the stiff foot prodding him awake. 'Catch up the mule,' his father said.

When he returned with the mule his father was standing in the black door, the rolled rug over his shoulder. 'Ain't you going to ride?' he said.

'No. Give me your foot.'

He bent his knee into his father's hand, the wiry, surprising power flowed smoothly, rising, he rising with it, on to the mule's bare back (they had owned a saddle once; the boy could remember it though not when or where) and with the same effortlessness his father swung the rug up in front of him. Now in the starlight they retraced the afternoon's path, up the dusty road rife with honeysuckle, through the gate and up the black tunnel of the drive to the lightless house, where he sat on the mule and felt the rough warp of the rug drag across his thighs and vanish.

'Don't you want me to help?' he whispered. His father did not answer and now he heard again that stiff foot striking the hollow portico with that wooden and clocklike deliberation, that outrageous overstatement of the weight it carried. The rug, hunched, not flung (the boy could tell that even in the darkness) from his father's shoulder struck the angle of wall and floor with a sound unbelievably loud, thunderous, then the foot again, unhurried and enormous; a light came on in the house and the boy sat, tense, breathing steadily and quietly and just a little fast, though the foot itself did not increase its beat at all, descending the steps now; now the boy could see him.

'Don't you want to ride now?' he whispered. 'We kin both ride now,' the light within the house altering now, flaring up and sinking. *He's coming down the stairs now*, he thought. He had already ridden the mule up beside the horse block; presently his father was up behind him and he doubled the reins over and slashed the mule across the neck, but before the animal could begin to trot the hard, thin arm came round him, the hard, knotted hand jerking the mule back to a walk.

In the first red rays of the sun they were in the lot, putting plow gear on the mules. This time the sorrel mare was in the lot before he heard it at all, the rider collarless and even bareheaded, trembling, speaking in a shaking voice as the woman in the house had done, his father merely looking up once before stooping again to the hame[9] he was buckling, so that the man on the mare spoke to his stooping back:

'You must realize you have ruined that rug. Wasn't there anybody here, any of your women . . .' he ceased, shaking, the boy watching him, the older brother leaning now in the stable door, chewing, blinking slowly and steadily at nothing apparently. 'It cost a hundred dollars. But you never had a hundred dollars. You never will. So I'm going to charge you twenty bushels of corn against your crop. I'll add it in your contract and when you come to the commissary you can sign it. That won't keep Mrs de Spain quiet but maybe it will teach you to wipe your feet off before you enter her house again.'

Then he was gone. The boy looked at his father, who still had not spoken or even looked up again, who was now adjusting the logger-head in the hame.

'Pap,' he said. His father looked at him – the inscrutable face, the shaggy brows beneath which the gray eyes glinted coldly. Suddenly the boy went toward him, fast, stopping as suddenly. 'You done the best you could!' he cried. 'If he wanted hit done different why didn't he wait and tell you how? He won't git no twenty bushels! He won't git none! We'll gether hit and hide hit! I kin watch . . .'

'Did you put the cutter back in that straight stock like I told you?'

'No, sir,' he said.

'Then go do it.'

That was Wednesday. During the rest of that week he worked steadily, at what was within his scope and some which was beyond it, with an industry that did not need to be driven nor even commanded twice; he had this from his mother, with the difference that some at least of what he did he liked to do, such as splitting wood with the half-size axe which his mother and aunt had earned, or saved money somehow, to present him with at Christmas. In company with the two older women (and on one afternoon, even one of the sisters), he built pens for the shoat[10] and the cow which were a part of his father's contract with the landlord, and one afternoon, his father being absent, gone somewhere on one of the mules, he went to the field.

They were running a middle buster now, his brother holding the plow straight while he handled the reins, and walking beside the straining mule, the rich black soil shearing cool and damp against his bare ankles, he thought *Maybe this is the end of it. Maybe even that twenty bushels that seems hard to have to pay for just a rug will be a cheap price for him to stop forever and always from being what he used to be*; thinking, dreaming now, so that his brother had to speak sharply to him to mind the mule: *Maybe he even won't collect the twenty bushels. Maybe it will all add up and balance and vanish – corn, rug, fire; the terror and grief, the being pulled two ways like between two teams of horses – gone, done with for ever and ever.*

Then it was Saturday; he looked up from beneath the mule he was harnessing and saw his father in the black coat and hat. 'Not that,' his father said. 'The wagon gear.' And then, two hours later, sitting in the wagon bed behind his father and brother on the seat, the wagon accomplished a final curve, and he saw the weathered paintless store with its tattered tobacco and patent-medicine posters and the tethered wagons and saddle animals below the gallery. He mounted the gnawed steps behind his father and brother, and there again was the lane of quiet, watching faces for the three of them to walk through. He saw the man in spectacles sitting at the plank table and he did not need to be told this was a Justice of the Peace; he sent one glare of fierce, exultant, partisan defiance at the man in collar and cravat now, whom he had seen but twice before in his life, and that on a galloping horse, who now wore on his face an expression not of rage but of amazed unbelief which the boy could not have known was at the incredible circumstance of being sued by one of his own tenants, and came and stood against his father and cried at the Justice: 'He ain't done it! He ain't burnt . . .'

'Go back to the wagon,' his father said.

'Burnt?' the Justice said. 'Do I understand this rug was burned too?'

'Does anybody here claim it was?' his father said. 'Go back to the wagon.' But he did not, he merely retreated to the rear of the room, crowded as that other had been, but not to sit down this time, instead, to stand pressing among the motionless bodies, listening to the voices:

'And you claim twenty bushels of corn is too high for the damage you did to the rug?'

'He brought the rug to me and said he wanted the tracks washed out of it. I washed the tracks out and took the rug back to him.'

'But you didn't carry the rug back to him in the same condition it was in before you made the tracks on it.'

His father did not answer, and now for perhaps half a minute there was no sound at all save that of breathing, the faint, steady suspiration of complete and intent listening.

'You decline to answer that, Mr Snopes?' Again his father did not answer. 'I'm going to find against you, Mr Snopes. I'm going to find that you were responsible for the injury to Major de Spain's rug and hold you liable for it. But twenty bushels of corn seems a little high for a man in your circumstances to have to pay. Major de Spain claims it cost a hundred dollars. October corn will be worth about fifty cents. I figure that if Major de Spain can stand a ninety-five dollar loss on something he paid cash for, you can stand a five-dollar loss you haven't earned yet. I hold you in damages to Major de Spain to the amount of ten bushels of corn over and above your contract with him, to be paid to him out of your crop at gathering time. Court adjourned.'

It had taken no time hardly, the morning was but half begun. He thought they would return home and perhaps back to the field, since they were late,[11] far behind all other farmers. But instead his father passed on behind the wagon, merely indicating with his hand for the older brother to follow with it, and crossed the road toward the blacksmith shop opposite, pressing on after his father, overtaking him, speaking, whispering up at the harsh, calm face beneath the weathered hat: 'He won't git no ten bushels neither. He won't git one. We'll . . .' until his father glanced for an instant down at him, the face absolutely calm, the grizzled eyebrows tangled above the cold eyes, the voice almost pleasant, almost gentle:

'You think so? Well, we'll wait till October anyway.'

The matter of the wagon – the setting of a spoke or two and the tightening of the tires – did not take long either, the business of the tires accomplished by driving the wagon into the spring branch behind the shop and letting it stand there, the mules nuzzling into the water from time to time, and the boy on the seat with the idle reins, looking up the slope and through the sooty tunnel of the shed where the slow hammer rang and where his father sat on an upended cypress bolt, easily, either talking or listening, still sitting there when the boy brought the dripping wagon up out of the branch and halted it before the door.

'Take them on to the shade and hitch,' his father said. He did so and returned. His father and the smith and a third man squatting on his heels inside the door were talking, about crops and animals; the boy, squatting too in the ammoniac dust and hoof-parings and scales of rust, heard his father tell a long and unhurried story out of the time before the birth of the older brother even when he had been a professional horsetrader. And then his father came up beside him where he stood before a tattered last year's circus poster on the other side of the store, gazing rapt and quiet at the scarlet horses, the incredible poisings and convolutions of tulle and tights and the painted leers of comedians, and said, 'It's time to eat.'

But not at home. Squatting beside his brother against the front wall, he watched his father emerge from the store and produce from a paper sack a segment of cheese and divide it carefully and deliberately into three with his pocket knife and produce crackers from the same sack. They all three squatted on the gallery and ate, slowly, without talking; then in the store again, they drank from a tin dipper tepid water smelling of the cedar bucket and of living beech trees. And still they did not go home. It was a horse lot this time, a tall rail fence upon and along which men stood and sat and out of which one by one horses were led, to be walked and trotted and then cantered back and forth along the road while the slow swapping and buying went on and the sun began to slant westward, they – the three of them – watching and listening, the older brother with his muddy eyes and his steady, inevitable tobacco, the father commenting now and then on certain of the animals, to no one in particular.

It was after sundown when they reached home. They ate supper by lamplight, then, sitting on the doorstep, the boy watched the night fully accomplish, listening to the whippoor-wills and the frogs, when he heard his mother's voice: 'Abner! No! No! Oh, God. Oh, God. Abner!' and he rose, whirled, and saw the altered light through the door where a candle stub now burned in a bottle neck on the table and his father, still in the hat and coat, at once formal and burlesque as though dressed carefully for some shabby and ceremonial violence, emptying the reservoir of the lamp back into the five-gallon kerosene can from which it had been filled, while the mother tugged at his arm until he shifted the lamp to the other hand and flung her back, not savagely or viciously, just hard, into the wall, her hands flung out against the wall for balance, her mouth open and in her face the same quality of hopeless despair as had been in her voice. Then his father saw him standing in the door.

'Go to the barn and get that can of oil we were oiling the wagon with,' he said. The boy did not move. Then he could speak.

'What . . .' he cried. 'What are you . . .'

'Go get that oil,' his father said. 'Go.'

Then he was moving, running, outside the house, toward the stable: this the old habit, the old blood which he had not been permitted to choose for himself, which had been bequeathed him willy nilly and which had run for so long (and who knew where, battening on what of outrage and savagery and lust) before it came to him. *I could keep on*, he thought. *I could run on and on and never look back, never need to see his face again. Only I can't. I can't*, the rusted can in his hand now, the liquid sploshing in it as he ran back to the house and into it, into the sound of his mother's weeping in the next room, and handed the can to his father.

'Ain't you going to even send a nigger?' he cried. 'At least you sent a nigger before!'

This time his father didn't strike him. The hand came even

faster than the blow had, the same hand which had set the can
on the table with almost excruciating care flashing from the
can toward him too quick for him to follow it, gripping him by
the back of his shirt and on to tiptoe before he had seen it quit
the can, the face stooping at him in breathless and frozen ferocity, the cold, dead voice speaking over him to the older
brother who leaned against the table, chewing with that steady,
curious, sidewise motion of cows:

'Empty the can into the big one and go on. I'll catch up with
you.'

'Better tie him up to the bedpost,' the brother said.

'Do like I told you,' the father said. Then the boy was moving, his bunched shirt and the hard, bony hand between his
shoulder-blades, his toes just touching the floor, across the
room and into the other one, past the sisters sitting with spread
heavy thighs in the two chairs over the cold hearth, and to
where his mother and aunt sat side by side on the bed, the
aunt's arms about his mother's shoulders.

'Hold him,' the father said. The aunt made a startled movement. 'Not you,' the father said. 'Lennie. Take hold of him. I
want to see you do it.' His mother took him by the wrist. 'You'll
hold him better than that. If he gets loose don't you know what
he is going to do? He will go up yonder.' He jerked his head
toward the road. 'Maybe I'd better tie him.'

'I'll hold him,' his mother whispered.

'See you do then.' Then his father was gone, the stiff foot
heavy and measured upon the boards, ceasing at last.

Then he began to struggle. His mother caught him in both
arms, he jerking and wrenching at them. He would be stronger
in the end, he knew that. But he had no time to wait for it.
'Lemme go!' he cried. 'I don't want to have to hit you!'

'Let him go!' the aunt said. 'If he don't go, before God, I am
going up there myself!'

'Don't you see I can't?' his mother cried. 'Sarty! Sarty! No!
No! Help me, Lizzie!'

Then he was free. His aunt grasped at him but it was too
late. He whirled, running, his mother stumbled forward on to
her knees behind him, crying to the nearer sister: 'Catch him,

Net! Catch him!' But that was too late too, the sister (the sisters
were twins, born at the same time, yet either of them now gave
the impression of being, encompassing as much living meat and
volume and weight as any other two of the family) not yet having begun to rise from the chair, her head, face, alone merely
turned, presenting to him in the flying instant an astonishing
expanse of young female features untroubled by any surprise
even, wearing only an expression of bovine interest. Then he
was out of the room, out of the house, in the mild dust of the
starlit road and the heavy rifeness of honeysuckle, the pale ribbon unspooling with terrific slowness under his running feet,
reaching the gate at last and turning in, running, his heart and
lungs drumming, on up the drive toward the lighted house, the
lighted door. He did not knock, he burst in, sobbing for breath,
incapable for the moment of speech; he saw the astonished face
of the Negro in the linen jacket without knowing when the
Negro had appeared.

'De Spain!' he cried, panted. 'Where's . . .' then he saw the
white man too emerging from a white door down the hall.
'Barn!' he cried. 'Barn!'

'What?' the white man said. 'Barn?'

'Yes!' the boy cried. 'Barn!'

'Catch him!' the white man shouted.

But it was too late this time too. The Negro grasped his
shirt, but the entire sleeve, rotten with washing, carried away,
and he was out that door too and in the drive again, and had
actually never ceased to run even while he was screaming into
the white man's face.

Behind him the white man was shouting, 'My horse! Fetch
my horse!' and he thought for an instant of cutting across the
park and climbing the fence into the road, but he did not know
the park nor how high the vine-massed fence might be and he
dared not risk it. So he ran on down the drive, blood and breath
roaring; presently he was in the road again though he could not
see it. He could not hear either: the galloping mare was almost
upon him before he heard her, and even then he held his course,
as if the very urgency of his wild grief and need must in a
moment more find him wings, waiting until the ultimate instant

to hurl himself aside and into the weed-choked roadside ditch as the horse thundered past and on, for an instant in furious silhouette against the stars, the tranquil early summer night sky which, even before the shape of the horse and rider vanished, strained abruptly and violently upward: a long, swirling roar incredible and soundless, blotting the stars, and he springing up and into the road again, running again, knowing it was too late yet still running even after he heard the shot and, an instant later, two shots, pausing now without knowing he had ceased to run, crying 'Pap! Pap!', running again before he knew he had begun to run, stumbling, tripping over something and scrabbling up again without ceasing to run, looking backward over his shoulder at the glare as he got up, running on among the invisible trees, panting, sobbing, 'Father! Father!'

At midnight he was sitting on the crest of a hill. He did not know it was midnight and he did not know how far he had come. But there was no glare behind him now and he sat now, his back toward what he had called home for four days anyhow, his face toward the dark woods which he would enter when breath was strong again, small, shaking steadily in the chill darkness, hugging himself into the remainder of his thin, rotten shirt, the grief and despair now no longer terror and fear but just grief and despair. *Father. My father*, he thought. 'He was brave!' he cried suddenly, aloud but not loud, no more than a whisper: 'He was! He was in the war! He was in Colonel Sartoris' cav'ry!' not knowing that his father had gone to that war a private in the fine old European sense, wearing no uniform, admitting the authority of and giving fidelity to no man or army or flag, going to war as Malbrouck[12] himself did: for booty – it meant nothing and less than nothing to him if it were enemy booty or his own.

The slow constellations wheeled on. It would be dawn and then sun-up after a while and he would be hungry. But that would be to-morrow and now he was only cold, and walking would cure that. His breathing was easier now and he decided to get up and go on, and then he found that he had been asleep because he knew it was almost dawn, the night almost over. He could tell that from the whippoorwills. They were everywhere now among the dark trees below him, constant and inflectioned and ceaseless, so that, as the instant for giving over to the day birds drew nearer and nearer, there was no interval at all between them. He got up. He was a little stiff, but walking would cure that too as it would the cold, and soon there would be the sun. He went on down the hill, toward the dark woods within which the liquid silver voices of the birds called unceasing – the rapid and urgent beating of the urgent and quiring[13] heart of the late spring night. He did not look back.

The Lost Decade

F. SCOTT FITZGERALD

All sorts of people came into the offices of the news-weekly and Orrison Brown had all sorts of relations with them. Outside of office hours he was 'one of the editors' – during work time he was simply a curly-haired man who a year before had edited the Dartmouth 'Jack-o-Lantern'[1] and was now only too glad to take the undesirable assignments around the office, from straightening out illegible copy to playing call-boy without the title.

He had seen this visitor go into the editor's office – a pale, tall man of forty with blond statuesque hair and a manner that was neither shy, nor timid, nor otherworldly like a monk, but something of all three. The name on his card, Louis Trimble, evoked some vague memory, but having nothing to start on Orrison did not puzzle over it – until a buzzer sounded on his desk, and previous experience warned him that Mr Trimble was to be his first course at lunch.

'Mr Trimble – Mr Brown,' said the Source of all luncheon money. 'Orrison – Mr Trimble's been away a long time. Or he *feels* it's a long time – almost twelve years. Some people would consider themselves lucky to've missed the last decade.'

'That's so,' said Orrison.

'I can't lunch today,' continued his chief. 'Take him to Voisins or "21"[2] or anywhere he'd like. Mr Trimble feels there're lots of things he hasn't seen.'

Trimble demurred politely.

'Oh, I can get around.'

'I know it, old boy. Nobody knew this place like you did once – and if Brown tries to explain the horseless carriage just send him back here to me. And you'll be back yourself by four, won't you?'

Orrison got his hat.

'You've been away ten years?' he asked while they went down in the elevator.

'They'd begun the Empire State Building,' said Trimble. 'What does that add up to?'

'About 1928. But as the chief said, you've been lucky to miss a lot.' As a feeler he added, 'Probably had more interesting things to look at.'

'Can't say I have.'

They reached the street, and the way Trimble's face tightened at the roar of traffic made Orrison take one more guess.

'You've been out of civilization?'

'In a sense.' The words were spoken in such a measured way that Orrison concluded this man wouldn't talk unless he wanted to – and simultaneously wondered if he could have possibly spent the thirties in a prison or an insane asylum.

'This is the famous "21,"' he said. 'Do you think you'd rather eat somewhere else?'

Trimble paused, looking carefully at the brownstone house.

'I can remember when the name "21" got to be famous,' he said, 'about the same year as Moriarty's.'[3] Then he continued almost apologetically, 'I thought we might walk up Fifth Avenue about five minutes and eat wherever we happened to be. Some place with young people to look at.'

Orrison gave him a quick glance and once again thought of bars and grey walls and bars; he wondered if his duties included introducing Mr Trimble to complaisant girls. But Mr Trimble didn't look as if that was in his mind – the dominant expression was of absolute and deepseated curiosity, and Orrison attempted to connect the name with Admiral Byrd's hideout at the South Pole[4] or flyers lost in Brazilian jungles. He was, or he had been, quite a fellow – that was obvious. But the only definite clue to his environment – and to Orrison the clue that led nowhere – was his countryman's obedience to the traffic lights and his predilection for walking on the side next to the shops and not the street. Once he stopped and gazed into a haberdasher's window.

'Crêpe ties,' he said. 'I haven't seen one since I left college.'

'Where'd you go?'

'Massachusetts Tech.'

'Great place.'

'I'm going to take a look at it next week. Let's eat somewhere along here –' They were in the upper Fifties. '– you choose.'

There was a good restaurant with a little awning just around the corner.

'What do you want to see most?' Orrison asked, as they sat down.

Trimble considered.

'Well – the back of people's heads,' he suggested. 'Their necks – how their heads are joined to their bodies. I'd like to hear what those two little girls are saying to their father. Not exactly what they're saying but whether the words float or submerge, how their mouths shut when they've finished speaking. Just a matter of rhythm – Cole Porter[5] came back to the States in 1928 because he felt that there were new rhythms around.'

Orrison was sure he had his clue now, and with nice delicacy did not pursue it by a millimeter – even suppressing a sudden desire to say there was a fine concert in Carnegie Hall tonight.

'The weight of spoons,' said Trimble, 'so light. A little bowl with a stick attached. The cast in that waiter's eye. I knew him once but he wouldn't remember me.'

But as they left the restaurant the same waiter looked at Trimble rather puzzled as if he almost knew him. When they were outside Orrison laughed:

'After ten years people will forget.'

'Oh, I had dinner there last May—' He broke off in an abrupt manner.

It was all kind of nutsy, Orrison decided – and changed himself suddenly into a guide.

'From here you get a good candid focus on Rockefeller Center,' he pointed out with spirit ' – and the Chrysler Building and the Armistead Building, the daddy of all the new ones.'

'The Armistead Building.' Trimble rubber-necked obediently. 'Yes – I designed it.'

Orrison shook his head cheerfully – he was used to going out with all kinds of people. But that stuff about having been in the restaurant last May . . .

He paused by the brass entablature in the cornerstone of the building. 'Erected 1928,' it said.

Trimble nodded.

'But I was taken drunk that year – every-which-way drunk. So I never saw it before now.'

'Oh.' Orrison hesitated. 'Like to go in now?'

'I've been in it – lots of times. But I've never seen it. And now it isn't what I want to see. I wouldn't ever be able to see it now. I simply want to see how people walk and what their clothes and shoes and hats are made of. And their eyes and hands. Would you mind shaking hands with me?'

'Not at all, sir.'

'Thanks. Thanks. That's very kind. I suppose it looks strange – but people will think we're saying good-bye. I'm going to walk up the avenue for awhile, so we *will* say good-bye. Tell your office I'll be in at four.'

Orrison looked after him when he started out, half expecting him to turn into a bar. But there was nothing about him that suggested or ever had suggested drink.

'Jesus,' he said to himself. 'Drunk for ten years.'

He felt suddenly of the texture of his own coat and then he reached out and pressed his thumb against the granite of the building by his side.

Now You Cookin' with Gas

ZORA NEALE HURSTON

Wait till I light up my coal-pot, and I'll tell you about this Ziga-boo called Jelly.

Well, all right now. He was a seal-skin brown and papa-tree-top-tall. Skinny in the hips and solid built for speed. He was born with this rough-dried hair, but when he laid on the grease and pressed it down over night with his stocking-cap, it looked just like that righteous moss, and had so many waves till you got seasick from looking. Solid, man, solid!

His mama named him Marvel, but after a month on Lennox Avenue, he changed all that to Jelly. How come? Well, he put it in the street that when it came to filling that long-felt need, sugar-curing the ladies' feelings, pimping, sweet-backing, he was in a class by himself and nobody knew his name, so he had to tell 'em. 'It must be Jelly, 'cause jam dont shake.' Therefore, his name was Jelly. He was a Scooter-pooker[1] from way back. That was what was on his sign. The stuff was there, and it was mellow. Whenever he was challenged by a hard-head or a frail eel[2] on the right of his title, he would eye-ball the idol-breaker with a slice of ice, and put on his ugly-laugh, made up out of scorn and pity and say, 'Youse just dumb to the fact, baby. If you dont know what you talking 'bout, you better ask Granny Grunt. I wouldnt mislead you, baby. I don't need to, – not with the help I got.' Then he would give the pimps' sign, and perco-late on down the avenue. You can't go behind a fact like that.

So this day he was airing out on the Avenue. It had to be late afternoon, or he would not have been out of bed. All you did by rolling out early was to stir your stomach up. That made you hunt for more dishes to dirty. The longer you slept, the less you had to eat. But you cant collar nods all day. No matter how long you stayed in bed, and how quiet you kept, sooner or later that big gut is going to reach over and grab that little one and start to gnaw. Thats confidential right from the Bible. You got to get out on the beat and collar yourself a hot.

So Jelly got into his zoot suit with the reet pleats³ and got out to skivver around and do himself some good. At 132nd Street, he spied one of his colleagues across the street, standing in front of a cafe. Jelly figured that if he bull-skated just right, he might confidence Sweet-Back out of a thousand on a plate. Maybe a shot of scrap-iron or a reefer. Therefore, Jelly took a quick backwards look at his shoesoles to see how his leather was holding out. The way he figured it after the peep was that he had plenty to get across and maybe do a little more cruising besides. So he stanched out into the street and made the crossing.

'Hi there, Sweet Back!' he exploded cheerfully, 'Gimme some skin!'

'Lay de skin on me, pal!' Sweet Back grabbed Jelly's outstretched hand and shook hard. 'Aint seen you since the last time, Jelly. Whats cookin'?'

'Oh, just like de bear – I aint nowhere. Like de bear's brother, – I aint no further. Like de bear's daughter – aint got a quarter.'

Right away, he wished he had not been so honest. Sweet Back gave him a top-superior cut-eye look. Looked at Jelly just like a showman looks at an ape. Just as far above Jelly as fried chicken is over branch water.

'Cold in hand, hunh?' He talked down to Jelly. 'A red hot pimp like you say you is, aint got no business in the barrel. Last night when I left you, you was beating up your gums and broadcasting about how hot you was. Just as hot as July-jam, you told me. What you doing cold in hand?'

'Aw, man, cant you take a joke? I was just beating up my gums when I said I was broke. How can I be broke when I got de best woman in Harlem? If I ask her for a dime, she'll give me a ten dollar bill; ask her for a drink of likker, and she'll buy me a whiskey still. If I'm lying, I'm flying!'

'Gar, dont hang out dat dirty washing in my back yard! Didnt

I see you last night with dat beat chick scoffing a hot dog? Dat chick you had was bet to de heels. Boy, you aint no good for what you live.'

'If you aint lying now, you flying. You aint got de first thin. You aint got nickel one.'

Jelly threw back the long skirt of his coat and rammed his hand down into his pants pocket.

'Put your money where your mouth is!' he challenged as he mock-struggled to haul out a huge roll. 'Back your crap with your money. I bet you five dollars!'

Sweet Back made the same gesture of hauling out non-existent money.

'I been raised in the church. I dont bet, but I'll doubt you. Five rocks!'

'I thought so!' Jelly crowed and hurriedly pulled his empty hand out of his pocket. 'I knowed you'd back up when I drawed my roll on you.'

'You ain't drawed no roll on me, Jelly. You aint drawed nothing but your pocket. You better stop dat boogerbooing. Next time I'm liable to make you do it.' There was a splinter of regret in his voice. If Jelly really had had some money, he might have staked him, Sweet Back to a hot. Good southern corn-bread with a piano[4] on a platter. Oh, well! The right browd would, or might come along.

'Who boogerbooing?' Jelly snorted. 'Jig, I dont have to. Talking about *me* with a beat chick scoffing a hot dog! Heh, heh! You must of not seen me, 'cause last night I was riding round in a Yellow Cab, with a yellow gal, drinking yellow likker and spending yellow money. Humph! Tell 'em 'bout me!'

'Git out of my face with that crap, Jelly! Dat broad I seen you with wasnt no pe-ola.[5] She was one of them coal-scuttle blondes with hair just as close to her head as ninety-nine is to a hundred. She look-ted like she had seventy-five pounds of clear bosom, guts in her feet, and she look-ted like six months in front and nine months behind. Buy you a whiskey still! Humph! Dat broad couldnt make the down payment on a pair of sox.'

'Sweet Back, you fixing to talk out of place.' Jelly stiffened.

'If you trying to jump salt, Jelly, thats your mammy.'

'Dont play in de family, Sweet Back. I dont play de dozens.[6] I done told you.'

'Who playing de dozens? You trying to get your hips up on your shoulders cause I said you was with a beat broad. One of them lam blacks.'[7]

'Who? Me? Long as you been knowing me, Sweet Back, you aint never seen me with nothing but pe-olas. I can get any frail eel I wants to. I can lay it! How come I'm up here in New York? You dont know, do you? Since youse dumb to the fact, I reckon I'll have to make you hep. I had to leave from down south cause Miss Anne used to worry me so bad to go with me. Who, Me? Man, I don't deal in no coal. Know what I tell 'em? If they's white, they's right! If they's yellow, they's mellow! If they's brown, they can stick around. But if they come black, they better git way back! Tell 'em bout me!'

'Aw, man, you trying to show your grandma how to milk ducks. Best you can do is to confidence some kitchen-mechanic out of a dime or two. Me, I knocks de pad with them cack-broads up on Sugar Hill,[8] and fills 'em full of melody. Man, I'm quick death and easy judgment. Youse just a home-boy, Jelly. Dont try to follow me.'

'Me follow *you*! Man, I come on like the Gang-Busters, and go off the MARCH OF TIME![9] If dat aint so, God is gone to Jersey City, and you know He wouldnt be messing round a place like that. Know what my woman done? We hauled off and went to church last Sunday, and when they passed round the plate for the *penny* collection, I throwed in a dollar. De man looked at me real hard for dat. Dat made my woman mad, so she called him back and throwed in a twenty dollar bill! Told him to take dat and go! Dats what he got for looking at me cause I throwed in a dollar.'

'Jelly, de wind may blow and de door may slam; dat what you shooting aint worth a damn!'

Jelly slammed his hand in his bosom as if to draw a gun. Sweet Back did the same.

'If you wants to fight, Sweet Back, the favor is in me.'

'I was deep-thinking then, Jelly. Its a good thing I aint short-tempered. Taint nothing to you. You aint hit me yet.'

'Oh, I flies hot quick' Jelly said. 'But I'm mighty easy cooled if de man I'm salty with is bigger than me.'

Both burst into a hearty laugh and changed from fighting to lounging poses.

'Dont get too yaller on me, Jelly. You liable to get hurt some day.'

'You over-sports your hand your ownself. I just dont pay you no mind. I know taint nothing to de bear but his curly hair. Lay de skin on me!'

They broke their hand-shake hurriedly because both of them looked up the Avenue and saw the same thing. It was a girl, and they both remembered that it was Wednesday afternoon. All of the domestics off for the afternoon with their pay in their pockets. Some of them bound to be hungry for love. That meant a dinner, a shot of scrap-iron, maybe room-rent and a reefer or two. Well, it did happen sometimes, so that gave vapor to hope that some women would buy them forty zoot suits, a Packard, and plenty of money to flash. This one looked prosperous. Both of the Scooter-Pookers hoped that the other one had other fish to fry, but neither retired. Both went into the pose, set lapels and put on the look.

'Big stars falling!' Jelly said out loud when she was in hearing distance. 'It must be just before day!' He put all the awe and admiration he could in his voice.

'Yeah Man!' Sweet Back agreed. 'Must be a recess in Heaven – pretty angel like that out on the ground.'

The girl drew abreast of them, long ear-rings swinging, reeling and rocking in her hips.

'I'd walk clear to Diddy-Wah-Diddy to get a chance to speak to a pretty lil' ground-angel like that.' Jelly went on.

'Aw, man, you aint willing to go very far. Me, I'd go slap to Ginny-Gall,[10] where they eat cow-rump, skin and all.'

The girl smiled, so Jelly set his hat like it was hanging on one louse-leg and just too mean to fall off, and took the plunge.

'Baby,' he crooned, 'Whats on de rail for de lizard?'

The girl halted and braced her hips with her hands. 'A Zigaboo down in Georgy where I come from asked a woman that one time, and the judge told him "ninety days".'

'Georgy!' Sweet Back pretended to be elated. 'Where 'bouts in Georgy is you from? Delaware?'

'Delaware?' Jelly snorted. 'My people! My people!! Free schools and dumb jigs![11] Man, how you going to put Delaware in Georgy? You ought to know dats in Maryland. Hah! Hah! Hah!'

'I never heard nothing about no Delaware – not in the part of Georgy I come from.'

'We dont care nothing bout no Delaware. Lets me and you go back down there in Georgy and settle down.' Sweet Back cooed.

'Go down in Georgy!' Jelly snorted. 'You crazy in the head? Christ walked de water to go *around* Georgy. What you want to go in it for?'

'Oh dont try to make out youse no northerner, you! Youse from right down in Bam your ownself!' The girl turned on Jelly.

'Yeah, I'm *from* there, and I aims to stay from there.'

'One of them Russians, eh?' The girl retorted. 'Rushed up here to get away from a job of work.'

'De work didnt worry me. Mister Charlie down there plays too rough to suit me. I aint none of them cowards like them shines down in Bam. I'm *mean!* I got Indian blood in *me.*[12] Them pecker-woods[13] down there liable to make me hurt some of 'em. So I just come on off to keep from killing somebody.'

'I know its de truth!' The girl snorted and laughed.

But that kind of talk was not leading towards the dinner table.

'But Baby!' Jelly gasped. 'Dat shape you got on you!' He dragged his eyes from her head to her feet. 'I bet the CocaCola Company is paying you good money for the patent!'

Their girl smiled with pleasure at this, so Sweet Back jumped in.

'I know youse somebody swell to know. Youse real people. You grins like a regular fellow.' He gave her his most killing look and let it simmer in. 'These dickty jigs round here tries to smile. Spose you and me go inside the cafe here and grab a hot?'

'You got any money?' The girl asked and stiffened like a ramrod. 'Nobody aint pimping on me. You dig me?'

'Aw, now, Baby!'

'I seen you two mullet-heads before. I was uptown when Joe
Brown had you all in the go-long last night. Ha! Ha! Dat cop
sure hates a pimp! All he needs to see is the pimps' salute, and
he will out with his night-stick and whip your head to the red.
Beat your head just as flat as a dime!' She went off into a great
blow of laughter.

'Aw, I wasnt scared of him.' Sweet Back tried to be casual. 'I
just know de fool is crazy. De way he carries on. You would
think I been fooling with some of his wives. He never hit *me*.
He just hit where I was.'

'You all really did turn on the fan!' The gile kept on laughing, and both of the men jumped salty. But nothing they said
showed it.

'Oh, seeing that he is one of my color, I let him go and call
him lucky.' Sweet Back went on. 'A cracker cop down in Georgy
got in my face one time and I shot him lightly and he died
politely.'[14]

'I know its de truth!' The girl smiled salty like. 'I bet you come
away from there so fast till your hip pockets was dipping sand.'

'Oh, lets us dont talk about the law. Lets talk about us.' Sweet
Back persisted. 'You going inside with me to holler "let one
come flopping! One come grunting! Snatch one from de rear!"'

'Naw indeed!' The girl laughed harshly. 'You skillets is trying to promote a meal on me. But it will never happen, brother.
You barking up the wrong tree. I wouldn't give you air if you
was stopped up in a jug. I'm not putting out a thing. I'm just
like the cemetery – I'm not putting out, I'm taking in!' She
reared back and regarded the two with scorn. 'Dig?'

'I'll tell you like the farmer told the potato – plant you now
and dig you later.'

The girl made a movement to switch on off. Sweet Back had
not dirtied a plate since the day before. He made a weak but
significant gesture.

'Trying to snatch my pocket-book,[15] eh?' She blazed. Instead
of running, she grabbed hold of Sweet Back's draping coat-tail
and made a slashing gesture. 'How much split you want back
here? If your feets dont hurry up and take you way from here
you'll *ride* away. I'll spread my lungs all over New York and

call the law. Go ahead, Bedbug! Touch me and I'll holler like a
pretty white woman!'

The boys were ready to flee, but she turned suddenly and
rocked on off with her ear-rings snapping and her heels popping.

'My people! My people!!' Sweet Back sighed when he was
calm enough to speak.

'I know you feel chewed,' Jelly said in an effort to make it
appear that he had had no part in the fiasco.

'Oh, let her go.' Sweet Back said magnanimously. 'When I
see people without the periodical principles they's supposed to
have, I just dont fool with 'em. What I want to steal her old
pocket-book with all the money I got? I could buy a beat chick
like her and give her away. I got money's mammy and Grandma's change. One of my women, and not the best one I got
neither, is buying me ten shag suits at one time. All I got to do
is to go round to the tailor shop and try 'em on.'

He glanced sidewise at Jelly to see if he was convincing. But
Jelly's thoughts were far away. He was remembering those full,
hot meals he had left back in Alabama to seek wealth and
splendor in Harlem without working. He had even forgotten
to look cocky and rich. He was thinking corroding thoughts
about the white folks in this man's town – so cold and finicky
about jobs. So mean about folks being on time and things had
to be done just so. They would call you 'Mister' all right, just
like he had been told that they would. But they kept their old
clothes and wore them themselves. You better not never ask
them about a loan before pay-day. Then too, these Harlem
landladies! They didnt want a thing out of you but your rent.
One thing had been over-rated. These lady-people wasnt as
lonesome for love as somebody had told him. His hunger
brought him back to the present. He decided he had better
mooch on around to a certain hair-dressing parlor. The woman
who ran it usually gave him a dime or two if he ran errands for
her, which was more work than he wanted to do, but which he
did when the hunting was poor.

'Well, I better get on down town and see if them folks at de
car place got my Packard ready for me. My woman just would

buy it. Told her I didnt want to be bothered with no car.' Jelly said this casually as if it bored him to death.

'Same here,' Sweet Back came back snappily. 'Okay, Jelly. See you in the funny papers.[16] If I dont see you no more in this world, I'll meet you in Africa.'

'Abyssinia,'[17] Jelly said. 'Dont get into no more scrapes like you done just now.'

'Oh, well, Jelly, if you dont bite, you dont taste.'

Both of them stiffened their arms at their sides, pointed their first fingers rigidly at the ground in the pimps' salute and went their separate ways.

The First Seven Years[1]

BERNARD MALAMUD

Feld, the shoemaker, was annoyed that his helper, Sobel, was so insensitive to his reverie that he wouldn't for a minute cease his fanatic pounding at the other bench. He gave him a look, but Sobel's bald head was bent over the last as he worked, and he didn't notice. The shoemaker shrugged and continued to peer through the partly frosted window at the nearsighted haze of falling February snow. Neither the shifting white blur outside nor the sudden deep remembrance of the snowy Polish village where he had wasted his youth could turn his thoughts from Max the college boy (a constant visitor in the mind since early that morning when Feld saw him trudging through the snow-drifts on his way to school), whom he so much respected because of the sacrifices he had made throughout the years – in winter or direst heat – to further his education. An old wish returned to haunt the shoemaker: that he had had a son instead of a daughter, but this blew away in the snow, for Feld, if anything, was a practical man. Yet he could not help but contrast the diligence of the boy, who was a peddler's son, with Miriam's unconcern for an education. True, she was always with a book in her hand, yet when the opportunity arose for a college education, she had said no, she would rather find a job. He had begged her to go, pointing out how many fathers could not afford to send their children to college, but she said she wanted to be independent. As for education, what was it, she asked, but books, which Sobel, who diligently read the classics, would as usual advise her on. Her answer greatly grieved her father.

A figure emerged from the snow and the door opened. At the counter the man withdrew from a wet paper bag a pair of battered shoes for repair. Who he was the shoemaker for a moment had no idea, then his heart trembled as he realized, before he had thoroughly discerned the face, that Max himself was standing there, embarrassedly explaining what he wanted done to his old shoes. Though Feld listened eagerly, he couldn't hear a word, for the opportunity that had burst upon him was deafening.

He couldn't exactly recall when the thought had occurred to him, because it was clear he had more than once considered suggesting to the boy that he go out with Miriam. But he had not dared speak, for if Max said no, how would he face him again? Or suppose Miriam, who harped so often on independence, blew up in anger and shouted at him for his meddling? Still, the chance was too good to let by: all it meant was an introduction. They might long ago have become friends had they happened to meet somewhere, therefore was it not his duty – an obligation – to bring them together, nothing more, a harmless connivance to replace an accidental encounter in the subway, let's say, or a mutual friend's introduction in the street? Just let him once see and talk to her and he would for sure be interested. As for Miriam, what possible harm for a working girl in an office, who met only loudmouthed salesmen and illiterate shipping clerks, to make the acquaintance of a fine scholarly boy? Maybe he would awaken in her a desire to go to college; if not – the shoemaker's mind at last came to grips with the truth – let her marry an educated man and live a better life.

When Max finished describing what he wanted done to his shoes, Feld marked them, both with enormous holes in the soles which he pretended not to notice, with large white-chalk X's and the rubber heels, thinned to the nails, he marked with O's, though it troubled him he might have mixed up the letters. Max inquired the price, and the shoemaker cleared his throat and asked the boy, above Sobel's insistent hammering, would he please step through the side door there into the hall. Though surprised, Max did as the shoemaker requested, and Feld went in after him. For a minute they were both silent, because Sobel had stopped banging, and it seemed they understood neither was to say anything until the noise began again. When it did, loudly, the shoemaker quickly told Max why he had asked to talk to him.

'Ever since you went to high school,' he said, in the dimly lit hallway, 'I watched you in the morning go to the subway to school, and I said always to myself, this is a fine boy that he wants so much an education.'

'Thanks,' Max said, nervously alert. He was tall and grotesquely thin, with sharply cut features, particularly a beak-like nose. He was wearing a loose, long, slushy overcoat that hung down to his ankles, looking like a rug draped over his bony shoulders, and a soggy old brown hat, as battered as the shoes he had brought in.

'I am a businessman,' the shoemaker abruptly said to conceal his embarrassment, 'so I will explain you right away why I talk to you. I have a girl, my daughter Miriam – she is nineteen – a very nice girl and also so pretty that everybody looks on her when she passes by in the street. She is smart, always with a book, and I thought to myself that a boy like you, an educated boy – I thought maybe you will be interested sometime to meet a girl like this.' He laughed a bit when he had finished and was tempted to say more but had the good sense not to.

Max stared down like a hawk. For an uncomfortable second he was silent, then he asked, 'Did you say nineteen?'

'Yes.'

'Would it be all right to inquire if you have a picture of her?'

'Just a minute.' The shoemaker went into the store and hastily returned with a snapshot that Max held up to the light.

'She's all right,' he said.

Feld waited.

'And is she sensible – not the flighty kind?'

'She is very sensible.'

After another short pause, Max said it was okay with him if he met her.

'Here is my telephone,' said the shoemaker, hurriedly handing him a slip of paper. 'Call her up. She comes home from work six o'clock.'

Max folded the paper and tucked it away into his worn leather wallet.

'About the shoes,' he said. 'How much did you say they will cost me?'

'Don't worry about the price.'

'I just like to have an idea.'

'A dollar – dollar fifty. A dollar fifty,' the shoemaker said.

At once he felt bad, for he usually charged $2.25 for this kind of job. Either he should have asked the regular price or done the work for nothing.

Later, as he entered the store, he was startled by a violent clanging and looked up to see Sobel pounding upon the naked last.[2] It broke, the iron striking the floor and jumping with a thump against the wall, but before the enraged shoemaker could cry out, the assistant had torn his hat and coat off the hook and rushed out into the snow.

So Feld, who had looked forward to anticipating how it would go with his daughter and Max, instead had a great worry on his mind. Without his temperamental helper he was a lost man, especially as it was years now since he had carried the store alone. The shoemaker had for an age suffered from a heart condition that threatened collapse if he dared exert himself. Five years ago, after an attack, it had appeared as though he would have either to sacrifice his business on the auction block and live on a pittance thereafter or put himself at the mercy of some unscrupulous employee who would in the end probably ruin him. But just at the moment of his darkest despair, this Polish refugee, Sobel, had appeared one night out of the street and begged for work. He was a stocky man, poorly dressed, with a bald head that had once been blond, a severely plain face, and soft blue eyes prone to tears over the sad books he read, a young man but old – no one would have guessed thirty. Though he confessed he knew nothing of shoemaking, he said he was apt and would work for very little if Feld taught him the trade. Thinking that with, after all, a landsman,[3] he would have less to fear than from a complete stranger, Feld took him on and within six weeks the refugee rebuilt as good a shoe as he, and not long thereafter expertly ran the business for the thoroughly relieved shoemaker.

Feld could trust him with anything and did, frequently going

home after an hour or two at the store, leaving all the money
in the till, knowing Sobel would guard every cent of it. The
amazing thing was that he demanded so little. His wants were
few; in money he wasn't interested – in nothing but books, it
seemed – which he one by one lent to Miriam, together with
his profuse, queer written comments, manufactured during his
lonely rooming house evenings, thick pads of commentary which
the shoemaker peered at and twitched his shoulders over as his
daughter, from her fourteenth year, read page by sanctified
page, as if the word of God were inscribed on them. To protect
Sobel, Feld himself had to see that he received more than he
asked for. Yet his conscience bothered him for not insisting that
the assistant accept a better wage than he was getting, though
Feld had honestly told him he could earn a handsome salary if
he worked elsewhere, or maybe opened a place of his own. But
the assistant answered, somewhat ungraciously, that he was
not interested in going elsewhere, and though Feld frequently
asked himself, What keeps him here? why does he stay? he
finally answered it that the man, no doubt because of his terrible experiences as a refugee, was afraid of the world.

After the incident with the broken last, angered by Sobel's
behavior, the shoemaker decided to let him stew for a week
in the rooming house, although his own strength was taxed
dangerously and the business suffered. However, after several
sharp nagging warnings from both his wife and daughter, he
went finally in search of Sobel, as he had once before, quite
recently, when over some fancied slight – Feld had merely asked
him not to give Miriam so many books to read because her eyes
were strained and red – the assistant had left the place in a huff,
an incident which, as usual, came to nothing, for he had
returned after the shoemaker had talked to him and taken his
seat at the bench. But this time, after Feld had plodded through
the snow to Sobel's house – he had thought of sending Miriam
but the idea became repugnant to him – the burly landlady at
the door informed him in a nasal voice that Sobel was not at
home, and though Feld knew this was a nasty lie, for where had
the refugee to go? still for some reason he was not completely
sure of – it may have been the cold and his fatigue – he decided

not to insist on seeing him. Instead he went home and hired a new helper.

Thus he settled the matter, though not entirely to his satisfaction, for he had much more to do than before, and so, for example, could no longer lie late in bed mornings because he had to get up to open the store for the new assistant, a speechless, dark man with an irritating rasp as he worked, whom he would not trust with the key as he had Sobel. Furthermore, this one, though able to do a fair repair job, knew nothing of grades of leather or prices, so Feld had to make his own purchases; and every night at closing time it was necessary to count the money in the till and lock up. However, he was not dissatisfied, for he lived much in his thoughts of Max and Miriam. The college boy had called her, and they had arranged a meeting for this coming Friday night. The shoemaker would personally have preferred Saturday, which he felt would make it a date of the first magnitude, but he learned Friday was Miriam's choice, so he said nothing. The day of the week did not matter. What mattered was the aftermath. Would they like each other and want to be friends? He sighed at all the time that would have to go by before he knew for sure. Often he was tempted to talk to Miriam about the boy, to ask whether she thought she would like his type – he had told her only that he considered Max a nice boy and had suggested he call her – but the one time he tried she snapped at him – justly – how should she know?

At last Friday came. Feld was not feeling particularly well so he stayed in bed, and Mrs Feld thought it better to remain in the bedroom with him when Max called. Miriam received the boy, and her parents could hear their voices, his throaty one, as they talked. Just before leaving, Miriam brought Max to the bedroom door and he stood there a minute, a tall, slightly hunched figure wearing a thick, droopy suit, and apparently at ease as he greeted the shoemaker and his wife, which was surely a good sign. And Miriam, although she had worked all day, looked fresh and pretty. She was a large-framed girl with a well-shaped body, and she had a fine open face and soft hair. They made, Feld thought, a first-class couple.

Miriam returned after 11:30. Her mother was already

asleep, but the shoemaker got out of bed and after locating his bathrobe went into the kitchen, where Miriam, to his surprise, sat at the table, reading.

'So where did you go?' Feld asked pleasantly.

'For a walk,' she said, not looking up.

'I advised him,' Feld said, clearing his throat, 'he shouldn't spend so much money.'

'I didn't care.'

The shoemaker boiled up some water for tea and sat down at the table with a cupful and a thick slice of lemon.

'So how,' he sighed after a sip, 'did you enjoy?'

'It was all right.'

He was silent. She must have sensed his disappointment, for she added, 'You can't really tell much the first time.'

'You will see him again?'

Turning a page, she said that Max had asked for another date.

'For when?'

'Saturday.'

'So what did you say?'

'What did I say?' she asked, delaying for a moment – 'I said yes.'

Afterwards she inquired about Sobel, and Feld, without exactly knowing why, said the assistant had got another job. Miriam said nothing more and went on reading. The shoemaker's conscience did not trouble him; he was satisfied with the Saturday date.

During the week, by placing here and there a deft question, he managed to get from Miriam some information about Max. It surprised him to learn that the boy was not studying to be either a doctor or lawyer but was taking a business course leading to a degree in accountancy. Feld was a little disappointed because he thought of accountants as bookkeepers and would have preferred 'a higher profession.' However, it was not long before he had investigated the subject and discovered that Certified Public Accountants were highly respected people, so he was thoroughly content as Saturday approached. But because Saturday was a busy day, he was much in the store and therefore did not see Max when he came to call for Miriam. From his wife he learned there had been nothing especially revealing about their greeting. Max had rung the bell and Miriam had got her coat and left with him – nothing more. Feld did not probe, for his wife was not particularly observant. Instead, he waited up for Miriam with a newspaper on his lap, which he scarcely looked at, so lost was he in thinking of the future. He awoke to find her in the room with him, tiredly removing her hat. Greeting her, he was suddenly inexplicably afraid to ask anything about the evening. But since she volunteered nothing he was at last forced to inquire how she had enjoyed herself. Miriam began something noncommittal, but apparently changed her mind, for she said after a minute, 'I was bored.'

When Feld had sufficiently recovered from his anguished disappointment to ask why, she answered without hesitation, 'Because he's nothing more than a materialist.'

'What means this word?'

'He has no soul. He's only interested in things.'

He considered her statement for a long time, then asked, 'Will you see him again?'

'He didn't ask.'

'Suppose he will ask you?'

'I won't see him.'

He did not argue; however, as the days went by he hoped increasingly she would change her mind. He wished the boy would telephone, because he was sure there was more to him than Miriam, with her inexperienced eye, could discern. But Max didn't call. As a matter of fact he took a different route to school, no longer passing the shoemaker's store, and Feld was deeply hurt.

Then one afternoon Max came in and asked for his shoes. The shoemaker took them down from the shelf where he had placed them, apart from the other pairs. He had done the work himself and the soles and heels were well built and firm. The shoes had been highly polished and somehow looked better than new. Max's Adam's apple went up once when he saw them, and his eyes had little lights in them.

'How much?' he asked, without directly looking at the shoemaker.

'Like I told you before,' Feld answered sadly. 'One dollar fifty cents.'

Max handed him two crumpled bills and received in return a newly minted silver half dollar.

He left. Miriam had not been mentioned. That night the shoemaker discovered that his new assistant had been all the while stealing from him, and he suffered a heart attack.

Though the attack was very mild, he lay in bed for three weeks. Miriam spoke of going for Sobel, but sick as he was Feld rose in wrath against the idea. Yet in his heart he knew there was no other way, and the first weary day back in the shop thoroughly convinced him, so that night after supper he dragged himself to Sobel's rooming house.

He toiled up the stairs, though he knew it was bad for him, and at the top knocked at the door. Sobel opened it and the shoemaker entered. The room was a small, poor one, with a single window facing the street. It contained a narrow cot, a low table, and several stacks of books piled haphazardly around on the floor along the wall, which made him think how queer Sobel was, to be uneducated and read so much. He had once asked him, Sobel, why you read so much? and the assistant could not answer him. Did you ever study in a college someplace? he had asked, but Sobel shook his head. He read, he said, to know. But to know what, the shoemaker demanded, and to know, why? Sobel never explained, which proved he read so much because he was queer.

Feld sat down to recover his breath. The assistant was resting on his bed with his heavy back to the wall. His shirt and trousers were clean, and his stubby fingers, away from the shoemaker's bench, were strangely pallid. His face was thin and pale, as if he had been shut in this room since the day he had bolted from the store.

'So when you will come back to work?' Feld asked him.

To his surprise, Sobel burst out, 'Never.'

Jumping up, he strode over to the window that looked out upon the miserable street. 'Why should I come back?' he cried.

'I will raise your wages.'

'Who cares for your wages!'

The shoemaker, knowing he didn't care, was at a loss what else to say.

'What do you want from me, Sobel?'

'Nothing.'

'I always treated you like you was my son.'

Sobel vehemently denied it. 'So why you look for strange boys in the street they should go out with Miriam? Why you don't think of me?'

The shoemaker's hands and feet turned freezing cold. His voice became so hoarse he couldn't speak. At last he cleared his throat and croaked, 'So what has my daughter got to do with a shoemaker thirty-five years old who works for me?'

'Why do you think I worked so long for you?' Sobel cried out. 'For the stingy wages I sacrificed five years of my life so you could have to eat and drink and where to sleep?'

'Then for what?' shouted the shoemaker.

'For Miriam,' he blurted – 'for her.'

The shoemaker, after a time, managed to say, 'I pay wages in cash, Sobel,' and lapsed into silence. Though he was seething with excitement, his mind was coldly clear, and he had to admit to himself he had sensed all along that Sobel felt this way. He had never so much as thought it consciously, but he had felt it and was afraid.

'Miriam knows?' he muttered hoarsely.

'She knows.'

'You told her?'

'No.'

'Then how does she know?'

'How does she know?' Sobel said. 'Because she knows. She knows who I am and what is in my heart.'

Feld had a sudden insight. In some devious way, with his books and commentary, Sobel had given Miriam to understand that he loved her. The shoemaker felt a terrible anger at him for his deceit.

'Sobel, you are crazy,' he said bitterly. 'She will never marry a man so old and ugly like you.'

Sobel turned black with rage. He cursed the shoemaker, but

then, though he trembled to hold it in, his eyes filled with tears and he broke into deep sobs. With his back to Feld, he stood at the window, fists clenched, and his shoulders shook with his choked sobbing.

Watching him, the shoemaker's anger diminished. His teeth were on edge with pity for the man, and his eyes grew moist. How strange and sad that a refugee, a grown man, bald and old with his miseries, who had by the skin of his teeth escaped Hitler's incinerators, should fall in love, when he had got to America, with a girl less than half his age. Day after day, for five years he had sat at his bench, cutting and hammering away, waiting for the girl to become a woman, unable to ease his heart with speech, knowing no protest but desperation.

'Ugly I didn't mean,' he said half aloud.

Then he realized that what he had called ugly was not Sobel but Miriam's life if she married him. He felt for his daughter a strange and gripping sorrow, as if she were already Sobel's bride, the wife, after all, of a shoemaker, and had in her life no more than her mother had had. And all his dreams for her – why he had slaved and destroyed his heart with anxiety and labor – all these dreams of a better life were dead.

The room was quiet. Sobel was standing by the window reading, and it was curious that when he read he looked young.

'She is only nineteen,' Feld said brokenly. 'This is too young yet to get married. Don't ask her for two years more, till she is twenty-one, then you can talk to her.'

Sobel didn't answer. Feld rose and left. He went slowly down the stairs but once outside, though it was an icy night and the crisp falling snow whitened the street, he walked with a stronger stride.

But the next morning, when the shoemaker arrived, heavy-hearted, to open the store, he saw he needn't have come, for his assistant was already seated at the last, pounding leather for his love.

A Late Encounter with the Enemy

FLANNERY O'CONNOR

General Sash was a hundred and four years old. He lived with his granddaughter, Sally Poker Sash, who was sixty-two years old and who prayed every night on her knees that he would live until her graduation from college. The General didn't give two slaps for her graduation but he never doubted he would live for it. Living had got to be such a habit with him that he couldn't conceive of any other condition. A graduation exercise was not exactly his idea of a good time, even if, as she said, he would be expected to sit on the stage in his uniform. She said there would be a long procession of teachers and students in their robes but that there wouldn't be anything to equal *him* in his uniform. He knew this well enough without her telling him, and as for the damn procession, it could march to hell and back and not cause him a quiver. He liked parades with floats full of Miss Americas and Miss Daytona Beaches and Miss Queen Cotton Products. He didn't have any use for processions and a procession full of schoolteachers was about as deadly as the River Styx[1] to his way of thinking. However, he was willing to sit on the stage in his uniform so that they could see him.

Sally Poker was not as sure as he was that he would live until her graduation. There had not been any perceptible change in him for the last five years, but she had the sense that she might be cheated out of her triumph because she so often was. She had been going to summer school every year for the past twenty because when she started teaching, there were no such things as degrees. In those times, she said, everything was normal but nothing had been normal since she was sixteen, and for the past twenty summers, when she should have been resting, she

had had to take a trunk in the burning heat to the state teacher's college; and though when she returned in the fall, she
always taught in the exact way she had been taught not to
teach, this was a mild revenge that didn't satisfy her sense of
justice. She wanted the General at her graduation because she
wanted to show what she stood for, or, as she said, 'what all
was behind her,' and was not behind them. This *them* was not
anybody in particular. It was just all the upstarts who had
turned the world on its head and unsettled the ways of decent
living.

She meant to stand on that platform in August with the General sitting in his wheel chair on the stage behind her and she
meant to hold her head very high as if she were saying, 'See
him! See him! My kin, all you upstarts! Glorious upright old
man standing for the old traditions! Dignity! Honor! Courage!
See him!' One night in her sleep she screamed, 'See him! See
him!' and turned her head and found him sitting in his wheel
chair behind her with a terrible expression on his face and with
all his clothes off except the general's hat and she had waked
up and had not dared to go back to sleep again that night.

For his part, the General would not have consented even to
attend her graduation if she had not promised to see to it that
he sit on the stage. He liked to sit on any stage. He considered
that he was still a very handsome man. When he had been able
to stand up, he had measured five feet four inches of pure game
cock. He had white hair that reached to his shoulders behind
and he would not wear teeth because he thought his profile was
more striking without them. When he put on his full-dress general's uniform, he knew well enough that there was nothing to
match him anywhere.

This was not the same uniform he had worn in the War
between the States.[2] He had not actually been a general in that
war. He had probably been a foot soldier; he didn't remember
what he had been; in fact, he didn't remember that war at all.
It was like his feet, which hung down now shriveled at the very
end of him, without feeling, covered with a blue-gray[3] afghan
that Sally Poker had crocheted when she was a little girl. He
didn't remember the Spanish-American War[4] in which he had

lost a son; he didn't even remember the son. He didn't have any use for history because he never expected to meet it again. To his mind, history was connected with processions and life with parades and he liked parades. People were always asking him if he remembered this or that – a dreary black procession of questions about the past. There was only one event in the past that had any significance for him and that he cared to talk about: that was twelve years ago when he had received the general's uniform and had been in the premiere.

'I was in that preemy they had in Atlanta,'[5] he would tell visitors sitting on his front porch. 'Surrounded by beautiful guls. It wasn't a thing local about it. It was nothing local about it. Listen here. It was a nashnul event and they had me in it – up onto the stage. There was no bob-tails at it. Every person at it had paid ten dollars to get in and had to wear his tuxseeder. I was in this uniform. A beautiful gul presented me with it that afternoon in a hotel room.'

'It was in a suite in the hotel and I was in it too, Papa,' Sally Poker would say, winking at the visitors. 'You weren't alone with any young lady in a hotel room.'

'Was, I'd a known what to do,' the old General would say with a sharp look and the visitors would scream with laughter. 'This was a Hollywood, California, gul,' he'd continue. 'She was from Hollywood, California, and didn't have any part in the pitcher. Out there they have so many beautiful guls that they don't need that they call them a extra and they don't use them for nothing but presenting people with things and having their pitchers taken. They took my pitcher with her. No, it was two of them. One on either side and me in the middle with my arms around each of them's waist and their waist ain't any bigger than a half a dollar.'

Sally Poker would interrupt again. 'It was Mr Govisky that gave you the uniform, Papa, and he gave me the most exquisite corsage. Really, I wish you could have seen it. It was made with gladiola petals taken off and painted gold and put back together to look like a rose. It was exquisite. I wish you could have seen it, it was . . .'

'It was as big as her head,' the General would snarl. 'I was tellin it. They gimme this uniform and they gimme this soward and they say, "Now General, we don't want you to start a war on us. All we want you to do is march right up on that stage when you're innerduced tonight and answer a few questions. Think you can do that?" "Think I can do it!" I say. "Listen here. I was doing things before you were born," and they hollered.'

'He was the hit of the show,' Sally Poker would say, but she didn't much like to remember the premiere on account of what had happened to her feet at it. She had bought a new dress for the occasion – a long black crepe dinner dress with a rhinestone buckle and a bolero – and a pair of silver slippers to wear with it, because she was supposed to go up on the stage with him to keep him from falling. Everything was arranged for them. A real limousine came at ten minutes to eight and took them to the theater. It drew up under the marquee at exactly the right time, after the big stars and the director and the author and the governor and the mayor and some less important stars. The police kept traffic from jamming and there were ropes to keep the people off who couldn't go. All the people who couldn't go watched them step out of the limousine into the lights. Then they walked down the red and gold foyer and an usherette in a Confederate cap and little short skirt conducted them to their special seats. The audience was already there and a group of UDC members[6] began to clap when they saw the General in his uniform and that started everybody to clap. A few more celebrities came after them and then the doors closed and the lights went down.

A young man with blond wavy hair who said he represented the motion-picture industry came out and began to introduce everybody and each one who was introduced walked up on the stage and said how really happy he was to be here for this great event. The General and his granddaughter were introduced sixteenth on the program. He was introduced as General Tennessee Flintrock Sash of the Confederacy, though Sally Poker had told Mr Govisky that his name was George Poker Sash and that he had only been a major. She helped him up from his seat but her heart was beating so fast she didn't know whether she'd make it herself.

The old man walked up the aisle slowly with his fierce white head high and his hat held over his heart. The orchestra began to play the Confederate Battle Hymn[7] very softly and the UDC members rose as a group and did not sit down again until the General was on the stage. When he reached the center of the stage with Sally Poker just behind him guiding his elbow, the orchestra burst out in a loud rendition of the Battle Hymn and the old man, with real stage presence, gave a vigorous trembling salute and stood at attention until the last blast had died away. Two of the usherettes in Confederate caps and short skirts held a Confederate and a Union flag crossed behind them.

The General stood in the exact center of the spotlight and it caught a weird moon-shaped slice of Sally Poker – the corsage, the rhinestone buckle and one hand clenched around a white glove and handkerchief. The young man with the blond wavy hair inserted himself into the circle of light and said he was *really* happy to have here tonight for this great event one, he said, who had fought and bled in the battles they would soon see daringly re-acted on the screen, and 'Tell me, General,' he asked, 'how old are you?'

'Niiiiiinnttty-two!' the General screamed.

The young man looked as if this were just about the most impressive thing that had been said all evening. 'Ladies and gentlemen,' he said, 'let's give the General the biggest hand we've got!' and there was applause immediately and the young man indicated to Sally Poker with a motion of his thumb that she could take the old man back to his seat now so that the next person could be introduced; but the General had not finished. He stood immovable in the exact center of the spotlight, his neck thrust forward, his mouth slightly open, and his voracious gray eyes drinking in the glare and the applause. He elbowed his granddaughter roughly away. 'How I keep so young,' he screeched, 'I kiss all the pretty guls!'

This was met with a great din of spontaneous applause and it was at just that instant that Sally Poker looked down at her feet and discovered that in the excitement of getting ready she had forgotten to change her shoes: two brown Girl Scout oxfords protruded from the bottom of her dress. She gave the

General a yank and almost ran with him off the stage. He was
very angry that he had not got to say how glad he was to be
here for this event and on the way back to his seat, he kept saying as loud as he could, 'I'm glad to be here at this preemy with
all these beautiful guls!' but there was another celebrity going
up the other aisle and nobody paid any attention to him. He
slept through the picture, muttering fiercely every now and then
in his sleep.

Since then, his life had not been very interesting. His feet
were completely dead now, his knees worked like old hinges,
his kidneys functioned when they would, but his heart persisted
doggedly to beat. The past and the future were the same thing
to him, one forgotten and the other not remembered; he had no
more notion of dying than a cat. Every year on Confederate
Memorial Day,[8] he was bundled up and lent to the Capitol City
Museum where he was displayed from one to four in a musty
room full of old photographs, old uniforms, old artillery, and
historic documents. All these were carefully preserved in glass
cases so that children would not put their hands on them. He
wore his general's uniform from the premiere and sat, with a
fixed scowl, inside a small roped area. There was nothing about
him to indicate that he was alive except an occasional movement in his milky gray eyes, but once when a bold child touched
his sword, his arm shot forward and slapped the hand off in an
instant. In the spring when the old homes were opened for pil-
grimages, he was invited to wear his uniform and sit in some
conspicuous spot and lend atmosphere to the scene. Some of
these times he only snarled at the visitors but sometimes he told
about the premiere and the beautiful girls.

If he had died before Sally Poker's graduation, she thought
she would have died herself. At the beginning of the summer
term, even before she knew if she would pass, she told the Dean
that her grandfather, General Tennessee Flintrock Sash of the
Confederacy, would attend her graduation and that he was a
hundred and four years old and that his mind was still clear as
a bell. Distinguished visitors were always welcome and could
sit on the stage and be introduced. She made arrangements
with her nephew, John Wesley Poker Sash,[9] a Boy Scout, to

come wheel the General's chair. She thought how sweet it would be to see the old man in his courageous gray and the young boy in his clean khaki – the old and the new, she thought appropriately – they would be behind her on the stage when she received her degree.

Everything went almost exactly as she had planned. In the summer while she was away at school, the General stayed with other relatives and they brought him and John Wesley, the Boy Scout, down to the graduation. A reporter came to the hotel where they stayed and took the General's picture with Sally Poker on one side of him and John Wesley on the other. The General, who had had his picture taken with beautiful girls, didn't think much of this. He had forgotten precisely what kind of event this was he was going to attend but he remembered that he was to wear his uniform and carry the sword.

On the morning of the graduation, Sally Poker had to line up in the academic procession with the B.S.'s[10] in Elementary Education and she couldn't see to getting him on the stage herself – but John Wesley, a fat blond boy of ten with an executive expression, guaranteed to take care of everything. She came in her academic gown to the hotel and dressed the old man in his uniform. He was as frail as a dried spider. 'Aren't you just thrilled, Papa?' she asked. 'I'm just thrilled to death!'

'Put the soward acrost my lap, damm you,' the old man said, 'where it'll shine.'

She put it there and then stood back looking at him. 'You look just grand,' she said.

'God damm it,' the old man said in a slow monotonous certain tone as if he were saying it to the beating of his heart. 'God damm every goddam thing to hell.'

'Now, now,' she said and left happily to join the procession.

The graduates were lined up behind the Science building and she found her place just as the line started to move. She had not slept much the night before and when she had, she had dreamed of the exercises, murmuring, 'See him, see him?' in her sleep but waking up every time just before she turned her head to look at him behind her. The graduates had to walk three blocks in the hot sun in their black wool robes and as she plodded

stolidly along she thought that if anyone considered this academic procession something impressive to behold, they need
only wait until they saw that old General in his courageous
gray and that clean young Boy Scout stoutly wheeling his chair
across the stage with the sunlight catching the sword. She imagined that John Wesley had the old man ready now behind the
stage.

The black procession wound its way up the two blocks and
started on the main walk leading to the auditorium. The visitors stood on the grass, picking out their graduates. Men were
pushing back their hats and wiping their foreheads and women
were lifting their dresses slightly from the shoulders to keep
them from sticking to their backs. The graduates in their heavy
robes looked as if the last beads of ignorance were being
sweated out of them. The sun blazed off the fenders of automo-
biles and beat from the columns of the buildings and pulled the
eye from one spot of glare to another. It pulled Sally Poker's
toward the big red Coca-Cola machine that had been set up by
the side of the auditorium. Here she saw the General parked,
scowling and hatless in his chair in the blazing sun while John
Wesley, his blouse loose behind, his hip and cheek pressed to
the red machine, was drinking a Coca-Cola. She broke from
the line and galloped to them and snatched the bottle away. She
shook the boy and thrust in his blouse and put the hat on the
old man's head. 'Now get him in there!' she said, pointing one
rigid finger to the side door of the building.

For his part the General felt as if there were a little hole
beginning to widen in the top of his head. The boy wheeled him
rapidly down a walk and up a ramp and into a building and
bumped him over the stage entrance and into position where he
had been told and the General glared in front of him at heads
that all seemed to flow together and eyes that moved from one
face to another. Several figures in black robes came and picked
up his hand and shook it. A black procession was flowing up
each aisle and forming to stately music in a pool in front of
him. The music seemed to be entering his head through the
little hole and he thought for a second that the procession
would try to enter it too.

He didn't know what procession this was but there was something familiar about it. It must be familiar to him since it had come to meet him, but he didn't like a black procession. Any procession that came to meet him, he thought irritably, ought to have floats with beautiful guls on them like the floats before the preemy. It must be something connected with history like they were always having. He had no use for any of it. What happened then wasn't anything to a man living now and he was living now.

When all the procession had flowed into the black pool, a black figure began orating in front of it. The figure was telling something about history and the General made up his mind he wouldn't listen, but the words kept seeping in through the little hole in his head. He heard his own name mentioned and his chair was shuttled forward roughly and the Boy Scout took a big bow. They called his name and the fat brat bowed. Goddam you, the old man tried to say, get out of my way, I can stand up! – but he was jerked back again before he could get up and take the bow. He supposed the noise they made was for him. If he was over, he didn't intend to listen to any more of it. If it hadn't been for the little hole in the top of his head, none of the words would have got to him. He thought of putting his finger up there into the hole to block them but the hole was a little wider than his finger and it felt as if it were getting deeper.

Another black robe had taken the place of the first one and was talking now and he heard his name mentioned again but they were not talking about him, they were still talking about history. 'If we forget our past,' the speaker was saying, 'we won't remember our future and it will be as well for we won't have one.' The General heard some of these words gradually. He had forgotten history and he didn't intend to remember it again. He had forgotten the name and face of his wife and the names and faces of his children or even if he had a wife and children, and he had forgotten the names of places and the places themselves and what had happened at them.

He was considerably irked by the hole in his head. He had not expected to have a hole in his head at this event. It was the slow black music that had put it there and though most of the

music had stopped outside, there was still a little of it in the
hole, going deeper and moving around in his thoughts, letting
the words he heard into the dark places of his brain. He heard
the words, Chickamauga, Shiloh, Johnston, Lee[11] and he knew
he was inspiring all these words that meant nothing to him. He
wondered if he had been a general at Chickamauga or at Lee.
Then he tried to see himself and the horse mounted in the middle of a float full of beautiful girls, being driven slowly through
downtown Atlanta. Instead, the old words began to stir in his
head as if they were trying to wrench themselves out of place
and come to life.

The speaker was through with that war and had gone on to
the next one and now he was approaching another and all his
words, like the black procession, were vaguely familiar and irritating. There was a long finger of music in the General's head,
probing various spots that were words, letting in a little light
on the words and helping them to live. The words began to
come toward him and he said, Dammit! I ain't going to have it!
and he started edging backwards to get out of the way. Then he
saw the figure in the black robe sit down and there was a noise
and the black pool in front of him began to rumble and to flow
toward him from either side to the black slow music, and he
said, Stop dammit! I can't do but one thing at a time! He couldn't
protect himself from the words and attend to the procession too
and the words were coming at him fast. He felt that he was running backwards and the words were coming at him like musket
fire, just escaping him but getting nearer and nearer. He turned
around and began to run as fast as he could but he found himself running toward the words. He was running into a regular
volley of them and meeting them with quick curses. As the
music swelled toward him, the entire past opened up on him
out of nowhere and he felt his body riddled in a hundred places
with sharp stabs of pain and he fell down, returning a curse for
every hit. He saw his wife's narrow face looking at him critic-
ally through her round gold-rimmed glasses; he saw one of his
squinting bald-headed sons; and his mother ran toward him
with an anxious look; then a succession of places – Chickamauga, Shiloh, Marthasville[12] – rushed at him as if the past

were the only future now and he had to endure it. Then suddenly he saw that the black procession was almost on him. He recognized it, for it had been dogging all his days. He made such a desperate effort to see over it and find out what comes after the past that his hand clenched the sword until the blade touched bone.

The graduates were crossing the stage in a long file to receive their scrolls and shake the president's hand. As Sally Poker, who was near the end, crossed, she glanced at the General and saw him sitting fixed and fierce, his eyes wide open, and she turned her head forward again and held it a perceptible degree higher and received her scroll. Once it was all over and she was out of the auditorium in the sun again, she located her kin and they waited together on a bench in the shade for John Wesley to wheel the old man out. That crafty scout had bumped him out the back way and rolled him at high speed down a flag-stone path and was waiting now, with the corpse, in the long line at the Coca-Cola machine.

Sunday Teasing

JOHN UPDIKE

Sunday morning: waking, he felt long as a galaxy, and just lacked the will to get up, to unfurl the great sleepy length beneath the covers and go be disillusioned in the ministry by some servile, peace-of-mind-peddling preacher. If it wasn't peace of mind, it was the integrated individual, and if it wasn't the integrated individual, it was the power hidden within each one of us. Never a stern old commodity like sin or remorse, never an open-faced superstition. So Arthur decided, without pretending that it was the preferable course as well as the easier, to stay home and read St Paul.[1]

His wife fussed around the apartment with a too-determined silence; whenever he read the Bible, she acted as if he were playing solitaire without having first invited her to play rummy, or as if he were delivering an oblique attack on Jane Austen and Henry Green,[2] whom she mostly read. Trying to bring her into the Sunday-morning club, he said, 'Here's my grandfather's favorite passage: First Corinthians eleven, verse three. "But I would have you know, that the head of every man is Christ; and the head of the woman is the man; and the head of Christ is God." He loved reading that to my mother. It infuriated her.'

A mulish perplexity ruffled Macy's usually smooth features. '*What?* The head? The head of every man. What does "the head" mean exactly? I'm sorry, I just don't understand.'

If he had been able to answer her immediately, he would have done so with a smile, but, though the sense of 'head' in the text was perfectly clear, he couldn't find a synonym. After a silence he said, 'It's so obvious.'

'Read me the passage again. I really didn't hear it.'

'No,' he said.

'Come on, please. "The head of the man is God . . ." '

'No.'

She abruptly turned and went into the kitchen. 'All you do is tease,' she said from in there. 'You think it's so funny.' He hadn't been teasing her at all, but her saying it put the idea into his head.

They were having a friend to the midday meal that Sunday, Leonard Byrne, a Jewish friend who, no matter what the discussion was about, turned it to matters of the heart and body. 'Do you realize,' he said halfway through the salad, a minute after a round of remarks concerning the movie *Camille*³ had unexpectedly died, 'that in our home it was nothing for my father to kiss me? When I'd come home from summer camp, he'd actually em*brace* me – physically embrace me. No inhibitions about it at all. In my home, it was *nothing* for men physically to show affection for one another. I remember my uncle when he came to visit had *no* inhibitions about warmly embracing my father. Now, that's one thing I find repugnant, personally re*pug*nant to me, about the American home. That there is none of that. It's evident that the American male has some innate fear of being mistaken for a homosexual. But *why*, that's the interesting thing, *why* should he be so protective of his virility? Why shouldn't the American father kiss the American son, when it's done in Italy, in Russia, in France?'

'It's the pioneer,' Macy said; she seldom volunteered her opinions, and in this case, Arthur felt, did it only to keep Leonard from running on and on and embarrassing himself. Now she was stuck with the words 'It's the pioneer,' which, to judge from her face, were beginning to seem idiotic to her. 'Those men *had* to be virile,' she gamely continued, 'they were out there alone, with Indians and bears.'

'By the way,' Leonard said, resting his elbow on the very edge of the table and tilting his head toward her, for suaveness, 'do you know, it has been established beyond all doubt that the American pioneer was a drunkard? But that's not the point. Yes, people say, "the pioneer," but I can't quite see how that affects me, as a second-generation American.'

'That's it,' Arthur told him. 'It doesn't. You just said yourself that your family wasn't American. They kissed each other. Now, take me. *I'm* an American. Eleventh-generation German. White, Protestant, Gentile, small-town, middle-class. I am *pure* American. And do you know, I have never seen my father kiss my mother. Never.'

Leonard, of course, was outraged ('That's shocking,' he said. 'That is truly shocking'), but Macy's reaction was what Arthur had angled for. It was hard to separate her perturbation at the announcement from the perturbation caused by her not knowing if he was lying or not. 'That's not true,' she told Leonard, but then asked Arthur, 'Is it?'

'Of course it's true,' he said, talking more to Leonard than to Macy. 'Our family dreaded body contact. Years went by without my touching my mother. When I went to college, she got into the habit of hugging me goodbye, and now does it whenever we go home. But in my teens, when she was younger, there was nothing of the sort.'

'You know, Arthur, that really frightens me,' Leonard said.

'Why? Why should it? It never occurred to my father to manhandle me. He used to carry me when I was little, but when I got too heavy, he stopped. Just like my mother stopped dressing me when I could do it myself.' Arthur decided to push the proposition further, since nothing he had said since 'I have never seen my father kiss my mother' had aroused as much interest. 'After a certain age, the normal American boy is raised by people who just see in him a source of income – moviehouse managers, garage attendants, people in luncheonettes. The man who ran the luncheonette where I ate did nothing but cheat us out of our money and crab about the noise we made, but I loved that man like a father.'

'That's *ter*rible, Arthur,' Leonard said. 'In my family we didn't really trust anybody outside the family. Not that we didn't have friends. We had lots of friends. But it wasn't quite the *same*. Macy, your mother kissed you, didn't she?'

'Oh, yes. All the time. And my father.'

'Ah, but Macy's parents are atheists,' Arthur said.

'They're Unitarians,'[4] she said.

Arthur continued, 'To go back to your *why* this should be so. What do we know about the United States other than the fact that it was settled by pioneers? It is a Protestant country, perhaps the only one. It and Norway. Now, what *is* Protestantism? A vision of attaining God with nothing but the mind. Nothing but the mind alone on a mountaintop.'

'Yes, yes, of course. We know that,' Leonard said, though in truth Arthur had just stated (he now remembered) not a definition of Protestantism but Chesterton's definition of Puritanism.[5]

'In place of the bureaucratic, interceding Church,' Arthur went on, trying to correct himself, flushing because his argument had chased him into the sacred groves of his mind, 'Luther's notion of Christ is substituted. The reason why in Catholic countries everybody kisses each other is that it's a huge family – God is a family of three, the Church is a family of millions, even heretics are kind of black sheep of the family. Whereas the Protestant lives all by himself, inside of himself. *Fide sola.*[6] Man *should* be lonely.'

'Yes, yes,' Leonard said, puzzling Arthur; he had meant the statements to be debatable.

Arthur felt his audience was bored, because they were eating again, picking at the anchovies and croutons. He said, as a punch line, 'I know when we have kids I'm certainly not going to kiss Macy in front of them.'

It was too harsh a thing to say, too bold; he was too excited. Macy said nothing, did not even look up, but her face was tense with an accusatory meekness.

'No, I don't mean that,' Arthur said. 'It's all lies, lies, lies, lies. My family was very close.'

Macy said to Leonard softly, 'Don't you believe it. He's been telling the truth.'

'I know it,' Leonard said. 'I've always felt that about Arthur's home ever since I met him. I really have.'

And though Leonard could console himself with this supposed insight, something uncongenial had been injected into the gathering, and he became sullen; his mood clouded the room, weighed on their temples like smog, and when, hours later, he left, both Arthur and Macy were unwilling to let him go because he had not had a good time. In a guilty spurt of hospitality, they chattered to him of future arrangements. Leonard walked down the stairs with his hat at an angle less jaunty than when he had come up those stairs – a somehow damp angle, as if he had confused his inner drizzle with a state of outer weather.

Suppertime came. Macy said that she didn't feel well and couldn't eat a bite. Arthur put Benny Goodman's 1938 Carnegie Hall concert on the record-player and, rousing his wife from the Sunday *Times*, insisted that she, who had been raised on Scarlatti and Purcell,[7] take notice of Jess Stacy's classic piano solo on 'Sing, Sing, Sing,'[8] which he played twice, for her benefit. He prepared some chicken-with-rice soup for himself, mixing the can with just half a can of water, since it would be for only one person and need not be too much thinned. The soup, heated to a simmer, looked so wholesome that he asked Macy if she really didn't want any. She looked up and thought. 'Just a cupful,' she said, which left him enough to fill a large bowl – plenty, though not a luxurious plenitude.

'Mm. That was so good,' she said after finishing.

'Feel better?'

'Slightly.'

Macy was reading through a collection of short stories, and Arthur brought the rocking chair from the bedroom and joined her by the lamp, with his paperback copy of *The Tragic Sense of Life*.[9] Here again she misunderstood him; he knew that his reading Unamuno depressed her, and he was reading the book not to depress her but to get the book finished and depress her no longer. She knew nothing of the contents except for his remark one time that according to the author the source of religion is our unwillingness to die; yet she was suspicious.

'Why don't you ever read anything except scary philosophy?' she asked him.

'It isn't scary,' he said. 'The man's a Christian, sort of.'

'You should read some fiction.'

'I will, I will, as soon as I finish this.'

Perhaps half an hour passed. 'Oh,' Macy said, dropping her book to the floor. 'That's *so* terrible, it's so *aw*ful.'

He looked at her inquiringly. She was close to tears. 'There's a story in here,' she explained. 'It just makes you sick. I don't want to think about it.'

'See, if you'd read Kierkegaard[10] instead of squalid fiction—'

'No, really. I don't even think it's a good story, it's so awful.'

He read the story himself, and Macy moved into the sling chair facing him. He was conscious of her body as clouds of pale color beyond the edge of the page, like a dawn, stirring with gentle unease. 'Very good,' Arthur said when he was done. 'Quite moving.'

'It's so horrible,' Macy said. 'Why was he so awful to his wife?'

'It's all explained. He was out of his caste. He was trapped. A perfectly nice man, corrupted by bad luck.'

'How can you *say* that? That's so ridiculous.'

'Ridiculous! Why, Macy, the whole pathos of the story lies in the fact that the man, for all his selfishness and cruelty, loves the woman. After all, *he's* telling the story, and if the wife emerges as a sympathetic character, it's because that's the way he sees her. The description of her at the train – here – "As the train glided away she turned toward me her face, calm and so sweet and which, in the instant before it vanished, appeared a radiant white heart."' The story, clumsily translated from the French, was titled 'Un Cœur blanc.' 'And then, later, remembering – "It gladdens me that I was able then to simulate a depth of affection that I did not at that time feel. She too generously repaid me, and in that zealous response was there not her sort of victory?" That's absolutely sympathetic, you see. It's a terrific image – this perceptive man caged in his own weak character.'

To his surprise, Macy had begun to cry. Tears mounted from the lower lids of eyes still looking at him. 'Macy,' he said, kneeling by her chair and touching his forehead to hers. He ardently wished her well at that moment, yet his actions seemed hurried and morbid. 'What is it? Of course I feel sorry for the woman.'

'You said he was a *nice* man.'

'I didn't mean it. I meant that the horror of the story lies in the fact that the man *does* understand, that he does love the woman.'

'It just shows, it shows how *different* we are.'

'No we're not. We're exactly alike. Our noses' – he touched hers, then his – 'are alike as two peas, our mouths like two turnips, our chins like two hamsters.' She laughed sobbingly, but the silliness of his refutation tended to confirm the truth of her remark.

He held her as long as her crying remained strenuous, and when it relented, she moved to the sofa and lay down, saying, 'It's awful when you have an ache and don't know if it's your head or your ear or your tooth.'

He put the palm of his hand on her forehead. He could never tell about fevers. Her skin felt warm, but then human beings were warm things. 'Have you taken your temperature?'

'I don't know where the thermometer is. Broken, probably.' She lay in a forsaken attitude, with one arm, the bluish underside uppermost, extended outward, supported in midair by the limits of its flexure. 'Oog,' she said, sticking out her tongue. 'This room is a mess.' The Bible had never been replaced in the row of books; it lay on its side, spanning four secular volumes. Several glasses, drained after dinner, stood like castle sentries on the windowsill, the mantel, and the lowest shelf of the bookcase. Leonard had left his rubbers[11] under the table. The jacket of the Goodman record lay on the rug, and the Sunday *Times*, that manifold summation of a week's confusion, was oppressively everywhere. Arthur's soup bowl was still on the table; Macy's cup, cockeyed in the saucer, rested by her chair, along with Unamuno and the collection of short stories. 'It's always so awful,' she said. 'Why don't you ever help to keep the room neat?'

'I will, I will. Now you go to bed.' He guided her into the other room and took her temperature. She kept the thermometer in her mouth as she undressed and got into her nightgown. He read her temperature as 98.8°. 'Very, very slight,' he told her. 'I prescribe sleep.'

'I look so pale,' she said in front of the bathroom mirror.

'We never should have discussed *Camille*.' When she was in bed, her face pink against the white pillow and the rest of her covered, he said, 'You and Garbo. Tell me how Garbo says, "You're fooling me."'

'You're fooling me,' she said in a fragile Swedish whisper.

Back in the living room, Arthur returned the books to the shelves, tearing neat strips from the *Times* garden section as bookmarks. He assembled the newspaper and laid it in the kitchen next to the trash can. He stood holding Leonard's rubbers for ten seconds, then dropped them in a corner. He took the record off the phonograph, slipped it into its envelope, and hid it in the closet with the others.

Lastly, he collected the dishes and glasses and washed them. As he stood at the sink, his hands in water which, where the suds thinned and broke, showed a silvery gray, the Sunday's events repeated themselves in his mind, bending like nacreous flakes around a central infrangible irritant,[12] becoming the perfect and luminous thought: *You don't know anything.*

Reunion

JOHN CHEEVER

The last time I saw my father was in Grand Central Station. I was going from my grandmother's in the Adirondacks to a cottage on the Cape that my mother had rented, and I wrote my father that I would be in New York between trains for an hour and a half, and asked if we could have lunch together. His secretary wrote to say that he would meet me at the information booth at noon, and at twelve o'clock sharp I saw him coming through the crowd. He was a stranger to me – my mother divorced him three years ago and I hadn't been with him since – but as soon as I saw him I felt that he was my father, my flesh and blood, my future and my doom. I knew that when I was grown I would be something like him; I would have to plan my campaigns within his limitations. He was a big, good-looking man, and I was terribly happy to see him again. He struck me on the back and shook my hand. 'Hi, Charlie,' he said. 'Hi, boy. I'd like to take you up to my club, but it's in the Sixties,[1] and if you have to catch an early train I guess we'd better get something to eat around here.' He put his arm around me, and I smelled my father the way my mother sniffs a rose. It was a rich compound of whiskey, after-shave lotion, shoe polish, woolens, and the rankness of a mature male. I hoped that someone would see us together. I wished that we could be photographed. I wanted some record of our having been together.

We went out of the station and up a side street to a restaurant. It was still early, and the place was empty. The bartender was quarreling with a delivery boy, and there was one very old waiter in a red coat down by the kitchen door. We sat down, and my father hailed the waiter in a loud voice. '*Kellner!*' he shouted. '*Garçon! Cameriere!*[2] *You!*' His boisterousness in the empty restaurant seemed out of place. 'Could we have a little service here!' he shouted. 'Chop-chop.' Then he clapped his hands. This caught the waiter's attention, and he shuffled over to our table.

'Were you clapping your hands at me?' he asked.

'Calm down, calm down, *sommelier*,' my father said. 'If it isn't too much to ask of you – if it wouldn't be too much above and beyond the call of duty, we would like a couple of Beefeater Gibsons.'[3]

'I don't like to be clapped at,' the waiter said.

'I should have brought my whistle,' my father said. 'I have a whistle that is audible only to the ears of old waiters. Now, take out your little pad and your little pencil and see if you can get this straight: two Beefeater Gibsons. Repeat after me: two Beefeater Gibsons.'

'I think you'd better go somewhere else,' the waiter said quietly.

'That,' said my father, 'is one of the most brilliant suggestions I have ever heard. Come on, Charlie, let's get the hell out of here.'

I followed my father out of that restaurant into another. He was not so boisterous this time. Our drinks came, and he cross-questioned me about the baseball season. He then struck the edge of his empty glass with his knife and began shouting again. '*Garçon! Kellner! Cameriere! You!* Could we trouble you to bring us two more of the same.'

'How old is the boy?' the waiter asked.

'That,' my father said, 'is none of your God-damned business.'

'I'm sorry, sir,' the waiter said, 'but I won't serve the boy another drink.'

'Well, I have some news for you,' my father said. 'I have some very interesting news for you. This doesn't happen to be the only restaurant in New York. They've opened another on the corner. Come on, Charlie.'

He paid the bill, and I followed him out of that restaurant into another. Here the waiters wore pink jackets like hunting coats, and there was a lot of horse tack on the walls. We sat down, and my father began to shout again. 'Master of the hounds! Tallyhoo and all that sort of thing. We'd like a little something in the way of a stirrup cup. Namely, two Bibson Geefeaters.'

'Two Bibson Geefeaters?' the waiter asked, smiling.

'You know damned well what I want,' my father said angrily. 'I want two Beefeater Gibsons, and make it snappy. Things have changed in jolly old England. So my friend the duke tells me. Let's see what England can produce in the way of a cocktail.'

'This isn't England,' the waiter said.

'Don't argue with me,' my father said. 'Just do as you're told.'

'I just thought you might like to know where you are,' the waiter said.

'If there is one thing I cannot tolerate,' my father said, 'it is an impudent domestic. Come on, Charlie.'

The fourth place we went to was Italian. '*Buon giorno*,' my father said. '*Per favore, possiamo avere due cocktail americani, forti, forti. Molto gin, poco vermut.*'[4]

'I don't understand Italian,' the waiter said.

'Oh, come off it,' my father said. 'You understand Italian, and you know damned well you do. *Vogliamo due cocktail americani. Subito.*'[5]

The waiter left us and spoke with the captain, who came over to our table and said, 'I'm sorry, sir, but this table is reserved.'

'All right,' my father said. 'Get us another table.'

'All the tables are reserved,' the captain said.

'I get it,' my father said. 'You don't desire our patronage. Is that it? Well, the hell with you. *Vada all' inferno.*[6] Let's go, Charlie.'

'I have to get my train,' I said.

'I'm sorry, sonny,' my father said. 'I'm terribly sorry.' He put his arm around me and pressed me against him. 'I'll walk you back to the station. If there had only been time to go up to my club.'

'That's all right, Daddy,' I said.

'I'll get you a paper,' he said. 'I'll get you a paper to read on the train.'

Then he went up to a newsstand and said, 'Kind sir, will you be good enough to favor me with one of your God-damned, no-good, ten-cent afternoon papers?' The clerk turned away from him and stared at a magazine cover. 'Is it asking too much, kind sir,' my father said, 'is it asking too much for you to sell me one of your disgusting specimens of yellow journalism?'[7]

'I have to go, Daddy,' I said. 'It's late.'

'Now, just wait a second, sonny,' he said. 'Just wait a second. I want to get a rise out of this chap.'

'Goodbye, Daddy,' I said, and I went down the stairs and got my train, and that was the last time I saw my father.

Wants

GRACE PALEY

I saw my ex-husband in the street. I was sitting on the steps of the new library.

Hello, my life, I said. We had once been married for twenty-seven years, so I felt justified.

He said, What? What life? No life of mine.

I said, OK. I don't argue when there's real disagreement. I got up and went into the library to see how much I owed them.

The librarian said $32 even and you've owed it for eighteen years. I didn't deny anything. Because I don't understand how time passes. I have had those books. I have often thought of them. The library is only two blocks away.

My ex-husband followed me to the Books Returned desk. He interrupted the librarian, who had more to tell. In many ways, he said, as I look back, I attribute the dissolution of our marriage to the fact that you never invited the Bertrams to dinner.

That's possible, I said. But really, if you remember: first, my father was sick that Friday, then the children were born, then I had those Tuesday-night meetings, then the war began. Then we didn't seem to know them anymore. But you're right. I should have had them to dinner.

I gave the librarian a check for $32. Immediately she trusted me, put my past behind her, wiped the record clean, which is just what most other municipal and/or state bureaucracies will not do.

I checked out the two Edith Wharton books I had just returned because I'd read them so long ago and they are more apropos now than ever. They were *The House of Mirth* and

The Children,[1] which is about how life in the United States in New York changed in twenty-seven years fifty years ago.

A nice thing I do remember is breakfast, my ex-husband said. I was surprised. All we ever had was coffee. Then I remembered there was a hole in the back of the kitchen closet which opened into the apartment next door. There, they always ate sugar-cured smoked bacon. It gave us a very grand feeling about breakfast, but we never got stuffed and sluggish.

That was when we were poor, I said.

When were we ever rich? he asked.

Oh, as time went on, as our responsibilities increased, we didn't go in need. You took adequate financial care, I reminded him. The children went to camp four weeks a year and in decent ponchos with sleeping bags and boots, just like everyone else. They looked very nice. Our place was warm in winter, and we had nice red pillows and things.

I wanted a sailboat, he said. But you didn't want anything.

Don't be bitter, I said. It's never too late.

No, he said with a great deal of bitterness. I may get a sailboat. As a matter of fact I have money down on an eighteen-foot two-rigger. I'm doing well this year and can look forward to better. But as for you, it's too late. You'll always want nothing.

He had had a habit throughout the twenty-seven years of making a narrow remark which, like a plumber's snake, could work its way through the ear down the throat, halfway to my heart. He would then disappear, leaving me choking with equipment. What I mean is, I sat down on the library steps and he went away.

I looked through *The House of Mirth*, but lost interest. I felt extremely accused. Now, it's true, I'm short of requests and absolute requirements. But I do want *something*.

I want, for instance, to be a different person. I want to be the woman who brings these two books back in two weeks. I want to be the effective citizen who changes the school system and addresses the Board of Estimate[2] on the troubles of this dear urban center.

I *had* promised my children to end the war[3] before they grew up.

I wanted to have been married forever to one person, my ex-husband or my present one. Either has enough character for a whole life, which as it turns out is really not such a long time. You couldn't exhaust either man's qualities or get under the rock of his reasons in one short life.

Just this morning I looked out the window to watch the street for a while and saw that the little sycamores the city had dreamily planted a couple of years before the kids were born had come that day to the prime of their lives.

Well! I decided to bring those two books back to the library. Which proves that when a person or an event comes along to jolt or appraise me I *can* take some appropriate action, although I am better known for my hospitable remarks.

The Flowers

ALICE WALKER

It seemed to Myop as she skipped lightly from hen house to pigpen to smokehouse that the days had never been as beautiful as these. The air held a keenness that made her nose twitch. The harvesting of the corn and cotton, peanuts and squash, made each day a golden surprise that caused excited little tremors to run up her jaws.

Myop carried a short, knobby stick. She struck out at random at chickens she liked, and worked out the beat of a song on the fence around the pigpen. She felt light and good in the warm sun. She was ten, and nothing existed for her but her song, the stick clutched in her dark brown hand, and the tat-de-ta-ta-ta of accompaniment.

Turning her back on the rusty boards of her family's share-cropper cabin, Myop walked along the fence till it ran into the stream made by the spring. Around the spring, where the family got drinking water, silver ferns and wildflowers grew. Along the shallow banks pigs rooted. Myop watched the tiny white bubbles disrupt the thin black scale of soil and the water that silently rose and slid away down the stream.

She had explored the woods behind the house many times. Often, in late autumn, her mother took her to gather nuts among the fallen leaves. Today she made her own path, bouncing this way and that way, vaguely keeping an eye out for snakes. She found, in addition to various common but pretty ferns and leaves, an armful of strange blue flowers with velvety ridges and a sweetsuds bush[1] full of the brown, fragrant buds.

By twelve o'clock, her arms laden with sprigs of her findings, she was a mile or more from home. She had often been as far

before, but the strangeness of the land made it not as pleasant
as her usual haunts. It seemed gloomy in the little cove in which
she found herself. The air was damp, the silence close and deep.

Myop began to circle back to the house, back to the peace-
fulness of the morning. It was then she stepped smack into his
eyes. Her heel became lodged in the broken ridge between
brow and nose, and she reached down quickly, unafraid, to free
herself. It was only when she saw his naked grin that she gave
a little yelp of surprise.

He had been a tall man. From feet to neck covered a long
space. His head lay beside him. When she pushed back the
leaves and layers of earth and debris Myop saw that he'd had
large white teeth, all of them cracked or broken, long fingers,
and very big bones. All his clothes had rotted away except
some threads of blue denim from his overalls. The buckles of
the overalls had turned green.

Myop gazed around the spot with interest. Very near where
she'd stepped into the head was a wild pink rose. As she picked
it to add to her bundle she noticed a raised mound, a ring,
around the rose's root. It was the rotted remains of a noose, a
bit of shredding plowline,[2] now blending benignly into the soil.
Around an overhanging limb of a great spreading oak clung
another piece. Frayed, rotted, bleached, and frazzled – barely
there – but spinning restlessly in the breeze. Myop laid down
her flowers.

And the summer was over.

I Bought a Little City

DONALD BARTHELME

So I bought a little city (it was Galveston, Texas[1]) and told everybody that nobody had to move, we were going to do it just gradually, very relaxed, no big changes overnight. They were pleased and suspicious. I walked down to the harbor where there were cotton warehouses and fish markets and all sorts of installations having to do with the spread of petroleum throughout the Free World,[2] and I thought, A few apple trees here might be nice. Then I walked out on this broad boulevard which has all these tall thick palm trees maybe forty feet high in the center and oleanders on both sides, it runs for blocks and blocks and ends up opening up to the broad Gulf of Mexico – stately homes on both sides and a big Catholic church that looks more like a mosque and the Bishop's Palace and a handsome red brick affair where the Shriners[3] meet. I thought, What a nice little city, it suits me fine.

It suited me fine so I started to change it. But softly, softly. I asked some folks to move out of a whole city block on I Street, and then I tore down their houses. I put the people into the Galvez Hotel which is the nicest hotel in town, right on the seawall, and I made sure that every room had a beautiful view. Those people had wanted to stay at the Galvez Hotel all their lives and never had a chance before because they didn't have the money. They were delighted. I tore down their houses and made that empty block a park. We planted it all to hell and put some nice green iron benches in it and a little fountain – all standard stuff, we didn't try to be imaginative.

I was pleased. All the people who lived in the four blocks surrounding the empty block had something they hadn't had before, a park. They could sit in it, and like that. I went and watched them sitting in it. There was already a black man there playing bongo drums. I hate bongo drums. I started to tell him to stop playing those goddamn bongo drums but then I said to myself, No, that's not right. You got to let him play his goddamn bongo drums if he feels like it, it's part of the misery of democracy, to which I subscribe. Then I started thinking about new housing for the people I had displaced, they couldn't stay in that fancy hotel forever.

But I didn't have any ideas about new housing, except that it shouldn't be too imaginative. So I got to talking to one of these people, one of the ones we had moved out, guy by the name of Bill Caulfield who worked in a wholesale-tobacco place down on Mechanic Street.

'So what kind of a place would you like to live in?' I asked him.

'Well,' he said, 'not too big.'

'Uh-huh.'

'Maybe with a veranda around three sides,' he said, 'so we could sit on it and look out. A screened porch, maybe.'

'Whatcha going to look out at?'

'Maybe some trees and, you know, the lawn.'

'So you want some ground around the house.'

'That would be nice, yeah.'

''Bout how much ground are you thinking of?'

'Well, not too much.'

'You see, the problem is, there's only x amount of ground and everybody's going to want to have it to look at and at the same time they don't want to be staring at the neighbors. Private looking, that's the thing.'

'Well, yes,' he said. 'I'd like it to be kind of private.'

'Well,' I said, 'get a pencil and let's see what we can work out.'

We started with what there was going to be to look at, which was damned difficult. Because when you look you don't want to be able to look at just one thing, you want to be able to shift your gaze. You need to be able to look at at least three things, maybe four. Bill Caulfield solved the problem. He showed me a box. I opened it up and inside was a jigsaw puzzle with a picture of the Mona Lisa on it.

'Lookee here,' he said. 'If each piece of ground was like a piece of this-here puzzle, and the tree line on each piece of property followed the outline of a piece of the puzzle – well, there you have it, QED and that's all she wrote.'

'Fine,' I said. 'Where are the folk going to park their cars?'

'In the vast underground parking facility,' he said.

'OK, but how does each householder gain access to his household?'

'The tree lines are double and shade beautifully paved walk-ways possibly bordered with begonias,' he said.

'A lurkway for potential muggists and rapers,' I pointed out.

'There won't be any such,' Caulfield said, 'because you've bought our whole city and won't allow that class of person to hang out here no more.'

That was right. I had bought the whole city and could prob-ably do that. I had forgotten.

'Well,' I said finally, 'let's give 'er a try. The only thing I don't like about it is that it seems a little imaginative.'

We did and it didn't work out badly. There was only one complaint. A man named A. G. Bartie came to see me.

'Listen,' he said, his eyes either gleaming or burning, I couldn't tell which, it was a cloudy day, 'I feel like I'm living in this gigantic jiveass jigsaw puzzle.'

He was right. Seen from the air, he was living in the middle of a titanic reproduction of the Mona Lisa, too, but I thought it best not to mention that. We allowed him to square off his prop-erty into a standard 60 x 100 foot lot and later some other people did that too – some people just like rectangles, I guess. I must say it improved the concept. You run across an occasional rectangle in Shady Oaks (we didn't want to call the development anything too imaginative) and it surprises you. That's nice.

I said to myself:

> Got a little city
> Ain't it pretty

By now I had exercised my proprietorship so lightly and if I do say so myself tactfully that I wondered if I was enjoying myself enough (and I had paid a heavy penny too – near to half my fortune). So I went out on the streets then and shot six thousand dogs. This gave me great satisfaction and you have no idea how wonderfully it improved the city for the better. This left us with a dog population of 165,000, as opposed to a human population of something like 89,000. Then I went down to the Galveston *News*, the morning paper, and wrote an editorial denouncing myself as the vilest creature the good God had ever placed upon the earth, and were we, the citizens of this fine community, who were after all free Americans of whatever race or creed, going to sit still while one man, *one man*, if indeed so vile a critter could be so called, etc. etc.? I gave it to the city desk and told them I wanted it on the front page in fourteen-point type, boxed. I did this just in case they might have hesitated to do it themselves, and because I'd seen that Orson Welles picture[4] where the guy writes a nasty notice about his own wife's terrible singing, which I always thought was pretty decent of him, from some points of view.

A man whose dog I'd shot came to see me.

'You shot Butch,' he said.

'Butch? Which one was Butch?'

'One brown ear and one white ear,' he said. 'Very friendly.'

'Mister,' I said, 'I've just shot six thousand dogs, and you expect me to remember Butch?'

'Butch was all Nancy and me had,' he said. 'We never had no children.'

'Well, I'm sorry about that,' I said, 'but I own this city.'

'I know that,' he said.

'I am the sole owner and I make all the rules.'

'They told me,' he said.

'I'm sorry about Butch but he got in the way of the big campaign. You ought to have had him on a leash.'

'I don't deny it,' he said.

'You ought to have had him inside the house.'

'He was just a poor animal that had to go out sometimes.'

'And mess up the streets something awful?'

'Well,' he said, 'it's a problem. I just wanted to tell you how I feel.'

'You didn't tell me,' I said. 'How do you feel?'

'I feel like bustin' your head,' he said, and showed me a short length of pipe he had brought along for the purpose.

'But of course if you do that you're going to get your ass in a lot of trouble,' I said.

'I realize that.'

'It would make you feel better, but then I own the jail and the judge and the po-lice and the local chapter of the American Civil Liberties Union.[5] All mine. I could hit you with a writ of mandamus.'[6]

'You wouldn't do that.'

'I've been known to do worse.'

'You're a black-hearted man,' he said. 'I guess that's it. You'll roast in Hell in the eternal flames and there will be no mercy or cooling drafts from any quarter.'

He went away happy with this explanation. I was happy to be a black-hearted man in his mind if that would satisfy the issue between us because that was a bad-looking piece of pipe he had there and I was still six thousand dogs ahead of the game, in a sense. So I owned this little city which was very, very pretty and I couldn't think of any more new innovations just then or none that wouldn't get me punctuated like the late Huey P. Long, former governor of Louisiana.[7] The thing is, I had fallen in love with Sam Hong's wife. I had wandered into this store on Tremont Street where they sold Oriental novelties, paper lanterns, and cheap china and bamboo birdcages and wicker footstools and all that kind of thing. She was smaller than I was and I thought I had never seen that much goodness in a woman's face before. It was hard to credit. It was the best face I'd ever seen.

'I can't do that,' she said, 'because I am married to Sam.'

'Sam?'

She pointed over to the cash register where there was a Chinese man, young and intelligent-looking and pouring that intelligent look at me with considered unfriendliness.

'Well, that's dismal news,' I said. 'Tell me, do you love me?'

'A little bit,' she said, 'but Sam is wise and kind and we have one and one-third lovely children.'

She didn't look pregnant but I congratulated her anyhow,

and then went out on the street and found a cop and sent him down to H Street to get me a bucket of Colonel Sanders' Kentucky Fried Chicken, extra crispy. I did that just out of meanness. He was humiliated but he had no choice. I thought:

> I own a little city
> Awful pretty
> Can't help people
> Can hurt them though
> Shoot their dogs
> Mess 'em up
> Be imaginative
> Plant trees
> Best to leave 'em alone?
> Who decides?
> Sam's wife is Sam's wife and coveting
> Is not nice.

So I ate the Colonel Sanders' Kentucky Fried Chicken, extra crispy, and sold Galveston, Texas, back to the interests. I took a bath on that deal, there's no denying it, but I learned something – don't play God. A lot of other people already knew that, but I have never doubted for a minute that a lot of other people are smarter than me, and figure things out quicker, and have grace and statistical norms on their side. Probably I went wrong by being too imaginative, although really I was guarding against that. I did very little, I was fairly restrained. God does a lot worse things, every day, in one little family, any family, than I did in that whole city. But He's got a better imagination than I do. For instance, I still covet Sam Hong's wife. That's torment. Still covet Sam Hong's wife, and probably always will. It's like having a tooth pulled. For a year. The same tooth. That's a sample of His imagination. It's powerful.

So what happened? What happened was that I took the other half of my fortune and went to Galena Park, Texas, and lived inconspicuously there, and when they asked me to run for the school board I said No, I don't have any children.

Collectors

RAYMOND CARVER

I was out of work. But any day I expected to hear from up north. I lay on the sofa and listened to the rain. Now and then I'd lift up and look through the curtain for the mailman.

There was no one on the street, nothing.

I hadn't been down again five minutes when I heard someone walk onto the porch, wait, and then knock. I lay still. I knew it wasn't the mailman. I knew his steps. You can't be too careful if you're out of work and you get notices in the mail or else pushed under your door. They come around wanting to talk, too, especially if you don't have a telephone.

The knock sounded again, louder, a bad sign. I eased up and tried to see onto the porch. But whoever was there was standing against the door, another bad sign. I knew the floor creaked, so there was no chance of slipping into the other room and looking out that window.

Another knock, and I said, Who's there?

This is Aubrey Bell, a man said. Are you Mr Slater?

What is it you want? I called from the sofa.

I have something for Mrs Slater. She's won something. Is Mrs Slater home?

Mrs Slater doesn't live here, I said.

Well, then, are you Mr Slater? the man said. Mr Slater . . . and the man sneezed.

I got off the sofa. I unlocked the door and opened it a little. He was an old guy, fat and bulky under his raincoat. Water ran off the coat and dripped onto the big suitcase contraption thing he carried.

He grinned and set down the big case. He put out his hand.

Aubrey Bell, he said.

I don't know you, I said.

Mrs Slater, he began. Mrs Slater filled out a card. He took cards from an inside pocket and shuffled them a minute. Mrs Slater, he read. Two-fifty-five South Sixth East? Mrs Slater is a winner.

He took off his hat and nodded solemnly, slapped the hat against his coat as if that were it, everything had been settled, the drive finished, the railhead reached.

He waited.

Mrs Slater doesn't live here, I said. What'd she win?

I have to show you, he said. May I come in?

I don't know. If it won't take long, I said. I'm pretty busy.

Fine, he said. I'll just slide out of this coat first. And the galoshes. Wouldn't want to track up your carpet. I see you do have a carpet, Mr . . .

His eyes had lighted and then dimmed at the sight of the carpet. He shuddered. Then he took off his coat. He shook it out and hung it by the collar over the doorknob. That's a good place for it, he said. Damn weather, anyway. He bent over and unfastened his galoshes. He set his case inside the room. He stepped out of the galoshes and into the room in a pair of slippers.

I closed the door. He saw me staring at the slippers and said, W. H. Auden[1] wore slippers all through China on his first visit there. Never took them off. Corns.

I shrugged. I took one more look down the street for the mailman and shut the door again.

Aubrey Bell stared at the carpet. He pulled his lips. Then he laughed. He laughed and shook his head.

What's so funny? I said.

Nothing. Lord, he said. He laughed again. I think I'm losing my mind. I think I have a fever. He reached a hand to his forehead. His hair was matted and there was a ring around his scalp where the hat had been.

Do I feel hot to you? he said. I don't know, I think I might have a fever. He was still staring at the carpet. You have any aspirin?

What's the matter with you? I said. I hope you're not getting sick on me. I got things I have to do.

He shook his head. He sat down on the sofa. He stirred at the carpet with his slippered foot.

I went to the kitchen, rinsed a cup, shook two aspirin out of a bottle.

Here, I said. Then I think you ought to leave.

Are you speaking for Mrs Slater? he hissed. No, no, forget I said that, forget I said that. He wiped his face. He swallowed the aspirin. His eyes skipped around the bare room. Then he leaned forward with some effort and unsnapped the buckles on his case. The case flopped open, revealing compartments filled with an array of hoses, brushes, shiny pipes, and some kind of heavy-looking blue thing mounted on little wheels. He stared at these things as if surprised. Quietly, in a churchly voice, he said, Do you know what this is?

I moved closer. I'd say it was a vacuum cleaner. I'm not in the market, I said. No way am I in the market for a vacuum cleaner.

I want to show you something, he said. He took a card out of his jacket pocket. Look at this, he said. He handed me the card. Nobody said you were in the market. But look at the signature. Is that Mrs Slater's signature or not?

I looked at the card. I held it up to the light. I turned it over, but the other side was blank. So what? I said.

Mrs Slater's card was pulled at random out of a basket of cards. Hundreds of cards just like this little card. She has won a free vacuuming and carpet shampoo. Mrs Slater is a winner. No strings. I am here even to do your mattress, Mr ... You'll be surprised to see what can collect in a mattress over the months, over the years. Every day, every night of our lives, we're leaving little bits of ourselves, flakes of this and that, behind. Where do they go, these bits and pieces of ourselves? Right through the sheets and into the mattress, *that's* where! Pillows, too. It's all the same.

He had been removing lengths of the shiny pipe and joining the parts together. Now he inserted the fitted pipes into the hose. He was on his knees, grunting. He attached some sort of scoop to the hose and lifted out the blue thing with wheels.

He let me examine the filter he intended to use.

Do you have a car? he asked.

No car, I said. I don't have a car. If I had a car I would drive you someplace.

Too bad, he said. This little vacuum comes equipped with a sixty-foot extension cord. If you had a car, you could wheel this little vacuum right up to your car door and vacuum the plush carpeting and the luxurious reclining seats as well. You would be surprised how much of us gets lost, how much of us gathers, in those fine seats over the years.

Mr Bell, I said, I think you better pack up your things and go. I say this without any malice whatsoever.

But he was looking around the room for a plug-in. He found one at the end of the sofa. The machine rattled as if there were a marble inside, anyway something loose inside, then settled to a hum.

Rilke[2] lived in one castle after another, all of his adult life. Benefactors, he said loudly over the hum of the vacuum. He seldom rode in motorcars; he preferred trains. Then look at Voltaire at Cirey with Madame Châtelet.[3] His death mask. Such serenity. He raised his right hand as if I were about to disagree. No, no, it isn't right, is it? Don't say it. But who knows? With that he turned and began to pull the vacuum into the other room.

There was a bed, a window. The covers were heaped on the floor. One pillow, one sheet over the mattress. He slipped the case from the pillow and then quickly stripped the sheet from the mattress. He stared at the mattress and gave me a look out of the corner of his eye. I went to the kitchen and got the chair. I sat down in the doorway and watched. First he tested the suction by putting the scoop against the palm of his hand. He bent and turned a dial on the vacuum. You have to turn it up full strength for a job like this one, he said. He checked the suction again, then extended the hose to the head of the bed and began to move the scoop down the mattress. The scoop tugged at the mattress. The vacuum whirred louder. He made three passes over the mattress, then switched off the machine. He pressed a lever and the lid popped open. He took out the filter. This filter is just for demonstration purposes. In normal use, all of this, this *material*, would go into your bag, here, he said. He pinched some of the dusty stuff between his fingers. There must have been a cup of it.

He had this look to his face.

It's not my mattress, I said. I leaned forward in the chair and tried to show an interest.

Now the pillow, he said. He put the used filter on the sill and looked out the window for a minute. He turned. I want you to hold onto this end of the pillow, he said.

I got up and took hold of two corners of the pillow. I felt I was holding something by the ears.

Like this? I said.

He nodded. He went into the other room and came back with another filter.

How much do those things cost? I said.

Next to nothing, he said. They're only made out of paper and a little bit of plastic. Couldn't cost much.

He kicked on the vacuum and I held tight as the scoop sank into the pillow and moved down its length – once, twice, three times. He switched off the vacuum, removed the filter, and held it up without a word. He put it on the sill beside the other filter. Then he opened the closet door. He looked inside, but there was only a box of Mouse-Be-Gone.

I heard steps on the porch, the mail slot opened and clinked shut. We looked at each other.

He pulled on the vacuum and I followed him into the other room. We looked at the letter lying face down on the carpet near the front door.

I started toward the letter, turned and said, What else? It's getting late. This carpet's not worth fooling with. It's only a twelve-by-fifteen cotton carpet with no-skid backing from Rug City. It's not worth fooling with.

Do you have a full ashtray? he said. Or a potted plant or something like that? A handful of dirt would be fine.

I found the ashtray. He took it, dumped the contents onto the carpet, ground the ashes and cigarets under his slipper. He got down on his knees again and inserted a new filter. He took off his jacket and threw it onto the sofa. He was sweating under the arms. Fat hung over his belt. He twisted off the scoop and attached another device to the hose. He adjusted his dial. He kicked on the machine and began to move back and forth, back and forth over the worn carpet. Twice I started for the letter. But he seemed to anticipate me, cut me off, so to speak, with his hose and his pipes and his sweeping and his sweeping . . .

I took the chair back to the kitchen and sat there and watched him work. After a time he shut off the machine, opened the lid, and silently brought me the filter, alive with dust, hair, small grainy things. I looked at the filter, and then I got up and put it in the garbage.

He worked steadily now. No more explanations. He came out to the kitchen with a bottle that held a few ounces of green liquid. He put the bottle under the tap and filled it.

You know I can't pay anything, I said. I couldn't pay you a dollar if my life depended on it. You're going to have to write me off as a dead loss, that's all. You're wasting your time on me, I said.

I wanted it out in the open, no misunderstanding.

He went about his business. He put another attachment on the hose, in some complicated way hooked his bottle to the new attachment. He moved slowly over the carpet, now and then releasing little streams of emerald, moving the brush back and forth over the carpet, working up patches of foam.

I had said all that was on my mind. I sat on the chair in the kitchen, relaxed now, and watched him work. Once in a while I looked out the window at the rain. It had begun to get dark. He switched off the vacuum. He was in a corner near the front door.

You want coffee? I said.

He was breathing hard. He wiped his face.

I put on water and by the time it had boiled and I'd fixed up two cups he had everything dismantled and back in the case. Then he picked up the letter. He read the name on the letter and looked closely at the return address. He folded the letter in half and put it in his hip pocket. I kept watching him. That's all I did. The coffee began to cool.

It's for a Mr Slater, he said. I'll see to it. He said, Maybe I will skip the coffee. I better not walk across this carpet. I just shampooed it.

That's true, I said. Then I said, You're sure that's who the letter's for?

He reached to the sofa for his jacket, put it on, and opened the front door. It was still raining. He stepped into his galoshes, fastened them, and then pulled on the raincoat and looked back inside.

You want to see it? he said. You don't believe me?

It just seems strange, I said.

Well, I'd better be off, he said. But he kept standing there. You want the vacuum or not?

I looked at the big case, closed now and ready to move on.

No, I said, I guess not. I'm going to be leaving here soon. It would just be in the way.

All right, he said, and he shut the door.

Communist

RICHARD FORD

My mother once had a boyfriend named Glen Baxter. This was in 1961. We – my mother and I – were living in the little house my father had left her up the Sun River, near Victory, Montana, west of Great Falls. My mother was thirty-two at the time. I was sixteen. Glen Baxter was somewhere in the middle, between us, though I cannot be exact about it.

We were living then off the proceeds of my father's life insurance policies, with my mother doing some part-time waitressing work up in Great Falls and going to the bars in the evenings, which I know is where she met Glen Baxter. Sometimes he would come back with her and stay in her room at night, or she would call up from town and explain that she was staying with him in his little place on Lewis Street by the GN yards.[1] She gave me his number every time, but I never called it. I think she probably thought that what she was doing was terrible, but simply couldn't help herself. I thought it was all right, though. Regular life it seemed, and still does. She was young, and I knew that even then.

Glen Baxter was a Communist and liked hunting, which he talked about a lot. Pheasants. Ducks. Deer. He killed all of them, he said. He had been to Vietnam as far back as then, and when he was in our house he often talked about shooting the animals over there – monkeys and beautiful parrots – using military guns just for sport. We did not know what Vietnam was then, and Glen, when he talked about that, referred to it only as 'the Far East.' I think now he must've been in the CIA[2] and been disillusioned by something he saw or found out about and been thrown out, but that kind of thing did not matter to us. He was a tall, dark-eyed man with short black hair, and was usually in a good humor. He had gone halfway through college in Peoria, Illinois, he said, where he grew up. But when he was around our life he worked wheat farms as a ditcher, and stayed out of work winters and in the bars drinking with women like my mother, who had work and some money. It is not an uncommon life to lead in Montana.

What I want to explain happened in November. We had not been seeing Glen Baxter for some time. Two months had gone by. My mother knew other men, but she came home most days from work and stayed inside watching television in her bedroom and drinking beers. I asked about Glen once, and she said only that she didn't know where he was, and I assumed they had had a fight and that he was gone off on a flyer back to Illinois or Massachusetts, where he said he had relatives. I'll admit that I liked him. He had something on his mind always. He was a labor man[3] as well as a Communist, and liked to say that the country was poisoned by the rich, and strong men would need to bring it to life again, and I liked that because my father had been a labor man, which was why we had a house to live in and money coming through. It was also true that I'd had a few boxing bouts by then – just with town boys and one with an Indian from Choteau – and there were some girlfriends I knew from that. I did not like my mother being around the house so much at night, and I wished Glen Baxter would come back, or that another man would come along and entertain her somewhere else.

At two o'clock on a Saturday, Glen drove up into our yard in a car. He had had a big brown Harley-Davidson that he rode most of the year, in his black-and-red irrigators[4] and a baseball cap turned backwards. But this time he had a car, a blue Nash Ambassador.[5] My mother and I went out on the porch when he stopped inside the olive trees my father had planted as a shelter belt, and my mother had a look on her face of not much pleasure. It was starting to be cold in earnest by then. Snow was down already onto the Fairfield Bench, though on this day a chinook was blowing, and it could as easily have been spring, though the sky above the Divide[6] was turning over in silver and blue clouds of winter.

'We haven't seen you in a long time, I guess,' my mother said coldly.

'My little retarded sister died,' Glen said, standing at the door of his old car. He was wearing his orange VFW[7] jacket and canvas shoes we called wino shoes, something I had never seen him wear before. He seemed to be in a good humor. 'We buried her in Florida near the home.'

'That's a good place,' my mother said in a voice that meant she was a wronged party in something.

'I want to take this boy hunting today, Aileen,' Glen said. 'There're snow geese down now. But we have to go right away, or they'll be gone to Idaho by tomorrow.'

'He doesn't care to go,' my mother said.

'Yes I do,' I said, and looked at her.

My mother frowned at me. 'Why do you?'

'Why does he need a reason?' Glen Baxter said and grinned.

'I want him to have one, that's why.' She looked at me oddly. 'I think Glen's drunk, Les.'

'No, I'm not drinking,' Glen said, which was hardly ever true. He looked at both of us, and my mother bit down on the side of her lower lip and stared at me in a way to make you think she thought something was being put over on her and she didn't like you for it. She was very pretty, though when she was mad her features were sharpened and less pretty by a long way. 'All right, then I don't care,' she said to no one in particular. 'Hunt, kill, maim. Your father did that too.' She turned to go back inside.

'Why don't you come with us, Aileen?' Glen was smiling still, pleased.

'To do what?' my mother said. She stopped and pulled a package of cigarettes out of her dress pocket and put one in her mouth.

'It's worth seeing.'

'See dead animals?' my mother said.

'These geese are from Siberia, Aileen,' Glen said. 'They're not like a lot of geese. Maybe I'll buy us dinner later. What do you say?'

'Buy what with?' my mother said. To tell the truth, I didn't know why she was so mad at him. I would've thought she'd be glad to see him. But she just suddenly seemed to hate everything about him.

'I've got some money,' Glen said. 'Let me spend it on a pretty girl tonight.'

'Find one of those and you're lucky,' my mother said, turning away toward the front door.

'I already found one,' Glen Baxter said. But the door slammed behind her, and he looked at me then with a look I think now was helplessness, though I could not see a way to change anything.

My mother sat in the backseat of Glen's Nash and looked out the window while we drove. My double gun was in the seat between us beside Glen's Belgian pump, which he kept loaded with five shells in case, he said, he saw something beside the road he wanted to shoot. I had hunted rabbits before, and had ground-sluiced pheasants and other birds, but I had never been on an actual hunt before, one where you drove out to some special place and did it formally. And I was excited. I had a feeling that something important was about to happen to me, and that this would be a day I would always remember.

My mother did not say anything for a long time, and neither did I. We drove up through Great Falls and out the other side toward Fort Benton, which was on the benchland[8] where wheat was grown.

'Geese mate for life,' my mother said, just out of the blue, as we were driving. 'I hope you know that. They're special birds.'

'I know that,' Glen said in the front seat. 'I have every respect for them.'

'So where were you for three months?' she said. 'I'm only curious.'

'I was in the Big Hole[9] for a while,' Glen said, 'and after that I went over to Douglas, Wyoming.'

'What were you planning to do there?' my mother asked.

'I wanted to find a job, but it didn't work out.'

'I'm going to college,' she said suddenly, and this was

something I had never heard about before. I turned to look at her, but she was staring out her window and wouldn't see me.

'I knew French once,' Glen said. '*Rosé's* pink. *Rouge's* red.' He glanced at me and smiled. 'I think that's a wise idea, Aileen. When are you going to start?'

'I don't want Les to think he was raised by crazy people all his life,' my mother said.

'Les ought to go himself,' Glen said.

'After I go, he will.'

'What do you say about that, Les?' Glen said, grinning.

'He says it's just fine,' my mother said.

'It's just fine,' I said.

Where Glen Baxter took us was out onto the high flat prairie that was disked for wheat and had high, high mountains out to the east, with lower heartbreak hills in between. It was, I remember, a day for blues in the sky, and down in the distance we could see the small town of Floweree, and the state highway running past it toward Fort Benton and the Hi-line.[10] We drove out on top of the prairie on a muddy dirt road fenced on both sides, until we had gone about three miles, which is where Glen stopped.

'All right,' he said, looking up in the rearview mirror at my mother. 'You wouldn't think there was anything here, would you?'

'*We're* here,' my mother said. 'You brought us here.'

'You'll be glad though,' Glen said, and seemed confident to me. I had looked around myself but could not see anything. No water or trees, nothing that seemed like a good place to hunt anything. Just wasted land. 'There's a big lake out there, Les,' Glen said. 'You can't see it now from here because it's low. But the geese are there. You'll see.'

'It's like the moon out here, I recognize that,' my mother said, 'only it's worse.' She was staring out at the flat wheatland as if she could actually see something in particular, and wanted to know more about it. 'How'd you find this place?'

'I came once on the wheat push,' Glen said.

'And I'm sure the owner told you just to come back and

hunt anytime you like and bring anybody you wanted. Come one, come all. Is that it?'

'People shouldn't own land anyway,' Glen said. 'Anybody should be able to use it.'

'Les, Glen's going to poach here,' my mother said. 'I just want you to know that, because that's a crime and the law will get you for it. If you're a man now, you're going to have to face the consequences.'

'That's not true,' Glen Baxter said, and looked gloomily out over the steering wheel down the muddy road toward the mountains. Though for myself I believed it was true, and didn't care. I didn't care about anything at that moment except seeing geese fly over me and shooting them down.

'Well, I'm certainly not going out there,' my mother said. 'I like towns better, and I already have enough trouble.'

'That's okay,' Glen said. 'When the geese lift up you'll get to see them. That's all I wanted. Les and me'll go shoot them, won't we, Les?'

'Yes,' I said, and I put my hand on my shotgun, which had been my father's and was heavy as rocks.

'Then we should go on,' Glen said, 'or we'll waste our light.'

We got out of the car with our guns. Glen took off his canvas shoes and put on his pair of black irrigators out of the trunk. Then we crossed the barbed wire fence, and walked out into the high, tilled field toward nothing. I looked back at my mother when we were still not so far away, but I could only see the small, dark top of her head, low in the backseat of the Nash, staring out and thinking what I could not then begin to say.

On the walk toward the lake, Glen began talking to me. I had never been alone with him, and knew little about him except what my mother said – that he drank too much, or other times that he was the nicest man she had ever known in the world and that someday a woman would marry him, though she didn't think it would be her. Glen told me as we walked that he wished he had finished college, but that it was too late now, that his mind was too old. He said he had liked the Far East very much, and that people there knew how to treat each other, and that he would go back some day but couldn't go now. He said also that he would like to live in Russia for a while and mentioned the names of people who had gone there, names I didn't know. He said it would be hard at first, because it was so different, but that pretty soon anyone would learn to like it and wouldn't want to live anywhere else, and that Russians treated Americans who came to live there like kings. There were Communists everywhere now, he said. You didn't know them, but they were there. Montana had a large number, and he was in touch with all of them. He said that Communists were always in danger and that he had to protect himself all the time. And when he said that he pulled back his VFW jacket and showed me the butt of a pistol he had stuck under his shirt against his bare skin. 'There are people who want to kill me right now,' he said, 'and I would kill a man myself if I thought I had to.' And we kept walking. Though in a while he said, 'I don't think I know much about you, Les. But I'd like to. What do you like to do?'

'I like to box,' I said. 'My father did it. It's a good thing to know.'

'I suppose you have to protect yourself too,' Glen said.

'I know how to,' I said.

'Do you like to watch TV,' Glen asked, and smiled.

'Not much.'

'I love to,' Glen said. 'I could watch it instead of eating if I had one.'

I looked out straight ahead over the green tops of sage that grew to the edge of the disked field, hoping to see the lake Glen said was there. There was an airishness and a sweet smell that I thought might be the place we were going, but I couldn't see it. 'How will we hunt these geese?' I said.

'It won't be hard,' Glen said. 'Most hunting isn't even hunting. It's only shooting. And that's what this will be. In Illinois you would dig holes in the ground and hide and set out your decoys. Then the geese come to you, over and over again. But we don't have time for that here.' He glanced at me. 'You have to be sure the first time here.'

'How do you know they're here now,' I asked. And I looked toward the Highwood Mountains twenty miles away, half in snow and half dark blue at the bottom. I could see the little town of Floweree then, looking shabby and dimly lighted in the distance. A red bar sign shone. A car moved slowly away from the scattered buildings.

'They always come November first,' Glen said.

'Are we going to poach them?'

'Does it make any difference to you,' Glen asked.

'No, it doesn't.'

'Well then, we aren't,' he said.

We walked then for a while without talking. I looked back once to see the Nash far and small in the flat distance. I couldn't see my mother, and I thought that she must've turned on the radio and gone to sleep, which she always did, letting it play all night in her bedroom. Behind the car the sun was nearing the rounded mountains southwest of us, and I knew that when the sun was gone it would be cold. I wished my mother had decided to come along with us, and I thought for a moment of how little I really knew her at all.

Glen walked with me another quarter-mile, crossed another barbed wire fence where sage was growing, then went a hundred yards through wheatgrass and spurge until the ground went up and formed a kind of long hillock bunker built by a farmer against the wind. And I realized the lake was just beyond us. I could hear the sound of a car horn blowing and a dog barking all the way down in the town, then the wind seemed to move and all I could hear then and after then were geese. So many geese, from the sound of them, though I still could not see even one. I stood and listened to the high-pitched shouting sound, a sound I had never heard so close, a sound with size to it – though it was not loud. A sound that meant great numbers and that made your chest rise and your shoulders tighten with expectancy. It was a sound to make you feel separate from it and everything else, as if you were of no importance in the grand scheme of things.

'Do you hear them singing,' Glen asked. He held his hand up to make me stand still. And we both listened. 'How many do you think, Les, just hearing?'

'A hundred,' I said. 'More than a hundred.'

'Five thousand,' Glen said. 'More than you can believe when you see them. Go see.'

I put down my gun and on my hands and knees crawled up the earthwork through the wheatgrass and thistle, until I could see down to the lake and see the geese. And they were there, like a white bandage laid on the water, wide and long and continuous, a white expanse of snow geese, seventy yards from me, on the bank, but stretching far onto the lake, which was large itself – a half-mile across, with thick tules on the far side and wild plums farther and the blue mountain behind them.

'Do you see the big raft?' Glen said from below me, in a whisper.

'I see it,' I said, still looking. It was such a thing to see, a view I had never seen and have not since.

'Are any on the land?' he said.

'Some are in the wheatgrass,' I said, 'but most are swimming.'

'Good,' Glen said. 'They'll have to fly. But we can't wait for that now.'

And I crawled backwards down the heel of land to where Glen was, and my gun. We were losing our light, and the air was purplish and cooling. I looked toward the car but couldn't see it, and I was no longer sure where it was below the lighted sky.

'Where do they fly to?' I said in a whisper, since I did not want anything to be ruined because of what I did or said. It was important to Glen to shoot the geese, and it was important to me.

'To the wheat,' he said. 'Or else they leave for good. I wish your mother had come, Les. Now she'll be sorry.'

I could hear the geese quarreling and shouting on the lake surface. And I wondered if they knew we were here now. 'She might be,' I said with my heart pounding, but I didn't think she would be much.

It was a simple plan he had. I would stay behind the bunker, and he would crawl on his belly with his gun through the wheatgrass as near to the geese as he could. Then he would simply stand up and shoot all the ones he could close up, both in the air and on the ground. And when all the others flew up, with luck some would turn toward me as they came into the wind, and then I could shoot them and turn them back to him, and he would shoot them again. He could kill ten, he said, if he was lucky, and I might kill four. It didn't seem hard.

'Don't show them your face,' Glen said. 'Wait till you think you can touch them, then stand up and shoot. To hesitate is lost in this.'

'All right,' I said. 'I'll try it.'

'Shoot one in the head, and then shoot another one,' Glen said. 'It won't be hard.' He patted me on the arm and smiled. Then he took off his VFW jacket and put it on the ground, climbed up the side of the bunker, cradling his shotgun in his arms, and slid on his belly into the dry stalks of yellow grass out of my sight.

Then, for the first time in that entire day, I was alone. And I didn't mind it. I sat squat down in the grass, loaded my double gun and took my other two shells out of my pocket to hold. I pushed the safety off and on to see that it was right. The wind rose a little, scuffed the grass and made me shiver. It was not the warm chinook now, but a wind out of the north, the one geese flew away from if they could.

Then I thought about my mother, in the car alone, and how much longer I would stay with her, and what it might mean to her for me to leave. And I wondered when Glen Baxter would die and if someone would kill him, or whether my mother would marry him and how I would feel about it. And though I didn't know why, it occurred to me that Glen Baxter and I would not be friends when all was said and done, since I didn't care if he ever married my mother or didn't.

Then I thought about boxing and what my father had taught me about it. To tighten your fists hard. To strike out straight from the shoulder and never punch backing up. How to cut a punch by snapping your fist inwards, how to carry your chin low, and to step toward a man when he is falling so you can hit him again. And most important, to keep your eyes open when you are hitting in the face and causing damage, because you need to see what you're doing to encourage yourself, and because it is when you close your eyes that you stop hitting and get hurt badly. 'Fly all over your man, Les,' my father said. 'When you see your chance, fly on him and hit him till he falls.' That, I thought, would always be my attitude in things.

And then I heard the geese again, their voices in unison, louder and shouting, as if the wind had changed again and put all new sounds in the cold air. And then a *boom*. And I knew Glen was in among them and had stood up to shoot. The noise of geese rose and grew worse, and my fingers burned where I held my gun too tight to the metal, and I put it down and opened my fist to make the burning stop so I could feel the trigger when the moment came. *Boom*, Glen shot again, and I heard him shuck a shell, and all the sounds out beyond the bunker seemed to be rising – the geese, the shots, the air itself going up. *Boom*, Glen shot another time, and I knew he was taking his careful time to make his shots good. And I held my gun and started to crawl up the bunker so as not to be surprised when the geese came over me and I could shoot.

From the top I saw Glen Baxter alone in the wheatgrass field, shooting at a white goose with black tips of wings that was on the ground not far from him, but trying to run and pull into the air. He shot it once more, and it fell over dead with its wings flapping.

Glen looked back at me and his face was distorted and strange. The air around him was full of white rising geese and he seemed to want them all. 'Behind you, Les,' he yelled at me and pointed. 'They're all behind you now.' I looked behind me, and there were geese in the air as far as I could see, more than I knew how many, moving so slowly, their wings wide out and working calmly and filling the air with noise, though their voices were not as loud or as shrill as I had thought they would be. And they were so close! Forty feet, some of them. The air around me vibrated and I could feel the wind from their wings and it seemed to me I could kill as many as the times I could shoot – a hundred or a thousand – and I raised my gun, put the muzzle on the head of a white goose, and fired. It shuddered in the air, its wide feet sank below its belly, its wings cradled out to hold back air, and it fell straight down and landed with an awful sound, a noise a human would make, a thick, soft, *hump* noise. I looked up again and shot another goose, could hear the pellets hit its chest, but it didn't fall or even break its pattern for flying. *Boom*, Glen shot again. And then again. 'Hey,' I heard him shout, 'Hey, hey.' And there were geese flying over me, flying in line after line. I broke my gun and reloaded, and thought to myself as I did: I need confidence here, I need to be sure with this. I pointed at another goose and shot it in the head, and it fell the way the first one had, wings out, its belly down, and with the same thick noise of hitting. Then I sat down in the grass on the bunker and let geese fly over me.

By now the whole raft was in the air, all of it moving in a slow swirl above me and the lake and everywhere, finding the wind and heading out south in long wavering lines that caught the last sun and turned to silver as they gained a distance. It was a thing to see, I will tell you now. Five thousand white geese all in the air around you, making a noise like you have never heard before. And I thought to myself then: this is something I will never see again. I will never forget this. And I was right.

Glen Baxter shot twice more. One he missed, but with the other he hit a goose flying away from him, and knocked it half falling and flying into the empty lake not far from shore, where it began to swim as though it was fine and make its noise.

Glen stood in the stubby grass, looking out at the goose, his gun lowered. 'I didn't need to shoot that one, did I, Les?'

'I don't know,' I said, sitting on the little knoll of land, looking at the goose swimming in the water.

'I don't know why I shoot 'em. They're so beautiful.' He looked at me.

'I don't know either,' I said.

'Maybe there's nothing else to do with them.' Glen stared at the goose again and shook his head. 'Maybe this is exactly what they're put on earth for.'

I did not know what to say because I did not know what he could mean by that, though what I felt was embarrassment at the great numbers of geese there were, and a dulled feeling like a hunger because the shooting had stopped and it was over for me now.

Glen began to pick up his geese, and I walked down to my two that had fallen close together and were dead. One had hit with such an impact that its stomach had split and some of its inward parts were knocked out. Though the other looked unhurt, its soft white belly turned up like a pillow, its head and jagged bill-teeth, its tiny black eyes looking as they would if they were alive.

'What's happened to the hunters out here?' I heard a voice speak. It was my mother, standing in her pink dress on the knoll above us, hugging her arms. She was smiling though she was cold. And I realized that I had lost all thought of her in the shooting. 'Who did all this shooting? Is this your work, Les?'

'No,' I said.

'Les is a hunter, though, Aileen,' Glen said. 'He takes his time.' He was holding two white geese by their necks, one in each hand, and he was smiling. He and my mother seemed pleased.

'I see you didn't miss too many,' my mother said and smiled. I could tell she admired Glen for his geese, and that she had done some thinking in the car alone. 'It *was* wonderful, Glen,' she said. 'I've never seen anything like that. They were like snow.'

'It's worth seeing once, isn't it?' Glen said. 'I should've killed more, but I got excited.'

My mother looked at me then. 'Where's yours, Les?'

'Here,' I said and pointed to my two geese on the ground beside me.

My mother nodded in a nice way, and I think she liked everything then and wanted the day to turn out right and for all of us to be happy. 'Six, then. You've got six in all.'

'One's still out there,' I said, and motioned where the one goose was swimming in circles on the water.

'Okay,' my mother said and put her hand over her eyes to look. 'Where is it?'

Glen Baxter looked at me then with a strange smile, a smile that said he wished I had never mentioned anything about the other goose. And I wished I hadn't either. I looked up in the sky and could see the lines of geese by the thousands shining silver in the light, and I wished we could just leave and go home.

'That one's my mistake there,' Glen Baxter said and grinned. 'I shouldn't have shot that one, Aileen. I got too excited.'

My mother looked out on the lake for a minute, then looked at Glen and back again. 'Poor goose.' She shook her head. 'How will you get it, Glen?'

'I can't get that one now,' Glen said.

My mother looked at him. 'What do you mean?'

'I'm going to leave that one,' Glen said.

'Well, no. You can't leave one,' my mother said. 'You shot it. You have to get it. Isn't that a rule?'

'No,' Glen said.

And my mother looked from Glen to me. 'Wade out and get it, Glen,' she said in a sweet way, and my mother looked young then, like a young girl, in her flimsy short-sleeved waitress dress and her skinny, bare legs in the wheatgrass.

'No.' Glen Baxter looked down at his gun and shook his head. And I didn't know why he wouldn't go, because it would've been easy. The lake was shallow. And you could tell that anyone could've walked out a long way before it got deep, and Glen had on his boots.

My mother looked at the white goose, which was not more than thirty yards from the shore, its head up, moving in slow circles, its wings settled and relaxed so you could see the black tips. 'Wade out and get it, Glenny, won't you, please?' she said. 'They're special things.'

'You don't understand the world, Aileen,' Glen said. 'This can happen. It doesn't matter.'

'But that's so cruel, Glen,' she said, and a sweet smile came on her lips.

'Raise up your own arms, 'Leeny,' Glen said. 'I can't see any angel's wings, can you, Les?' He looked at me, but I looked away.

'Then you go on and get it, Les,' my mother said. 'You weren't raised by crazy people.' I started to go, but Glen Baxter suddenly grabbed me by my shoulder and pulled me back hard, so hard his fingers made bruises in my skin that I saw later.

'Nobody's going,' he said. 'This is over with now.'

And my mother gave Glen a cold look then. 'You don't have

a heart, Glen,' she said. 'There's nothing to love in you. You're just a son of a bitch, that's all.'

And Glen Baxter nodded at my mother, then, as if he understood something he had not understood before, but something that he was willing to know. 'Fine,' he said, 'that's fine.' And he took his big pistol out from against his belly, the big blue revolver I had only seen part of before and that he said protected him, and he pointed it out at the goose on the water, his arm straight away from him, and shot and missed. And then he shot and missed again. The goose made its noise once. And then he hit it dead, because there was no splash. And then he shot it three times more until the gun was empty and the goose's head was down and it was floating toward the middle of the lake where it was empty and dark blue. 'Now who has a heart?' Glen said. But my mother was not there when he turned around. She had already started back to the car and was almost lost from sight in the darkness. And Glen smiled at me then and his face had a wild look on it. 'Okay, Les?' he said.

'Okay,' I said.

'There're limits to everything, right?'

'I guess so,' I said.

'Your mother's a beautiful woman, but she's not the only beautiful woman in Montana.' And I did not say anything. And Glen Baxter suddenly said, 'Here,' and he held the pistol out at me. 'Don't you want this? Don't you want to shoot me? Nobody thinks they'll die. But I'm ready for it right now.' And I did not know what to do then. Though it is true that what I wanted to do was to hit him, hit him as hard in the face as I could, and see him on the ground bleeding and crying and pleading for me to stop. Only at that moment he looked scared to me, and I had never seen a grown man scared before – though I have seen one since – and I felt sorry for him, as though he was already a dead man. And I did not end up hitting him at all.

A light can go out in the heart. All of this happened years ago, but I still can feel now how sad and remote the world was to me. Glen Baxter, I think now, was not a bad man, only a man scared of something he'd never seen before – something soft in himself – his life going a way he didn't like. A woman with a son. Who could blame him there? I don't know what makes people do what they do, or call themselves what they call themselves, only that you have to live someone's life to be the expert.

My mother had tried to see the good side of things, tried to be hopeful in the situation she was handed, tried to look out for us both, and it hadn't worked. It was a strange time in her life then and after that, a time when she had to adjust to being an adult just when she was on the thin edge of things. Too much awareness too early in life was her problem, I think.

And what I felt was only that I had somehow been pushed out into the world, into the real life then, the one I hadn't lived yet. In a year I was gone to hard-rock mining and no-paycheck jobs and not to college. And I have thought more than once about my mother saying that I had not been raised by crazy people, and I don't know what that could mean or what difference it could make, unless it means that love is a reliable commodity, and even that is not always true, as I have found out.

Late on the night that all this took place I was in bed when I heard my mother say, 'Come outside, Les. Come and hear this.' And I went out onto the front porch barefoot and in my underwear, where it was warm like spring, and there was a spring mist in the air. I could see the lights of the Fairfield Coach in the distance, on its way up to Great Falls.

And I could hear geese, white birds in the sky, flying. They made their high-pitched sound like angry yells, and though I couldn't see them high up, it seemed to me they were everywhere. And my mother looked up and said, 'Hear them?' I could smell her hair wet from the shower. 'They leave with the moon,' she said. 'It's still half wild out here.'

And I said, 'I hear them,' and I felt a chill come over my bare chest, and the hair stood up on my arms the way it does before a storm. And for a while we listened.

'When I first married your father, you know, we lived on a street called Bluebird Canyon, in California. And I thought that was the prettiest street and the prettiest name. I suppose no one brings you up like your first love. You don't mind if I say that, do you?' She looked at me hopefully.

'No,' I said.

'We have to keep civilization alive somehow.' And she pulled her little housecoat together because there was a cold vein in the air, a part of the cold that would be on us the next day. 'I don't feel part of things tonight, I guess.'

'It's all right,' I said.

'Do you know where I'd like to go?'

'No,' I said. And I suppose I knew she was angry then, angry with life, but did not want to show me that.

'To the Straits of Juan de Fuca.[11] Wouldn't that be something? Would you like that?'

'I'd like it,' I said. And my mother looked off for a minute, as if she could see the Straits of Juan de Fuca out against the line of mountains, see the lights of things alive and a whole new world.

'I know you liked him,' she said after a moment. 'You and I both suffer fools too well.'

'I didn't like him too much,' I said. 'I didn't really care.'

'He'll fall on his face. I'm sure of that,' she said. And I didn't say anything because I didn't care about Glen Baxter anymore, and was happy not to talk about him. 'Would you tell me something if I asked you? Would you tell me the truth?'

'Yes,' I said.

And my mother did not look at me. 'Just tell the truth,' she said.

'All right,' I said.

'Do you think I'm still very feminine? I'm thirty-two years old now. You don't know what that means. But do you think I am?'

And I stood at the edge of the porch, with the olive trees before me, looking straight up into the mist where I could not see geese but could still hear them flying, could almost feel the air move below their white wings. And I felt the way you feel when you are on a trestle all alone and the train is coming, and you know you have to decide. And I said, 'Yes, I do.' Because that was the truth. And I tried to think of something else then and did not hear what my mother said after that.

And how old was I then? Sixteen. Sixteen is young, but it can also be a grown man. I am forty-one years old now, and I think about that time without regret, though my mother and I never talked in that way again, and I have not heard her voice now in a long, long time.

Starving Again

LORRIE MOORE

Dennis's ex-wife had fallen in love with a man she said was like out of a book. Dennis forgot to ask what book. He was depressed and barely dating. 'I should have said to her, "Yeah, and what book?"' Dennis was always kicking himself on the phone, not an easy thing, the tricky ouch of it. His friend Mave tended to doodle a lot when talking to him, slinky items with features, or a solitary game of tick-tack-toe. Sometimes she even interrupted him to ask what time it was. Her clock was in the other room.

'But you know,' Dennis was saying, 'I've got my own means of revenge: If she wants to go out with other men, I'm going to sit here and just let her.'

'That's an incredibly powerful form of revenge,' said Mave. She was not good on the phone. She needed the face, the pattern of eyes, nose, trembling mouth. When she was on the phone she often had to improvise Dennis's face from a window: the pug nose of the lock, the paned eyes, the lip jut of the sill. Or else she drew another slinky item with features. People talking were meant to look at a face, the disastrous cupcake of it, the hide-and-seek of the heart dashing across. With a phone, you said words, but you never watched them go in. You saw them off at the airport but never knew whether there was anyone there to greet them when they got off the plane.

They met for dinner at some sort of macrobiotic place, because Dennis had recently become obsessed. Before his wife left him, his idea of eating healthy had been to go to McDonald's and order the Filet-o-Fish, but now he had whole books about miso. And about tempeh. Mostly, however, he had books about love. He believed in studying his own heart this way. Men were like that, Mave had noticed. They liked to look in the mirror. For women, mirrors were a chore: Women looked, frowned, got out equipment, and went to work. But for men mirrors were sex: Men locked gazes with their own reflections, undressed themselves with their eyes, and stared for a shockingly long time. Mave believed that not being able to see your life clearly, to scrutinize it intelligently, meant that probably you were at the dead center of it, and that couldn't possibly be a bad thing.

This month Dennis was reading books written supposedly for women, titles like *Get Real, Smarting Cookie, Get Real* and *Why I Hate Myself*. 'Those books are trouble,' said Mave. 'Too many well-adjusted people will endanger the arts in this country. To say nothing of the professions.' She studied Dennis's flipped-over tie, the soft, torn eye of its clipped label. 'You choose to be healthy, and you leave too many good people behind.'

But Dennis said he identified, that the books were amazing, and he reached into the book bag he now carried with him everywhere and read passages aloud. 'Here,' he said to Mave, who had brought her own whiskey to the place and was pouring it into a water glass from which she had drunk all the water and left only the ice. She had had to argue with the waitress to get ice. 'Oh, no – here,' Dennis said. He had found another passage from *Why I Hate Myself* and started to read it, loud and with expression, when suddenly he broke into a disconsolate weep, deep and from the belly. 'Oh, God, I'm sorry.'

Mave shoved her whiskey glass across the table toward him. 'Don't worry about it,' she murmured. He took a sip, then put the book away. He dug through his book bag and found Kleenex to dab at his nose.

'I didn't get like this on my own,' he said. 'There are people responsible.' Inside his bag Mave could see a news magazine with the exasperated headline: ETHIOPIA: WHY ARE THEY STARVING THIS TIME?[1]

'Boredom is heartless,' said Dennis, the tears slowing. He indicated the magazine. 'When the face goes into a yawn, the blood to the chest gets constricted.'

'Are you finished with my drink?'

'No.' He took another gulp and winced. 'I mean, yes,' and he handed it back to Mave, wiped his mouth with a napkin. Mave looked at Dennis's face and was glad no one had broken up with her recently. When someone broke up with you, you became very unattractive, and it confirmed all the doubts that person had ever had about you to begin with. 'Wait, just one more sip.' Someone broke up with you and you yelled. You blistered, withered, and flushed. You apologized to inanimate objects and drank when you swore you wouldn't. You went around humming the theme to *Valley of the Dolls*,[2] doing all the instruments even, lingering on the line about *gotta get off, gonna get, have to get* . . . It wasn't good to go out on that kind of limb for love. You went out on a limb for food, but not for love. Love was not food. Love, thought Mave, was more like the rest rooms at the Ziegfeld: sinks in the stalls, big deal. Mave worked hard to forget very quickly afterward what the men she went out with even looked like. This was called sticking close to the trunk.

'All yours,' said Dennis. He was smiling now. The whiskey brought the blood to his face in a nice way.

Mave looked down at her menu. 'There's no spaghetti and meatballs here. I wanted to order the child's portion of the spaghetti and meatballs.'

'Oh, that reminds me,' said Dennis, shaking a finger for emphasis. With his books away and the whiskey in him, he seemed more confident. 'Did I tell you the guy my wife's seeing is Italian? Milanese, not Brooklyn. What do you suppose that means, her falling in love with an Italian?'

'It means she's going to feel scruffy all the time. It means that he will stare at all the fuzzies on her shirt while she is telling him something painful about a childhood birthday party nobody came to. Let's face it: She's going to start to miss the fact, Dennis, that your hair zooms out all over the goddamn place.'

'I'm getting it cut tomorrow.'

Mave put on her reading glasses. 'This is not a restaurant. Restaurants serve different things from this.'

'You know, one thing about these books for women, I have to tell you. The whole emphasis on locating and accepting your homosexual side is really very powerful. It frees and expands some other sort of love in you.'

Mave looked up at him and smiled. She was drawn to the insane because of their blazing minds. 'So you've located and accepted?'

'Well, I've realized this. I like boys. *And* I like girls.' He leaned toward her confidentially. 'I just don't like *berls*.' Dennis reached again for Mave's whiskey. 'Of course, I am completely in the wrong town. May I?' He leaned his head back, and the ice cubes knocked against his teeth. Water beaded up on his chin. 'So, Mave, who are *you* romancing these days?' Dennis was beginning to look drunk. His lips were smooth and thick and hung open like a change purse.

'These days?' There were little ways like this of stalling for time.

'These right here.'

'Right here. These. I've been seeing Mitch again a little.'

Dennis dropped his forehead into his palm, which had somehow flown up from the table, so that the two met midair in an unsightly smack. 'Mitch! Mave, he's such a womanizer!'

'So I needed to be womanized. I was losing my sheen.'

'You know what you do? You get all your boyfriends on sale. It's called Bargain Debasement. Immolation by desire.'

'Look, you need to be womanized, you go to a womanizer. I don't take these things seriously anymore. I make it a point now to forget what everybody looks like. I'm being Rudolf Bing.[3] I've lost my mind and am traipsing around the South Seas with an inappropriate lover, and I believe in it. I think everybody in a love affair is being Rudolf Bing anyway, and they're vain to believe otherwise . . . Oh, my God, that man in the sweater is feeling his girlfriend's lymph nodes.' Mave put away her reading glasses and fumbled around in her bag for the whiskey flask. That was the thing with hunger: It opened up something dangerous in you, something endless, like a universe, or a cliff. 'I'm sorry. Rudolf Bing is on my mind. He's really been on my mind. I feel like we're all almost like him.'

'Almost like Bing in love,' said Dennis. '*What a day this has been. What a rare mood I'm in.*'[4] Mave was in a long sip. 'I've been listening to that *Live at Carnegie Hall* tape too much.'

'Music! Let's talk about music! Or death! Why do we always have to talk about love?'

'Because our parents were sickos, and we're starved for it.'

'You know what I've decided? I don't want to be cremated. I used to, but now I think it sounds just a little too much like a blender speed. Now I've decided I want to be embalmed, and then I want a plastic surgeon to come put in silicone implants everywhere. Then I want to be laid out in the woods like Snow White, with a gravestone that reads *Gotta Dance.*'[5] The whiskey was going down sweet. That was what happened after a while, with no meal to assist – it had to do the food work on its own. 'There. We talked about death.'

'That's talking about death?'

'What exactly is *kale?* I don't understand why they haven't taken our order yet. I mean, it's crowded now, but it wasn't ten minutes ago. Maybe it was the ice thing.'

'You know what else my wife says about this Italian? She says he goes around singing this same song to himself. You know what it is?'

' "Santa Lucia." '[6]

'No. It's the "Addams Family"[7] theme song: *Their house is a museum, when people come to see-um . . .*'

'Your wife tells you this?'

'We're friends.'

'Don't tell me you're friends. You hate her.'

'We're friends. I don't hate her.'

'You think she's a user and a tart. She's with some guy with great shoes whose coif doesn't collapse into hairpin turns across his part.'

'You used to be a nice person.'

'I never was a nice person. I'm still a nice person.'

'I don't like this year,' said Dennis, his eyes welling again.

'I know,' said Mave. 'Eighty-eight. It's too Sergio Mendes[8] or something.'

'You know, it's OK not to be a nice person.'

'I need your permission? Thank you.' This was what Dennis had been doing lately: granting everyone permission to feel the way they were going to feel regardless. It was the books. Dennis's relationship to his own feelings had become tender, curatorial. Dismantling. Entomological. Mave couldn't be like that. She treated her emotional life the way she treated her car: She let it go, let it tough it out. To friends she said things like 'I know you're thinking this looks like a '79, but it's really an '87.' She finally didn't care to understand all that much about her emotional life; she just went ahead and did it. The point, she thought, was to attend the meager theater of it, quietly, and not stand up in the middle and shout, 'Oh, my God, you can see the crew backstage!' There was a point at which the study of something became a frightening and naive thing.

'But, Dennis, really, why do you think so much about love, of someone loving you or not loving you? That is all you read about, all you talk about.'

'Put the starving people of the world together in a room, and what you get is a lot of conversation about roast beef. They should be talking about the Napoleonic Code?'[9] At the mention of roast beef, Mave's face lit up, greenish, fluorescent. She looked past Dennis and saw the waitress coming toward their table at last: she was moving slowly, meanly, scowling; there was a large paper doily stuck to her shoe. 'I mean . . .' Dennis was saying, looking pointedly at Mave, but Mave was watching the waitress approach. *Oh, life, oh, sweet, forgiven for the ice* . . . He grabbed Mave's wrist. There was always an emergency. And then there was love. And then there was another emergency. That was the sandwiching of it. Emergency. Love. Emergency. 'I mean, it's not as if you've been dozing off,' Dennis was saying, his voice reaching her now, high and watery. 'I mean, correct me if I'm wrong,' he said, 'but I don't think I've been having this conversation alone.' He tightened his grip. 'I mean, have I?'

The Third and Final Continent

JHUMPA LAHIRI

I left India in 1964 with a certificate in commerce and the equiva-
lent, in those days, of ten dollars to my name. For three weeks I
sailed on the SS *Roma*, an Italian cargo vessel, in a third-class
cabin next to the ship's engine, across the Arabian Sea, the Red
Sea, the Mediterranean, and finally to England. I lived in north
London, in Finsbury Park, in a house occupied entirely by penni-
less Bengali bachelors like myself, at least a dozen and sometimes
more, all struggling to educate and establish ourselves abroad.

I attended lectures at LSE[1] and worked at the university
library to get by. We lived three or four to a room, shared a
single, icy toilet, and took turns cooking pots of egg curry,
which we ate with our hands on a table covered with newspapers. Apart from our jobs we had few responsibilities. On
weekends we lounged barefoot in drawstring pajamas, drinking tea and smoking Rothmans, or set out to watch cricket at
Lord's. Some weekends the house was crammed with still more
Bengalis, to whom we had introduced ourselves at the green-
grocer, or on the Tube, and we made yet more egg curry, and
played Mukhesh on a Grundig reel-to-reel,[2] and soaked our
dirty dishes in the bathtub. Every now and then someone in
the house moved out, to live with a woman whom his family
back in Calcutta had determined he was to wed. In 1969, when
I was thirty-six years old, my own marriage was arranged.
Around the same time I was offered a full-time job in America,
in the processing department of a library at MIT. The salary
was generous enough to support a wife, and I was honored
to be hired by a world-famous university, and so I obtained a
sixth-preference green card,[3] and prepared to travel farther still.

By now I had enough money to go by plane. I flew first to Calcutta, to attend my wedding, and a week later I flew to Boston, to begin my new job. During the flight I read *The Student Guide to North America*, a paperback volume that I'd bought before leaving London, for seven shillings six pence on Tottenham Court Road, for although I was no longer a student I was on a budget all the same. I learned that Americans drove on the right side of the road, not the left, and that they called a lift an elevator and an engaged phone busy. 'The pace of life in North America is different from Britain as you will soon discover,' the guidebook informed me. 'Everybody feels he must get to the top. Don't expect an English cup of tea.' As the plane began its descent over Boston Harbor, the pilot announced the weather and time, and that President Nixon had declared a national holiday: two American men had landed on the moon.[4] Several passengers cheered. 'God bless America!' one of them hollered. Across the aisle, I saw a woman praying.

I spent my first night at the YMCA in Central Square, Cambridge, an inexpensive accommodation recommended by my guidebook. It was walking distance from MIT, and steps from the post office and a supermarket called Purity Supreme. The room contained a cot, a desk, and a small wooden cross on one wall. A sign on the door said cooking was strictly forbidden. A bare window overlooked Massachusetts Avenue, a major thoroughfare with traffic in both directions. Car horns, shrill and prolonged, blared one after another. Flashing sirens heralded endless emergencies, and a fleet of buses rumbled past, their doors opening and closing with a powerful hiss, throughout the night. The noise was constantly distracting, at times suffocating. I felt it deep in my ribs, just as I had felt the furious drone of the engine on the SS *Roma*. But there was no ship's deck to escape to, no glittering ocean to thrill my soul, no breeze to cool my face, no one to talk to. I was too tired to pace the gloomy corridors of the YMCA in my drawstring pajamas. Instead I sat at the desk and stared out the window, at the city hall of Cambridge and a row of small shops. In the morning I reported to my job at the Dewey Library, a beige fort-like building by Memorial Drive. I also opened a bank account, rented a post office box, and bought a plastic bowl and a spoon at Woolworth's, a store whose name I recognized from London. I went to Purity Supreme, wandering up and down the aisles, converting ounces to grams and comparing prices to things in England. In the end I bought a small carton of milk and a box of cornflakes. This was my first meal in America. I ate it at my desk. I preferred it to hamburgers or hot dogs, the only alternative I could afford in the coffee shops on Massachusetts Avenue, and, besides, at the time I had yet to consume any beef. Even the simple chore of buying milk was new to me; in London we'd had bottles delivered each morning to our door.

In a week I had adjusted, more or less. I ate cornflakes and milk, morning and night, and bought some bananas for variety, slicing them into the bowl with the edge of my spoon. In addition I bought tea bags and a flask, which the salesman in Woolworth's referred to as a thermos (a flask, he informed me, was used to store whiskey, another thing I had never consumed). For the price of one cup of tea at a coffee shop, I filled the flask with boiling water on my way to work each morning, and brewed the four cups I drank in the course of a day. I bought a larger carton of milk, and learned to leave it on the shaded part of the windowsill, as I had seen another resident at the YMCA do. To pass the time in the evenings I read the *Boston Globe* downstairs, in a spacious room with stained-glass windows. I read every article and advertisement, so that I would grow familiar with things, and when my eyes grew tired I slept. Only I did not sleep well. Each night I had to keep the window wide open; it was the only source of air in the stifling room, and the noise was intolerable. I would lie on the cot with my fingers pressed into my ears, but when I drifted off to sleep my hands fell away, and the noise of the traffic would wake me up again. Pigeon feathers drifted onto the windowsill, and one evening, when I poured milk over my cornflakes, I saw that it had soured. Nevertheless I resolved to stay at the YMCA for six weeks, until my wife's passport and green card were ready. Once she arrived I would have to rent a proper apartment, and from time to time I studied the classified section of the newspaper, or stopped in at the housing office at MIT during my lunch break, to see what was available in my price range. It was in this manner that I discovered a room for immediate occupancy, in a house on a quiet street, the listing said, for eight dollars per week. I copied the number into my guidebook and dialed from a pay telephone, sorting through the coins with which I was still unfamiliar, smaller and lighter than shillings, heavier and brighter than *paisas*.

'Who is speaking?' a woman demanded. Her voice was bold and clamorous.

'Yes, good afternoon, madame. I am calling about the room for rent.'

'Harvard or Tech?'

'I beg your pardon?'

'Are you from Harvard or Tech?'

Gathering that Tech referred to the Massachusetts Institute of Technology, I replied, 'I work at Dewey Library,' adding tentatively, 'at Tech.'

'I only rent rooms to boys from Harvard or Tech!'

'Yes, madame.'

I was given an address and an appointment for seven o'clock that evening. Thirty minutes before the hour I set out, my guidebook in my pocket, my breath fresh with Listerine. I turned down a street shaded with trees, perpendicular to Massachusetts Avenue. Stray blades of grass poked between the cracks of the footpath. In spite of the heat I wore a coat and a tie, regarding the event as I would any other interview; I had never lived in the home of a person who was not Indian. The house, surrounded by a chain-link fence, was off-white with dark brown trim. Unlike the stucco row house I'd lived in in London, this house, fully detached, was covered with wooden shingles, with a tangle of forsythia bushes plastered against the front and sides. When I pressed the calling bell, the woman with whom I had spoken on the phone hollered from what seemed to be just the other side of the door, 'One minute, please!'

Several minutes later the door was opened by a tiny, extremely old woman. A mass of snowy hair was arranged like a small sack on top of her head. As I stepped into the house she

sat down on a wooden bench positioned at the bottom of a
narrow carpeted staircase. Once she was settled on the bench,
in a small pool of light, she peered up at me with undivided
attention. She wore a long black skirt that spread like a stiff
tent to the floor, and a starched white shirt edged with ruffles at
the throat and cuffs. Her hands, folded together in her lap, had
long pallid fingers, with swollen knuckles and tough yellow
nails. Age had battered her features so that she almost resembled a man, with sharp, shrunken eyes and prominent creases
on either side of her nose. Her lips, chapped and faded, had
nearly disappeared, and her eyebrows were missing altogether.
Nevertheless she looked fierce.

'Lock up!' she commanded. She shouted even though I stood
only a few feet away. 'Fasten the chain and firmly press that
button on the knob! This is the first thing you shall do when
you enter, is that clear?'

I locked the door as directed and examined the house. Next
to the bench on which the woman sat was a small round table,
its legs fully concealed, much like the woman's, by a skirt of
lace. The table held a lamp, a transistor radio, a leather change
purse with a silver clasp, and a telephone. A thick wooden cane
coated with a layer of dust was propped against one side. There
was a parlor to my right, lined with bookcases and filled with
shabby claw-footed furniture. In the corner of the parlor I saw
a grand piano with its top down, piled with papers. The piano's
bench was missing; it seemed to be the one on which the woman
was sitting. Somewhere in the house a clock chimed seven
times.

'You're punctual!' the woman proclaimed. 'I expect you
shall be so with the rent!'

'I have a letter, madame.' In my jacket pocket was a letter
confirming my employment from MIT, which I had brought
along to prove that I was indeed from Tech.

She stared at the letter, then handed it back to me carefully,
gripping it with her fingers as if it were a dinner plate heaped
with food instead of a sheet of paper. She did not wear glasses,
and I wondered if she'd read a word of it. 'The last boy was
always late! Still owes me eight dollars! Harvard boys aren't

what they used to be! Only Harvard and Tech in this house!
How's Tech, boy?'

'It is very well.'

'You checked the lock?'

'Yes, madame.'

She slapped the space beside her on the bench with one
hand, and told me to sit down. For a moment she was silent.
Then she intoned, as if she alone possessed this knowledge:

'There is an American flag on the moon!'

'Yes, madame.' Until then I had not thought very much about
the moon shot. It was in the newspaper, of course, article upon
article. The astronauts had landed on the shores of the Sea of
Tranquillity, I had read, traveling farther than anyone in the
history of civilization. For a few hours they explored the moon's
surface. They gathered rocks in their pockets, described their
surroundings (a magnificent desolation, according to one astronaut), spoke by phone to the president, and planted a flag in
lunar soil. The voyage was hailed as man's most awesome achievement. I had seen full-page photographs in the *Globe*, of the
astronauts in their inflated costumes, and read about what certain people in Boston had been doing at the exact moment the
astronauts landed, on a Sunday afternoon. A man said that he
was operating a swan boat with a radio pressed to his ear; a
woman had been baking rolls for her grandchildren.

The woman bellowed, 'A flag on the moon, boy! I heard it
on the radio! Isn't that splendid?'

'Yes, madame.'

But she was not satisfied with my reply. Instead she commanded, 'Say "splendid"!'

I was both baffled and somewhat insulted by the request. It
reminded me of the way I was taught multiplication tables as a
child, repeating after the master, sitting cross-legged, without
shoes or pencils, on the floor of my one-room Tollygunge
school. It also reminded me of my wedding, when I had repeated
endless Sanskrit verses after the priest, verses I barely understood, which joined me to my wife. I said nothing.

'Say "splendid"!' the woman bellowed once again.

'Splendid,' I murmured. I had to repeat the word a second

time at the top of my lungs, so she could hear. I am soft-spoken by nature and was especially reluctant to raise my voice to an elderly woman whom I had met only moments ago, but she did not appear to be offended. If anything the reply pleased her because her next command was:

'Go see the room!'

I rose from the bench and mounted the narrow carpeted staircase. There were five doors, two on either side of an equally narrow hallway, and one at the opposite end. Only one door was partly open. The room contained a twin bed under a sloping ceiling, a brown oval rug, a basin with an exposed pipe, and a chest of drawers. One door, painted white, led to a closet, another to a toilet and a tub. The walls were covered with gray and ivory striped paper. The window was open; net curtains stirred in the breeze. I lifted them away and inspected the view: a small back yard, with a few fruit trees and an empty clothesline. I was satisfied. From the bottom of the stairs I heard the woman demand, 'What is your decision?'

When I returned to the foyer and told her, she picked up the leather change purse on the table, opened the clasp, fished about with her fingers, and produced a key on a thin wire hoop. She informed me that there was a kitchen at the back of the house, accessible through the parlor. I was welcome to use the stove as long as I left it as I found it. Sheets and towels were provided, but keeping them clean was my own responsibility. The rent was due Friday mornings on the ledge above the piano keys. 'And no lady visitors!'

'I am a married man, madame.' It was the first time I had announced this fact to anyone.

But she had not heard. 'No lady visitors!' she insisted. She introduced herself as Mrs Croft.

My wife's name was Mala. The marriage had been arranged by my older brother and his wife. I regarded the proposition with neither objection nor enthusiasm. It was a duty expected of me, as it was expected of every man. She was the daughter of a schoolteacher in Beleghata. I was told that she could cook, knit, embroider, sketch landscapes, and recite poems by Tagore,[5] but these talents could not make up for the fact that she did not possess a fair complexion, and so a string of men had rejected her to her face. She was twenty-seven, an age when her parents had begun to fear that she would never marry, and so they were willing to ship their only child halfway across the world in order to save her from spinsterhood.

For five nights we shared a bed. Each of those nights, after applying cold cream and braiding her hair, which she tied up at the end with a black cotton string, she turned from me and wept; she missed her parents. Although I would be leaving the country in a few days, custom dictated that she was now a part of my household, and for the next six weeks she was to live with my brother and his wife, cooking, cleaning, serving tea and sweets to guests. I did nothing to console her. I lay on my own side of the bed, reading my guidebook by flashlight and anticipating my journey. At times I thought of the tiny room on the other side of the wall which had belonged to my mother. Now the room was practically empty; the wooden pallet on which she'd once slept was piled with trunks and old bedding. Nearly six years ago, before leaving for London, I had watched her die on that bed, had found her playing with her excrement in her final days. Before we cremated her I had cleaned each of her fingernails with a hairpin, and then, because my brother could not bear it, I had assumed the role of eldest son, and had touched the flame to her temple, to release her tormented soul to heaven.

The next morning I moved into the room in Mrs Croft's house. When I unlocked the door I saw that she was sitting on the piano bench, on the same side as the previous evening. She wore the same black skirt, the same starched white blouse, and had her hands folded together the same way in her lap. She looked so much the same that I wondered if she'd spent the whole night on the bench. I put my suitcase upstairs, filled my flask with boiling water in the kitchen, and headed off to work. That evening when I came home from the university, she was still there.

'Sit down, boy!' She slapped the space beside her.

I perched beside her on the bench. I had a bag of groceries with me – more milk, more cornflakes, and more bananas, for my inspection of the kitchen earlier in the day had revealed no spare pots, pans, or cooking utensils. There were only two saucepans in the refrigerator, both containing some orange broth, and a copper kettle on the stove.

'Good evening, madame.'

She asked me if I had checked the lock. I told her I had.

For a moment she was silent. Then suddenly she declared, with the equal measures of disbelief and delight as the night before, 'There's an American flag on the moon, boy!'

'Yes, madame.'

'A flag on the moon! Isn't that splendid?'

I nodded, dreading what I knew was coming. 'Yes, madame.'

'Say "splendid"!'

This time I paused, looking to either side in case anyone were there to overhear me, though I knew perfectly well that the house was empty. I felt like an idiot. But it was a small enough thing to ask. 'Splendid!' I cried out.

Within days it became our routine. In the mornings when I left for the library Mrs Croft was either hidden away in her bedroom, on the other side of the staircase, or she was sitting on the bench, oblivious to my presence, listening to the news or classical music on the radio. But each evening when I returned the same thing happened: she slapped the bench, ordered me to sit down, declared that there was a flag on the moon, and declared that it was splendid. I said it was splendid, too, and then we sat in silence. As awkward as it was, and as endless as it felt to me then, the nightly encounter lasted only about ten minutes; inevitably she would drift off to sleep, her head falling abruptly toward her chest, leaving me free to retire to my room. By then, of course, there was no flag on the moon. The astronauts, I had read in the paper, had taken it down before flying back to Earth. But I did not have the heart to tell her.

Friday morning, when my first week's rent was due, I went to the piano in the parlor to place my money on the ledge. The piano keys were dull and discolored. When I pressed one, it made no sound at all. I had put eight one-dollar bills in an envelope and written Mrs Croft's name on the front of it. I was not in the habit of leaving money unmarked and unattended. From where I stood I could see the profile of her tent-shaped skirt. She was sitting on the bench, listening to the radio. It seemed unnecessary to make her get up and walk all the way to the piano. I never saw her walking about, and assumed, from the cane always propped against the round table at her side, that she did so with difficulty. When I approached the bench she peered up at me and demanded:

'What is your business?'

'The rent, madame.'

'On the ledge above the piano keys!'

'I have it here.' I extended the envelope toward her, but her fingers, folded together in her lap, did not budge. I bowed slightly and lowered the envelope, so that it hovered just above her hands. After a moment she accepted, and nodded her head.

That night when I came home, she did not slap the bench, but out of habit I sat beside her as usual. She asked me if I had checked the lock, but she mentioned nothing about the flag on the moon. Instead she said:

'It was very kind of you!'

'I beg your pardon, madame?'

'Very kind of you!'

She was still holding the envelope in her hands.

On Sunday there was a knock on my door. An elderly woman introduced herself: she was Mrs Croft's daughter, Helen. She walked into the room and looked at each of the walls as if for signs of change, glancing at the shirts that hung in the closet, the neckties draped over the doorknob, the box of cornflakes on the chest of drawers, the dirty bowl and spoon in the basin. She was short and thick-waisted, with cropped silver hair and bright pink lipstick. She wore a sleeveless summer dress, a row of white plastic beads, and spectacles on a chain that hung like a swing against her chest. The backs of her legs were mapped with dark blue veins, and her upper arms sagged like the flesh of a roasted eggplant. She told me she lived in Arlington, a town farther up Massachusetts Avenue. 'I come once a week to bring Mother groceries. Has she sent you packing yet?'

'It is very well, madame.'

'Some of the boys run screaming. But I think she likes you. You're the first boarder she's ever referred to as a gentleman.'

'Not at all, madame.'

She looked at me, noticing my bare feet (I still felt strange wearing shoes indoors, and always removed them before entering my room). 'Are you new to Boston?'

'New to America, madame.'

'From?' She raised her eyebrows.

'I am from Calcutta, India.'

'Is that right? We had a Brazilian fellow, about a year ago. You'll find Cambridge a very international city.'

I nodded, and began to wonder how long our conversation would last. But at that moment we heard Mrs Croft's electrifying voice rising up the stairs. When we stepped into the hallway we heard her hollering:

'You are to come downstairs immediately!'

'What is it?' Helen hollered back.

'Immediately!'

I put on my shoes at once. Helen sighed.

We walked down the staircase. It was too narrow for us to descend side by side, so I followed Helen, who seemed to be in no hurry, and complained at one point that she had a bad knee. 'Have you been walking without your cane?' Helen called out. 'You know you're not supposed to walk without that cane.' She paused, resting her hand on the banister, and looked back at me. 'She slips sometimes.'

For the first time Mrs Croft seemed vulnerable. I pictured her on the floor in front of the bench, flat on her back, staring at the ceiling, her feet pointing in opposite directions. But when we reached the bottom of the staircase she was sitting there as usual, her hands folded together in her lap. Two grocery bags were at her feet. When we stood before her she did not slap the bench, or ask us to sit down. She glared.

'What is it, Mother?'

'It's improper!'

'What's improper?'

'It is improper for a lady and gentleman who are not married to one another to hold a private conversation without a chaperone!'

Helen said she was sixty-eight years old, old enough to be my mother, but Mrs Croft insisted that Helen and I speak to each other downstairs, in the parlor. She added that it was also improper for a lady of Helen's station to reveal her age, and to wear a dress so high above the ankle.

'For your information, Mother, it's 1969. What would you do if you actually left the house one day and saw a girl in a miniskirt?'

Mrs Croft sniffed. 'I'd have her arrested.'

Helen shook her head and picked up one of the grocery bags. I picked up the other one, and followed her through the parlor and into the kitchen. The bags were filled with cans of soup, which Helen opened up one by one with a few cranks of a can opener. She tossed the old soup in the saucepans into the sink, rinsed the pans under the tap, filled them with soup from the newly opened cans, and put them back in the refrigerator. 'A few years ago she could still open the cans herself,' Helen said. 'She hates that I do it for her now. But the piano killed her hands.' She put on her spectacles, glanced at the cupboards, and spotted my tea bags. 'Shall we have a cup?'

I filled the kettle on the stove. 'I beg your pardon, madame. The piano?'

'She used to give lessons. For forty years. It was how she raised us after my father died.' Helen put her hands on her hips, staring at the open refrigerator. She reached into the back, pulled out a wrapped stick of butter, frowned, and tossed it into the garbage. 'That ought to do it,' she said, and put the unopened cans of soup in the cupboard. I sat at the table and watched as Helen washed the dirty dishes, tied up the garbage bag, watered a spider plant over the sink, and poured boiling water into two cups. She handed one to me without milk, the string of the tea bag trailing over the side, and sat down at the table.

'Excuse me, madame, but is it enough?'

Helen took a sip of her tea. Her lipstick left a smiling pink stain on the inside rim of the cup. 'Is what enough?'

'The soup in the pans. Is it enough food for Mrs Croft?'

'She won't eat anything else. She stopped eating solids after she turned one hundred. That was, let's see, three years ago.'

I was mortified. I had assumed Mrs Croft was in her eighties, perhaps as old as ninety. I had never known a person who had lived for over a century. That this person was a widow who lived alone mortified me further still. It was widowhood that had driven my own mother insane. My father, who worked as a clerk at the General Post Office of Calcutta, died of encephalitis when I was sixteen. My mother refused to adjust to life without him; instead she sank deeper into a world of darkness from which neither I, nor my brother, nor concerned relatives, nor psychiatric clinics on Rashbihari Avenue could save her. What pained me most was to see her so unguarded, to hear her burp after meals or expel gas in front of company without the slightest embarrassment. After my father's death my brother abandoned his schooling and began to work in the jute mill he would eventually manage, in order to keep the household running. And so it was my job to sit by my mother's feet and study for my exams as she counted and recounted the bracelets on her arm as if they were the beads of an abacus. We tried to keep an eye on her. Once she had wandered half naked to the tram depot before we were able to bring her inside again.

'I am happy to warm Mrs Croft's soup in the evenings,' I suggested, removing the tea bag from my cup and squeezing out the liquor. 'It is no trouble.'

Helen looked at her watch, stood up, and poured the rest of her tea into the sink. 'I wouldn't if I were you. That's the sort of thing that would kill her altogether.'

That evening, when Helen had gone back to Arlington and Mrs Croft and I were alone again, I began to worry. Now that I knew how very old she was, I worried that something would happen to her in the middle of the night, or when I was out during the day. As vigorous as her voice was, and imperious as she seemed, I knew that even a scratch or a cough could kill a person that old; each day she lived, I knew, was something of a miracle. Although Helen had seemed friendly enough, a small part of me worried that she might accuse me of negligence if anything were to happen. Helen didn't seem worried. She came and went, bringing soup for Mrs Croft, one Sunday after the next.

In this manner the six weeks of that summer passed. I came home each evening, after my hours at the library, and spent a few minutes on the piano bench with Mrs Croft. I gave her a bit of my company, and assured her that I had checked the lock, and told her that the flag on the moon was splendid. Some evenings I sat beside her long after she had drifted off to sleep, still in awe of how many years she had spent on this earth. At times I tried to picture the world she had been born into, in 1866[6] – a world, I imagined, filled with women in long black skirts, and chaste conversations in the parlor. Now, when I looked at her hands with their swollen knuckles folded together in her lap, I imagined them smooth and slim, striking the piano keys. At times I came downstairs before going to sleep, to make sure she was sitting upright on the bench, or was safe in her bedroom. On Fridays I made sure to put the rent in her hands. There was nothing I could do for her beyond these simple gestures. I was not her son, and apart from those eight dollars, I owed her nothing.

At the end of August, Mala's passport and green card were ready. I received a telegram with her flight information; my brother's house in Calcutta had no telephone. Around that time I also received a letter from her, written only a few days after we had parted. There was no salutation; addressing me by name would have assumed an intimacy we had not yet discovered. It contained only a few lines. 'I write in English in preparation for the journey. Here I am very much lonely. Is it very cold there. Is there snow. Yours, Mala.'

I was not touched by her words. We had spent only a handful of days in each other's company. And yet we were bound together; for six weeks she had worn an iron bangle on her wrist, and applied vermilion powder to the part in her hair, to signify to the world that she was a bride. In those six weeks I regarded her arrival as I would the arrival of a coming month, or season – something inevitable, but meaningless at the time.

So little did I know her that, while details of her face sometimes rose to my memory, I could not conjure up the whole of it.

A few days after receiving the letter, as I was walking to work in the morning, I saw an Indian woman on the other side of Massachusetts Avenue, wearing a sari with its free end nearly dragging on the footpath, and pushing a child in a stroller. An American woman with a small black dog on a leash was walking to one side of her. Suddenly the dog began barking. From the other side of the street I watched as the Indian woman, startled, stopped in her path, at which point the dog leapt up and seized the end of the sari between its teeth. The American woman scolded the dog, appeared to apologize, and walked quickly away, leaving the Indian woman to fix her sari in the middle of the footpath, and quiet her crying child. She did not see me standing there, and eventually she continued on her way. Such a mishap, I realized that morning, would soon be my concern. It was my duty to take care of Mala, to welcome her and protect her. I would have to buy her her first pair of snow boots, her first winter coat. I would have to tell her which streets to avoid, which way the traffic came, tell her to wear her sari so that the free end did not drag on the footpath. A five-mile separation from her parents, I recalled with some irritation, had caused her to weep.

Unlike Mala, I was used to it all by then: used to cornflakes and milk, used to Helen's visits, used to sitting on the bench with Mrs Croft. The only thing I was not used to was Mala. Nevertheless I did what I had to do. I went to the housing office at MIT and found a furnished apartment a few blocks away, with a double bed and a private kitchen and bath, for forty dollars a week. One last Friday I handed Mrs Croft eight one-dollar bills in an envelope, brought my suitcase downstairs, and informed her that I was moving. She put my key into her change purse. The last thing she asked me to do was hand her the cane propped against the table, so that she could walk to the door and lock it behind me. 'Good-bye, then,' she said, and retreated back into the house. I did not expect any display of emotion, but I was disappointed all the same. I was only a boarder, a man who paid her a bit of money and passed in and out of her home for six weeks. Compared to a century, it was no time at all.

At the airport I recognized Mala immediately. The free end of her sari did not drag on the floor, but was draped in a sign of bridal modesty over her head, just as it had draped my mother until the day my father died. Her thin brown arms were stacked with gold bracelets, a small red circle was painted on her forehead, and the edges of her feet were tinted with a decorative red dye. I did not embrace her, or kiss her, or take her hand. Instead I asked her, speaking Bengali for the first time in America, if she was hungry.

She hesitated, then nodded yes.

I told her I had prepared some egg curry at home. 'What did they give you to eat on the plane?'

'I didn't eat.'

'All the way from Calcutta?'

'The menu said oxtail soup.'

'But surely there were other items.'

'The thought of eating an ox's tail made me lose my appetite.'

When we arrived home, Mala opened up one of her suit-cases, and presented me with two pullover sweaters, both made with bright blue wool, which she had knitted in the course of our separation, one with a V neck, the other covered with cables. I tried them on; both were tight under the arms. She had also brought me two new pairs of drawstring pajamas, a letter from my brother, and a packet of loose Darjeeling tea. I had no present for her apart from the egg curry. We sat at a bare table, each of us staring at our plates. We ate with our hands, another thing I had not yet done in America.

'The house is nice,' she said. 'Also the egg curry.' With her left hand she held the end of her sari to her chest, so it would not slip off her head.

'I don't know many recipes.'

She nodded, peeling the skin off each of her potatoes before eating them. At one point the sari slipped to her shoulders. She readjusted it at once.

'There is no need to cover your head,' I said. 'I don't mind. It doesn't matter here.'

She kept it covered anyway.

I waited to get used to her, to her presence at my side, at my table and in my bed, but a week later we were still strangers. I still was not used to coming home to an apartment that smelled of steamed rice, and finding that the basin in the bathroom was always wiped clean, our two toothbrushes lying side by side, a cake of Pears soap from India resting in the soap dish. I was not used to the fragrance of the coconut oil she rubbed every other night into her scalp, or the delicate sound her bracelets made as she moved about the apartment. In the mornings she was always awake before I was. The first morning when I came into the kitchen she had heated up the leftovers and set a plate with a spoonful of salt on its edge on the table, assuming I would eat rice for breakfast, as most Bengali husbands did. I told her cereal would do, and the next morning when I came into the kitchen she had already poured the cornflakes into my bowl. One morning she walked with me down Massachusetts Avenue to MIT, where I gave her a short tour of the campus. On the way we stopped at a hardware store and I made a copy of the key, so that she could let herself into the apartment. The next morning before I left for work she asked me for a few dollars. I parted with them reluctantly, but I knew that this, too, was now normal. When I came home from work there was a potato peeler in the kitchen drawer, and a tablecloth on the table, and chicken curry made with fresh garlic and ginger on the stove. We did not have a television in those days. After dinner I read the newspaper, while Mala sat at the kitchen table, working on a cardigan for herself with more of the bright blue wool, or writing letters home.

At the end of our first week, on Friday, I suggested going out. Mala set down her knitting and disappeared into the bathroom. When she emerged I regretted the suggestion; she had put on a clean silk sari and extra bracelets, and coiled her hair with a flattering side part on top of her head. She was prepared as if for a party, or at the very least for the cinema, but I had no such destination in mind. The evening air was balmy. We walked several blocks down Massachusetts Avenue, looking into the windows of restaurants and shops. Then, without thinking, I led her down the quiet street where for so many nights I had walked alone.

'This is where I lived before you came,' I said, stopping at Mrs Croft's chain-link fence.

'In such a big house?'

'I had a small room upstairs. At the back.'

'Who else lives there?'

'A very old woman.'

'With her family?'

'Alone.'

'But who takes care of her?'

I opened the gate. 'For the most part she takes care of herself.'

I wondered if Mrs Croft would remember me; I wondered if she had a new boarder to sit with her on the bench each evening. When I pressed the bell I expected the same long wait as that day of our first meeting, when I did not have a key. But this time the door was opened almost immediately, by Helen. Mrs Croft was not sitting on the bench. The bench was gone.

'Hello there,' Helen said, smiling with her bright pink lips at Mala. 'Mother's in the parlor. Will you be visiting awhile?'

'As you wish, madame.'

'Then I think I'll run to the store, if you don't mind. She had a little accident. We can't leave her alone these days, not even for a minute.'

I locked the door after Helen and walked into the parlor. Mrs Croft was lying flat on her back, her head on a peach-colored cushion, a thin white quilt spread over her body. Her hands were folded together on top of her chest. When she saw me she pointed at the sofa, and told me to sit down. I took my place as directed, but Mala wandered over to the piano and sat on the bench, which was now positioned where it belonged.

'I broke my hip!' Mrs Croft announced, as if no time had passed.

'Oh dear, madame.'

'I fell off the bench!'

'I am so sorry, madame.'

'It was the middle of the night! Do you know what I did, boy?'

I shook my head.

'I called the police!'

She stared up at the ceiling and grinned sedately, exposing a crowded row of long gray teeth. Not one was missing. 'What do you say to that, boy?'

As stunned as I was, I knew what I had to say. With no hesitation at all, I cried out, 'Splendid!'

Mala laughed then. Her voice was full of kindness, her eyes bright with amusement. I had never heard her laugh before, and it was loud enough so that Mrs Croft had heard, too. She turned to Mala and glared.

'Who is she, boy?'

'She is my wife, madame.'

Mrs Croft pressed her head at an angle against the cushion to get a better look. 'Can you play the piano?'

'No, madame,' Mala replied.

'Then stand up!'

Mala rose to her feet, adjusting the end of her sari over her head and holding it to her chest, and, for the first time since her arrival, I felt sympathy. I remembered my first days in London, learning how to take the Tube to Russell Square, riding an escalator for the first time, being unable to understand that when the man cried 'piper' it meant 'paper,' being unable to decipher, for a whole year, that the conductor said 'mind the gap' as the train pulled away from each station. Like me, Mala had traveled far from home, not knowing where she was going, or what she would find, for no reason other than to be my wife. As strange as it seemed, I knew in my heart that one day her death would affect me, and stranger still, that mine would affect her. I wanted somehow to explain this to Mrs Croft, who was still scrutinizing Mala from top to toe with what seemed to be placid disdain. I wondered if Mrs Croft had ever seen a woman in a sari, with a dot painted on her forehead and bracelets stacked on her wrists. I wondered what she would object to. I wondered if she could see the red dye still vivid on Mala's feet, all but obscured by the bottom edge of her sari. At last Mrs Croft declared, with the equal measures of disbelief and delight I knew well:

'She is a perfect lady!'

Now it was I who laughed. I did so quietly, and Mrs Croft did not hear me. But Mala had heard, and, for the first time, we looked at each other and smiled.

I like to think of that moment in Mrs Croft's parlor as the moment when the distance between Mala and me began to lessen. Although we were not yet fully in love, I like to think of the months that followed as a honeymoon of sorts. Together we explored the city and met other Bengalis, some of whom are still friends today. We discovered that a man named Bill sold fresh fish on Prospect Street, and that a shop in Harvard Square called Cardullo's sold bay leaves and cloves. In the evenings we walked to the Charles River to watch sailboats drift across the water, or had ice cream cones in Harvard Yard. We bought an Instamatic camera with which to document our life together, and I took pictures of her posing in front of the Prudential building,[7] so that she could send them to her parents. At night we kissed, shy at first but quickly bold, and discovered pleasure and solace in each other's arms. I told her about my voyage on the SS *Roma*, and about Finsbury Park and the YMCA, and my evenings on the bench with Mrs Croft. When I told her stories about my mother, she wept. It was Mala who consoled me when, reading the *Globe* one evening, I came across Mrs Croft's obituary. I had not thought of her in several months – by then those six weeks of the summer were already a remote interlude in my past – but when I learned of her death I was stricken, so much so that when Mala looked up from her knitting she found me staring at the wall, the newspaper neglected in my lap, unable to speak. Mrs Croft's was the first death I mourned in America, for hers was the first life I had admired; she had left this world at last, ancient and alone, never to return.

As for me, I have not strayed much farther. Mala and I live in a town about twenty miles from Boston, on a tree-lined street much like Mrs Croft's, in a house we own, with a garden that saves us from buying tomatoes in summer, and room for guests. We are American citizens now, so that we can collect social security when it is time. Though we visit Calcutta every

few years, and bring back more drawstring pajamas and Darjeeling tea, we have decided to grow old here. I work in a small
college library. We have a son who attends Harvard University.
Mala no longer drapes the end of her sari over her head, or
weeps at night for her parents, but occasionally she weeps for
our son. So we drive to Cambridge to visit him, or bring him
home for a weekend, so that he can eat rice with us with his
hands, and speak in Bengali, things we sometimes worry he
will no longer do after we die.

Whenever we make that drive, I always make it a point to
take Massachusetts Avenue, in spite of the traffic. I barely recognize the buildings now, but each time I am there I return
instantly to those six weeks as if they were only the other day,
and I slow down and point to Mrs Croft's street, saying to my
son, here was my first home in America, where I lived with a
woman who was 103. 'Remember?' Mala says, and smiles,
amazed, as I am, that there was ever a time that we were
strangers. My son always expresses his astonishment, not at
Mrs Croft's age, but at how little I paid in rent, a fact nearly as
inconceivable to him as a flag on the moon was to a woman
born in 1866. In my son's eyes I see the ambition that had first
hurled me across the world. In a few years he will graduate and
pave his way, alone and unprotected. But I remind myself that
he has a father who is still living, a mother who is happy and
strong. Whenever he is discouraged, I tell him that if I can sur-
vive on three continents, then there is no obstacle he cannot
conquer. While the astronauts, heroes forever, spent mere hours
on the moon, I have remained in this new world for nearly
thirty years. I know that my achievement is quite ordinary. I am
not the only man to seek his fortune far from home, and certainly I am not the first. Still, there are times I am bewildered
by each mile I have traveled, each meal I have eaten, each person
I have known, each room in which I have slept. As ordinary as it
all appears, there are times when it is beyond my imagination.

The Caterpillar

LYDIA DAVIS

I find a small caterpillar in my bed in the morning. There is no good window to throw him from and I don't crush or kill a living thing if I don't have to. I will go to the trouble of carrying this thin, dark, hairless little caterpillar down the stairs and out to the garden.

He is not an inchworm, though he is the size of an inchworm. He does not hump up into the middle but travels steadily along on his many pairs of legs. As I leave the bedroom, he is quite speedily walking around the slopes of my hand.

But halfway down the stairs, he is gone – my hand is blank on every side. The caterpillar must have let go and dropped. I can't see him. The stairwell is dim and the stairs are painted dark brown. I could get a flashlight and search for this tiny thing, in order to save his life. But I will not go that far – he will have to do the best he can. Yet how can he make his way down to the back door and out into the garden?

I go on about my business. I think I've forgotten him, but I haven't. Every time I go upstairs or down, I avoid his side of the stairs. I am sure he is there trying to get down.

At last I give in. I get the flashlight. Now the trouble is that the stairs are so dirty. I don't clean them because no one ever sees them here in the dark. And the caterpillar is, or was, so small. Many things under the beam of the flashlight look rather like him – a very slim splinter of wood or a thick piece of thread. But when I poke them, they don't move.

I look on every step on his side of the stairs, and then on both sides. You get somewhat attached to any living thing once you try to help it. But he is nowhere. There is so much dust and dog hair on the steps. The dust may have stuck to his little body and made it hard for him to move or at least to go in the direction he wanted to go in. It may have dried him out. But why would he even go down instead of up? I haven't looked on the landing above where he disappeared. I will not go that far.

I go back to my work. Then I begin to forget the caterpillar. I forget him for as long as one hour, until I happen to go to the stairs again. This time I see that there is something which is just the right size, shape, and color on one of the steps. But it is flat and dry. It can't have started out as him. It must be a short pine needle or some other plant part.

The next time I think of him, I see that I have forgotten him for several hours. I think of him only when I go up or down the stairs. After all, he is really there somewhere, trying to find his way to a green leaf, or dying. But already I don't care as much. Soon, I'm sure, I will forget him entirely.

Later there is an unpleasant animal smell lingering about the stairwell, but it can't be him. He is too small to have any smell. He has probably died by now. He is simply too small, really, for me to go on thinking about him.

Notes

'The Little Man in Black', Washington Irving (pp. 1–8)

1. *sugar-loaf hat*: a conical hat, thought to resemble a pile of refined sugar, which was worn during the Tudor and Stuart periods and associated with the Puritans.
2. *Raw-head-and-bloody-bones himself*: the bogeyman. A British phrase that spread to America, and, according to John Locke (1632–1704), was often used 'to awe children, and keep them in subjection'.
3. *turnspit*: a short-legged, long-bodied dog, bred to turn the roasting-spit by running within a kind of tread-wheel connected to it. A lowly breed.
4. *familiar*: a pet, but also suggestive of a demon.
5. *necromancy*: the art of predicting the future by communication with the dead, or, more generally, divination, sorcery, witchcraft, enchantment.
6. *the wicked cease from troubling*: from Job 3: 17.
7. *Linkum Fidelius*: the sayings of this fictional character are quoted throughout *Salmagundi*, the periodical written by Irving, his brother and a friend from 1807 to 1808. Irving may have been thinking of the town of Linkum, a made-up place featured in Scots ballads such as 'Lord Livingston' and 'Fair Janet'; 'Linkum' may also be a corruption of linkman, or torch-bearer.

'Young Goodman Brown', Nathaniel Hawthorne (pp. 9–22)

1. *Salem village*: the village, now known as Danvers, is twenty miles from Boston and was the centre of the 1692 witch trials. One hundred and forty-one people were arrested, nineteen were hanged as witches and one was crushed to death. Not to be confused with the town of Salem where Hawthorne was born.
2. *of all nights in the year*: perhaps 31 October, Hallowe'en.

3. *errand*: an expedition for a specific purpose. Perhaps also an allu-
    sion to Samuel Danforth's 1670 sermon 'Errand into the Wilderness'.

4. *justified*: in Puritan thought, to be justified also meant being
    chosen or elected by God.

5. *the Old South*: the Old South Meeting House in Boston.

6. *King William's court*: the court of William of Orange, who ruled
    England from 1689 to 1702.

7. *kept covenant*: kept to the arrangement. Covenant also has a theo-
    logical meaning: Calvinist thought emphasized God's contractual
    promises – with Christ, concerning human salvation, but also
    with men and women, making it clear what their duties were.

8. *Quaker woman*: the Puritans viewed Quakers as heretics.

9. *to set fire to an Indian village, in King Philip's war*: the war
    between English colonists and the Native American inhabitants
    of southern New England (1675–6) is named after the latter's
    leader, Metacom (1639–76), known to the English as King Philip.
    Captain William Hathorne (1645–78), Hawthorne's first American
    forebear, took part in the campaign and in the burning of a
    Narragansett village fort in 1675.

10. *catechism*: several critics have identified this as John Cotton's
    catechism, *Milk for Babes* (1646), which emphasizes humanity's
    innate depravity.

11. *Goody Cloyse*: the historical Sarah Cloyse was accused of witch-
    craft and imprisoned but she was later freed.

12. *gossip*: from 'god-sibb', a person spiritually related to another
    through sponsorship at a baptism; a godparent.

13. *that unhanged witch, Goody Cory . . . the juice of smallage and
    cinque-foil and wolf's-bane*: the historical Martha Cory was
    hanged for witchcraft in 1692. Made of wild celery, potentilla
    and (poisonous) aconite the potion was supposed to endow its
    drinker with the power to fly.

14. *the Egyptian Magi*: the Magi demonstrated their magical powers
    to Moses by turning their rods into serpents. See Exodus 7: 11–13.

15. *figure*: the word substituted for the more definite 'apparition' in
    the story's earlier versions.

16. *Martha Carrier . . . queen of hell*: Martha Carrier was hanged as
    a witch in 1692.

'The Tell-Tale Heart', Edgar Allan Poe (pp. 23–8)

1. *all things in the heaven and in the earth*: a paraphrase of Philip-
    pians 2: 10.

2. *with a film over it*: suggesting cataract.
3. *death watches in the wall*: beetles which eat the timber of buildings.
4. *tattoo*: a regular, drum-like beat.
5. *scantlings*: small beams of wood supporting the floor.

'Aunt Hetty on Matrimony',
Fanny Fern (pp. 29–30)

1. *antimonial*: vomit-inducing. Antimony is a chemical element which was used as an emetic.
2. *lucifer-match*: one of the first commercial friction matches.

'Jim Smiley and His Jumping Frog',
Mark Twain (pp. 31–7)

1. *Mr A. Ward*: Twain had promised a contribution to a book edited by Artemus Ward, a famous humorist. 'Jim Smiley and His Jumping Frog' arrived too late but was passed on to the New York *Saturday Press*.
2. *'49*: 1849, the year the California Gold Rush began.
3. *the big flume*: a waterway used to transport logs and perhaps also to sift gold from sediment.
4. *straddle-bug*: a long-legged beetle.
5. *spraddling up*: sprawling.
6. *Andrew Jackson*: (1767–1852); the dog is named for the seventh President, who was associated with the frontier and with a tough and scrappy populism.
7. *Dan'l Webster*: (1782–1852); the Whig senator from Massachusetts was often caricatured as a frog because of his big belly and style of oratory. In *The Adventures of Tom Sawyer* (1876), the village mayor emulates his eloquence.
8. *a red*: a one-cent coin was made of copper. Often used to refer to a trivial amount of money.

'The Wonderful Tar-Baby Story',
Joel Chandler Harris (pp. 38–9)

1. *calamus root*: *Acorus calamus* or *Acorus americanus* (Sweet Flag) is used medicinally and as a stimulant; some believe it to be hallucinogenic.

'Two Friends',
Mary Wilkins Freeman (pp. 40–52)

1. *meetly enough*: fittingly enough.
2. *pillow-tick*: pillow case.

'The Wife of His Youth',
Charles W. Chesnutt (pp. 53–65)

1. *The Wife of His Youth*: see Proverbs 5: 18–20.
2. *a pillar of cloud by day and of fire by night*: see Exodus 13: 21.
3. *Groveland*: modelled on Chesnutt's home town of Cleveland, Ohio; perhaps a verbal play on Grover Cleveland, President in1885–9 and 1893–7.
4. *With malice towards none, with charity for all*: from Abraham Lincoln's second inaugural address, 1865.
5. *Tennyson*: Alfred, Lord Tennyson (1809–92), English poet. As well as 'A Dream of Fair Women' (1832), Ryder reads from 'Margaret' (1832) and 'Sir Launcelot and Queen Guinevere' (1842).
6. *triflin'es'*: good-for-nothing.
7. *words that we all know*: he quotes *Hamlet*, I, iii, 78–80.

'The Real Right Thing',
Henry James (pp. 66–79)

1. *a Johnson and a Scott, with a Boswell and a Lockhart to help*: James Boswell (1740–95) published *The Life of Samuel Johnson* in 1791; John Gibson Lockhart (1794–1854) was the author of *The Life of Sir Walter Scott* (1837–9).
2. *decadent*: a term used, mainly by hostile critics, to describe the self-consciously elaborate and daring style of a number of late-nineteenth-century artists and writers.

'An Episode of War',
Stephen Crane (pp. 80–84)

1. *blue infantry*: the Union Army wore blue uniforms during the Civil War.

'Hearts and Hands', O. Henry (pp. 85–7)

1. *the eastbound B. & M. express*: the Burlington and Missouri River Railroad.

'The Untold Lie', Sherwood Anderson (pp. 88–93)

1.   *the down train*: the southbound train.

'Out of Season', Ernest Hemingway (pp. 94-100)

1.   *a musette*: a canvas and leather shoulder bag used by American officers during World War I.
2.   *Cortina*: Cortina d'Ampezzo, the ski resort in the Dolomites where Hemingway and his wife stayed (at the Hotel Bellevue) in the spring of 1923.
3.   *Max Beerbohm*: an English writer and caricaturist (1872–1956) associated with the late-nineteenth-century Decadent movement.
4.   *Geld:* money (German); *lire* were the Italian currency.
5.   *Was wollen sie?*: What do you want?(German).
6.   *vecchio*: old man (Italian).
7.   *Senta, caro!*: Listen, mate (Italian).
8.   *Pane, salami, formaggio*: bread, sausage, cheese (Italian).
9.   *Carleton Club*: Hemingway is presumably thinking of the Carlton Club – the oldest and most elite Conservative club in London.

'Atrophy', Edith Wharton (pp. 101–12)

1.   *'sixties*: 1860s.
2.   *Bath chair*: a kind of wheelchair invented in Bath in the 1750s and, in a modified form, still in use in the 1920s.
3.   *A resuscitated fly buzzed*: perhaps an allusion to Emily Dickinson's poem 'I heard a Fly buzz – when I died' (1862).

'The Whistle', Eudora Welty (pp. 117–22)

1.   *Almanac*: an annual book of tables, containing a calendar, with astronomical data and calculations, ecclesiastical anniversaries and other notable dates.

'Barn Burning', William Faulkner (pp. 123–42)

1.   *the scarlet devils and the silver curve of fish*: logos used by the Underwood canned food company.
2.   *Colonel Sartoris Snopes*: Sarty has been named after John Sartoris, whom he mistakenly thinks his father fought under during the Civil War. The Colonel was introduced in Faulkner's first Yoknapatawpha novel, *Sartoris* (1929).

3. *a Confederate provost's man*: a military policeman for the southern secessionist army.

4. *locusts*: in North America the locust-tree is a kind of acacia (*Robinia pseudoacacia*).

5. *blue or gray*: blue was the uniform colour of the Union army, gray that of the Confederates.

6. *owning me body and soul for the next eight months*: Abner Snopes is a sharecropper on a fixed contract. Landlords lent a portion of land, equipment and other goods to a tenant in return for an agreed share of the crop produced. The system, which became widespread after the Civil War, exploited landless farmers whose 'share' remained at subsistence level.

7. *Cherokee roses*: *Rosa laevigata* grows along the Trail of Tears, the route that the Cherokee and other Native American nations followed in their forced relocation to Oklahoma in the 1830s. The white petals of the rose are said to represent Cherokee tears, the yellow centre their stolen gold, and the seven leaves on each stem the seven clans of the nation.

8. *whippoorwill*: a nightjar with a haunting song, frequently evoked in American literature.

9. *hame*: either of the two curved bars holding the traces of the harness on a plough. Faulkner later refers to different parts of the plough: the 'logger-head', the U-shaped hook which attaches the hame to the traces; the 'straight stock', the plough's frame; and the 'cutter', a blade that makes a vertical cut, clearing the way for the plough share's horizontal cut. A 'middle buster', mentioned further on, is a shallow plough designed to move earth to either side of a central furrow and was often used between rows of established cotton plants. Its use implies that Sarty and his brother are working in a field that has already been ploughed and planted by someone else.

10. *shoat*: a young weaned pig.

11. *late*: corn should be planted in March, not May.

12. *Malbrouck*: the popular name of John Churchill, first Duke of Marlborough, who was notorious for embezzlement and taking bribes during the War of the Spanish Succession (1701–14).

13. *quiring*: resounding, like music sung by a choir.

'The Lost Decade', F. Scott Fitzgerald (pp. 143–6)

1. *Dartmouth 'Jack-o-Lantern'*: a humour magazine at Dartmouth College. This reference supports the view that Orrison Brown is

a portrait of the novelist Budd Schulberg (1914–2009), who befriended Fitzgerald in 1939.

2. *Voisins or '21'*: fashionable, expensive restaurants in Manhattan. Voisins was at 375 Park Avenue, and '21' is still at 21 West 52nd Street.

3. *Moriarty's*: a famous Irish pub in Philadelphia.

4. *Admiral Byrd's hideout at the South Pole*: an explorer and aviator, Richard E. Byrd (1888–1957) made four expeditions to the Antarctic. The second trip, in 1933, included five solitary months holed up in his base camp. Byrd wrote about the experience in a 1938 book entitled *Alone*.

5. *Cole Porter*: (1891–64); an American composer, song-writer and acquaintance of Fitzgerald who lived in Europe during the 1920s.

'Now You Cookin' with Gas',
Zora Neale Hurston (pp. 147–55)

A number of the following notes, marked (H), are drawn from Hurston's own glossary to this story (see 'Harlem Slanguage', *The Complete Stories*, HarperCollins, 1995).

1. *Jelly . . . sweet-backing . . . Scooter-pooker*: 'jelly' means 'sex'. A 'jelly bean', like a 'sweet back', a 'scooter-pooker' and 'pimp', is 'a man who lives by sex' (H).

2. *frail eel*: pretty girl.

3. *zoot suit with the reet pleats*: 'Harlem style suit, padded shoulders, 43-inch trousers at the knee with cuff so small it needs a zipper to get into, high waist line, fancy lapels, bushels of buttons, etc.' (H). They were also known as 'shag suits'.

4. *a piano*: spare-ribs.

5. *pe-ola*: very light-skinned woman, like Peola Johnson in Fannie Hurst's 1933 novel *Imitation of Life*.

6. *play de dozens*: 'low-rating the ancestors of your opponent' (H).

7. *lam blacks*: very dark-skinned people.

8. *I knocks de pad . . . on Sugar Hill*: 'I have sex.' Sugar Hill was an area in north-west Harlem where the wealthy could experience the 'sweet life'.

9. *Gang Busters . . . MARCH OF TIME*: *Gang Busters* was a popular radio drama (1935–57) offering 'authentic police case histories'. Its opening sound effects (whistles, sirens, guns, tyres, etc.) resulted in a popular catchphrase 'come on like Gang Busters'. Launched in 1931, *March of Time* was the first network

dramatized news radio programme. In 1935, a companion monthly newsreel was launched. The radio programme continued until 1945 and the newsreel to 1951.

10. *Diddy-Wah-Diddy ... Ginny-Gall*: both are described as suburbs of Hell in Hurston's glossary.

11. *My people! My people!! Free schools and dumb jigs*: 'My people! My people!!' is 'The saddest and funniest expression in the Negro language ... when a progressive Negro observes the backwardness of some members' (H). 'Free schools and dumb jigs' is said 'when something particularly stupid is done' (H).

12. *I got Indian blood in me*: Hurston begins her 1928 essay 'How It Feels to Be Colored Me' with the ironic comment that she is 'the only Negro in the United States whose grandfather on the mother's side was *not* an Indian chief'.

13. *pecker-woods*: a derogatory term for poor Southern whites, who were thought to resemble red-headed woodpeckers. 'Cracker', another contemptuous term, is used later on. Georgia was known as 'the Cracker State'.

14. *I shot him lightly and he died politely*: 'I completely outdid him' (H).

15. *my pocket-book*: handbag or purse. Also a slang term for vagina.

16. *See you in the funny papers*: the newspaper comic strips. A popular farewell.

17. *Abyssinia*: inspired by Psalm 68: 31 ('Ethiopia shall soon stretch out her hands unto God'), many African Americans thought of the country in allegorical terms, as an ancestral homeland. Of particular threat to this idea was Mussolini's invasion in 1935.

'The First Seven Years', Bernard Malamud (pp. 156–66)

1. *The First Seven Years*: this alludes to the Genesis story (29: 20) of Jacob's labour to win Rachel as his wife. Jacob's first seven years end when he is tricked by her father Laban into marrying her sister Leah; another seven will follow before he is able to make Rachel his wife.

2. *last*: a model for shaping or repairing a shoe or boot.

3. *landsman*: a Jew who has emigrated from the same country.

'A Late Encounter with the Enemy',
Flannery O'Connor (pp. 167–77)

1. *River Styx*: the river that encircles Hades, marking a boundary between it and the world of the living. The dead were ferried across.

2.   *the War between the States*: the Civil War (1861–5).

3.   *blue-gray*: combining the colours of the Union and Confederate armies.

4.   *the Spanish-American War*: an 1898 conflict between the United States and Spain, at the end of which Spain ceded Puerto Rico, the Philippine Islands and Guam.

5.   *that preemy they had in Atlanta*: presumably a reference to the 1939 Atlanta premiere of *Gone with the Wind*, the film adaptation of Margaret Mitchell's 1936 novel.

6.   *a group of UDC members*: the United Daughters of the Confederacy was founded in 1874 for women descendants of Confederate veterans.

7.   *the Confederate Battle Hymn*: 'Dixie's Land' (also known as 'Dixie') by Daniel Decatur Emmett (1815–1904).

8.   *Confederate Memorial Day*: eight states observe a holiday to commemorate those who died fighting for the Confederacy. Different dates are chosen; in Georgia, it's 26 April, the anniversary of the surrender of General Joseph E. Johnston to Union General William Sherman in 1865.

9.   *John Wesley Poker Sash*: Sally's nephew is named after the eighteenth-century founder of Methodism John Wesley (1703–91), who spent nearly two years in Savannah, Georgia – O'Connor's home town. She used the name again – for a brattish eight-year-old in 'A Good Man is Hard to Find' (1955) and for Mrs May's 'intellectual' son who hates everything in 'Greenleaf' (1965).

10. *the B.S.'s*: the Bachelor of Science students.

11. *Chickamauga, Shiloh, Johnston, Lee*: a rather mixed-up list of Civil War battles and generals: Chickamauga was won by the Confederates in September 1863; Shiloh by the Union Army in April 1862. Confederate General Albert Sidney Johnston (1803–62) died at Shiloh but General Robert E. Lee (1807–70) was not present at either.

12. *Marthasville*: the previous name of Atlanta, Georgia. It was changed in 1845.

'Sunday Teasing', John Updike (pp. 178–85)

1.   *St Paul*: the epistles of St Paul are the thirteen books of the New Testament attributed to the apostle.

2.   *Jane Austen*: Jane Austen (1775–1817) is an English novelist, as is Henry Green, the nom de plume of Henry Yorke (1903–73).

3. *the movie Camille*: there are several film adaptations of Alexandre Dumas's *La Dame aux Camélias* (1848), which ends with the heroine's death from tuberculosis. They are referring to the 1936 movie, directed by George Cukor and starring the Swedish actress Greta Garbo.

4. *Unitarians*: Unitarianism is a liberal branch of nontrinitarian Protestantism which maintains the compatibility of reason and faith and which emphasizes ethics rather than theology.

5. *Chesterton's definition of Puritanism*: in his *Short History of England* (1917), the Roman Catholic English novelist G. K. Chesterton (1874–1936) defined Puritanism as 'the principle that the mind of man can alone directly deal with the mind of God'.

6. *Fide sola*: by faith alone (Latin). The theological doctrine that historically distinguished Protestantism from Roman Catholicism and Eastern Orthodoxy.

7. *Scarlatti and Purcell*: Giuseppe Domenico Scarlatti (1685–1757) was a Neapolitan composer especially noted for his keyboard sonatas. Henry Purcell (1659–95) was an English composer of both secular and sacred music.

8. *Jess Stacy's classic piano solo on 'Sing, Sing, Sing'*: this version of the 1936 Louis Prima song featured as the climax of Benny Goodman's 1938 concert at Carnegie Hall.

9. *The Tragic Sense of Life*: *The Tragic Sense of Life in Men and Nations* (1912) by the Spanish writer and philosopher Miguel de Unamuno (1864–1936). Unamuno maintained that contradiction was the fundamental fact of the spiritual life. In his view what made life tragic is that faith requires we live as if we were destined by God for eternity while reason denies that possibility.

10. *Kierkegaard*: Søren Kierkegaard (1813–1855), the Danish philosopher, who also explored the relationship between objective reason and subjective faith.

11. *rubbers*: overshoes.

12. *nacreous flakes ... infrangible irritant*: iridescent flakes; like mother of pearl (another term for nacre). 'Infrangible': not capable of being broken or separated into parts.

'Reunion', John Cheever (pp. 186–9)

1. *the Sixties*: that is, twenty blocks north of Grand Central.

2. *Kellner! ... Garçon!, Cameriere!*: Waiter! (German, French and Italian).

3. *a couple of Beefeater Gibsons*: a martini made with Beefeater gin and served with a pearl onion.
4. *Buon giorno ... Per favore, possiamo avere due cocktail americani, forti, forti. Molto gin, poco vermut*: Good day. Please may we have two American cocktails, strong, strong. A lot of gin, a little vermouth (Italian).
5. *Vogliamo due cocktail americani. Subito*: We want two American cocktails. Immediately (Italian).
6. *Vada all' inferno*: Go to hell (Italian).
7. *yellow journalism*: the term (shortened from 'yellow-kid journalism') refers to sensationalist reporting and was coined in the late nineteenth century to describe the rival newspapers of Joseph Pulitzer (1847–1911) and William Randolph Hearst (1863–1951). Their competition extended to comic strips featuring the 'Yellow Kid'.

'Wants', Grace Paley (pp. 190–2)

1. *The House of Mirth* and *The Children*: published in 1905 and 1928 respectively.
2. *the Board of Estimate*: the governmental body responsible for budget and land-use decisions in New York City until 1990.
3. *to end the war*: the Vietnam war ended in April 1975.

'The Flowers', Alice Walker (pp. 193–4)

1. *sweetsuds bush*: perhaps a local name for Carolina allspice (*Calycanthus floridus*), also known as sweetshrub, which grows throughout the south-eastern states.
2. *plowline*: the rope used to attach a horse or mule to the plough.

'I Bought a Little City', Donald Barthelme (pp. 195–200)

1. *Galveston, Texas*: a port on Galveston island in the Gulf of Mexico about forty-five miles south-east of Houston.
2. *the Free World*: a Cold War term used to describe states not under the control of the Soviet Union or other communist nations.
3. *the Shriners*: the Ancient Arabic Order of the Nobles of the Mystic Shrine (AAONMS) was founded in 1870 and is linked to Freemasonry. The Shriners are very active in community projects.
4. *that Orson Welles picture*: Citizen Kane (1941).

5.   *American Civil Liberties Union*: the stated mission of the ACLU
     is to 'defend and preserve the individual rights and liberties guar-
     anteed to every person in this country by the Constitution and
     the laws of the US'.
6.   *a writ of mandamus*: a formal written command from a superior
     jurisdiction that commands an inferior court or corporation to
     perform or refrain from performing a particular act, the per-
     formance or omission of which is a legal obligation.
7.   *Huey P. Long, former governor of Louisiana*: Long served as
     Governor (1928–32) and Senator (1932–5). He undertook
     an unprecedented public works programme, building roads,
     bridges, hospitals and educational institutions, but his oppon-
     ents accused him of dictatorial tendencies. Assassinated in 1935,
     his final words were reputedly 'God, don't let me die, I have so
     much left to do.'

'Collectors', Raymond Carver (pp. 201–7)

1.   *W. H. Auden*: the English poet (1907–73) visited China in 1938.
2.   *Rilke*: Rainer Maria Rilke (1875–1926) was an Austro-German
     poet and writer.
3.   *Voltaire at Cirey with Madame Châtelet*: François-Marie Arouet
     (1694–1778), who wrote under the name Voltaire, lived in the
     Chateau of Cirey between 1734 and 1749 having been offered
     protection by the Marquise de Châtelet following the publica-
     tion of his controversial *Philosophical Letters* (1733).

'Communist', Richard Ford (pp. 208–25)

1.   *the GN yards*: the Great Northern Railway yards.
2.   *the CIA*: in June 1954 Ngo Dinh Diem was installed as leader of
     South Vietnam by the CIA, which then continued to operate
     behind the scenes. In November 1961, when the story is set,
     President Kennedy pledged to send more financial aid and mili-
     tary advisers, effectively (if secretly) taking over South Vietnam's
     fight against the communist guerrillas.
3.   *a labor man*: a trade unionist.
4.   *irrigators*: rubber boots or waders.
5.   *Nash Ambassador*: the top-of-the-line model in the Nash range;
     production stopped in 1957.
6.   *the Divide*: the mountains of the Continental Divide run diag-
     onally through Montana from north-west to south central.

7. *VFW*: Veterans of Foreign Wars, the largest American organiza-
    tion of combat veterans.
8. *benchland*: a level tract between a river and neighbouring hills.
9. *the Big Hole*: the Big Hole valley is in south-western Montana.
10. *the Hi-line*: the area of Northern Montana along which High-
    way 2 and the Great Northern Railway line run.
11. *the Straits of Juan de Fuca*: a 95-mile-long body of water con-
    necting the Puget Sound to the Pacific Ocean and providing part
    of the boundary between Canada and the United States.

'Starving Again', Lorrie Moore (pp. 226–31)

1. *Why are they starving THIS time*: in May 1988 the *New York
    Times* reported that two million lives were at risk in Ethiopia –
    twice the number who died in 1984–5, when the Live Aid and
    We Are the World concerts drew attention to the famine.
2. *the theme to Valley of the Dolls*: written by Dory and André
    Previn, the theme to the 1967 film, based on Jacqueline Susann's
    1966 roman à clef, was a number-one hit for Dionne Warwick.
3. *Rudolf Bing*: Austrian-born opera impresario (1902–97). The
    story's conversation, which takes place in 1988, refers to his
    marriage the previous year to Carroll Douglass and their Carib-
    bean travels. The tabloids were fascinated because he was
    eighty-five and had been diagnosed with Alzheimer's disease,
    while she was forty-seven, and had three previous marriages to
    older men. In 1989 an American court declared Bing incompe-
    tent and annulled the marriage.
4. *'What a day this has been. What a rare mood I'm in'*: lyric from
    'Almost Like Being in Love' by Alan Jay Lerner (music by Frederick
    Loewe). It features on *Judy at Carnegie Hall*, a famous recording of
    a Judy Garland concert that took place on 23 April 1961.
5. *Gotta Dance*: lyric from 'Broadway Rhythm' by Arthur Freed
    (music by Nacio Herb Brown). The song featured in *Broadway
    Melody 1936* (1935) and *Singin' in the Rain* (1952).
6. *'Santa Lucia'*: a traditional Neapolitan song.
7. *the Addams Family*: a TV show (1964–6) based on Charles Add-
    ams's cartoon series of the same name, which ran in the *New
    Yorker* from 1938 to 1988, when Addams died. Vic Mizzy wrote
    the theme song.
8. *Sergio Mendes*: a Brazilian songwriter and bandleader (1941–).
9. *Napoleonic Code*: the French Civil Code, established by Napo-
    leon in 1804.

'The Third and Final Continent', Jhumpa Lahiri (pp. 232–52)

1. *LSE*: London School of Economics. Later, *MIT*: Massachusetts Institute of Technology (Tech).

2. *Mukhesh on a Grundig reel-to-reel*: Mukhesh Chand Mathur (1923–76), a famous Bollywood playback singer – that is, he recorded the songs that the actors mimed. A reel-to-reel is a type of tape recorder which preceded the cassette recorder.

3. *sixth-preference green card*: an identification card for a permanent resident who does not have US citizenship and who is considered 'capable of performing specified skilled or unskilled labor, not of a temporary or seasonal nature, for which a shortage of employable persons exists.' (US Immigration Act of 1965)

4. *two American men had landed on the moon*: Neil Armstrong and Edwin (Buzz) Aldrin landed on the moon on 20 July 1969. Armstrong famously announced 'one small step for man, one giant leap for mankind'.

5. *Tagore*: Rabindranath Tagore (1861–1941), a Bengali poet, playwright, novelist, musician and painter.

6. *1866*: the year that the Civil Rights Act was passed, declaring that everyone born in the United States was a citizen, 'without regard to race, color, or previous condition of slavery or involuntary servitude'.

7. *the Prudential building*: upon its completion in 1964, the 228-metre-high Prudential Tower was – for a while – the tallest building in the world outside of New York City.

Biographical Notes

Sherwood Anderson was born in 1876 in Camden, Ohio, and grew up in various small towns in the state. When he was thirty-six, he had a nervous breakdown and gave up his job as a paint manufacturer to become a writer. The author of numerous novels, memoirs and collections of stories, he is mainly remembered today for *Winesburg, Ohio* (1919), an immensely influential collection of linked tales about 'small town life', of which 'The Untold Lie' is one. Anderson died in 1941.

Donald Barthelme was born in 1931 and grew up in Houston, Texas, to which he returned shortly before his death in 1989. Closely involved in the art world (he was director of Houston's Contemporary Arts Museum before moving to New York in 1962), Barthelme was a regular contributor of stories and sketches to the *New Yorker* during the 1960s and 70s. He is the author of fourteen books, including four short novels and several collections of essays, but his best work was in the short story. He died in 1989.

Raymond Carver was born in Clatskanie, Oregon, in 1938 and lived a peripatetic life, working, studying and writing. His first collection, *Will You Please Be Quiet, Please?* (1976), gathered together stories (including 'Collectors') which had been published in a variety of places over the previous decade. *What We Talk About When We Talk About Love* (1981) made him famous and he subsequently published two further major collections: *Cathedral* (1983) and, shortly before he died in 1988, *Where I'm Calling From*. He also wrote essays and several volumes of poetry. Several further selections and editions of stories have appeared since his death.

John Cheever was born in Quincy, Massachusetts, in 1912. His first story (about being expelled from school) was published in the *New Republic* when he was just eighteen. He went on to publish many more stories (141 in the *New Yorker*) and in 1978 *The Stories of John*

Cheever was a huge bestseller. Cheever also wrote four short novels, including *Falconer* (1977). He died in 1982.

Charles W. Chesnutt was born in Cleveland, Ohio, in 1858, the son of free black parents from North Carolina. After working as a teacher, school principal, newspaper reporter, accountant and lawyer, he began publishing stories in the late 1880s. 'The Goophered Grapevine', the first story by an African American to appear in the *Atlantic*, opens a collection of plantation stories called *The Conjure Woman* (1899). That year he also published *The Wife of His Youth and Other Stories of the Color Line*, the title story of which is included here. A series of essays, three novels and a biography of Frederick Douglass followed, but after 1905 Chesnutt largely gave up writing and returned to his legal career and to social and political activism. He died in 1932.

Stephen Crane, who was born in Newark, New Jersey, in 1871, specialized in short forms. His life too was short (he died of tuberculosis in 1900 when he was just twenty-nine), but he published over 300 sketches, stories and reports, two collections of poetry and five novels. A champion of realism, his subject matter ranged from the New York Bowery to the American West to the experience of war. *The Red Badge of Courage* (1895) made him famous, but Crane later said it was 'too long'.

Lydia Davis was born in Northampton, Massachusetts, in 1947. She has had two careers – as a translator of French literature (including works by Proust and Flaubert) and as a writer of stories (a term she argues is less prescriptive than 'short stories'). Since 1976 she has published six collections, and in 2009 a *Collected Stories*. She is also the author of a novel, *The End of the Story* (1995).

William Faulkner was born in 1897 in Mississippi and, apart from brief periods in New Orleans and Hollywood, spent most of his life living in, and describing, his own 'little postage-stamp of soil'. Many of his stories and fifteen of his novels – including *The Sound and the Fury* (1929) and *Absalom, Absalom!* (1936) – dissect Yoknapatawpha County, an 'apocryphal' version of Mississippi's Lafayette County. His *Collected Stories*, opening with 'Barn Burning', was published in 1950. Faulkner died in 1962.

Born in 1811, Sara Payson Willis adopted the pseudonym **Fanny Fern** when she took up writing in the early 1850s, after the death of one husband and divorce from a second. The author of two novels and a notoriously well-paid newspaper columnist, she was one of the most successful writers of the period. Her best vignettes were collected in *Fern Leaves from Fanny's Port-Folio* (1853) and subsequent volumes. She died in 1872.

F. Scott Fitzgerald was born in St Paul, Minnesota, in 1896. His first novel, *This Side of Paradise* (1920), was a huge hit, enabling him to marry his long-standing fiancée, Zelda Sayre. Fitzgerald went on to write four further novels, notably *The Great Gatsby* (1925) and *Tender is the Night* (1934), along with numerous short stories, most of which he didn't rate highly. He died in 1940.

Richard Ford was born in Jackson, Mississippi, in 1944 but moved to Arkansas when he was eight. Since 1976 he has published five novels and three collections of stories, set in (among other places) Montana, Mississippi, New Orleans and Paris. Best known for his 'Frank Bascombe' trilogy – *The Sportswriter* (1986), *Independence Day* (1995), and *The Lay of the Land* (2006) – Ford has done much of his best work in the short story, a form he describes as a 'streamlined little verbal torpedo'.

Mary Wilkins Freeman was born in 1852 in Randolph, Massachusetts, and spent most of her life in Massachusetts and Vermont. She was still a teenager when she began to publish children's and adult fiction to support her family. 'Two Friends' was the twenty-fifth of her stories to appear in *Harper's Bazaar*. Over her lifetime she published over 200 stories, but today she is known primarily as the author of *The New England Nun and Other Stories* (1891). Freeman died in 1930.

Born in Georgia, around 1848, **Joel Chandler Harris** began work at thirteen, as a printer's apprentice on Joseph Addison Turner's plantation newspaper, the *Countryman*. He later worked on various newspapers before becoming editor of the *Atlanta Constitution* in 1876. In 1880, Harris began a new career as the bestselling author of ten volumes of stories narrated by 'Uncle Remus', which had their origin in the African-American folk tales told by George Terrell, a slave on Turner's plantation, Turnwold. Harris died in 1908.

Born in 1804 in Salem, Massachusetts, **Nathaniel Hawthorne** was a descendant of both Daniel Hathorne, a revolutionary war hero, and

John Hathorne, one of the judges in the Salem witch trials. In 1842, he settled in Concord and became part of a circle of Transcendentalist writers, including Emerson, Thoreau and Fuller. Hawthorne's early work was mostly anonymously published short fiction, and he only began to establish a reputation when his stories were collected, in *Twice-Told Tales* (1837) and *Mosses from an Old Manse* (1846). Following the huge success of *The Scarlet Letter* (1850), which drew on his Puritan heritage, he devoted himself to novel-writing. Hawthorne died in 1864.

Ernest Hemingway was born in the Chicago suburb of Oak Park in 1899. He served as an ambulance driver in Italy during the later stages of the First World War, and after the war, returned to Europe as a foreign correspondent. While his first stories were initially published with the help of Paris's avant-garde expatriate community, his breakthrough came with the 1925 New York publication of *In Our Time*, which introduced a style that would be widely imitated. Hemingway consolidated his reputation with *The Sun Also Rises* (1926) and went on to publish many more stories and novels, many of which drew on his adventures in Spain, Cuba and elsewhere. But his early work was his best. Hemingway committed suicide in 1961.

William Sidney (he later changed it to Sydney) Porter was born in Greensboro, North Carolina, in 1862. While working as a bank teller in Austin, Texas, he was indicted on charges of embezzlement. His first story was published while he was a prisoner at the Ohio Penitentiary. On leaving jail, he adopted the pen-name **O. Henry**, under which he published over 600 stories. A hugely popular writer, he was famous for ending his stories with an ironic or sentimental twist or 'snapper'. He died in 1910.

Zora Neale Hurston was born in 1891 in Notasulga, Alabama, but soon moved to the brand-new all-black town of Eatonville, Florida – the setting for her best-known novel, *Their Eyes Were Watching God* (1937). In 1925 Hurston became the first black student to attend New York's Barnard College, where she studied anthropology with Franz Boas. A leading light of the Harlem Renaissance, she also conducted fieldwork into folk culture in Florida and in Haiti, some of which was published as *Mules and Men* (1935). She died in 1960.

Washington Irving was born into a mercantile family in New York in 1783. He began publishing in 1802 as 'Jonathan Oldstyle, Gent.' and in 1807–8 collaborated with his brother and a friend on *Salmagundi*, the serial from which 'The Little Man in Black' is taken. He found it difficult to make a living as a writer and so pursued a career in law and business for many years, much of it in Europe. Irving's breakthrough came with another collection of pieces supposedly gathered by an 'old bachelor', *The Sketch Book of Geoffrey Crayon, Gent.* (1819–20). The book's success, in Britain as well as the US, made him America's first celebrity author. He died in 1859.

Henry James was born in New York in 1843. By the time he was in his early twenties, he had already placed stories in many of the major American magazines. When he was thirty-two he moved to Europe, eventually settling in England, where he spent the last forty years of his life. He published twenty novels – including *The Portrait of a Lady* (1881) and *The Golden Bowl* (1904) – and 112 tales of varying lengths. He resented the constraints of the short story, preferring the scope for development allowed by the 'blest *nouvelle*' – a form which provoked much of his best work, including *Daisy Miller* (1878) and *In the Cage* (1898). James died in 1916.

Born in London to Bengali parents in 1967, **Jhumpa Lahiri** moved to the United States when she was three. She has written two collections of short stories: *Interpreter of Maladies* (1999), which concludes with 'The Third and Final Continent', and *Unaccustomed Earth* (2008). She has also published a novel, *The Namesake* (1993).

Bernard Malamud was born in Brooklyn in 1914. He wrote eight novels and is best known for his first, *The Natural* (1952), a mythic treatment of baseball, and *The Assistant* (1957). The latter shares a milieu with 'The First Seven Years', which appeared in his acclaimed first story collection, *The Magic Barrel* (1958). Malamud died in 1986 and a *Complete Stories* was published in 1997.

Lorrie Moore was born in 1957 and grew up in Glens Fall, New York. Her first story was published when she was just 19 and she is now the author of three novels and three collections of stories. She has taught at the University of Wisconsin since 1984. 'Starving Again' is included in *Like Life* (1990) and her *Collected Stories* (2008).

Flannery O'Connor was born in 1925 in Savannah, Georgia. One of the first recipients of a Master of Fine Arts (MFA) degree from the Iowa Writers' Workshop in 1947, she moved to New York to work on her first novel, *Wise Blood* (1952). But in 1950, diagnosed with lupus erythematosis, she returned to Milledgeville, Georgia, where she remained until her death in 1964. She completed a further novel, *The Violent Bear It Away* (1960), but is best known for two collections of short stories, *A Good Man Is Hard to Find* (1955) and the posthumous *Everything That Rises Must Converge* (1965).

The daughter of Russian-Jewish immigrants, **Grace Paley** was born in the Bronx in 1922 and spent her life in New York and, later, Vermont. She began (and continued) as a poet and essayist but made her mark as a political activist and the author of three collections of stories, *The Little Disturbances of Man* (1959), *Enormous Changes at the Last Minute* (1974) and *Later the Same Day* (1985). A *Collected Stories* was published in 1994, but she continued to write until her death in 2007.

Dorothy Parker was born Dorothy Rothschild in Long Branch, New Jersey, in 1893. A member of the Algonquin 'vicious circle' (a group of writers, critics and editors who traded wisecracks and witticisms over lunch at the Algonquin Hotel during the 1920s), Parker wrote stories, sketches and poems for the smart New York magazines and, in the 30s and 40s, numerous screenplays for Hollywood. She was also a passionate anti-fascist and Civil Rights campaigner. Parker died in 1967.

Edgar Allan Poe was born in Boston in 1809, the second child of a couple of itinerant actors. After his mother died, he was taken in by a prosperous couple from Virginia, with whom he later fell out. Influenced by German and British Romanticism, he began as a poet but turned to magazine fiction to support himself and his cousin Virginia, whom he married in 1836 when she was thirteen. His first collection, *Tales of the Grotesque and Arabesque*, appeared in 1839 and he had an instant success with 'The Raven', a poem, in 1845. Poe also devoted a great deal of energy to the business of setting up and editing journals. Credited with having invented the detective story and science fiction, and with developing a still influential theory of the short story, he died in mysterious circumstances in 1849.

Born in 1835, Samuel L. Clemens grew up in Hannibal, Missouri, on the Mississippi River. After his father died when he was twelve, he worked as a printer and a riverboat pilot before heading west to try his luck, first as a prospector and then as a reporter. He adopted the river pilot's cry of **Mark Twain** (meaning two fathoms of water, deep enough for a steamboat to pass) as his pen-name in 1863 and first tasted national fame in 1865 with 'Jim Smiley and His Jumping Frog'. He moved on to longer and more complex narratives but his very best work, like *The Adventures of Huckleberry Finn* (1885), retained links to the vernacular tall-tale tradition. Clemens died in 1910.

Born in 1932, **John Updike** grew up in Shillington, Pennsylvania (the model for the town of 'Olinger' in many of his stories). Only a few months after graduating from Harvard in 1955, he had a story accepted by the *New Yorker*: the magazine subsequently published hundreds of his stories, reviews, essays and poems. Updike also wrote more than twenty novels, most notably the 'Rabbit' series. He died in 2009.

Alice Walker was born in Eatonton, Georgia, in 1944. Active in the Civil Rights movement, she published her first short story in 1967 and her first novel, *Meridian*, in 1970. Best known today for the novel *The Color Purple* (1982), she has published numerous works of non-fiction and poetry as well as three collections of stories. 'The Flowers' can be found in *Love and Trouble: Stories of Black Women* (1973) and *The Complete Stories* (1994).

Eudora Welty was born in 1909 in Jackson, Mississippi, where she lived (she said) a 'sheltered life' until her death in 2001. After graduating from college, she worked as a publicity officer for the Works Progress Administration and as a photographer. Her first story was published in 1936 and her first book, *A Curtain of Green*, including 'The Whistle', appeared in 1941. Welty wrote three further collections of stories, five novels, a memoir and numerous essays, many of which explore the nuances of the short-story form.

Edith Wharton was born Edith Jones in 1862 into one of the wealthiest and most socially prominent New York families. Her great-aunts were supposed to have inspired the phrase 'keeping up with the Joneses'. When she was thirty-five, and, not very happily, Mrs Edward Wharton, she published her first book, *The Decoration of Houses*. By the time of her death, forty years later in 1937, she had published at least one more every year: travel books, stories, poems, essays, memoirs and novels. Today Wharton is largely remembered as the author of *The House of Mirth* (1905) and *The Age of Innocence* (1920).

Sources

'The Little Man in Black', Washington Irving
First published in *Salmagundi* (November 1807).

'Young Goodman Brown', Nathaniel Hawthorne
First published in the *New-England Magazine* (April 1835) and then, in
the revised form included here, in *Mosses from an Old Manse* (1851).

'The Tell-Tale Heart', Edgar Allan Poe
First published in the *Pioneer* (January 1843) and then, in the revised
form included here, in the *Broadway Journal* (August 1845).

'Aunt Hetty on Matrimony', Fanny Fern
First published in the *Olive Branch* (December 1851) and then in *Fern
Leaves from Fanny's Port-Folio* (1853).

'Jim Smiley and His Jumping Frog', Mark Twain
First published in the *Saturday Press* (November 1865). Twain subsequently revised the story several times and renamed it 'The Notorious
Jumping Frog of Calaveras County' and then 'The Celebrated Jumping Frog of Calaveras County'.

'The Wonderful Tar-Baby Story', Joel Chandler Harris
First published in the *Atlantic Constitution* (November 1879) and
then in *Uncle Remus: His Songs and his Sayings* (1880).

'Two Friends', Mary Wilkins Freeman
First published in *Harper's Bazaar* (June 1887).

'The Wife of His Youth', Charles W. Chesnutt
First published in the *Atlantic Monthly* (July 1898) and then in *The
Wife of His Youth and Other Stories of the Color Line* (1899).

'The Real Right Thing', Henry James
First published in *Collier's Weekly* (December 1899) and then in *The Soft Side* (1900).

'An Episode of War', Stephen Crane
First published in *The Gentlewoman* (December 1899) and then in *Wounds in the Rain* (1900).

'Hearts and Hands', O. Henry
First published, under the name Sydney Porter, in *Everybody's Magazine* (December 1902) and then in *Waifs and Strays* (1917).

'The Untold Lie', Sherwood Anderson
First published in *The Seven Arts* (January 1917) and then in *Winesburg, Ohio* (1919).

'Out of Season', Ernest Hemingway
First published in the small-press *Three Stories and Ten Poems* (1923) and then, in the revised form included here, in *In Our Time* (1925).

'Atrophy', Edith Wharton
First published in the *Ladies' Home Journal* (November 1927) and then in *Certain People* (1930).

'New York to Detroit', Dorothy Parker
First published in *Vanity Fair* (October 1928).

'The Whistle', Eudora Welty
First published in *Prairie Schooner* (Fall 1938) and then, in the revised form included here, in *A Curtain of Green and Other Stories* (1941).

'Barn Burning', William Faulkner
First published in *Harper's Magazine* (June 1939) and then as the opening story of Faulkner's *Collected Stories* (1950).

'The Lost Decade', F. Scott Fitzgerald
First published in *Esquire* (December 1939).

'Now You're Cookin' with Gas', Zora Neale Hurston
An edited version was published as 'Story in Harlem Slang' in the *American Mercury* (July 1942). The unedited version first appeared in Zora Neale Hurston, *The Complete Stories* (1995), accompanied by

'Harlem Slanguage', a glossary which has been drawn upon in the
Explanatory Notes.

'The First Seven Years', Bernard Malamud
First published in *Partisan Review* (September–October 1950) and
then in *The Magic Barrel* (1958).

'A Late Encounter with the Enemy', Flannery O'Connor
First published in *Harper's Bazaar* (September 1953) and then in *A
Good Man is Hard to Find* (1955).

'Sunday Teasing', John Updike
First published in *The New Yorker* (October 1956) and then in *The
Same Door* (1959).

'Reunion', John Cheever
First published in *The New Yorker* (October 1962) and then in *The
Brigadier and the Golf Widow* (1964).

'Wants', Grace Paley
First published as part of 'Two Stories: 1. "Debts", 2. "Wants"' in
Atlantic (May 1971) and then in *Enormous Changes at the Last Min-
ute* (1974).

'The Flowers', Alice Walker
First published in *Love and Trouble: Stories of Black Women* (1973).

'I Bought a Little City', Donald Barthelme
First published in *The New Yorker* (November 1974) and then in
Amateurs (1977).

'Collectors', Raymond Carver
First published in *Esquire* (August 1975) and then in *Will You Please
Be Quiet, Please* (1976).

'Communist', Richard Ford
First published in *Antaeus* (Autumn 1985) and then in *Rock Springs*
(1987).

'Starving Again', Lorrie Moore
First published in *Cosmopolitan* (May 1990) and then in *Like Life*
(1990).

'The Third and Final Continent', Jhumpa Lahiri
First published in *The New Yorker* (June 1999) and then in *Interpreter of Maladies* (1999).

'The Caterpillar', Lydia Davis
First published in *NOON* (2006) and then in *Varieties of Disturbance* (2007).

Acknowledgements

The editor gratefully acknowledges the following for permission to reprint copyright material:

'I Bought a Little City' from *Sixty Stories* by Donald Barthelme, reprinted by permission of The Wylie Agency. Copyright © 1981, 1982 by Donald Barthelme. All rights reserved.

'Collectors' from *Will You Please Be Quiet, Please?* by Raymond Carver, reprinted by permission of Harvill Vintage, an imprint of The Random House Group Ltd and The Wylie Agency. Copyright © by Raymond Carver 1976, Tess Gallagher 1989. All rights reserved.

'Reunion' from *The Stories of John Cheever* by John Cheever, reprinted by permission of Jonathan Cape, an imprint of The Random House Group Ltd, and Alfred A. Knopf, a division of Random House, Inc. Copyright © 1978 by John Cheever.

'The Caterpillar' from *The Collected Stories of Lydia Davis*, reprinted by permission of Hamish Hamilton and Farrar Straus & Giroux. Copyright © 2010 by Lydia Davis.

'Barn Burning' from *Collected Stories of William Faulkner* by William Faulkner, reprinted by permission of Chatto & Windus, an imprint of The Random House Group Ltd, and Random House, Inc. Copyright 1950 by Random House, Inc. Copyright renewed © 1977 by Jill Faulkner Summers.

'Communist' from *Rock Springs* by Richard Ford, reprinted by permission of the author c/o Rogers, Coleridge & White Ltd, 20 Powis Mews, London W11 1JN, and Grove/Atlantic, Inc. Copyright © 1987 by Richard Ford.

'Out of Season' from *The Short Stories of Ernest Hemingway* by Ernest Hemingway, reprinted by permission of Jonathan Cape, an imprint of The Random House Group Ltd, and Scribner, a division of Simon & Schuster, Inc. Copyright © 1925 by Charles Scribner's Sons; copyright renewed © 1953 by Ernest Hemingway. All rights reserved.

'Now You Cookin' with Gas' from *The Complete Stories* by Zora Neale Hurston (HarperCollins, 1995), Introduction copyright © 1995 by Henry Louis Gates Jr and Sieglinde Lemke. Compilation © 1995 by Vivian Bowden, Lois J. Hurston Gaston, Clifford Hurston, Lucy Ann Hurston, Winifred Hurston Clark, Zora Mack Goins, Edgar Hurston Sr and Barbara Hurston Lewis. Afterword and bibliography copyright © 1995 by Henry Louis Gates. Reprinted by permission of HarperCollins Publishers.

'The Third and Final Continent' from *Interpreter of Maladies* by Jhumpa Lahiri, reprinted by permission of Houghton Mifflin Harcourt Publishing Company and HarperCollins Publishers Ltd. Copyright © 1999 by Jhumpa Lahiri. All rights reserved.

'The First Seven Years' from *The Stories of Bernard Malamud* by Bernard Malamud, reprinted by permission of Chatto & Windus, an imprint of The Random House Group Ltd, and Farrar Straus & Giroux. Copyright © 1983, 1984 by Bernard Malamud.

'Starving Again' from *Like Life* by Lorrie Moore, reprinted by permission of Faber & Faber Ltd and Alfred A. Knopf, a division of Random House, Inc. Copyright © 1988, 1989, 1990 by Lorrie Moore.

'A Late Encounter with the Enemy' from *The Complete Stories* by Flannery O'Connor, reprinted by permission of the Mary Flannery O'Connor Charitable Trust via Harold Matson Company, Inc. Copyright © 1956, 1957, 1958, 1960, 1961 by Flannery O'Connor. Copyright renewed © 1993 by Regina Cline O'Connor. All rights reserved.

'Wants' from *The Collected Stories* by Grace Paley, reprinted by permission of Markson Thoma Literary Agency. Copyright © 1994 by Grace Paley.

'New York to Detroit' from *The Portable Dorothy Parker/The Collected Dorothy Parker* by Dorothy Parker, reprinted by permission of Gerald Duckworth & Co. Ltd and Viking Penguin, a division of

Penguin Group (USA) Inc. Copyright 1928, renewed © 1956 by Dorothy Parker, copyright © 1973, 2006 by The National Association of Colored People.

'Sunday Teasing' from *Early Stories 1953–1975* by John Updike, reprinted by permission of Penguin Group (UK) and Alfred A. Knopf, a division of Random House, Inc. Copyright © 2003 by John Updike.

'The Flowers' from *In Love and Trouble: Stories of Black Women* by Alice Walker, reprinted by permission of David Higham Associates and Houghton Mifflin Harcourt Publishing Company. Copyright © 1973 by Alice Walker.

'The Whistle' from *A Curtain of Green and Other Stories* by Eudora Welty, reprinted by permission of Russell & Volkening, Inc., as agents for the author. Copyright © 1941 by Eudora Welty, renewed in 1969.

For their considerable help on various aspects of the book, the editor would also like to thank Kristina Blagojevitch, Andrew Boddy, Tracy Bohan, Anna Hervé, Alexis Kirschbaum, Claire Péligry, Barbara Placido and David Trotter.